Also by Lisa Gornick

A Private Sorcery

TINDERBOX

LISA GORNICK

SARAH CRICHTON BOOKS

FARRAR, STRAUS AND GIROUX

NEW YORK

TINDERBOX

Sarah Crichton Books
Farrar, Straus and Giroux
18 West 18th Street, New York 10011

Copyright © 2013 by Lisa Gornick
All rights reserved
Printed in the United States of America
First edition, 2013

Library of Congress Control Number: 2013941742
ISBN: 978-0-374-27786-4

Designed by Jonathan D. Lippincott

Farrar, Straus and Giroux books may be purchased for educational, business, or
promotional use. For information on bulk purchases, please contact the
Macmillan Corporate and Premium Sales Department at 1-800-221-7945,
extension 5442, or write to specialmarkets@macmillan.com.

www.fsgbooks.com
www.twitter.com/fsgbooks • www.facebook.com/fsgbooks

1   3   5   7   9   10   8   6   4   2

To Lila and Marian

once in a while,
you can creep out of your own life
and become someone else—

—Mary Oliver, "Acid"

ONE

1

Myra cradles the phone to her ear as she gives the *yes* that she knows even now, this April Saturday morning, should be a *no*. Her yes is not even a yes, since Adam, her fragile second child—acrophobic, claustrophobic, equinophobic screenwriter of grade-B Westerns—is too avoidant to make a request, though the request is so clearly implied, it might as well be granted words.

"Rachida's head was still in Morocco when she chose dermatology," Adam says in the mumbly voice that has followed him from childhood, muffled now by the scraggly beard he grew at thirty with the hope of no longer being mistaken for a teen. "There, so many diseases present with the skin, dermatology is frontline medicine. Here, in Detroit, with her office in a shopping mall, she feels like a glorified aesthetician. She rolls her eyes when her patients complain about pimples. She scowls when they ask for Botox."

Pools of gold light spill onto the dining terrace, where Myra has spent the past hour planting terra-cotta pots that by summer will be filled with blooming thyme, Kirby cucumbers, and grape tomatoes sweet as cherries. The loamy scent of potting soil wafts through the open sliding doors into the kitchen of the Manhattan brownstone where she lives alone and keeps her psychotherapy office as she pieces together that her chronically angry Moroccan-Jewish dermatologist daughter-in-law has accepted a one-year respecialization fellowship in primary care at a hospital less than a mile away.

"They offered us housing in the medical student high rises.

A junior four on the nineteenth floor . . ." Adam's voice trails off as banks of gleaming elevators he would never enter fill Myra's mind—and then the image of her six-year-old grandson, Omar, trudging on his sturdy little legs behind his panting father up flight after flight of stairs.

2

Caro studies Myra's long smooth forearms. Is there a cosmic lesson to be learned in this second year of the new millennium from her mother's effortless beauty? Does Beauty, outraged by her mother's indifference, seek her out?

It is Sunday, their weekly dinner at the Amsterdam Avenue macrobiotic place, neither of them vegetarian but neither with a taste for trendier restaurants. Caro spears a wedge of organic yam as her mother places her chopsticks on her plate and folds her hands.

"Adam called yesterday. Rachida is going to do her fellowship here. They'll be coming at the end of June, as soon as Omar finishes school."

There is a twinge of discomfort as Caro recognizes that neither Adam nor Rachida has phoned to tell her, a reminder of the excessive reserve she has felt with them since their marriage. A problem, Caro thinks, rooted in confusion over Rachida, not really about loyalties, though it is hard to trace where those lie, but rather about who knows whom best—Caro having met Rachida first, at Rachida's parents' home in Essaouira, which Adam, afraid to fly, has never seen.

"Great," Caro murmurs, the word hollow even to her own ears. But why would she not mean it? Even if they have drifted apart, she loves her brother, her little brother, as she still thinks of him, despite there being only two years between them. Her greater ease at making a way in the world—her Harvard degree and semester abroad, with Adam unable to leave the city for college; her big job, with Adam still scraping by—has so long been the warp and woof of their lives, it has left no room for poisonous rivalry. And how could there be after all those years of Adam's fears and phobias: elevators, which complicated considerably their childhood in New York City, and airplanes, which required their mother to escort them by train each March to visit their cardiologist father installed in his fantasy casita outside of Tucson, and horses, of which their father and his second wife had kept six. The annual battle between their father and Adam over Adam's refusal to ride until the wrangler hired to teach Adam sat their father down and said, *Doc, you know how to listen to a heart, but me, I know horses and how people and horses get along, and one thing you can't do is force a human to ride a horse, which is what you're trying to do with that boy of yours.*

Her mother passes her fingers through her gunmetal hair, cut in a blunt downtown way that makes the color look more chosen than fated. "They're going to live with me for the year."

Caro holds herself very still in an effort not to react, not to blurt out anything, but it is useless. Her brows knit together, a habit since childhood. Then, her mother would smooth the flat of her hand over Caro's broad forehead, inheritance from a line of Jewish peasant women with faces round as cabbages that somehow skipped over her and Adam's sculpted visages. "Poor Caro," her mother once whispered, "fated to be the most sensible of us all," as though in Caro's features her personality is sealed.

"The housing they offered Rachida is on the nineteenth floor. Obviously impossible for Adam. With only Rachida's fellowship salary and the pittance he got for the option on his last screenplay, they'd have to live in Yonkers or Queens. Where would Omar go to school?"

"Where's he going to go if he lives with you? Even if they could afford private school, it's too late to apply."

Her mother takes a long drink from her glass of triple-filtered water. She fixes her cornflower-blue eyes on Caro's chocolate-brown ones. "I was thinking that with your school connections you could find them something."

Caro sighs.

"I'll handle the tuition."

Had anyone asked her, she would not have agreed that she is the most sensible of them all. The least squeaky wheel, yes, but not the most sensible. Built like the field hockey player she once was—short, stocky, and a little bowlegged, she has been slender only once in her life: the semester she spent in Paris that rolled into the summer she met Rachida and her family in Essaouira. Now she lives alone, with not so much as a goldfish, the 120 children at the East Harlem preschool where she is the director quite enough company for her, thank you.

"Where will you put them?"

Her mother produces a pale green sheet of paper torn from one of the steno pads in which she keeps her patient notes, a pad for each patient, each tucked like children's jackets in their assigned slots inside the rolltop desk she locks every night. Under each slot is a label marked with the patient's appointment time: 8:45, 9:30, 10:15, 11:00. Then, in the afternoon, 2:30, 3:15, 4:00, and 4:45. Monday, Tuesday, Thursday, and Friday. Not until Caro graduated from college and returned to New York did she understand that not all therapists keep the same schedule every day and don't see patients on Wednesdays—not to mention, write every morning from five to eight, walk every noon hour around the reservoir, or take up, as her mother had at the age of fifty, the piano.

On the paper, her mother has sketched her four-story house in cross section. In the front fourth-floor room, down the hall from her mother's own room in the back, in what had been Adam's room, there is an *O* for what Caro assumes will be Omar's room. On the third floor, in Caro's old room with the branches from the neighbors' backyard tree nearly touching the window, there is *A&R*, in what apparently will be Adam and Rachida's room.

"In here," her mother points to the front third-floor room they had called the TV room and that now houses her grand piano, "Adam can set up a desk. I'm never there during the day."

The parlor level—with the roll-armed couch that once belonged to her mother's parents and the cream Corbusier swivel chairs and black Barcelona chairs her parents bought when her father got his first job after his residency, in the front by the bay windows filled with the southern light—appears unchanged. Separating the seating and kitchen areas is the weathered farm table her mother found in an antique store in the Bronx before catalogue furniture companies began selling knock-off versions. At the back is the kitchen with the soapstone counters and the dining deck that looks out over the garden her mother created from a patch of torn-up concrete.

The entrance to the garden is through her mother's ground-floor office, the French doors sketched ajar, as she keeps them when the weather is warm. Summers, on the side table next to the patient chair, a vase of heritage roses sits by the tissue box. Next to the waiting room is a tiny bedroom and miniature bath, which the architect who designed the space called the au pair's suite, the necessity of which he had insisted, and which her mother has sporadically rented to a graduate student.

Caro studies the sketch. She can find no holes in her mother's plan. All she knows is that her mouth has gone dry and her mind has drifted to the pint of Chunky Monkey ice cream she will buy on her way home.

3

Myra learns about Eva three days later from Ursula, her cousin from the Peruvian branch of her family, who learned about Eva an hour before from her sister Alicia, who learned about Eva that morning from her cheeky maid Marina, who met Eva the night before when Eva showed up unexpectedly at Marina's boyfriend's two-room apartment. Eva and her sister and father had lived on the street in Iquitos where Marina's boyfriend grew up. They are *paisanos*. Marina's boyfriend had no choice but to let her stay. His mother would set a *maligno*, an evil spirit, on him if he did anything less.

Marina had expected to eat rice and beans with her boyfriend, watch TV together, and then have sex on the couch before her boyfriend's roommate arrived home from his nightshift job. Instead, she found herself sitting at her boyfriend's greasy table listening to Eva's story about a great-great-grandfather on her mother's side who was Jewish, a secret Eva's mother had kept from Eva's father but had given Eva an amulet shaped like a hand to prove; Eva's account of the hardships of studying Hebrew in Iquitos, where there is no rabbi and the makeshift synagogue is in the back of a flooring store; and Eva's fervent wish to emigrate to Israel.

None of what Eva said was comprehensible to Marina—everyone knows that Indians aren't Jews, rich people in Miraflores and San Isidro are Jews—but she, nonetheless, repeated it in the morning to her employer, Mrs. Alicia, whom Marina hoped to enlist in the service of Eva's removal from her boyfriend's living-room floor.

Alicia immediately recognized Eva as one of the mestizo self-proclaimed Jews from Iquitos over which her Lima synagogue has been divided for years—most of the Ashkenazi congregation wanting nothing to do with these third- and fourth-generation offspring of Sephardic turn-of-the-century rubber traders and their Indian common-law wives, whom they view as having no legitimate claim to Jewish identity, while a vocal few, including two of the synagogue elders, proclaim it monstrous for the congregation not to respond to pleas for Jewish education, no matter the bloodlines of the seekers.

Retreating to her bedroom, the only place in the house safely out of the maid's earshot, Alicia reached for the phone, hitting the automatic dial button for the cell phone of her sister, Ursula.

Ursula was in her backyard, examining the sloppy work of her gardener. "This," Ursula said, after hearing her sister's story about Eva, "could be a disaster. Remember the four Indians last year from Iquitos who wanted Rabbi Menendez to circumcise them? When Menendez said no since they'd all been baptized and couldn't understand why they couldn't also worship Jesus Christ, Clara Bejan contacted that kooky rabbi from St. Louis, who flew down to meet them. I heard Clara's children were dropped from everyone's bar-mitzvah-party list."

Ursula looked over the top of the wall that separates Alicia's property from her own, behind which she can see the roof of her sister's pool house. It annoyed her that Alicia had called when she was so close.

"I have to do something," Alicia said. "You know Marina, my maid. She's very cocky. She'll gossip and turn me into a brute."

"Marina probably just wants the girl away from her boyfriend. Is she pretty?"

"She has a nice little figure. But when you look at her up close, she seems unhealthy. Her hair is too thin, like a woman our age, and her nose is spotted with blackheads."

"Men don't notice those things. Marina just doesn't want this Eva camping out with her boyfriend."

"She's very bright. Her English is excellent, as good as ours, and she says she's been teaching herself Hebrew too. There's just something a little strange about her. Marina said her boyfriend told her the family had problems."

With *a woman our age*, Ursula thought of her cousin Myra, a mousy, bookish wallflower when they'd first met—Ursula a sophomore at Sarah Lawrence, Myra a freshman at nearby Barnard—but now the handsomest woman she knew of their generation.

"I'll call Myra. Maybe she knows someone who could use the girl in New York. They never have proper help there."

4

Myra picks up after the third ring. It being a Wednesday, a day she doesn't see patients, she has spent the morning writing at the farm table: a meditation on the teleology of love on which she has been working now for nearly a year. Strangely, she had been thinking about Ursula and Ursula's obsession with her own breasts, which this morning struck Myra as rooted in the maternal starvation of children raised by maids. Too sharp in the nose and broad in the beam to be called beautiful when they first met, Ursula had been, nonetheless, stunningly sensual. Men and women alike longed for the dark nipples hinted at beneath the pointy-tipped brassieres she wore under her red cashmere sweaters in winter, her boat-necked dresses in summer. There was nothing, she would tell Myra, that she loved more than to unsnap her brassiere, cup her large, soft breasts in her hands, and feel a warm mouth (man's or woman's made no difference to her) clamped on those nipples and then moving down her flawless olive skin.

Myra listens to her cousin's latest soap opera. Her father and Ursula's father had been brothers, the yin and yang male bookends of the family: Myra's father, a string-beany fourteen when he left Ukraine in the fall of 1910, never again to see his roly-poly baby brother or any other member of his immediate family aside from his older sister, Misha, whom he'd been conscripted to chaperone on her voyage to New York to join her fiancé—a fiancé who failed to meet the boat, having left days before it docked for a prospecting scheme in Utah, from which, if he ever returned, he never notified Misha.

She sips her now cold coffee while Ursula tells her about

Eva and Marina and the Sturm und Drang in her synagogue—
the synagogue founded by Ursula's father, who, three years after Myra's father landed in New York, emigrated with the rest
of the family to Lima, where, as an adult, he transformed the
import-export business his father had started into an impressive
enterprise diversified in real estate and shopping malls, and
then built a fantastic villa in Miraflores with a swimming pool
and trampoline and five maids, who did the mopping and
cooking and tending of his vain wife and two daughters.

Having no experience herself with South American maids
and the normativeness of their duplicities or the extent of the
responsibility entailed, Myra tells her cousin that of course she
will keep her ears open for a position for Eva.

"Anything, sweetheart, ironing, cooking, babysitting. I'd
find her something myself, but . . . It's a crime the way they
snub these people in Lima."

5

The idea that she might herself hire Eva arrives in the evening
while Myra is watering her garden, her thoughts cycling between her ambivalence about giving up her solitude and her
happiness about having her son and his family, especially Omar,
with her for the year. What she is not looking forward to is a
year of laundry and cooking and dishes. Perhaps she could hire
this Eva, bright and hardworking, Ursula said, to help with the
housework and Omar.

Myra waits until she assumes Omar will be in bed before
telephoning Adam and Rachida to hear their thoughts.

"Hi, Grandma," Omar says.

"You're up late. Don't you have school tomorrow?"

"Rachida's still at her office. She said she'd give me my bath
when she got home. I'm watching a DVD about the human

body. Did you know that children have more bones than grown-ups? I have almost one hundred bones more than you!"

During the first few years of Omar's life, Myra struggled, not with her behavior, which she has always kept in check, but with her inclination to make private judgments about the way Adam and Rachida handle Omar: their looseness regarding bedtime, their permissiveness with letting him eat whatever he wants (for years, almost exclusively grilled cheese), Rachida's allowing him to call her by her first name. It has all seemed rife with the overindulgence of first-time parents, with the difficulty she has seen in so many of her patients with feeling that they are, in fact, the adults. Her son and his wife have never asked her advice on anything, and she has known better than to offer it. Now, though, with Omar six and a half, she has to admit that whatever they are doing, different as it might be from what seems sensible to her, Omar is a sweet and thoughtful child.

"Can I talk to your dad?"

Not until Adam squeals, "Iquitos? She's from Iquitos?" does Myra make the connection of Iquitos with *Fitzcarraldo*, the movie that launched Adam at twelve on the course of becoming a screenwriter. By the time he was fifteen, he'd seen the movie, set and filmed in Iquitos, a dozen times and watched the documentary about the making of the movie nearly as many times—the parallel between the grandiose project of the film's protagonist, Fitzcarraldo, who attempts to drag a ship over a mountain so as to reach otherwise inaccessible rubber trees with which he hopes to finance the building of an opera house in Iquitos, and that of the filmmaker, Werner Herzog, with his insistence that he film a real boat being dragged over a real mountain in a real jungle, having struck Adam as nothing short of mystical.

"Why don't you talk it over with Rachida?" Myra suggests. "If she's interested, I could let Eva come a few weeks before you arrive as a trial."

6

Rachida finds Omar asleep on the couch and Adam staring at his computer screen.

"What the hell is going on here? I tried to call you half a dozen times to say I was going to be late, but no one picked up."

"Did you know that there are several hundred offspring of Moroccan Jews living along the Amazon? At the turn of the twentieth century, hundreds of young Moroccan-Jewish men, a lot of them were kids, not even twenty years old, traveled up the Amazon, starting in Belém in Brazil and eventually making their way to Iquitos in Peru in these crude boats they made themselves."

"Did you give Omar his bath?"

Adam takes off his glasses and rubs his eyes. He pulls his beard. Fourteen years ago, when they first met, he still had vestiges of his childhood beauty: his mother's slender form and delicate features. Now he has the ungainly middle-aged flab of a once-skinny child who never developed the muscles to use his arms and legs in a powerful way, and his face is half-hidden by the scruffy beard. Without his glasses, he squints in the harsh light. He swivels in his chair so that he faces Rachida, whose outline—the cropped hair, the practical clothes—she knows he can barely make out.

"It's an amazing story. These guys basically became the brokers between the native Indian rubber tappers and the shipowners who transported the raw rubber to Europe. By 1910, two hundred Moroccan-Jewish men were living in Iquitos, and there were businesses named, I'm not joking, Casa Khan, Casa Israel, and Casa Cohen. These guys kept their Moroccan wives, but they also took common-law Indian wives and had lots of babies. Then this English botanist smuggled 70,000 rubber seeds from Brazil and planted them in the Royal Botanic Gardens to see if they could survive in a different climate. When they did, the seedlings were sent to Malaysia and other parts of Asia, where transportation was easier and the plantation owners didn't have to deal with unruly labor who carried poison darts, and, poof, end of the Amazonian rubber boom. The Jewish guys just packed up and went back to Fez or Rabat or Tangier, leaving behind their common-law wives and all the kids."

"Why are you talking about this?"

"This girl my mother wants to hire to help with Omar and the housework. She's from this community that's existed now for nearly a century—the great-great-grandchildren of those Moroccan-Jewish guys, Indians basically, who identify themselves as Jews even though they've almost all gone to Catholic schools and have only the vaguest ideas about Judaism."

Rachida doesn't even try to stifle her sigh. Adam should know that she doesn't give a fuck about Moroccan Jews. When she left Essaouira fifteen years ago, it was to get away from the dying community there. She just wants to get off her aching feet. She looks around for somewhere to sit other than the folding chair that came with the card table, but with Adam in the desk chair and Omar on the couch, there is nowhere else.

When they first moved in, she intended, not to decorate— she hates that word, which reminds her of her mother's pompous aspirations to Europeanize their mellah home—but to make the rooms comfortable. She wanted to buy an armchair for the empty corner of the living room and a real desk for the dining alcove and some shelving for Omar's toys. But the house quickly turned into an endless series of problems, the leaking roof, the fuses blowing if they run the microwave with the air conditioner on, and Adam incapable of producing the tone of voice required to get the landlord to respond. Then there has been her father, no longer able to stand for hours at his jewelry bench, so that she's taken to sending him a few hundred dollars a month, the money she might have spent on furniture (money she's not mentioned to Adam and is certain her father has not mentioned to her mother), and she reached the breaking point with her practice and it has been all she can do to keep up her office hours and take care of Omar and fill out the respecialization fellowship applications.

Rachida opens the folding chair and leans down to untie her shoes. It has been years since she's been charmed by Adam's obsessions, and her patience with stories about the valiant efforts of Jews to worship throughout the Diaspora runs to minutes, but this particular story about Moroccan Jews in South America does ring a bell with something her father once told her.

"Some of the women from this community, Ursula told my mother, sent the women's group at her synagogue a letter asking for instruction in Jewish cooking and family planning and including the question if someone could please explain to them why they couldn't have pictures of Jesus in their houses. A lot of the younger members, like Eva, have developed the ambition of emigrating to Israel. Ursula says her synagogue has treated the emissaries the Iquitos Jews have sent to Lima abysmally, refusing their pleas for bar mitzvahs and circumcisions on the grounds that not having had Jewish mothers, they're not Jews."

"Who is Eva?"

Adam puts his glasses back on. Reading the scrolling text on his computer screen has left him with a throbbing behind his eyes. He wishes he could go upstairs and lock the bedroom door and look at one of the magazine pictures he keeps stashed in a large envelope in a file box at the bottom of his closet. Thinking about the photographs gives him a half erection, and for a moment he imagines getting up to touch his wife, but it strikes him as preposterous. He is afraid she would laugh out loud.

Rachida pulls off her socks. Adam watches while she massages her feet: wide across the arches and surprisingly small.

For a long time, Rachida had been the one who would get things started between them. Both of them lacked any prior experience, but she knew exactly what she wanted and gave detailed directions. After Omar was born, she stopped initiating. Adam's desire for her has similarly diminished, but there are still moments like this one, with his erection now pressing against his briefs, when he wants to have sex and feels no aversion at the thought of it being with her. What he has never figured out, though, is how to shift from talking about who will take the laundry to the laundromat to the language of hands and tongues and more.

"Are you going to answer my question? Who is Eva?"

"This girl Ursula asked my mother to help find work in New York. My mother is thinking about hiring her to be a housekeeper for when we come. If we like her, she could help out with Omar after school."

Rachida sits up. Her glossy black hair, the envy of her sister and mother with their frizzy heads, settles back into place. Irritated by their constant playing with her hair, she chopped it off herself when she was ten, refusing ever since to grow it past her ears. Now she cuts both her and Omar's hair by tracing the outlines of a bowl on their heads.

"So, let's see. My choice is, I have Omar watch DVDs while you cruise the Internet looking up whatever bizarre piece of history you're into that day or he gets taken to the park after school by an Indian maid whose great-great-grandfather was a Jew from Morocco?"

7

If Ursula's version of Eva's story foregrounded the internecine struggles between the Limian maids and their San Isidro employers, Myra's version is inflected through her psychotherapist's lens. Related to Caro the following Sunday over the pot of chai tea that follows their dinner, it features a Jewish girl from the Amazon who needs to get away from a troubling family situation.

"A family situation?" Caro asks. "What does that mean?"

"Darling, I talked with the girl for half an hour on the phone. We talked about her work experience and the job description. Ursula said she thinks the mother died in some kind of disaster, but I certainly wasn't going to ask about it over the phone."

"What's her experience with kids?"

"She's done lots of babysitting and worked in the children's program of an Amazonian lodge that caters to tourists. She loves kids. Alicia had her fill in when one of her maids was out sick. She said Eva cleans like a demon and irons like a dream."

"As if Adam or Rachida wear clothes that are ironed. Not to be a stickler for details, but does she have references?"

Myra catches the waitress's eye, makes a writing gesture on the palm of her hand. It is hard for her to explain her attachment to Alicia and Ursula. Having met neither of them until after she'd left her parents' home and never having been to Peru, she would not say that she is close with them. Nonetheless, they are the closest link she has to her father, whose story—he'd traversed the years of the First World War driving an ice truck while he studied bookkeeping at night, his sister Misha, unable to learn English or convert her humiliated rage after she'd been jilted by her fiancé into something productive, his ward—still makes her sad. After the war, her father had accepted an offer from the ice manufacturer's cousin, who assumed from his humorless honesty and balding pate that he was a man twice his age, to become comptroller for a kosher meat-processing plant in Baltimore. Misha had spent the allowance he gave her on magazines and chocolates and trips to the movies, untroubled by leaving the cleaning, shopping, and laundry for him to do on Sundays. When at forty-nine years of age and over two hundred pounds, she dropped dead of a heart attack, Myra's father appeared so desiccated that the rabbi called in for the service thought he was Misha's father. Once he learned the truth, a lightbulb had gone off for the rabbi: a match for his equally dour thirty-six-year-old spinster sister. Myra's conception, she imagines, was the result of the only intimate relations the two of them ever had, her Baltimore childhood spent in an immaculately clean row house as barren of talk as it was of dust or beauty, the frugality of which had yielded her rather significant inheritance.

"The first month will be a trial period. Alicia and Ursula are going to buy Eva a ticket with an open return date. She'll come in the middle of June, a few weeks before Adam, Rachida, and Omar arrive. I'll know within a week if she's unsuitable, which would leave me time to find someone else."

For a moment, Caro thinks she detects a trace of anxiety on her mother's face, but by the time the waitress arrives with a bill that her mother whisks away from Caro's outstretched hand, her mother's eyes and mouth are relaxed, so that it is only later, looking back, that Caro can see what any preschool director would tell you: first impressions are always right. About Eva, her mother hasn't a clue.

8

As she walks home, it occurs to Caro that until she was seven, she believed they were a plain-vanilla family, with a mom who picked up the children at school and escorted them to ballet and to karate and to get their teeth cleaned, even if she was reading all the time, and a dad who was a cardiologist who got home in time for dinner and left the house on the days when he conducted teaching rounds before anyone else got up, and four grandparents: her mother's parents in Baltimore, whom they visited at Thanksgiving and hardly saw otherwise, and her father's parents, who lived nearby and had a house in the Catskills where they stayed every Memorial Day and Labor Day. Then, in the space of one year, her mother's parents died, an event most remarkable for the fact that these pursed-mouth people, who'd insisted that Myra, their only child, wear the neighbor's hand-me-down coats, had socked away quite a bit of money.

For reasons Caro cannot explain, since there would have been enough money before (perhaps her mother needed it to be her own), the inheritance led to her mother returning to school to become a psychologist. Three nights a week, she disappeared for her classes, nights when it seemed that their father was always forgetting something and going back to his office or the hospital—the super's wife, who wore a hairnet and smelled of talcum powder, willing to oblige for last-minute babysitting—until, several years into it all, there was a night when voices were raised and suitcases packed and her father moved in with the receptionist from his office.

During the six months her father lived with the receptionist (Sharon or Sheri or maybe it was Shirley), Caro and Adam spent weekends at the receptionist's apartment, weekends during which their mother raced to finish her dissertation and Adam, then eight, refused to take a shower (Sharon or Sheri or whatever her name was had no tub) or, to their father's great irritation, sleep without the television on. Doctorate completed, her mother cashed in her inherited saving bonds and IBM stock to buy the then decrepit brownstone. When they moved in a year later, after the crackled tiles in the bathrooms had been acid-cleaned and the kitchen redone with the soapstone counters and her mother's office installed on the street level, the block housed a group home for the mentally ill, a drug detox clinic, and two buildings rented out by the room. Now, twenty-two years later, her mother's neighbors are investment bankers and partners in law firms.

If her mother got her brownstone from her parents' penny-pinching, Caro acquired her own apartment as expiation from her father, Larry—which was exactly how she put it when he hemmed and hawed—for ruining forever, she told him, her prospects for a healthy relationship by cheating on her mother.

"You left at a critical time," Caro had lectured her father, "the eve of the transition from concrete to formal operations." It was the summer after her Harvard graduation. They were dining by the pool of her father's Tucson casita, ten feet from the spot where on Caro's last visit he'd proudly shot a rattle-snake curled at the foot of an enormous saguaro cactus.

"Don't give me your mother's psychoanalytic crap," her father said, cutting too quickly to the chase for Caro to clarify that this was Piaget, Developmental Psych 101, not Freud. So she'd switched to dollars and cents, a language that he and his cardiology partners spoke with a frightful fluency.

"Actually, Daddy, what I'm asking for is really an exchange. Do you remember how you always promised you'd send me to medical school if I wanted to go? Well, I don't. What I want is"—she paused and looked him in the eye—"a two-bedroom apartment, paid for in full, which, if I do what I'm planning to do, I'll never be able to afford." A good deal, she continued, truly, and then pulled out the *pièce de résistance*, a Lotus spread-sheet, which proved what a bargain her proposition was if he took into account the opportunity costs of medical school tuition.

She complimented the pork chops dished out by her father's second soon-to-be ex-wife, ignorant about anything not found in a women's magazine but sufficiently cunning to act as though she did not understand the transaction taking place.

9

The plan Myra makes with Ursula is that Eva will arrive on a Saturday in the middle of June, two weeks before Adam and his family. Myra will meet Eva at the airport and then have the weekend to get her oriented. On the first Thursday in June, however, the phone rings minutes before Myra's 8:45 patient.

"Myra, sweetheart," Ursula says, "there's been a tiny problem, nothing to worry about, just something between Alicia and the maid whose boyfriend is the *paisano* of Eva. Alicia lost her patience and went, stupid woman, and changed Eva's ticket for tomorrow before I could even check with you. So, please, sweetheart, forgive me, but she will be arriving tomorrow at four. I told Alicia, Tomorrow is Friday, Myra will be working, and she said, Just have Eva take a bus to her house. Of course I can't let the poor thing take the bus, but I will give her some American dollars so she can take a taxi to you."

Throughout the morning, Myra finds her thoughts drifting to Eva: it does not seem right to have the girl try to negotiate a taxi at Kennedy airport. For all the years of her practice, however, Myra has done her best not to cancel her patients unless absolutely necessary. It is part of her covenant to her patients. They are to hold inside all of the tempestuous feelings the work stirs up between sessions; on her end, she promises to do her best to be there at the appointed time.

It pains Myra to ask Caro, even though she knows it will really not be a hardship for Caro, her reaction a carryover from her childhood when she'd hated asking anything of her own mother (always, in Myra's memory, on the floor on her hands and knees with a rag scouting out crumbs Myra assumed from her mother's pinched face Myra had created), so that she'd struggled to button the backs of her dresses, to make her own sandwiches, to not ask for new shoes until her feet hurt. Now, though, she can hear the soft, accented voice of her former analyst, Dreis, chastising her: *And what is the favor? You are hiring the girl to help your son, you want her met at the airport because you think this the kindest welcome, you don't want to disturb the work with your patients. This is your mother inside you. She could not tolerate that you were a human child who made messes, and now you cannot tolerate that you are human and do not have three hands and cannot be in two places at the same time . . .*

At lunchtime, Myra calls Caro at work. "But it's no problem," Caro says. "We only have twenty-six children who stay for the afternoon and there are three teachers plus the assistant director. They'll be happy to have me out of their hair."

"Thank you, darling. You can take my car. I'll leave the picture Ursula sent me of Eva with the guys at the garage."

10

Caro sleeps with the shades open so she can see the morning sky, now lightening with streaks of dove and pearl.

With all the talk about her brother's move these past few weeks, she has not asked her mother about her project: something her mother calls the teleology of love. Knowing that most people consider a philosophical project pretentious or a sign of someone whose head is in the clouds, her mother does not discuss it unless asked directly. In her mother's case, though, neither could be further from the truth. She is deeply practical: interested in ideas only to the extent that they touch on human dilemmas of real import. And she is the antithesis of pretentious. Because she believes modesty to be fundamentally false, a reaction formation, she once said, against the urge to boast, she is not modest. Rather, she feels no need to hijack others to be her audience.

When her mother first told Caro about her project, Caro had to ask for a definition. "Teleology," her mother answered, "is the study of the purposes or goals in either nature or history. You know that I don't believe in such ideas: that we are part of a deity-created design, that history is unfolding toward an end. I'm stealing the word for my own purposes."

"Which are?"

"To understand human desire." Her mother smiled shyly. As a girl, she has told Caro, her shoulders had hunched with chronic embarrassment. She was nearly thirty before she stood sufficiently tall for it to be noted that she has the neck and carriage of a Russian dancer, something she has not yet lost, as though her late blooming has been compensated for by a delayed demise. Caro can understand entirely why her father fell in love with her mother, and how devastated he must have been when she was willing to throw herself on the rocks, body and soul, time and again, in her effort to have a third child. Why he had to cheat so as not to feel enthralled or crushed.

"I don't mean this in a grandiose, absolutist way. I'm not talking about universal truths, just the commonalities in experience between people due to our shared biologies and histories. I've reached the age when the end seems nearer than the beginning, when reflection is a stronger impulse than fantasy. You'll see, or perhaps you've already seen"—she paused to check Caro's face—"what one wants changes. I'm trying to understand the evolution of that change. I'm using myself, not because I'm exemplary, but rather because I'm the case I know best."

While Caro was in high school and college, her mother had written half a dozen papers on quirky subjects, such as secret-keepers, gossip, arrogance as an expression of sadomasochism, papers that without fanfare gathered an audience. The teleology is her mother's first long project. The idea, her mother has told her, was inspired by a conversation they once had over dinner at an outdoor café in Riverside Park. They'd fallen into one of their familiar riffs, remarking on the dichotomies among the four of them. Her father, a doer, a fixer of clogged hearts, screened doors, horse bits. A fact junkie—a filing cabinet of information on diplomatic and military history, pharmaceutical and surgical cardiac interventions, medical practice economics, the care and breeding of horses. Adam, his opposite, a thinker and imaginer, a translator of stories into images—and yet also a collector of arcane knowledge. Her mother, an intellectual from the era before specialization and technology and career pigeonholing trumped the ambition of a thinking person to be sufficiently broadly informed so as to reflect on current affairs, history, the full spectrum of human experience.

"In a way," Caro said, "my work with preschoolers is the applied version of yours with your patients. I try to engineer for my children the outcomes—self-esteem, self-control, a love of learning—that when missing send adults running to you."

A few tables away, a man and a woman were trying to coax a toddler into a high chair. The child squirmed, landing an impressive punch to the man's jaw before she was forcibly strapped into the seat.

"Ten seconds," Caro said, "until that kid flings her plate onto the ground."

Her mother glanced at the embarrassed and exasperated parents. "I had Adam and you before the bring-your-kids-with-you-everywhere ethos. When your father was in medical school, the fifties' imperative of maintaining a baby's schedule still ruled. He would never have allowed either of you to go out to dinner with us at that age."

The plate crashed to the ground.

"I don't think of you as an engineer," her mother continued. "That's a bit Orwellian for my taste."

"I'm exaggerating. But don't we need a vision of what we think would be optimal, me for my three- and four-year-olds, you for your patients?"

Her mother leaned back in her chair and inhaled slowly,

a sign, Caro has learned, that she is mulling something over. "I hope I do better with my patients than I did with you and Adam." She glanced sideways, as though gathering her thoughts. "That sounds terrible. I mean that I failed both of you in so many ways, not through lack of love, but because I stifled you. Like all parents, I suppose, it was impossible not to want for my children things I could not achieve. Because I don't love my patients in the same way, I can see them more clearly, let them unfold with less imposition."

Caro walked her mother home. When they reached the brownstone, her mother took her hand. "Coming back to your idea that you are the engineer, do you really think we can do anything more than respond, encourage, discourage, what is already unfolding? As I look back on my life, it seems like this series of tectonic plates, one layer shifting into another, so that what I wanted at twenty hardly touches what I want now. It makes me wonder if there's some inevitability to it, something greater than my own personal history."

Her mother kissed her cheek. The kiss rested like dew. Two months passed before her mother said anything about her project, which by then, with a little self-deprecating smile, she described as the study of desire from conception to death.

11

At seven, Caro walks to her mother's garage. Waiting for the attendant to bring down the car, she studies the picture her mother left, which looks as if it was taken in a photo booth. In it, Eva has dark recessed eyes, angry and scared, like an animal encountered at night.

She crosses Central Park and drives north on Third Avenue. Beyond 100th Street, the city changes, the surprise of a hill, the signs and voices all in Spanish. She parks outside the building that houses the school, handing five dollars for watching the car to Simon, the homeless man who, years ago, she tried to help get into a shelter but who prefers his squat behind the steps of the bakery where every morning she buys him a café con leche and a roll with melted cheese.

"Love, they have to take me out before anyone touch your car." Simon makes a little boxing move. It is already seventy degrees, but he is dressed in several layers of clothes, one a hooded Harvard sweatshirt that was once hers.

When she first came to work at the school, twelve years ago, it was housed in the basement of a church a block away. There were rats in the tiny yard where the children played and peeling paint in the two classrooms. It took her a month to realize that what she needed was a crash course in community politics and a grant writer. She invited the city councilwoman and a friend who worked for the Ford Foundation to visit the school. Minutes before they came, she opened the garbage cans in the courtyard so the place stank and unscrewed two of the ceiling's fluorescent lights. The city councilwoman covered her nose and then told Caro about a nearby fire station that was being shut down. The Ford Foundation friend offered to help Caro write the grants that led to the station's transformation into six light-filled classrooms with water tables and sand tables and cozy book corners and an award-winning indoor playground in the former fire truck garage.

Now, 120 children, ages three and four, attend the school. Hot lunches are served family style. Because so few of the children have a pediatrician, Caro has organized a liaison with Mount Sinai Hospital so that every week pediatric residents come to the school. Vaccinations and flu shots are given on-site. Last year, Caro managed to have the program extended to include the siblings of her little students. For five years now, psych interns have run parenting groups for the mothers—groups that remained empty until Caro thought to provide free coffee and doughnuts and to hire two college students to watch the babies in tow.

Her father teases her, calling her East Harlem's Jane Addams. In one of the many articles that have been written about the school, a radical education professor from Teachers College was quoted in a way that implied that the school is a Band-Aid in the community, something politicians can point to and say, See how much we're doing, when in fact it is just a drop in the bucket.

"What knee-jerk baloney," her mother responded. "It's a line of reasoning that can be used with any good deed. It reminds me of one of my patients who gets enraged when her parents do something nice for her because it's evidence contrary to her theory about what brutes they are. You could make the same argument about my work. I treat perhaps thirty-five different patients in a year. But if half those patients truly change, who knows how many people they'll touch."

Her mother brushed her hair from her eyes. "Hard to accept that we can't part the seas or turn water into wine."

12

Walking into the light of the airport, Eva seems only scared, a girl dressed in nappy black pants and chunky boots with a fake leather jacket and an L.A. Lakers duffel bag. She stares straight ahead so that Caro has to tap her on the shoulder to get her attention.

"Eva? Are you Eva?"

The girl stands perfectly still. When Caro first heard that Eva came from the Amazon, she imagined a hut surrounded by toucans and monkeys. She was surprised when Adam informed her that although Iquitos is landlocked, accessible only by boat or plane, with a jungle market where you can buy everything from crocodile meat to the hallucinogenic aya-huasca, it is, nonetheless, a modern city with Internet cafés and banks, the avenues teeming with motorcycle-driven rickshaws.

A look of confusion passes over the girl's face. For a moment Caro wonders if Eva speaks English, as her mother was assured by Ursula. Or perhaps Eva is experiencing the shock Caro can still recall from her first weeks in Paris, when her college French seemed unrelated to what she was hearing, the words stuck together so she couldn't tell where one started and the next ended.

"I'm Caro, Myra's daughter."

Slowly, Eva's face clears. "I know. I know the whole family. Mrs. Ursula explain everything to me. There is your mother, Doctor M., and you and your brother. His wife is also a doctor, and the child is Omar." Eva smiles when she says Omar's name, revealing a front tooth with a little chip. "I love children! I have a present for him."

She drops the duffel bag at her feet and digs inside. When she stands up, there is a red stuffed animal that looks like a monkey under her arm.

"Mrs. Ursula tell me the child is six. When I work at the jungle lodge, I babysit many children five, six, seven years of age."

"That's adorable. I'm sure he will love it," Caro says, though, in truth, it is hard to imagine Omar, whose phone conversations at four were about the extinction of dinosaurs due to the climate change caused when a meteorite crashed into the earth, playing with this toy.

"We have these monkeys nearby where I come from. They are called howler monkeys because they scream all night. Me, I am used to it, but the Americans, when they stay in the lodges, sometimes they complain they cannot sleep from all of the noise."

"I've seen photos of them." One of her teachers had come

back from Belize with slides of howler monkeys, no larger than cats, hidden in the upper branches of a thicket of trees—too unlike the picture-book monkeys the children knew to capture their interest. "Let's get your luggage."

Eva points at the duffel. "I have everything in here. Mrs. Ursula buy me two jeans and this jacket. My friend, he give me the suitcase. You know the Lakers?"

"I'm not much of a sports fan."

"You know Shaquille O'Neal? He is my favorite player."

"I've heard of him." Caro picks up the duffel and slings it over her shoulder. "With traffic, it's about an hour's drive back to the city. Do you need to use the bathroom, get a snack before we go?" She points at the food court ahead. "We could stop and get a sandwich if you'd like."

The frightened expression from when Caro tapped Eva's shoulder returns to the girl's face. Eva lowers her chin, covering her nose and mouth with her hand. Caro can see the oyster color of her scalp. "Are you okay?"

"I smell something burning. There is something burning over there."

Caro inhales. There is the slightest scent of cooking meat. "I think that's hamburgers on a grill. Would you like to get something?"

Eva bolts ahead so that Caro, weighed down with the duffel, has to struggle to catch up with her. There is a bead of sweat at Eva's hairline. Caro shifts the duffel to her other shoulder and takes Eva's elbow. "Slow down. You're going to lose me."

"I don't like the smell . . ."

Caro points to the coffee stand on their right, the candy kiosk on their left. "There are plenty of other places. Are you hungry?"

"Hungry?" Eva tilts her head. It is hard to tell if she is contemplating the meaning of the word or the state of her gut.

"Yes," she whispers. "I am very, very hungry."

13

By the time Caro arrives at the brownstone with Eva, her mother has finished with her afternoon patients. She double-parks as her mother comes down the steps. Eva reaches in back for her bag and opens the car door. She stands still as Myra holds out her hand and then, not receiving a hand in return, touches Eva lightly on the arm.

Myra leans over to kiss Caro through the open window.

"Will you be okay?" Caro asks softly.

"Of course—and thank you."

Caro returns her mother's car to the garage, and then walks home. Reaching her building, she gives a half smile to her doorman, who, after seventeen years at the job, can distinguish the residents' personalities and moods: who wants to chat, who wants to pass through the lobby without intrusion. A man who knows that during the twelve years she has owned her apartment, she has never brought anyone home or unexpectedly failed to return for a night.

She unlocks her front door and takes off her shoes. She finds it comforting that when she comes back in the evening, nothing inside her apartment is ever altered. It is the panorama outside her windows that changes: a cityscape of water towers and rooftops with the Hudson River beyond, steel gray and white-capped in winter, a palate of blues in summer. At night, the lights of Edgewater across the water; mornings, the buildings brushed with pink from the eastern light.

Eva's disorientation this afternoon had brought back her own experience as a foreigner during the semester she'd spent in Paris. Eager to save money to travel, she'd eschewed the dorms offered by the study program, taking instead a job as an au pair for two children, five and seven. The mother had been a concert pianist who wore her hair severely pulled back from

her face and did not hesitate to pinch either Caro or the children when she was displeased. Her chubby engineer husband
escaped the pinches by strategic retreats to a little workshop off
the kitchen where he made birdcages. The children would torment Caro by bounding ahead of her in the street and pulling
their mouths horizontally until their eyes looked as if they
would pop. She had been so miserable she lost her appetite, unable to swallow the celery rémoulade and boeuf bourguignon
the pianist made each Sunday, the buttery gratins and smelly
cheeses she served in the evenings. For the first time, her collarbones emerged. Misery gave her a waistline. No longer over-
shadowed by belly and hips, her breasts seemed enormous.
The engineer took to watching her as she leaned over to tie the
children's shoes.

One night, she was awakened by a sound in the keyhole of
the maid's room where she slept. The chubby engineer stood
over her bed, an enormous erection pointing at her face. She
wanted to scream, but she was afraid of waking the children
and receiving a vicious pinch from the pianist. The engineer
smiled at her. Even in the dark, his teeth appeared brown. He
offered her a chocolate truffle. Too scared to refuse, she put it
in her mouth. He locked the door and gently pulled back her
covers. He massaged the crotch of her white cotton underwear.
She felt humiliated that her pelvis arched toward his fingers
and the crotch of her underwear grew wet. Chocolate drooled
out of her mouth. It was her first orgasm, though she'd not
understood that at the time. The engineer laughed. Afterward,
she felt something warm and sticky on the tops of her thighs.
In the morning, when the children had left for school and the
pianist had disappeared behind the glass doors of the salon to
practice, he handed her an envelope with two thousand francs
and told her to leave before *le déjeuner.*

Ma petite putain, the engineer had called her. My little
whore.

14

The first morning Eva is in the house, Myra wakes, as usual, at four-thirty. Opening her bedroom door, she nearly hits Eva's sleeping body, curled on the hallway floor. Eva is wearing yellow pajamas and sucking her thumb.

Myra gently rouses Eva, guiding her into the front bedroom, to the twin bed that was Adam's and that Myra has now designated to be Omar's. She pulls the south-facing blinds and covers Eva with the blanket folded at the bottom of the bed. The girl turns onto her side and puts her thumb back into her mouth.

The kitchen is still dark. Myra makes a pot of coffee and brings a mug downstairs to her office. Her desk faces the French doors leading to the garden, invisible at this hour. She tries to settle down to work but cannot focus on her writing. When they first moved into the house, Adam, then nine, had also rebelled against the sleeping arrangements, refusing to stay in his room one floor below hers despite Caro's offer to keep her door open so he could sit up in bed and see her. After two nights of having him in her bed, Myra relented and moved his things to the room down the hall from hers, a room she had intended to be a television–guest room.

Then, there was no need to look for an explanation. Adam's insistence on sleeping nearer to her was part of his package of phobias and fears, foreshadowed by the clutching, easily startled temperament he'd shown as a baby and toddler, his poor appetite, the ectomorphic form he'd inherited from her, and then cemented when his father had left the house. With Eva, though . . . She stops herself. The girl has been here less than a day.

Eva is eating at the kitchen table by the time Myra comes back upstairs. She is humming between spoonfuls of cereal, a tune that is vaguely familiar. She smiles at Myra, a shy smile, but without any trace of embarrassment.

"You moved upstairs."

Eva giggles. "I am sorry."

"Were you uncomfortable in your room?"

"It is so lonely all the way down there. At home, we have one floor. My sister and I share a room. In Lima, I sleep in the room with my friend."

"That's going to be Omar's room when he gets here, but you can sleep there for the next two weeks. Maybe by then everything will seem more familiar."

Eva nods. As she stands to clear her bowl, she resumes her humming. Now Myra recognizes the tune. It is "Edelweiss" from *The Sound of Music.*

"Small and white / Clean and bright / You look happy to meet me."

The Sound of Mucous, Larry had called it. He'd chase the children around the house bellowing, "Big and green / Dirty and mean / You look happy to eat me."

The humming stops. "Thank you," Eva says.

15

Usually a sound sleeper, Caro is woken in the middle of the night by a dream of howler monkeys. She is in a basket suspended from a tree. One of the monkeys has climbed in and is clinging to her, its claws digging so hard into her skin she can see beads of blood. Unable to shake the creepy feeling of the dream, she wanders into her kitchen, where she stands at the counter eating grapes, imagining her mother on the fourth floor of the dark brownstone with Eva three stories below. When the grapes are gone, she takes a bagel from the freezer and defrosts it in the microwave. She eats it slathered with peanut butter and then opens a carton of frozen yogurt, which she eats to the bottom.

In the morning, she feels sick from the nighttime eating. No amount of toothpaste will remove the revolting taste from her mouth. She puts on her running shoes and jogs slowly across Eighty-sixth Street and then into Central Park. She circles the reservoir twice, once on the path by the water, once on the bridle path, hating herself for the useless calories. She can identify the impetus for stuffing herself—the anxiety about Eva, the memories she'd unleashed—but the understanding never stops the compulsive hand to mouth that leaves her with a self-loathing in comparison to which the original discomfort would have been a pleasure.

With her head finally clear after the second lap, she calls her mother. The answering machine picks up. "Hi," Caro says. "It's me. I thought I'd stop by and see how you and Eva are doing."

Ten minutes later, she climbs the steps to the brownstone. Two urns overflowing with verbena and hollyhocks flank the door. She rings the bell, and then uses her key to let herself in.

Her mother and Eva are at the farm table that separates the kitchen and parlor. Through the doors opening onto the dining deck, Caro can see the mugs left on the outdoor table. The canvas umbrella is open, casting shade over the terra-cotta pots. Below, in the garden, a path leads from the shaded lower deck to a fountain installed the year Adam left for college, if his at best partial residence in his N.Y.U. dorm can be called leaving, by her mother's first lover, a photographer with a penchant for tinkering that resulted in a hidden pump that makes the water gurgle over a tiny wheel. Beyond the fountain and the brick-edged beds of plantings—low pachysandra, bushy oat grass, miscanthus interspersed with daylilies and purple irises—is the huppah under which Adam and Rachida were married seven years ago, Omar's presence in Rachida's belly obvious to all. The huppah is home now to a hammock, installed by her mother's last lover, an itinerant lecturer of mathematics whose jealous scenes had led to what her mother has told her was a decision that "last" means not latest but final, a final she now views in the context of her teleology of love as progress rather than retreat.

"Hello, darling," Myra says. "We're just working out a schedule for Eva, first for the next two weeks before the others arrive, and then for after that. Come take a look and see if we've forgotten anything."

Caro pulls up a chair and pours herself a glass of lemon water from the pitcher on the table. Although she and everyone else admire her mother's keen organizational skills, applied these days primarily to herself and her own pursuits, they also provoke in Caro a kind of dread, a silent rebelliousness, as though she is being asked to conform to a grim military regime. When she once confessed this to her mother, her mother said, "I'm so sorry. How awful for you. You need to remember that I'm only trying to control myself. An orderly external life allows my mind to wander freely. It's an occupational hazard for therapists. We overvalue order, since it's the unchanging routine of the sessions that lets the unconscious flow."

Her mother's love of order, Caro has come to understand, runs even deeper. For her mother, there is a harmonic beauty in a household where the precise number of cartons of milk needed for a week are loaded face forward on the bottom refrigerator shelf every Wednesday afternoon, where each closet has its designated function, where the mattresses are turned left to right, top to bottom, in alternating seasons. Unlike Caro, her mother eats the foods her body needs at the times they are needed. Her days are laid out so that each includes fresh air, work, solitude, conversation, and time at her piano. They are works of art unto themselves, something that fills Caro alternately with awe and horror—awe because her mother, in fact, accomplishes more in a day than anyone else she knows, horror because it seems inhuman to be able to keep destructive impulses so entirely leashed.

Caro studies the first column of the schedule her mother has drawn up for Eva. It is labeled *Daily Tasks*: Mondays for laundry, Tuesdays for washing linens and ironing, Wednesdays for cleaning the baths and kitchen, Thursdays for vacuuming and dusting, Fridays for food shopping and errands. She skips to the column labeled *Omar School Pickup*. Caro had leaned on all her connections to find a first-grade spot for Omar, with a friend in the admissions office at the City School having come through only last week thanks to a family that was unexpectedly moving. On the schedule, there is Adam for Monday, Eva for Tuesday, her mother for Wednesday, Rachida for Thursday, and her own name next to Friday with a question mark.

"I wondered if you want to do one day a week. I put down Fridays, since that's usually a lighter day for you."

Caro imagines Omar holding up his hand in delight, the miracle of a finger for each weekday, a day for each caregiver. "Sure," she says, a beat too slowly, her response like a card poorly played as it dawns on her that her brother's move is pulling them both back home.

16

At first, Eva brings only her pajamas upstairs to the room Myra intends for Omar. By the second week, though, Myra notices that Eva has brought up the remainder of her possessions: the pair of black pants, the two pairs of jeans, a handful of T-shirts, the fake leather jacket, the Lakers' duffel bag, a dog-eared Old Testament, and a small wooden box that she puts on the dresser. Eva's toothbrush sits in a glass atop the fourth-floor hallway bathroom sink. A bottle of her shampoo rests on the side of the tub.

It is Tuesday. Adam, Rachida, and Omar are due on Saturday. In the evening, Myra will remind Eva that she needs to move back downstairs before Omar arrives. When Myra comes upstairs from her office, though, Eva is so exuberant about her plans—in the fall, she will find a class to study Hebrew and maybe one to improve her English as well; she has been reading Dr. M.'s New York guidebooks about places she can take Omar—that Myra puts off raising the subject for another day.

At two, Myra wakes to the sound of a scream. She reaches the hall with Eva's second scream. She knocks on Eva's door, then pushes it open. Eva is sitting upright in the bed.

"Eva?"

Her eyes are open, fixed straight ahead. She screams again.

Myra places a hand on Eva's back. The girl does not move or speak. She seems to be still asleep. Gently, Myra rubs Eva's back, speaking to her softly, the way she had with Adam when he would have a night terror.

Eva squeezes her eyes tight, then opens them wide. She looks at Myra, unsure, it seems, who she is.

"It's Myra. Dr. M."

Eva vigorously shakes her head as though rejecting Myra's words. Then she seems to come to. She covers her face with her hands.

"What happen?" Eva asks.

"You had a nightmare. You were screaming in your sleep."

"I am so embarrassed."

"Don't be embarrassed. Everyone has nightmares on occasion." Myra pauses. It is true that everyone has nightmares, but only children rouse the household with screams.

"It happen before, but not in a very long time."

"Would you like some water?"

"Yes, please."

Myra goes into the bathroom and fills a paper cup with water. When she returns, Eva is still sitting up in the bed. She drinks the water, then crumples the cup between her hands.

"I promise it will not happen again."

On Eva's face is what Myra thinks of as the lovesick-puppy look. When the children were little, she would see it on occasion with a playmate: a child who would respond to cookies and milk and a hand on her shoulder by reaching out her arms and calling *Mama*. On occasion, the look will appear in the eyes of a patient whose hunger for love is so profound that the patient's awareness that Myra is a therapist—listening with genuine care and interest, with what she has come to recognize is a kind of love on her part but remains at heart a job, a job she puts down at night and on weekends and during August so she can care for her own family and herself—is eclipsed by a voracious demand for more.

"Go back to sleep. We can talk in the morning." Myra holds out her hand to take the crumpled cup.

"My father, when he hear me scream, he slap me. My sister, she put a sock in my mouth so he does not hear me."

Eva studies Myra's face. "You are worrying it will happen after Omar arrives? Don't worry. It is only because I was not used to it here. I am used to it now."

17

In the morning, Myra cannot concentrate on her work. She sits in front of her computer, but her thoughts will not budge from Eva's scream. Should she send the girl back to Lima? But for what? For being afraid to sleep alone on the ground floor? For having a night terror?

At eight, she calls Ursula's cell phone. It rings in Paris, where Ursula is on an extended shopping trip, on the rose quartz marble ledge of the enormous bath where she is soaking, in her suite at the George V Hotel.

Ursula listens to her cousin's concerns about Eva's night terrors, her worry that perhaps New York is too much for the girl. She thinks about the problem Eva could make for Alicia and her in their San Isidro synagogue, where her eldest grandson will soon be seeking his bar mitzvah date, were Eva to ask for Hebrew lessons or Jewish education or, God forbid, to join the congregation.

"Well, of course, sweetheart, if you need to send her back . . ." Ursula sighs. She climbs out of the tub, her brown nipples covered with milk foam. Her waist has thickened considerably since she reached menopause, a decade ago, but in her hand-sewn Parisian lingerie, her breasts and bottom—with the help of her trainer and ample French emollients—have retained sufficient firmness, in tandem with her Centurion American Express card, to attract the occasional twenty-something lover, such as the young Spaniard now splayed naked on the floral quilted spread of the hotel bed.

"Well, I suppose I might find her a job in one of the knitting factories on the outskirts of the city. Only, they treat the girls there like slaves, paying them piece work for hats and sweaters. Fifty cents a hat. Two dollars a sweater."

Wrapped in a towel, Ursula enters the dressing room, the chaise longue and telephone table littered by now, her third day in Paris, with shopping receipts and clothing boxes, one of which produces a red lace brassiere and a matching pair of tap pants.

She glances at the Spanish boy, who has produced an erection which he is fondly stroking.

"Sweetheart, I have to go. I will call you later. I promise. But perhaps you might give it just a teensy bit more time?"

Ursula feels a heaviness in her breasts and an urgency between her legs. "Kiss, kiss. Bye."

The Spaniard grins when he sees the red lace.

"Be rough," she orders.

18

By the time Myra has finished her midday walk around the reservoir, showered, eaten her lunch, and returned to her desk by the open French doors, the solution is clear. She will have to reorganize the sleeping arrangements. On the fourth floor, where she had planned for Omar to take the front room while she kept her bedroom overlooking the garden, she will let Eva stay put. She will give Rachida and Adam her bedroom. Omar can have the back bedroom on the third floor, and Adam can still have the music room for his office. She will move downstairs into the small room she'd planned for Eva.

She gets up to look at the room. It is narrow, with a twin bed under the window. A small wooden dresser and a card table are the room's only other furnishings. A pegboard with hooks serves as a makeshift closet. If she empties the closet in her office, there will be enough space for her clothes. In a way, it will be better. She won't have to worry about Eva moving around while her patients are in the office.

Fifty cents a hat. Two dollars a sweater.

It is a more logical arrangement, she tells herself.

19

After the chubby engineer threw her out, Caro had camped in the fifth-floor walk-up apartment of Anne-Marie, a girl from Brussels she'd met at the Parc Monceau. Pooling the money from the envelope the engineer had given her and the allowance Anne-Marie received from her banker father, they left in June for Greece, after which they took the train west to Spain, the ferry from Algeciras to Tangier, and then another train south to Casablanca. Terrified of the overtures of a Coca-Cola distributorship heir which had taken a nasty turn, but more, really, of herself and who she'd become during the months since her employer had pulled back her sheets, she fled Casablanca, taking the first departing bus.

The bus had gone to Essaouira, a town she knew nothing about. She spent three days in bed with what she thought was a case of tourista before she ventured out, wandering through a maze of narrow streets just wide enough for a wheelbarrow or donkey cart, the white light and briny smell from the adjacent sea lending a holiday atmosphere.

At the jewelers' souk, she found a silver bracelet for her mother, a braided cuff over which she bargained with the bearded shop owner to reach a price of 550 dirham. "A very rare piece," the owner said. "I am losing money selling it to you."

Two stores down, the identical cuff was displayed in the window. "How much?" she inquired of the young man behind the counter.

"I will give you a very good deal. Three hundred dirham."

Indignant, Caro returned to the first shop to protest.

"That," the man sneered, "that bracelet you saw, to mention it in the same breath as mine is an insult. I will give you the benefit of the doubt. You are ignorant about the differences in the quality of silver."

The man had a long face with a bulbous nose. His cheeks were flecked with broken capillaries. It was clear that, from his point of view, inflating prices for a tourist was acceptable practice, the exchange between them entirely within the realm of principle.

Her eyes wandered to a shelf where there was a candelabrum that looked like a menorah. "Can I see that?"

Very carefully, the shop owner reached for the object, which he placed on the glass countertop. There was a star of David on the base of the piece. He peered at her. "You are a Jew?"

She did not answer.

"You want this instead?"

She nodded.

"For you, I will rob myself. Rob my own family. But no more discussion of the quality of my silver. You will come to my home tomorrow for the Sabbath dinner."

And so Caro met Uri and his vain, hypochondriacal wife, Raquel, and then their brainy angry daughter, Rachida, and her sweet older sister, Esther, the mother's handmaiden and an image of how Rachida might have looked had she not felt her life depended on being as unlike her sister and mother as possible.

Esther and Raquel fingered Caro's clothes, the hem of the loose blouse and the folds of the long skirt she'd worn to walk the streets alone.

"These are shoes for a girl?" Esther asked, giggling as she slipped her tiny soft feet inside Caro's beat-up Birkenstocks.

Uri batted Esther's leg. "Excuse this rude child of mine."

Before dinner, Raquel lit candles. The family held hands, Rachida grimacing as she placed hers inside Caro's, and Uri said the blessing over the wine, the same *baruch atah Adonai Eloheinu Melekh haolam, borei p'ri hagafen* Caro dimly recalled her mother's uncle saying on their annual visits to her mother's parents' home.

"Your parents, they keep the Sabbath?" Uri asked as Raquel served the couscous.

"Not really. They both had uncles who were rabbis, but neither of them is religious."

"Your father should have insisted. That is the job of the father."

She did not want to say that her parents were divorced, her father remarried to a woman who wasn't Jewish, but before she could decide what to say, Rachida blurted out, the first words Caro can remember her having said, her face locked until that moment in a bored scowl, "In America, they are not still in the Dark Ages. There are Jews who actually use their minds."

A vein throbbed in Uri's temple. When he spoke, it was as

though he were releasing his words one by one. "My daughter, she thinks that she is more intelligent than her father. She thinks her science is wiser than the Talmud. But she will learn. Our ancestors have been here since the time of the Romans. My father was a Berber. My grandfather was a Berber. My great-great-great-great-grandfather was a Berber. We are the Jews who came here directly from the Holy Land. Not the Jews who fled Spain. Not the Jews who pretended to be Christians. Before there were Muslims here, before there were kings—when there were only tribes of people. Our people have brought our trades to every corner of the world: to China, to India, to South America, to Canada. And always, always we have kept Sabbath, obeyed the kosher laws, observed the High Holidays. But no, my brilliant daughter, she is smarter than thousands of years of our people."

At "brilliant," Uri slammed his fist on the table, toppling his glass of wine. Raquel reached over to right the glass and blot up the wine. Esther froze, a forkful of couscous midair, and Rachida pushed back her chair, mumbling something that Caro was sure must be *fuck you* in Arabic.

After the meal, Rachida reappeared. She grilled Caro about New York City, where—she lowered her voice to tell Caro, her parents didn't know yet—she was applying to medical school.

A year later, Rachida began medical school in the Bronx. She had been living across from the school for a month when she first called Caro, home for the summer with a job at a Head Start program. They spent several evenings together, the first of which was marked by what Caro knew was Rachida's surprise to see the changes in her, her curves hidden beneath the twenty pounds she'd regained on her return to Harvard, when, unable to sleep, she'd begun the secretive night eating in her dorm room as she tried not to think about what had happened with the chubby engineer in Paris and then afterward.

The evenings with Rachida passed with awkward pauses, continued on Caro's end out of a sense of guilt at the thought of

abandoning a foreigner, but also due to a begrudging admiration of Rachida's frank bitterness—about her father's mi-
sogyny, that he never got over not having a son; about the
foolishness of her mother and sister, who couldn't understand
Rachida's lack of interest in clothing and domestic adornment;
about the other medical students, who awkwardly avoided
political conversations in her presence, assuming her to be a
Muslim foe of Israel.

A few days before Caro returned to Boston, in a last-ditch
effort to be hospitable, she introduced Rachida to Adam, about
to start his first year at N.Y.U. Perhaps he would take Rachida
on as a movie partner—his ironic love of lowbrow movies com-
panionable, she thought, with Rachida's enjoyment of them for
exactly what they are. Romance between the two of them never
crossed her mind, not only because of their age difference, Rachida's twenty-two to Adam's eighteen, but also because it was
hard to imagine physical contact between them, Rachida too
brusque to seem amorous, Adam looking like a kid whose hand
needed to be held.

By the time Caro came home for Thanksgiving, Adam and
Rachida were a couple, even then, though, more like an old
married couple than young lovers. When Rachida left for her
dermatology residency in Detroit, still believing she would ul-
timately return to Morocco, Adam followed—neither of them
prepared for the other female residents with complexions out
of cosmetic advertisements and tight skirts worn under their
lab coats, all headed for lucrative nine-to-five practices that
would require no evening beepers and permit ample time for
family ski trips and home-beautification projects. They married
three months before Omar's birth, after which Rachida gave up
the idea of going back to Morocco. In the fifth year of her shopping mall practice, she devised the plan of a respecialization
fellowship in primary care that would allow her afterward to
work at a clinic serving the Arabic community in Detroit.

Now, in two days, Rachida, Adam, and Omar would be here. *You should be happy,* Caro tells herself. She pinches her arm. *You really should.*

20

"It's the summer solstice," Omar announces as he tumbles out of the backseat of the stuffed Honda wagon. His bangs, navy-black like his mother's, hang over his forehead. "Rachida explained it to me. The way that the axis of the earth to the sun changes with the seasons."

Rachida had given Omar her mini-astronomy lecture somewhere around Ohio, part of her scientific education program, prophylactic, she believes, to a vulnerability to religion. She dislodges herself from behind the driver's seat and glances at her son. Like her, he rarely smiles, his seriousness so familiar to her, she had never thought about it until Omar's preschool teacher mentioned it—not with alarm, she was careful to say, Omar is passionate about so many things and plays so nicely with the other children, but rather because it is so unusual to see a child so lacking in, well, she blushed as she said it, childishness.

Standing on the steps of the brownstone are Myra, Caro, and a girl with stringy dark hair who, Rachida realizes, must be Eva. In one hand, she is holding a blue helium balloon that says WELCOME, in the other a stuffed animal.

"It's the longest day of the year! Rachida said I could stay up as late as I want." Omar disappears into the arms of his grandmother and aunt. Adam groans as he unfolds himself from the passenger seat, pulling on his beard and his wrinkled khaki shorts. Caro hugs him, a hug that ends in a little poke to the belly that in the last year has begun to overhang his belt.

Rachida cocks her head in Omar's direction. She can feel

the circle of perspiration that has formed on her back. "He slept all afternoon."

The rounds of hugging with introductions of Eva continue until Rachida pops the trunk and begins lifting out the bags. Omar goes inside with Eva to look at the box of his father's old toys that Eva has unpacked in the third-floor room that will be his. By the time Rachida arrives with a duffel filled with Omar's clothes, Omar and Eva are flopped on the rug, their noses inches apart as they sort through the pieces of an Erector set.

Myra announces that dinner will be on the kitchen deck. Rachida washes her hands and face in the kitchen sink, aware that it would be more appropriate to go upstairs to wash up and change her shirt with its slightly unpleasant odor—that she is under the sway of the oppositionalism her mother-in-law's graciousness sets off in her, Myra's good manners eliciting her own rudest inclinations. When she'd once mentioned this to Caro, Caro had laughingly chided, "Trust me, I understand. But you'd better get over it. There's so much my mother does well. If you become a contrarian with her, the only things left for you to do will be to suck your teeth and play poker."

With her face still wet, she steps onto the deck. Votive candles are perched on the railing. From the garden below, she can hear the fountain, a hypnotic gurgling that brings her back to an afternoon in Fez with her father and sister, a square with a blue-and-white-tiled fountain where students from the nearby madrasa would come to wash.

Eva has come downstairs and is now helping Myra carry the food to the outdoor table: shrimp done on skewers on the grill, baby potatoes roasted with olive oil and dill from one of the terra-cotta pots, a corn-bread and green salad that Myra says are both Eva's doing. Eva beams. With each platter she places on the table, she looks up at Myra to check her reaction. Rachida counts the plates. Six. She knows there is no acceptable alternative to having Eva eat with them, but it will be a chore to carry on a conversation with her, grating to see the glances Eva gives Myra, Myra's small nods of encouragement.

Myra sends Eva to get the others. When everyone is on the deck, she motions for Rachida to take the seat at the end of the table across from her, Omar and Eva along one side, Adam and Caro on the other.

"I can't believe you're from Iquitos," Adam says, looking at Eva. "*Fitzcarraldo* is one of my absolute favorite movies. I've seen it and *Burden of Dreams*, the documentary about Herzog's making of the film, dozens of times. You probably know some of the people that were in it. There were over a thousand extras. My God, Herzog, the megalomaniac, actually dragged that ship over the mountain. Everyone thought he was insane. He makes his character Fitzcarraldo seem like a measured man."

Rachida feels her irritation rising, her impatience with Adam's cinematic obsessions. If they were not at her mother-in-law's table, she would tell him to zip it. Eva looks at her plate, which Rachida notices has no shrimp. Does Eva keep kosher?

"Perhaps Eva doesn't know about the film," Myra says.

"Impossible. Herzog took over Iquitos. The Amazon was filled with canoes confronting the steamship, which they really drove over the rapids."

Eva continues to stare at her plate. Rachida sees Omar reach under the table to take Eva's hand, the way she once saw Caro do with Adam when their father, Larry, had launched one of his bellicose lectures on the grandeur of a man riding a horse.

"It's a movie, Eva," Myra says, "that was filmed in Iquitos. When was it made, Adam?"

"It was released in 1982. But they began preproduction in the mid-seventies. It took so long because Jason Robards, who originally played Fitzcarraldo, got sick and had to resign, and then Mick Jagger, who played his sidekick, a Sancho to

Robards's Quixote, quit because he'd run out of time before his next tour. Herzog had to virtually start over. For a while, he planned to play Fitzcarraldo himself, but then Kinski insisted that he would be better and had to do it."

"Eva would have been a young child while they were filming. It's unlikely she'd know the extras."

"I am very sorry. My parents never go to the movies. My father drive a speedboat for one of the jungle lodges, and he always go to a bar after work. For fun, my mother play this tile game with the ladies on our street. She is a very religious person. The only movie she ever watch is *The Sound of Music*. We watch it on television every year together." Eva's face brightens. "Do you know the movie? I know all the songs!" Softly, Eva begins to sing: "The hills are alive with the sound of music / With songs they have sung for a thousand years . . ."

As a child, Rachida had loved that movie. She, too, can remember watching it on television with her mother and sister, Julie Andrews singing in a dubbed French. *"Collines que j'aime / Vous chantez au monde / Des airs qu'autrefois / J'entendais chez moi . . ."* Once, she'd tried to get Adam to watch it with her, but he'd said, "You've got to be kidding. It's kitsch through and through."

"You must have heard people talk about Herzog making *Fitzcarraldo*," Adam persists. "Your parents or other people who were involved?"

Her annoyance like a sneeze that can no longer be controlled, Rachida blurts, "Stop interrogating her. Can't you see that she doesn't know anything about it?"

Now it is Omar's turn to look into his plate.

"Oh Jesus, I'm sorry." Rachida sighs. "Just, Adam, enough already." She looks at Omar, but when he lifts his face, his expression is impassive, as though he long ago resigned himself to his mother's sharp tongue and his father's way of never seeing that he is annoying the shit out of everyone.

"We'll have to watch it after dinner," Adam says. "It opens with this fabulous scene of Klaus Kinski and Claudia Cardinale, both in gorgeous white finery, racing to get to the Teatro Amazonas in Manaus in time to hear Caruso sing."

21

When they are done eating, Adam goes to look for his copy of *Fitzcarraldo*. Rachida and Myra take Omar upstairs to help him get ready for bed, and Eva clears the table. Caro follows Adam into the music room, where her mother has set up a table under the window for him to use as a desk. She watches her brother rifling through the file boxes he has brought with him, wondering if she should ask how things are going with Rachida.

"It's got to be in here. I'd never have left it behind." Adam splits the tape on a box labeled *The Searchers* and begins emptying out cassettes and files. Caro examines the labels on the other boxes: Contracts & Bills, Screenplays/Books. Only one is unlabeled.

"How about this one? Could it be in here?" she asks, tapping the box.

Adam intercepts her arm so quickly, he lands her a shove. Their eyes lock and her hands clench. It shocks her, this taste of sibling violence that for them had been blessedly rare, squashed by her feelings of pity and protectiveness toward her scrawny brother.

"It's not in there." He pushes the box out of her reach, his clutter having already defiled their mother's serene order, so that Caro has to fight an urge to chastise him, to order him to put his things away—the vestigial, bossy, older-sister feeling that he is hers but also that he is her responsibility.

"I'm going to call it a night," Caro says.

22

"We're doing great," Myra reports when Caro telephones a few days later to inquire. "On Sunday, Adam took Omar to the park, where he met a child who'll also be in first grade at City. The mother told Adam about the camp at the school. Adam and Omar went over to see if there were any openings, and there was one space left. They let him start right away. He loves it. They're doing a unit on reptiles and have two snakes and a gecko in a terrarium. Adam was thrilled, because it means he can get down to work now rather than having to wait for September. I was going to call you tonight to see if you wanted to do pickup on Friday."

Something about the way her mother's words are inflected leaves the impression of an imperative rather than an interrogative. Only once has Caro heard her father, who has never let go of his mantle as the aggrieved party, as though it were her mother, not he, who'd busted up their marriage, voice anything that sounds like a criticism of her. *The softest-spoken tyrant you'll ever meet,* he'd said. *A will of steel.*

On Friday, Caro meets Omar in the classroom that serves as home base for his camp group. He is sitting at one of the child-sized tables reading a junior encyclopedia, his head arced over the book so she can see the cowlick at the top of his soft neck. He doesn't notice her arrival until she kisses his hair.

"Auntie Caro, can I finish my page?" Caro glances at the book, open to a section on insects and spiders. A diagram shows the butterfly life cycle: egg, caterpillar, chrysalis, adult.

"Okay. Where's your stuff? I'll gather it up."

Omar points to a wall of cubbies where a group of boys are gathered like a squirming beast, poking one another with the action figures they are allowed, with the day now over, to remove from their camp bags. She retrieves Omar's bag, damp, with a faint scent of chlorine from the balled-up bathing trunks inside.

Once they are outside, Caro takes Omar's hand. They walk to Broadway for ice cream while Omar describes the way a caterpillar makes a chrysalis, and how when it splits open—he unfurls his fingers so his hands are pinwheels—there's no more caterpillar, just a butterfly!

She watches her nephew's ice-cream cone, expecting the splatters to which she is accustomed from her preschoolers, but Omar manages his cone with careful expertise so that the only residue is a pale vanilla spot on his nose. With it half-uneaten, he hands it to her. "I'm full. I've had enough."

Is there something worrisome about a child not finishing an ice-cream cone, something too restrained for his age?

"Do you know how many horns the styracosaurus had? Six horns on its head plus one on its nose."

"I didn't know that."

"Do you know which dino is my very favorite one?"

"Let me think. Mmmm . . . The polkadotateratops?"

Omar looks at his sneakers, as though sparing her the humiliation of discovering that her joke is not funny. "The parasaurolophus. It had only one horn on its head and it was a herbivore."

He stops—so suddenly Caro nearly drops the remains of the now dripping cone—and leans over, pointing at a chewed-up piece of gum on the sidewalk. "A bird or a squirrel could choke on that."

"Don't touch. I'll get it." She picks up the gum with one of the napkins she'd wrapped around the cone. At the corner, she tosses the cone and the gum in a trash can.

"Eva is a vegetarian," Omar continues, slipping his hand into Caro's now empty one. "Did you know that some vegetarians don't eat anything that comes from animals?"

"They're called vegans. Is Eva a vegan?"

"She doesn't eat meat or chicken or fish. Rachida told me it's not because of her religion. She just doesn't like it."

When they arrive back at the house, Eva is in the kitchen washing lettuce and boiling water for pasta.

"Hi, Miss Caro. Hi, Omar. You like something to drink?" Eva asks, having been carefully instructed, Caro imagines, by her mother to offer Omar plenty of fluids.

"Yes, please. What are you making?"

"Macaroni and cheese pie."

Eva tilts her head toward an index card propped against the tile backsplash. She looks at Caro. "Your mother write the recipe for me. She is teaching me how to cook. Did she teach you?"

"A few things. Omar says you're a vegetarian."

Eva wipes her hands on the hips of her pants. "The smell of cooking animal, it makes me sick to the stomach. Your mother is so nice. She says it is okay if I prepare everything else, she will make the meat. She washes and seasons it so I don't have to touch it."

"Are you allergic?" Omar asks. "There's a boy in my camp who's allergic to nuts. He has to keep this special pen that's really a needle in his backpack."

"I don't like the smell." Eva crinkles her nose. With a shudder of her shoulders, she turns back to the stove.

23

Over dinner, Adam announces that he has begun a new project, a remake of *The Searchers*.

"I've been thinking about it a long time, debating the dramatic circumstances. Then this week it came to me. Eva inspired me." He smiles in her direction, a smile she responds to with what strikes Myra as a look of frozen fear.

"I've been reading about the boomtown atmosphere of Iquitos in the 1890s. All of these people descended on the town to make their fortunes with rubber, with no regard for the people who'd lived there for centuries. I've recast Ethan Edwards as a Jew from Tangier searching for the missing daughter his brother had with a common-law Indian wife."

"*The Searchers*," Myra says. "I must have seen the original, but I can't remember it."

"It's fabulous! We can watch it after dinner. I have a copy upstairs. It's John Ford's finest film. You could learn how to paint, how to photograph, how to be a novelist just by studying that film."

Rachida, who has made an extra effort to be home for dinner since she was on call the night before, rolls her eyes, but before she can make a caustic remark, Myra says that would be lovely and Omar is pleading to watch too.

"Please, Rachida, I don't have camp tomorrow."

"How many people of color are slaughtered in this thing?" Rachida asks.

"There are ways of seeing the film that transcend the old cowboys-and-Indians genre. It's really a profound critique of racism, about Ethan Edwards's projection of the savage part of himself onto the Native Americans."

"Pleeeeese . . . pretty please with a cherry on top." Omar holds up his hand. "I give my word of honor."

"It's scary," Adam says, "but nothing is really shown."

"I'll cover my eyes if it's inappropriate."

"Why don't you get into your pj's and brush your teeth first," Myra suggests.

Adam heads upstairs to help Omar and to get the video set up in the music room while Myra goes out to water her garden. Rachida says she has to make a work call, leaving Caro to help Eva with the dishes.

Caro assumes the position at the sink, rinsing the dishes and them handing them to Eva to load into the dishwasher. She can see her mother in the garden below moving among the plant beds with her snaky hose. Leaning over to prune the

white begonias, her mother appears in the soft dusk slender
and limber as a girl.

Stuffed with the macaroni and cheese, Caro feels old and
heavy. She watches her mother rewind the hose and then disappear, heading inside, Caro assumes, through the doors to her
office. A few minutes later, Caro hears her mother's steps on
the front stairs, and then the piano as she begins to play.

"Your mother, she plays so beautifully," Eva says. She looks
at Caro shyly. "I never hear anyone play so beautifully."

"She does." Caro listens, trying to identify the music—one
of the Bach Inventions. Despite her persistent efforts, her mother
had not been able to get either of her children to stick with an
instrument. Adam had hung in for two years of clarinet, before hurling it on the floor in a moment of frustration. Caro
had quit the guitar after six months of lessons, during which
she'd developed painful calluses and failed to tune the damn
thing.

For her fiftieth birthday, her mother, having never played
anything more than a schoolgirl's "Chopsticks," bought herself
a grand piano. Even the bow-tied salesperson questioned the
purchase; perhaps, he suggested, she would like to rent a con-
sole on which to take her first lessons. Her mother was reso-
lute. She had already found a teacher, an Austrian man who'd
looked at her hands and had her sing the melody of a Chopin
waltz before declaring that she would be playing the Mozart
Sonata in C by the end of a year.

On the day the piano arrived, her mother began her practice schedule: one hour, five nights a week. Indeed, by the end
of her first year of study, she was playing the easy Mozart so-
natas, Beethoven's "Für Elise," and the Chopin Waltz in A
Minor.

The first time Caro heard her mother play, she was filled
with wonder tinged with a strange resentment. Glancing up
from the keys, her mother had seen Caro's expression.

"Yes?" her mother said, placing her hands in her lap.

"I can't believe how well you play. After so little time."

Her mother raised her eyebrows.

"It's a little overwhelming to have a mother who can do so many things. It leaves me feeling like a klutz."

On her mother's face was a familiar quizzical look whose melancholic undertones, depending on Caro's mood, provoked the wish either to get away as fast as possible or to wrap her arms around her mother. "You were lucky," Caro said. "All your mother could do was clean."

"Very lucky. All I ever saw was my mother's backside sticking up in the air as she crawled around on her hands and knees scouting for dirt."

Caro smiled, imagining her shrunken, dour grandmother. "But if it were you, it would be a perfect backside that would make mine look enormous in comparison."

"Oh yes, my pathetic daughter. Phi Beta Kappa from Harvard, director at twenty-six of a preschool she's since made nationally renowned."

"Seriously, Mom, how do you do it?"

Myra closed her music books. She set them on the side of the music stand. "Once you learn to apply yourself, to dig deep and push for excellence, you can do it with anything. Cooking, gardening, writing. It's like learning to use a muscle—only this is a psychological muscle."

"How come I don't have it?"

Her mother hesitated, as though debating if she should acknowledge that it is true that Caro has never done anything that has required her to apply herself 100 percent. "Everything you've done, you've been able to do with a small piece of yourself. It's a different experience when you have to use every fiber of your being."

"So how did you learn?"

Her mother came to sit next to her on the couch. She

picked up Caro's hand and, sensing no resistance, held it lightly. "Actually," she said, "it was with you. When you were a baby. You were a little colicky, not terribly so, and it didn't last that long, but I was very anxious, which you sensed, and that made you even fussier. Your father was a resident and hardly home. On a resident's salary, we couldn't even consider babysitting help. I didn't understand then that the real problem was my own lack of experience being mothered. I had to figure out how to soothe you, on no sleep, with no inner model or help. That was the first time I had to dig deep. I did it again with your brother, and then again when I wrote my thesis. Eventually, it became ingrained, a way of being."

Caro hands the last of the dinner plates to Eva. There is an almost ecstatic look on Eva's face as she glances up at the ceiling through which Myra's playing can be heard. "Your mother, Omar wants her to teach him. Do you think she will let me watch?"

Caro imagines her mother on the piano bench, Omar beside her looking down at the keys, Eva on a nearby chair with her eyes fixed on them. The image leaves her with a queasy feeling. "You'll have to ask her."

She gives Eva the dishwasher detergent and turns to scrubbing the sink.

24

The Searchers begins with TEXAS 1868 against a black background.

"It was filmed in Monument Valley," Adam whispers to Caro. "Do you remember, we went there once with Dad?"

"In Arizona?"

"Ford, the director, loved Monument Valley. It was totally unspoiled in the fifties, the farthest point anywhere in the country from a railroad. He thought the landscape looked more like Texas than Texas itself. He would set up tent cities and live out on the desert with his actors and crew. He and John Wayne were great buddies. They'd finish a bottle of wine together and then spend a couple of hours smoking cigars and playing cards."

Last summer, Adam had taken Rachida and Omar on a long-planned car trip from Detroit to Riggins, Idaho, with the intention of showing his wife and son the land he mythologized in the Westerns he wrote for third-world markets. The week before they left, wildfires had broken out, ravaging hundreds of thousands of acres of land. Crushed at the idea of canceling the trip, Adam had convinced Rachida to persevere. They arrived in Montana to find that entire mountainsides had burned in a matter of days and flames were leaping across Route 80. The craggy peaks of the Crazy Mountains, usually crystalline clear in August, were hidden by sooty gray sky.

The trip culminated with a rafting sojourn on the Salmon River led by a guide Adam had found on the Internet: a former Deadhead turned ardent Native Americanist who met them dressed in a blue loincloth, his hand-crafted drums under one arm. On their first day, they drifted past hills orange with flame, the fleeing elk and deer and moose racing along the banks of the river. Late afternoon, the Deadhead guide set up camp on a sandy beachhead. Omar raced up the dunes, whooping as he flung himself down the mounds of white sand, while Adam squinted into the smoke at prop planes passing overhead.

"Smoke jumpers from the McCall base," the Deadhead told Adam. "Headed into the Nez Percé."

"Smoke jumpers?"

"Guys who jump into fires so they can fight them inside out."

"Pretty heroic."

"Yup. Ninety-nine point nine percent of them."

"And the rest?"

"Don't quote me. Let's just say it might not be past a disgruntled guy to add a few days' work by dropping a burning briquette on the way to a jump site."

In the middle of the night, Adam awoke to a red glow hovering over the ridge of the opposite bank of the river and Omar's cheeks dusted with ashes. Back in Detroit, there was a letter from his mother with a copy of an editorial she'd clipped on the misguided zealousness of the old Smokey Bear policy: the snuffing out of all fires had prevented the natural clearing of the underbrush by smaller conflagrations, leaving a tinderbox primed to set off the inferno then taking place. Across the top of the Smokey Bear clipping, she'd printed in her precise hand *The Tragedy of Good Intentions*.

Adam picks up the remote. "This shot here, wait, I'll stop it."

He hits the pause button, freezing an image of a woman, her back to the camera, framed by a rough-hewn doorway, her eyes presumably locked on something she sees in the distance.

"If you're going to butcher this by talking through the whole thing and stopping it every five seconds, I'm going to go take a shower," Rachida says.

Myra surveys her family. Her grandson is lying on the couch with his head in her lap, his legs propped on Eva's thighs. Rachida is perched on the desk chair, no longer looking at the screen. Caro sits in the velvet wing chair with her feet up on the piano bench. Adam, still standing, is fiddling with the remote.

In the next scene, the reverend, who is also the captain of the Texas Rangers, arrives to round up volunteers for a band of men to retrieve some stolen cattle. The reverend stares into the camera while the departing Ethan Edwards bends to tenderly kiss his brother's wife on the brow. Again, Adam stops the film. "The entire motivation for the film is captured in this frame."

Rachida stands. Myra exchanges glances with her daughter. Caro shrugs her shoulders. Oblivious, it seems, to Rachida's departure, Adam restarts the film, which, like the mood in the room, is taking a darker and darker cast as the fear of an Indian raid falls over the adults who have remained to tend to the homestead. Realizing what her parents are suspecting, the older daughter, a teenager, breaks into an eye-popping scream.

Myra looks at Omar and then at Adam to see if he wants to stop the movie, perhaps it is too much for a six-year-old, but Adam's gaze is fixed on the screen. The phone rings. Before Myra can untangle herself from Omar to get it, the ringing stops.

Forty miles away, Ethan, with inhuman calm, informs the search party that they have been duped: the cattle theft, he understands now, was a ploy to draw them away from the homestead so the remaining settlers could be ambushed. In an excruciating display of discipline, Ethan waters and feeds his exhausted horse before beginning the long journey back to his brother's family.

To Myra's relief, Omar turns inward on the couch. With his deepening breath, he appears to be falling asleep. Myra strokes her grandson's dark head of hair, her fingers massaging his scalp. She can't shake the thought that Rachida picked up the phone knowing the call would be for her—her angry departure over Adam's annotations a ploy like the cattle theft.

Eva has drawn her knees up to her chest and is chewing a finger.

As Ethan approaches the homestead, the camera cuts away from John Wayne's face to the valley below. A red swatch of flame defines the roof of the burning homestead, drawing nearer and nearer with each pound of the horse's hooves.

Eva gasps. She buries her face between her knees.

TWO

1

For as long as Adam can remember, there has been a divide in the family about the house his father's father, Max, commenced building the year he turned fifty-one. The divide, Adam has come to understand, is, in fact, about Frank Lloyd Wright, whose Wisconsin Taliesin home was its inspiration—to the ire of Adam's grandmother, Ida, prime minister of the hate-the-house or, more precisely, hate-Frank-Lloyd-Wright faction of the family, his father, Larry, her secretary of state. Once Adam reached an age when he could verbalize an opinion, he became his grandfather's most vociferous ally in support of the house, an attitude he only later understood he had absorbed from his mother's quiet admiration for the sentiments of his grandfather which the house embodied. In Adam's case, though, his allegiances are seen as of questionable motive. As his father is fond of saying, Adam would have become a cannibal had Larry been a vegetarian.

Max, who died five years ago, had made by the standards of the family a substantial amount of money as an entertainment lawyer with a client list that Ida, dead herself now for nearly two years, never missed an opportunity to report had included at various times Zero Mostel, Dean Martin, and Doris Day. His own father had been a diamond merchant in Frankfurt who came to America in the 1880s and opened a jewelry store in South Orange, New Jersey, on whose bread-and-butter trade of gold wedding bands, silver charm bracelets, and sensible watches he raised three sons who went on to become a rabbi, a teacher, and, in Max's case, a lawyer.

As a young man, Max had been dapper and dilettantish, in love with cloisonné pens and platinum cuff links, limited-edition pocket knives, engraved leather folios. By the time Larry was old enough to play in his father's dressing room, there were shelves of Italian-made shoes, drawers of silk pajamas, and a cedar closet housing baskets of cashmere socks, piles of merino wool sweaters, a collection of fox-lined hats.

Then everything changed. The change took place almost overnight. It was the spring of 1952, and Max had taken his family—Ida, unhappy that they were not going to Palm Beach; Larry, an awkward and moody thirteen; and Henry, then nine—to Phoenix, where he had business to conduct for a client. The client invited all of them to his home, a house, it turned out, that had been designed by Frank Lloyd Wright. It was unlike anything any of them had ever seen: low to the ground, with cement panels and periwinkle-blue beams and ceiling-to-floor glass windows—an abode that Ida politely complimented to the owner's face but later declared to be the ugliest house ever built.

Standing inside, looking out at the green lawn and the palm trees and the desert sky, Max, a man who until that moment had been an unadvertised atheist, felt for the first time that he had seen God—seen that the duty of mankind is to honor nature and to live in harmony with the earth and all her creatures. Simultaneously shattered and filled with joy, he'd experienced in his bones the paradox of the infinitesimal scale of each human being, the earth itself but a speck of dust in the universe, existing in concert with the infinite potential of each individual.

On his arrival home, Max vowed to live the rest of his years clothed in what he already owned. To Ida's horror, he donated his silk pajamas and platinum cuff links and Hermès cravats to the used-clothing store run by the local B'nai B'rith ladies (from which she secretly reclaimed the cuff links for her sons), keeping for himself seven changes of clothing for each season, which he wore until they were threadbare. A month later, on a Thursday morning, he left his Riverdale home, as he did every weekday, in his yellow Cadillac. Instead of turning south toward his office in the Flatiron building, he drove north along the Taconic Parkway into the Catskills, where he remained alone for three nights, purchasing before his return an eighteen-acre lot in the township of Willow, with the intention, he informed Ida, of having Frank Lloyd Wright design them a home.

Max commenced a correspondence with the eighty-four-year-old Wright, their exchange of letters, which he showed Adam, mired in Max's elegiac descriptions of the mountain vistas and Wright's compulsive iterations of his contractual policies. After one visit to the bug-infested land over a particularly rainy June week during which the family stayed at a dingy hotel with lumpy mattresses and attended a cacophonic atonal concert at a nearby avant-garde music colony, Ida dug in her heels, refusing to discuss the construction of anything in what she called that godforsaken corner of the world. By the time Max was able to convince her that a nearby country home would be nice for the boys, Wright had died and his sons were both already in college. Never having wavered from the vision he'd had on the Arizona trip, Max hired an architect who had spent a brief time at Wright's Arizona studio, Taliesin West. The architect designed a hodgepodge Prairie and Usonian house with signature Wrightian features, such as casement windows that opened wide enough for a small person to be able to crawl in and out, and a cruciform design centered on a flagstone fireplace.

Unfortunately, what was primarily needed was a proper siting of the house on the property, which was adjacent to a pond that, in the summers, attracted wild geese whose abundant fecal deposits drew all species of flying insects, including mosquitoes, wasps, and bees that nested in the low eaves formed by the flat roof. Without a basement, the flagstone floor remained damp spring, summer, and fall, with pods of black mold forming in the corners. Winters, the subfloor would constrict and thin slivers of ice would push through the blackened grout.

When Larry and Myra married, in 1967, Ida had already ceased her visits to the house. Although Max maintained a stubborn allegiance to the property, which he'd named Max's Tali in homage to Wright's Taliesin (a name which he pretended not to know was twisted by his sons into Max's Folly), he was beginning to appear worn down by the seamless way the never-quite-completed construction had merged into ceaseless repairs of termite-ridden beams and rusting casement hinges.

On Myra's first night at the house, the August before she married Larry, she donned the obligatory bug spray and joined Max on the terrace, while Larry stayed inside watching a baseball game. It was too overcast to see the moon or the stars, the air somehow both muggy and chilly, the only sound that of the mosquitoes sizzling as they flew into the citronella candles. In his soon-to-be daughter-in-law, Max found an open ear for his thoughts about Frank Lloyd Wright as a descendant of Emerson and Thoreau and a recipient of the most elevated strains of Americanism—an Americanism not about property and a New World Industrial Revolution but about the nation as the embodiment of an ideal in which spirit and equality reigned supreme over tradition and greed. It was the first time Myra had ever considered the possibility that being an American was something to cultivate and honor. For her own perpetually exhausted father, America had been a place to get ahead, the home of a grim, godless modernity, an idea about which he'd had neither the energy nor the inclination to attach any moral valence.

Until their divorce, Larry and Myra took their children

every Memorial Day and Labor Day to the Willow house—
trips, Adam would later learn, that were largely bolstered by
his mother's admiration of his grandfather's vision, a sentiment
which earned her a permanent place in Max's circle of deepest
affection.

2

At the beginning of July, Larry calls Caro to tell her that he
and Betty, his third wife, will be spending the first two weeks
of August at Max's Folly, the name they have all taken to calling the house now that Max is gone. Since Ida's death, Larry
and his brother, Henry, have rented the house to two sculptors.
The lease will run out at the end of the month, and Larry and
Henry intend to put the house up for sale after Labor Day.
During Larry's trip, he will arrange for some painting and
minor repairs to be done. Would Caro like to come for a visit
with Adam, Rachida, and Omar? Not wanting to sound mor-
bid, Caro thinks, her father refrains from saying *final visit*,
though this is obviously the case.

"Actually, if you don't mind having the workers around,
you could stay until Labor Day. I'm having the pool liner re-
placed next week, and the Ping-Pong table is still set up in the
dining room."

"Did you ask Adam?"

Her father clears his throat. The tension between her
brother and father has only increased with the addition of Rachida to the family. *What kind of hypocritical bullshit is that?*
Adam sputtered when her father responded to the news of his
plan to marry Rachida by asking if their children would be
American or Moroccan. *All my life you lecture me on the impor-
tance of marrying a Jewish woman. Not that you've seemed to
think, since Mom, that it applied to you. What you really meant*

was have your babies with a white Jewish woman. Only the Ash-kenazi need apply.

Adam's comments, Caro knows, had cut her father to the quick. Her father thinks of himself as a reasonable man, an enlightened person, a man with his feet firmly planted in science but with a healthy respect for his heritage and the history of his people. In his mind, his feelings are utterly distinct from racial prejudice, even if he cannot articulate exactly how when Adam accuses him of precisely this.

"Well, I was hoping you could do that. You know Adam. If I ask, he'll say no. Think it over, okay? I've got to run."

Caro remains holding the phone, filled with the sort of uncomfortable feelings that make her want to put something in her mouth, which, in fact, she does: the rest of a box of cereal followed by the remaining third of a jar of peanut butter. By the time she reaches the jar bottom, she is too sedated and filled with disgust at her lack of self-control to think about her brother.

Adam's response when Caro calls the following evening to convey their father's offer comes as a surprise. "Sure. That would be great. Omar's camp will be over early August. We can go for a week while Dad's there and then stay for another week after that. I'll bring Eva so she can watch Omar and I can get some work done. Rachida can come up on the weekends."

"What do you mean *we*? I wasn't thinking of staying after Dad leaves."

When Adam speaks again, it is in the voice Caro has known since childhood: the boy who, having understood that he was too old to get into bed with their mother after a bad dream, would creep downstairs to climb in with her, the trellising details of the dream described while she tried to make herself comfortable in half of a twin bed. "Come on, Caro, your school's closed in August. You know I can't go without you."

3

With Larry's move to Arizona, Caro and Adam's Memorial Day and Labor Day visits to Max's Tali came to a halt. Instead, each August their father would travel east and they would take a two-week vacation with him, the destinations limited by Adam's plane phobia to locales reachable by car or train, with a few days first at the Willow house. By then, with the help of abundant chemical sealants and an expert who'd succeeded in removing the geese from the property by placing poison in the pond, Max had managed to hold his own against nature's attack on the property, and Ida, won over by the presence of her grandchildren, begrudgingly agreed to summer visits. Max built a swimming pool with a black rubber liner safe from cracks in the winter at the cost of making the water ominously opaque and installed a Ping-Pong table in the dining room, where they held nightly round-robin doubles tournaments, the pairings—plump Ida and clumsy Adam, tanned Larry and bespectacled Max—amusingly reported by Caro in her nightly calls home to her mother.

Adam can no longer recall when they ceased the August visits to Willow. It must have been, he thinks, when his father finally threw in the towel on those summer trips, all of which involved endless car drives during which Adam would try to mitigate the boredom by reading in the backseat, resulting in a car sickness whose progression could be measured in the accelerating yellow cast to his skin. Having arrived at their destination, a mountain or lake or beach cottage somewhere, Adam would stay inside with his nose in a book, a choice that yielded the satisfaction of substantially pissing off his father.

It was on one of those occasions that he discovered the story of Wright's original Taliesin home. He'd run out of reading material before they left Willow and borrowed a book about Wright from his grandfather's bookcase for the trip, which that year was to a cottage on Prince Edward Island that bordered the St. Lawrence Sound. His father and Caro had just come in from an afternoon at an empty, duned beach, an excursion which his father had first attempted to cajole him to join, then threatened punishment if he did not, before reaching a final peevish "Suit yourself, your loss, not ours."

Larry was on the back patio shaking the sand out of the towels and tote bags when Adam, whose late pubescence had left him beached in a place neither child nor man, swung open the screen door.

"Did you know that the original Taliesin burned to the ground?"

"No, I never heard that." Larry sat down on the picnic bench and began working on a recalcitrant sandal strap.

"Mamah Borthwick Cheney, Wright's mistress"—Adam could not hide the pleasure in being able to use this last word—"and two of her children and three other people were ax-murdered."

"Really."

Adam was dancing from foot to foot, approaching a state when he would get so excited his voice would crack, his father yelling, "Jesus Christ, calm the fuck down," and Adam shouting, "Look at you, look at you, fuck fuck fuck . . ." before he stormed out—which here would entail climbing down the red clay cliffs to the water's edge, where, knobby-kneed and weak-ankled, he might slip on the rocks and, Adam's imagination jumping ahead, flail in the crashing waves.

"Ax-murdered," Adam repeated in a mock spooky voice.

Larry sat up, a sandal in each hand. "What are you talking about?"

"The servant from Barbados doused the dining room with gasoline, sealed off all the doors but one, lit a match, and then stood at the remaining door axing everyone as they came out."

Adam sank down on his haunches and swung an imaginary ax through the damp hot air. His father stared at him with a look of disgust, as though he were holding back from saying something along the lines of *Don't you think you're a little old for this sort of stuff? At your age, I was sneaking* Playboy *magazines under my bed.*

"So, how did Frank Lloyd Wright survive this carnage?" Larry asked.

"He wasn't there." Although Adam had not intended for there to be an analogy drawn to his absent father, recognizing the potential, he lingered on the last syllable and then, without a backward glance, picked up his book and returned inside.

Since then, Adam has read different versions of the first Taliesin fire. (The house was rebuilt and then caught fire again.) In some accounts, the culprit was, as he'd originally read, a man from Barbados. In others, he was a recently fired servant enraged by his dismissal; a manservant abusively treated by Wright's lover, Mamah Cheney; a cook driven mad by the immorality of Wright and Cheney, both of whom had left their spouses and children to travel together to Europe, living openly together without so much as a hint of shame. *Hussy*, Mamah would hear the cook mumbling as he diced apples for cobbler and onions for pork stuffing. In some versions, all egresses from the Wright dining room were sealed. In others, certain members of Wright's studio escaped through the casement windows. In all of them, it was the fire in the luncheon room that sent the victims into the arms of the man with the ax.

4

They leave at two o'clock on a Saturday afternoon, Eva and Omar in the backseat with the cooler Myra has filled with cold drinks and snacks, Adam in the passenger seat, Caro behind the wheel. Rachida is on call for the weekend, her goodbyes whispered to Adam and Omar while they were still half-asleep.

Myra stands on the street watching the last-minute loading of bags and buckling of seat belts.

For the past week, Caro has tried to convince her mother to come up the following Saturday with Rachida, by which time her father and Betty will have left.

"Thank you, darling. It's sweet of you to invite me, but I wouldn't feel comfortable."

"I'd tell Dad. I'm sure he'd have no problem with your staying with us."

"It's not him. It's me. You know that I don't enjoy nostalgia trips. I've never even gone back to see my parents' house in Baltimore."

By the time they reach the thruway, Omar and Eva have both fallen asleep. Adam opens his window and closes his eyes.

It's five when they arrive at the Willow house. Larry comes out to the driveway in time to see his daughter drive up with three inert bodies. "I'm glad everyone's so excited to be here."

Adam opens the car door, stumbles toward the bushes, leans over the blue hydrangeas, and throws up.

"Jesus," Larry calls out. "Are you all right?"

Adam picks up his glasses, which have fallen onto the gravel. He wipes his mouth on the back of his arm, points at the house, and heads inside.

Caro shakes Eva and Omar awake. When she turns around, Betty is there, barefoot in micro white shorts that hug her broad bottom and show off her long, tanned legs. Betty pinches her nose. "What is that foul smell?"

Caro kisses Betty on the cheek. "Adam puked in the bushes."

Omar climbs out of the car and hugs his grandfather. Eva stands with the coolor pressed against her middle, looking around.

"Betty, Dad—this is Eva. Eva—this is my father, Larry, and Betty. Wow, it is nasty smelling . . ."

"I'll get the hose." Betty blows kisses at everyone, then heads to the side of the house. Larry takes the cooler from Eva.

"It is so beautiful here," Eva says. "I never see anything like this except in *The Sound of Music*. At the beginning, where Maria sings."

"It's the Catskills, not the Alps," Larry says. "But it is pretty."

Betty drags the hose over to the bushes and begins spraying them. The kitchen door bangs and Adam reappears, clammy and pale. "I should do that," he says.

"I got it, lovey. Remember, I grew up on a ranch in New Zealand. This is nothing next to what the dogs would drag home. Chewed-up rabbits and worse."

"Go," Caro directs, "rest by the pool. I'll unload the car."

"Turn off the stove," Betty hollers. "Swedish meatballs should be done."

Caro and Larry carry the bags inside, the bedroom arrangements having been worked out over the phone: Adam in the guest room with the queen bed, so there will be space for Rachida when she comes, Eva and Omar in the bunk beds in what Grandma Ida had called the children's room, Caro on the couch in the den until her father and Betty leave, when she will move into what had been her grandparents' room.

Caro pulls on her black tank suit, covering up her excesses with an oversized T-shirt. Most of the time, she feels at peace that she is never going to be anyone to look at, her brief foray with having a sexy figure the year she lived abroad having borne nothing worthwhile. Given one wish, it would not be to have that body again but, rather, to eat normally: three meals a day and a snack here and there. Around her father, though, she is always thrown back into the feeling she has had since her solid child's body morphed into something with bulges in the right, but also in too many of the wrong, places—that she has disappointed him by not being a beauty.

She climbs the flagstone steps to the pool, where Eva and

Omar are already in the water, squealing as they take turns throwing a basketball into a floating hoop left by the tenants. Eva has on a tomato-red bathing suit with an attached skirt and a stiff built-in brassiere, absurdly large on her, a hand-me-down, perhaps, from Ursula or Alicia.

Her father and Betty are seated under an umbrella with drinks in their hands. Adam is sprawled on a chaise at the edge of the pool with his eyes closed.

"Miss Caro, Miss Caro!" Eva waves.

"You found your suits."

"Dr. M. tell me to pack them on top of the suitcases so Omar can swim right away. Omar show me the way Mr. Adam used to go to the pool. Through the window!"

Caro had forgotten this, that Adam would leave the screen propped against the bedroom wall so he could come and go through the window.

Betty pours Caro a drink that looks like a melted lollipop. "Have a meatball," she says, pointing at the platter. "Nice, isn't it? I like seeing the mountains. And it's so cool compared to Arizona. You can't even be outside in August there."

Betty flings her legs up so that her bunioned but well-manicured feet rest on Larry's thighs. Caro feels her jaw tighten as she recalls her last visit to Tucson, when an evening had similarly commenced with a pitcher of something too sweet and had then proceeded to Betty pressing her pelvis against her father and calling him her baby cucumber.

"I have to admit, for the first time, this visit, I understand why my father loved it here."

Adam opens his eyes.

"Where did you say Eva's from?" Betty asks Adam. "She seems like a sweet girl."

"Iquitos. That's a city on the Amazon in northern Peru."

"I didn't know the Amazon went through Peru. Geography." Betty laughs. "Well, school in general, was never my thing."

"Eva," Adam says to Betty, "is what you would call one of us. Her great-great-grandfather was a Jew from Morocco."

"She knew Rachida?"

Adam raises the back of the chaise so he is sitting up. He sniffs his drink. "Eva's great-great-grandfather was a rubber trader from Rabat who lived in the Amazon at the turn of the century. The rest of her heritage is Bora Indian."

"So she's an Indian Jew?" her father asks. "I never heard of that."

"Grow up, Dad. There are Chinese Jews. There are Pakistani Jews. Judaism is a religion, not a blood type."

Caro stands. "I'm going for a swim." She shoots her father a look. He nods and rises to his feet. Caro takes Adam's drink from his hand while her father yanks Adam's glasses from his nose.

"You grow up," Caro says as she and her father tip Adam into the pool.

5

It is the first evening Myra has been alone in the house in nearly two months. She sits in the garden with her notebook in hand, pleased but also a bit disoriented by the solitude.

At the front of the notebook, she keeps her master list, her evolving teleology of love, which she has titled "A History of One Woman's Passions." At first, as for all mammals, she has written, there is the breast or, in her case, the substitute bottle, since she was born at a time when breastfeeding was viewed as slightly barbaric. Only for her, the bottle had been simply that—a disembodied receptacle with no sensual body attuned to hers. Anything more would have terrified her mother. Where her appetite should have been, Myra was left with a hole, so that to this day food brings her no pleasure; she eats to squelch hunger and acquire fuel, having to remind herself in the same way she has to pay attention to put gas in her car. *But, of course,* Dreis, her former analyst, said, *you were starved for love. No cookie would do.*

Looking out from her crib, she saw the shadows of the venetian blinds on the walls, the shift as the sun rose in the sky and the room lightened. Then later, the love of *I can do it*: walk, talk, ride, draw, and then read, which led to books, her first passion, the world opening from the pages. Books remained preeminent through her discovery of her own late-blooming body, not dwarfed until she found men: a boy in high school who read poetry and kissed her on a damp summer lawn, a boy in college who played the cello and had long lean legs and thick dirty blond hair. She slept naked with him, let him make her come with his fingers. It had been he, not she, who was too scared to have intercourse. With Larry, there had been her first and only deep romantic love, but it paled, or perhaps simply faded, with the onslaught of the love of her children, when she knew that she could survive the loss of him but not of them.

There had been the twisted attachment, a sort of love, really, Dreis proclaimed, that she developed for pain: the miscarriages, over and over; her parents' deaths, which left her not with a feeling of loss but with a sense of utter aloneness as she recognized that she had never been able to love either of them because neither had loved her. They had taken care of her the way a turtle does her young: providing until the season when the offspring can manage on its own. Foods with adequate nutrients, given without pleasure, so they were stripped of taste, shelter scrubbed so it felt more like an institution than a home, protection that forbade joy but left her limbs intact. Her parents died so quickly, there was no opportunity for her to take care of them (even that, it seemed, they had deprived her of), to transform what they'd not given her into something she would do for them.

With Dreis, she felt for the first time what it was like to be seen and understood by another; with her patients, she learned that the experience was equally profound when she was the one with the mirror to show them who they were, the vision of what they could be. After the divorce, there was love of nature, which she found in her garden and terra-cotta pots, in her daily walks in the park—the world transformed from the ammonia scent of her mother's house into a thing of beauty. And then, with her fiftieth birthday, there was the piano, the awe she felt when the patterns in the Bach Inventions began to reveal themselves to her, when she could glimpse the logic of a Chopin mazurka.

Briefly, she'd thought she might discover a love of God, but a month of Saturdays in a synagogue left her embarrassed, sadly aware that it was too late for her not to experience the rituals as false or, worse, silly. When she discovered that, for her, God is grace, the pieces fell into place. That she could do. She would aspire to live with grace, even more, to embody grace, her home infused with as much beauty and generosity as she could muster. It was with this idea, this latest stage of her teleology, that she had opened her home to Adam and Rachida and Omar, with the hope that Adam would finish a screenplay he could sell for some respectable money and Rachida would do her fellowship and Omar would march his little self through first grade. Opened her home, she'd not recognized at the time but had to now, to Eva as well. Eva with her dreams of next year in Jerusalem.

At dusk, Myra waters the flowering beds and blooming herbs, then locks the terrace door, leaving her garden clogs on the deck. Barefoot, she climbs the stairs to the music room, where she sits down to play without the sound of footsteps overhead. She begins with the major scales, advancing by fifths, first hands separate, triple octaves, then hands in tandem, and then one ascending while the other descends, a pattern, her teacher showed her, which creates a series of chords while keeping the fingering between the hands the same. She proceeds to arpeggios, saving the sevenths for last: the progression from the joyful third, celebration of life, to the melancholic seventh, mournful reminder of its fading.

When she first learned the cycle of fifths, it had taken her breath away, the mathematical perfection, the way the magic happens no matter the scale. As a child, she'd loved mathematics, not for the pyrotechnics of computation, but for the mystical nature of an invention that insists on utter independence from its creator, an invisible system more discovered than constructed, so that studying trigonometry or doing geometric proofs felt like unveiling the laws of the universe—as if those were not also a fiction of man. Larry had also loved mathematics. But what he loved was the use to which numbers could be put—the prediction of velocities and markets and weather patterns—a kind of exploitation, Myra had felt, of mathematics for man's purposes rather than a reverence for its poetry.

Larry found these thoughts of hers very sweet, very feminine. Her mind literally turned him on. He'd listen to her talk and wrap his arms around her or fondle her breasts and press his groin against hers. It took her years to realize how degrading she found this, how his actions implied that her ideas were soft next to the harder qualities of his, and how his amusement at her mind was for him a metaphor of sexual conquest, of being able to pin her against a wall or hold her beneath him in bed.

When she'd discovered Larry's affair and told him to leave, her father-in-law, Max, sixty-six and in his last year of work, seemed more heartbroken than his son, who, at first, seemed half-relieved. Not knowing what else to do, Max invited her to lunch. Seated across the table from her at La Caravelle, he asked her to consider the implications of her decision for the children.

Silently, Myra, who in the prior five years had miscarried six times and buried both her parents, wept into her leek soup.

Max offered her his handkerchief, which she blotched with her tears and then accidentally dropped in her soup.

"I'm sorry," he said. "It's unfair of me to ask you that. Larry is just so goddamned weak. Smart but weak. He couldn't bear your grief over your miscarriages. The girl, the secretary, receptionist, whatever the hell she is, he was trying to keep you from getting pregnant again."

Her head bent, Myra nodded. What Max said was so true, she immediately recognized it as something she already knew. And although it did not make her feel she could trust Larry again or remain married to him, it had changed everything, because she could no longer hate him. To the contrary, with the truth of her father-in-law's comment in mind, she had come to feel toward Larry a mild, neutered affection, a feeling not unlike what she might have for a former schoolteacher or neighbor, an affection that allowed her to go forward unencumbered by powerful emotions.

Before Larry's infidelity, she'd visualized the four of them—Larry, Caro, Adam, and herself—as a four-sided form: a square, a rectangle, a parallelogram, a quadrilateral, a tetrahedron. Afterward, they became a pentagon: the fifth position occupied first by the receptionist and then by each of Larry's subsequent two wives. When she invited Adam, Rachida, and Omar to stay with her this year, she imagined again a four-sided form. Now, though, there is Eva. Again, a fifth.

6

The week that Caro, Adam, Omar, and Eva spend with Larry and Betty proceeds with surprising ease. Larry has purchased a month's membership to the local country club. Each morning, he leaves with Eva and Omar to spend the day teaching them the rudiments of golf and tennis, buying them lunch at the clubhouse, goofing around with them on the shuffleboard court. Around noon, Adam disappears into his room with the door closed, at work on his rewrite of *The Searchers*, and Betty heads out to go shopping for what she calls antiques—napkin rings, a ceramic spoon rest, a wooden duck—leaving the pool area deliciously free for Caro to read and swim.

Every day, over breakfast, Larry and Adam debate the merits of various Westerns in preparation for the choice of the evening's viewing. Caro had forgotten that Adam's love of these movies came from her father, who now sees them as a ratification of his decision to move to Arizona. For Adam, it is as though his expertise about Westerns compensates for his being unable to do any of the things the men in these stories routinely do: ride a horse, shoot a gun, woo a woman, punch a man. With Eva's reaction to *The Searchers*, Caro at first worries about her watching the other movies Adam and her father choose, but whatever bothered Eva in *The Searchers* does not seem to do so with *The Magnificent Seven*, *The Naked Spur*, *Stagecoach*, *Shane*.

On Wednesday afternoon, the phone rings while Caro is at the pool. When Adam fails to pick up, Caro races down the steps.

"Hey," Rachida says.

"Is everything okay?"

"Yeah. Only I have to cancel coming up. I'm on call."

Caro can hear the tension in Rachida's voice. "I'll find Adam."

"Just tell him, okay? I'll talk to him when Omar calls before bed. I've got to get to rounds."

"Sure." Caro looks at her watch. It is two o'clock. From what she remembers with her father, rounds are usually first thing in the morning and then at the end of the day.

Annoyed that Adam didn't answer the phone, she knocks on his door. She knocks again and then, in the way of family members, turns the knob.

The door is locked. "One minute," Adam calls out. She waits, wondering what the hell she is waiting for.

When Adam opens the door, he looks disheveled. The blinds are shut and the bed is unmade. There's a musky smell in the room. Her stomach turns.

"Did I wake you?"

"Just a little snooze."

"That was Rachida. She can't come this weekend. She's on call."

Adam knits his brows. "How can she be on call? She was on call last weekend."

Caro examines her brother. Everything needs to be trimmed: hair, beard, fingernails. She hates feeling caught between him and Rachida. "That's what she said. She said she'd talk to you about it tonight."

7

It is past midnight when Myra hears Rachida come in. Unable to fall back asleep, she sits in her office with a blanket over her knees, looking out at a milky moon hovering over a treetop. She tries to read, her concentration pierced by memories of the Willow house, where her children now are, and the early years of her marriage, before *the call*, before everything halted, when she'd spent so much time there herself.

The call. For years, it had felt as though it had taken up permanent residence in her consciousness, that she was locked in its confines, in the supra-intensity of those moments. Now, though, it has been years since she has thought about it at all.

Still, it's all there: Caro in the kitchen doing her third-grade homework; Adam in the tub, blowing bubbles through a wand, just old enough to be left alone in the water, with firm instructions not to stand up while Myra went to answer the phone in her bedroom.

"Is he home?"

It was a woman's voice, loud and demanding, so that Myra, with her mind still on Adam in the tub, jumped to the easiest conclusion: a patient who had somehow gotten hold of their number, even though Larry kept it unlisted so that patients would have to go through his service to reach him on evenings and weekends.

"Where is he?"

In fact, Myra could not say. She had stopped trying to keep track of Larry's schedule. Sometimes he arrived home in time to kiss the children good night, sometimes not. There were women she knew from the playground who considered taming the hour of their husband's return home as the index of their control in the marriage, but on her end, aside from wishing the children would get to see more of their father, it didn't much matter. Her evening routine with Adam and Caro, in fact, went more smoothly when Larry came home after they were asleep. On those nights, she would sit with him while he ate a reheated plate of whatever she'd prepared earlier for the children, her mind already on the reading or other work she needed to do for her next day's classes.

The woman on the other end of the line began to cry.

"Is there something I can help you with?" Myra asked.

"You can tell that prick if he doesn't leave you, he's going to be sorry. Real sorry."

"Excuse me," Myra said. Her voice was small and hollow. "I have to get my son out of the bath."

Myra hung up. Her heart was pounding so wildly she had to sit down on the edge of the bed. The phone rang again. She let it ring and ring. When she finally picked up, the woman screamed, "Eight months. Eight goddamned months." She made a sound that was either a sob or a laugh. "That bastard's been screwing me for eight goddamned months, telling me goddamned lies."

Myra hung up again. She leaned down to unplug the phone. Already, the phone was ringing again. The jack was behind the bed, and she had to go onto her hands and knees to reach it. When she stood back up, she held on to the headboard to keep from blacking out.

In the bathroom, Adam had moved on to playing with his pirate boat. At seven, he was on the verge of becoming too old for playing in the tub. Too old for bubbles and pirate boats. Too young to go through a divorce, but in the time she'd walked from her bedroom back into the bathroom, she'd seen into the months and years ahead to what would happen.

She got Adam out of the tub, dried him, and sent him to get into his pajamas. Then she knelt next to the toilet, a wave of nausea yielding the dinner she'd had with the children. The eight months made perfect sense. It coincided precisely with the last time she and Larry had had sex, with the polite chill that had fallen between them. With the way that her marriage had come to occupy fewer and fewer of her thoughts, slipping lower on her list of priorities, behind the children, behind her classes, behind her work with Dreis on the backlog of grief she felt about the six miscarriages which had left her afraid to try again but still longing for another child—a longing Dreis had gently begun to show her had its origins in never having felt longed for herself, her parents' deaths having made finite what had never taken place.

She rinsed out her mouth at the sink. She knew women who had gone insane with jealous rage after discovering their husbands' affairs. When her neighbor downstairs had learned in the ninth month of her pregnancy that her vain husband had slept with another woman on an out-of-town business trip, she put as many of his prized Ferragamo shoes as she could fit into the oven and roasted them until they turned into something resembling beef jerky. Another woman from the playground tore her husband's photographs of his mother, who'd died when he was eleven, into confetti and then, weeping, flushed the pieces with her wedding ring down the toilet. Afterward, she begged him to come back.

Myra washed her face. The woman had sounded thirtyish. Myra imagined her having peroxided blond hair and big breasts. She imagined Larry atop her, thrusting and grunting. She imagined the woman sucking Larry while he sat upright in his desk chair, swallowing his cum, the way she could never bring herself to do. She imagined Larry mounting the woman from behind and holding on to her squishy breasts.

The images had brought with them a sharp pain that started in her throat and moved into her gut. The pain was not about Larry touching someone else. It was not because she wanted to be the woman. The images brought pain because, with this breach, she knew she would never again be able to sleep in the same bed with Larry or let him touch her in any way. They brought pain because this was the father of her children, the man with whom she had conceived eight times (with this thought, which came after the good-night kiss she gave Adam and the chapter of *Little Women* she read to Caro, the sobs came hard and fast), because now there would be no more children and Adam and Caro would have to be told all the stupid unbelievable things children of divorce are told about how their parents no longer love each other but will still always love them.

8

For their last evening in the Willow house, Larry suggests that they grill salmon steaks. Betty buys corn on the cob and tomatoes from the farmers' market and Caro and Omar bake brownies for dessert. Adam, Larry notices, actually changes his shirt.

Eva and Omar ring the terrace with citronella candles,

paltry defense against the mosquitoes, so they can eat outside. The divide in the family about the merits of the house had been mirrored in the divide between who did and did not get bitten by mosquitoes. Larry and his mother, Ida, had been eaten alive; Max (always lobbying to dine on the terrace), Myra, and Adam had never been touched.

Larry sprays his arms and legs with insecticide and, out of homage to his father, takes his glass of wine outside. He turns on the grill. The last time he can recall eating on the terrace was with Myra. It must have been her suggestion, to please his father, who, she argued, had paid his doghouse dues for the house.

His father had loved Myra from the moment Larry introduced them. *A woman with a soul,* his father announced. Myra was twenty-three, an assistant at a publishing house. Larry was thirty, in the last year of his cardiology residency. He had slept with thirteen girls, the first few, girls from his set, well versed on the pros and cons of Bergdorf's versus Bendel's, with good tennis serves and strong opinions on the diamond settings they expected. He had broken off two engagements, one because he'd developed an aversion to the way the girl smelled, the second because he'd decided after six months of her endless complaining—how her dresses came back from the cleaners, the temperature of a consommé, the hours he watched baseball on television—that he would rather kill himself than spend the rest of his life listening to her.

It had been a fluke that he even met Myra, at a book party, an event he never would have attended had another resident, a cousin of the author, not brought him along on the way to a bar they frequented. It was the first time he'd been at a book party and he'd not known quite what to do. Myra was behind the table where they were selling copies of the book. She had small breasts, dark hair pulled back in a ponytail, and a thin prominent nose that made it impossible to call her pretty but that he would later realize made her quite beautiful. She was dressed in a long Indian skirt and embroidered shoes. He bought a copy of the book so as to be able to talk with her.

She was like no girl he'd ever dated. She read Rilke in French and Marcuse and Virginia Woolf and grew dozens of plants in her tiny apartment on the fourth floor of a brownstone on Seventy-fourth Street. She spent her meager salary on tickets for nosebleed seats to hear Glenn Gould play the *Goldberg Variations* at Carnegie Hall. His mother, disapproving of Myra's clothes, unhinged by her stillness, the strangeness of a girl who didn't make chirpy entertaining conversation, pursed her lips before issuing a damning *She seems very nice.*

Larry had understood his father's comment that Myra had a soul to mean that he himself lacked depth. It hurt him because he had chosen cardiology precisely because of the metaphors, which he believed, about the heart. It hurt him because he knew it was true. He was loud. He drank a lot. He loved to play tennis, ski, watch sports on television. He'd been fucking regularly since he was fifteen. He and Myra, he believed, were yin and yang. With her, he believed, he would gain access to a river of meaning that ran beneath the surface of things, a river he'd been aware of on rare occasions, sometimes after sitting with his mother in synagogue for most of the Yom Kippur day, once when his father had taken his brother, Henry, and him on a mule trip into the Grand Canyon and they'd slept outside so they could watch the shooting stars.

And indeed, at first he and Myra had felt like two pieces of a puzzle that fit together. He'd taught her to ski, lifted her high in the air, skis and all, when she'd made it down the bunny slope the first time, her cheeks red, her eyes glistening with pride. He'd taken her on her first airplane ride, to a hotel in Puerto Rico where he'd ordered rum drinks for them both from the swim-up bar in the pool and chartered a sailing boat for the afternoon. And although she had been shy and inexperienced in bed, she'd let him teach her about her body and then his.

Caro pokes her head out the door. "Are you ready for the fish?"

"Sure."

Larry watches his daughter carry the platter, an oven mitt and a long spatula squeezed under an arm. Adam had inherited Myra's graceful form, hidden now under his middle-aged tire and schlumpy gait. In Caro, it is his mother's body reincarnate—the heavy breasts, the short legs—and his own narrow, deeply set brown eyes. He watches his daughter the way he might watch a patient or even a stranger, with an odd distance between them that he would not say distresses him but leaves him feeling disconnected from himself, his love for her absolutely there but out of sight, like the shed on the distant edge of his land.

She smiles at him as she sets the platter next to the grill. A wave of gratitude passes over him that she has always been sweet to him, that, unlike Adam, she has not held the divorce against him. Not that she isn't tough. She had driven a hard bargain when she wanted to buy her apartment, but he had admired her shrewdness and not resented her for it. Like her mother, who has always been meticulously fair with him about money, something he knows from his divorced friends is virtually unheard of, his daughter holds firm to a standard of reasonableness and equity.

Larry puts the salmon on the grill and hands the platter to Caro to take back inside. He sits on the stone wall of the terrace waiting for the steaks to cook on the first side. When the children were little, he'd been besotted with them. He'd prided himself on being a hands-on father: changing diapers, giving baths, taking the children on Saturdays to the park so Myra could have some time for herself. Saturday nights, there had been a standing babysitter, and he and Myra would go out to dinner, laughing that they seemed mostly to talk about the kids, on occasion leaving before dessert, unable to stay away any longer from their sleeping babes, and then, after paying the babysitter, having sex, sometimes on the living-room floor, while Myra chastised him about Caro and Adam being able to hear them if they awoke, but mostly in their bed, where Larry would marvel that he lusted even more for his wife since they'd had children together.

Then came the miscarriages, each at ten to eleven weeks. Myra had braved the first and second with a stiff upper lip. Her gynecologist reassured her that one out of four conceptions miscarry. Larry can no longer remember the exact order of things after that: the progesterone suppositories, which left her so sluggish she could barely stay awake; her parents dying within ten months of one another; her decision to use the money she'd inherited to go to graduate school. Another miscarriage, this time with so much bleeding he had to rush her to the emergency room. The night he called her a selfish bitch, *Jesus fucking Christ*, he yelled, *we have two beautiful children who you're fucking neglecting now, either sleeping all the time or off at your useless classes.* He still remembers the devastated look on her face as she took her pillow so she could sleep on the couch, and then, in the middle of the night, hearing her throwing up in the bathroom and realizing she was pregnant again.

After the sixth miscarriage, he found himself devising excuses to stay later at the office. He would look up at the clock and it would be nearly eight. With the children already in bed, there seemed no reason not to go out to eat by himself. No reason not to schedule the racquet ball games he'd always squeezed into his lunch hour for after work.

The less time he spent with his kids, the less satisfying the time with them became. He no longer knew which was Adam's latest favorite bedtime story. He missed Caro's transition from bathtub to shower, was not aware that she had made

it to the twelves on the multiplication table. On the rare evenings when he was home before the children went to bed, Adam
would insist that his mother read to him and Caro would forget to give him a good-night kiss. Myra stopped leaving food
covered with foil for him in the fridge. Then came the night
when he told his receptionist, Sheri, who, he had to admit, he'd
hired in part because of her enormous boobs, and his nurse,
who hated his receptionist for those appendages, to go home, he
would lock up. His nurse called out a goodbye as she left. Was
he truly surprised when Sheri appeared at his office door with
her blouse unbuttoned and her size D brassiere on display?

9

Larry flips the salmon steaks, basting them with the marinade
Betty made. Through the kitchen window, he can see Betty
putting pats of butter on the corn, Caro tossing the salad.

Strangely, thinking back, he'd not been angry at Sheri for
calling Myra. He moved his clothing into her apartment in
Yorkville, never arguing with Myra about the children's visita-
tion schedule, which he let her set, all the while certain that
after Myra finished her Ph.D. and the renovation on the brownstone she'd bought with her inheritance, they would have a serious talk in which they would agree to stop this silly charade
about getting divorced and he would stop fucking Sheri and
move into the house with the children and her.

When, eight months after he'd moved out, he phoned Myra
to suggest a dinner, the venue, he imagined, for the serious
talk, she seemed already to know what he intended to tell her.

"We're collaborating so well about the children," she said.
"Let's not ruin it by saying a lot of painful things that we won't
be able to forget."

"What do you mean?" A bitter taste was filling his mouth.

"Larry, don't ask me." For a moment, he thought perhaps she was crying. "The answer is no. It's as no as no can ever be. I cannot go backward. I'll have my Ph.D. in a month. The children and I are moving into the brownstone in June."

"We have our entire lives before us. The kids are only eight and ten. Think of them. How much happier they'd be if we got back together."

"You should have thought about that before you slept with Sheri."

"Sheri is nothing. Something that never would have happened had we not been falling apart."

"And why were we falling apart? Have you thought about that?"

The truth was he had not.

"Your father told me it was because you couldn't tolerate the pain I was in."

"When did he say that?"

"He took me out to lunch, right after we separated."

Then he did something stupid, something he can understand only as desperation, desperation at the vision of his life stretching before him, the life of a divorced father, the distance that would develop with his children, the shallowness of Sheri and the others who would follow. Or perhaps it was hurt that his father, who had hardly talked with him since he'd moved in with Sheri, had talked, instead, with Myra. "We could keep trying," he said. "We could get pregnant again."

He heard Myra suck in her breath. Then the line went dead.

In the morning, he called a realtor, who by week's end had found him a two-bedroom apartment in a building with a garage and health club. He gave Sheri three weeks' severance pay and a pair of gold earrings. He went to Bloomingdale's and in an afternoon bought a leather sectional couch, a glass coffee table, a dining-room set, a king-sized bed for the master bedroom, twin beds for the room where the kids would stay on their alternate weekend visits, and a wall unit for the expensive television and stereo equipment he purchased the next day. He leased a Porsche for the garage and bought a silk bathrobe that he hung in his closet for the want-to-be models and actresses happy to sleep with a thirty-nine-year-old cardiologist with plenty of money for nice restaurants and weekends in the Hamptons. And still, all the while, he imagined that sometime, not now, but not too long from now, when the time was right, he'd have his dinner with Myra and his life would return to . . . the word he thought, over and over, was *normal*.

After two years had passed, he had to acknowledge that this time was not going to come. He fell into a depression that left him with a pit in his stomach and unable to sleep, which he dug himself out of by the move to Tucson to join a practice that even in his sickened state of mind he had the instinct to know would make him rich.

With his move, he had seen the children for two weeks each August, during the time between Christmas and New Year's, when he'd stay in a suite at the Stanhope (even Adam unable to resist the pleasures of room service and television in bed and a visit to F.A.O. Schwarz), and then during their March break, when Myra would bring them by train to Tucson to stay with him in the house he'd bought on the west side of town, a Spanish-style casita with a ten-stall barn and a four-car garage and a gunite pool with an attached hot tub. Myra would do a house exchange with a retired French professor from the University of Tucson, an arrangement about which Larry had been deeply grateful, since Adam, even at thirteen, would not have been able to manage ten days without seeing his mother.

Each year, he picked up what he still thought of as his family at the train station, the children grumpy, dragging the backpacks out of which they'd lived for two days, Myra astonishingly crisp in her tailored pants and white blouse. Because of his car sickness, Adam would sit in the front seat, Caro and

Myra in the back, while they drove to the French professor's house, a bungalow near the university, close enough to shopping that Myra didn't have to rent a car. He'd carry Myra's suitcase to the front door while she hugged the children goodbye, reminding Adam to take his allergy medicine, the pill at bedtime, the nose spray in the morning, promising Caro that she'd call them every night.

Larry tests the salmon steaks with a fork. "I need a serving platter," he calls out.

He can no longer remember how many of those March trips there had been, or on which of them he'd made a fool of himself with Myra, only that he'd already introduced Caro and Adam to Linda, whose lingerie model's body, on exhibit in her tight T-shirts and horsewoman's jeans and boots, embarrassed them—her spending problem, centered on shoes and handbags, still unknown to him.

The children had been old enough to be left alone at the house for a few hours, which he did one evening while he went to check on a patient at the hospital. His patient, who'd had quadruple bypass surgery at six in the morning, was staring at the ceiling while his wife busied herself rearranging the objects on the bedside stand, preoccupied in the anxious way of people visiting someone truly ill with an attempt to be useful. Larry asked her to step outside, not because he intended to examine his patient—that would be left to the surgical resident—but rather because he knew that a break from the sickroom, which she would do only on doctor's orders, would rejuvenate her for the long night ahead.

When he took his patient's hand, the man looked at him with the terror of someone whose chest has been sawed open, who in some inchoate way knew how close he had traveled to death.

"I feel like shit."

"I bet you do."

"I'm afraid I'm not going to pull through."

"If you weren't here, you wouldn't. But you are here, and you will."

For the remainder of the ten minutes Larry spent with his patient, the man said nothing. He closed his eyes, not asleep, but too deeply fatigued for any more visual input. Early in his career, Larry had learned how powerful a few words of reassurance could be to his patients. It had surprised him to find this capacity in himself, a patience he had never achieved with his children or Myra or anyone else. When he'd expressed as much to Myra, she'd said, "But it's common that a person will have his best self emerge in a context that's less personal. It's easier."

"It's not quite real?"

"It's real. You're no less real as a doctor. You're just more conflicted about being your strongest best self outside of that role."

Leaving the hospital, he stopped to buy a bottle of wine. He'd told Linda he would try to drop by her condo on the way home. He lingered for a few moments, talking with the store owner about the year's new Beaujolais, all the while thinking about Myra, about the conversation so many years ago about his best self, about the children in the casita watching television. Would Myra be at the bungalow at this hour? She'd never liked red wine; it reminded her of the Manischewitz her father had poured at Passover, the one night each year he would have wine in the house.

He bought a bottle of an already chilled Sancerre.

Parking outside the French professor's bungalow, he felt absurdly nervous. There was a light on in the living room, but when he rang the bell, no one came to the door. He stood awkwardly on the step outside, shifting from foot to foot, before trying the bell again.

"Larry?"

He started, the awareness that the voice was Myra's coming

as he turned, his ankle twisting beneath him. He leaned against the door. "Fuck."

"Is everything okay?"

"I twisted my ankle."

"With the children?"

"They're fine." He sat down on the step, gripping his ankle.

"Let me get you some ice."

"You spooked me, coming out of the bushes like that."

"I was on the patio out back. You spooked me, coming over without calling."

"Can I come in? I'll just ice my ankle and then let you be."

He followed his ex-wife inside. She was wearing a loose cotton dress with a sweater on top. Her long thin legs and feet were bare. From the back, she looked like a girl of twenty. The bungalow was filled with books and a perfumy smell from some flowers she had set on the dining table in the tiled front room. She brought him a dampened towel knotted with ice inside. He sat down at the table and rested his foot on the opposite chair. She had been here less than a week, but still the house felt the way he remembered their home together to have been.

Myra handed him a glass of lemon water.

"I brought you a bottle of wine. It's in the front seat of the car. Only I'm too much of a klutz to be able to go get it."

"You haven't told me why you're here."

"Be kind to an injured guy and go get the bottle of wine and then I'll tell you."

When Myra returned, it was with the bottle of wine, two glasses, and a corkscrew. She gave him the corkscrew and he opened the bottle, pouring each of them a glass. She sat in the chair next to him and took a small sip. He took a large one.

"I just wanted to talk with you. I never get to talk with you."

"Is Linda with the kids?"

"You know about Linda?"

"They told me about her. They said she's very nice." Larry knew that his children had said no such thing. "Caro said she's very glamorous and a skilled horsewoman. You must like that."

"They're by themselves, watching TV. It's fine. The house has an alarm, but it's so safe out there, I usually don't even lock the doors."

"You left them with the doors unlocked?"

"Of course not. I locked up tight. And no one could get past the dogs."

"Maybe we should call them."

"I called before I left the hospital. They were watching *M*A*S*H*."

Larry took the ice off his ankle. Like most doctors, he hated being a patient. Luckily, he had his mother's stolid constitution, so years would go by without his suffering more than a winter sniffle or summer cold. He could recall only one occasion during the years they'd been married that he'd been sick enough to stay in bed. Instead of enjoying Myra's ministrations, the bed trays she'd brought him, the cool washcloths she placed on his feverish forehead, he'd snapped at her.

"So what did you want to talk about?"

He bit his tongue so as not to blurt out *That I still love you.* "There's nothing specific. I just miss you."

"I miss you sometimes too."

He took Myra's hand, so cool and light after his patient's clammy paw. "It was a mistake, what I did."

She put down her glass of wine. "I haven't eaten yet tonight. This will go to my head and I'll do something I regret."

He leaned toward his ex-wife. He took her other hand so that both of her hands were cupped between his. "Do something you'll regret."

He edged his chair next to hers, cringing at the screeching sound of the legs on the tile. She let him kiss her. She tasted the same. She smelled the same. He kissed her several times. His breath deepened. The bedroom was behind them. If he stood, would he be able to lead her there?

Her hands were on his chest. She pushed him back and stood up.

She moved to the armchair, curling her legs under her. He hobbled, one shoe on, the other off, to the couch. She looked at him with what at first glance, in the dim light, seemed like amusement, but, on second glance, did not.

"You sure know how to make a guy feel ridiculous."

"Don't talk to me about making someone feel ridiculous." She covered her eyes with her fingertips, pressing along the sockets. Had his ankle not been throbbing, he would have gotten up from the couch and pried her fingers away. Instead, he waited for her to lower her hands.

"Some women might feel flattered to have the man who cheated on them then try to cheat with them on someone else. But I just feel debased. I'm sorry to sound cruel, but in my professional opinion, you don't know what you want. This is pathetic, your being here, my letting you touch me."

He had not waited for her to kick him out again. He'd gathered up his shoe and left.

10

Adam comes through the kitchen door with an empty platter. He scampers, barefoot, like a mole emerging from a burrow. Larry feels the familiar irritation at his son rising in him, curbs the impulse to tell him to put on his goddamned shoes.

He lifts the first of the salmon steaks from the grill onto the platter.

"Boo!" Startled, Larry turns toward the voice. Omar is climbing out the casement window. "Boo, Grandpa! Boo!"

"Jesus," Larry says. Eva climbs out behind Omar. She giggles as she straightens herself up. "I nearly dropped the fish."

"I scared you?" Omar asks. He smiles shyly.

"Nearly scared the pants off of me." It is good to see the kid acting like a kid. "Your father used to do the same thing—crawl out of the window to come to dinner. Spook us."

Adam laughs. "I used to pretend I was one of Mamah Cheney's kids jumping out of the dining-room window after the servant set the house on fire."

Eva stares at Adam.

Larry examines his thirty-two-year-old son, the face that seems still only half-formed. The almost twenty-five years since Myra kicked him out have passed in a heartbeat.

"Sometimes I'd get Caro to climb out the window," Adam continues, "and then I'd chase her, pretending I was the ax murderer." Adam raises his hand as though there were an ax in it and bolts toward Omar, who screams with terrified delight as he runs from his father. Adam chases Omar around the edge of the terrace.

"He-elp!" Omar yells. "Help!"

Larry lifts the last of the fish steaks onto the platter. In his mind's eye, he can still see Myra lowering her hands from her face while he nursed his injured ankle. Even in the dim light of the bungalow, there had been no question about it. Her eyes were dry.

"Save me from this dangerous man!" Omar cries, now on his second lap around the terrace.

"Got ya, got ya," Adam yells, swinging his arms. Omar veers toward Larry. He darts between Larry and the picnic table, his father close behind.

Adam stumbles. "Shit!" he cries, crashing into Larry.

The platter falls to the ground, breaking into two jagged halves as the fish tumbles onto the flagstones.

Larry looks at the broken platter. There are shards of porcelain on the steaks. "Idiot. Look what you've done."

Adam leans over to pick up the fish. "I stubbed my toe," he mumbles. He holds a piece of fish in each hand, looking helplessly for somewhere to put them.

Betty arrives with a new platter. Caro follows with a broom, her eyes moving from person to person. "Here," Betty says, taking the fish from Adam and then picking up the other pieces from the ground. "Nothing a quick rinsey under the water and two more minutes on the grill won't cure. Just don't cut your feet."

Omar buries his face in Eva's side. She puts an arm around him.

Larry touches Adam's shoulder. He feels like a bully. A monster. "Sorry, son. I didn't mean that. Are you okay?"

"It was stupid of me to be running like that."

The worst part is that Larry knows that Adam thinks he is right. That he is an idiot. "Is your toe okay?"

"Yeah, it's fine."

Adam sits on the picnic bench. He clutches his foot. Omar sits next to him. He leans over to examine the toe. Caro sweeps the plate shards into the dustbin.

Larry turns the grill back on. He takes a gulp of his wine. "Okay, another adventure at Max's Folly." His voice sounds artificial, the cheerfulness disingenuous even to his own ears.

Betty musses Omar's hair as she passes behind him with the fish, but he does not respond. He is watching Eva, who has raised her palms so they form a cup under her chin. She spits into them. Three times in quick succession.

"Why'd you do that, Eva?" Omar asks. "Spit in your hands?"

"Because of the story of the wicked man who burn down the house and use his ax on the people."

"That's just a story, right, Daddy?" Omar turns to look at his father. "It's not real."

"Oh, it happened all right."

Caro glares at Adam. "It was a long time ago, Omar. A freak event."

Eva spits in her hands again. "Four." She spits again. "Five."

"Why do you keep doing that?" Omar asks.

"My grandmother teach me. It is how you keep away the evil."

Omar counts the bodies. "There are five of us out here. You spit five times because there are five of us."

"One time for each finger," Eva says.

"But you have ten fingers. Don't you have to spit ten times?"

"Five. There are five fingers on a hamsa. You spit five times."

"What's a hamsa?" Omar asks.

Eva wipes her palms on the sides of her pants. She lifts the chain that hangs around her neck so the hand-shaped silver amulet that had been inside her shirt rests momentarily between her thumb and forefinger. She raises it to her lips, then tucks it back beneath her shirt.

11

Of them all, only Adam believes in the significance of coincidence. As a child, he would study lists of notable dates. With great solemnity, he would announce the connections: Did his parents know that Charlie Chaplin died on the birthday of Houdini? That the Great Fire in San Francisco occurred on the same day as an eruption of Mount St. Helens? His father would attempt to debunk the significance with his layman's statistical proofs: in a room of twenty-three people, there is a greater chance of two or more persons having the same birthday than not. But none of it had mattered to Adam. Once he believed something, not even God, had he believed in a deity, would have been able to sway him.

Back in the city, Adam is struck with the first coincidence

to get under his skin in a very long time. The quiver of uncanniness he felt so often as a child envelops him one afternoon as he is reading about the rubber boom in Iquitos. In 1909 in Iquitos, the rubber trade was approaching its precipitous end, the 70,000 rubber seeds Sir Henry Wickham smuggled out of Brazil having taken hold in neatly organized rubber plantations halfway across the world. In 1909, Frank Lloyd Wright and Mamah Cheney left their respective families in Chicago to sail to Europe together, the prequel to the disaster to befall them.

Adam gets up from his desk. He stretches his arms overhead. He can hear the front door opening, Omar and Eva laughing together. Why does Omar rarely laugh when he is with Rachida or him?

Surely, Adam thinks, one of the rubber traders must have traveled from Manaus to New York, booking passage to Europe on the same boat on which Frank and Mamah fled together, all of them with children and spouses left behind.

12

For the first few weeks after Adam, Omar, and Eva return from Willow, Myra maintains her routine: her morning sessions followed by a brisk walk around the Central Park reservoir, a shower, then a simple lunch, which she eats, when the weather is nice, on the deck off the kitchen. She'd initially protested when Eva began making her lunch, but Eva is so eager to do it, Myra lets her.

In general, the girl seems happier. She chatters about Omar, who loves her, Adam says, because she plays with him like another kid. Coming up the stairs after seeing her last patient, Myra will hear the laughter that accompanies Eva and Omar's ongoing card tournament, the centerpiece of which is a game called Spit that involves whooping yells.

At the beginning of September, Eva tells Myra about a mother she met in the park who has offered to introduce Eva to the rabbi at the nearby West End Avenue synagogue. Eva asks Myra if she can shift her hours so she can attend the services Friday evenings and the adult Hebrew classes Tuesday and Thursday mornings.

Eva's first visit to the synagogue is on the Friday before Rosh Hashanah. "I never was in a synagogue before," she tells Myra when she returns. "I think it will be something very strange, maybe like a crypt, but it looks like the cathedral we have at home. There is a man who sings. He has the most beautiful voice."

"The cantor."

"The cantor," Eva repeats. She begins to hum, a mournful melody that Myra dimly recalls from the synagogue where her uncle had been the rabbi. Her mother had never liked going to services, had seemed relieved when Myra announced at eleven that she no longer wanted to attend. During the few weeks, now nearly a decade ago, Myra tried attending services again, she visited the same West End Avenue synagogue where Eva now goes: a grand, crumbling edifice with peeling pink paint and stained-glass windows clouded with decades of dirt. The rabbi had been interested in radical theology and a messianism that had made Myra think of men in black coats davenning at the Wailing Wall.

"In Iquitos," Eva continues, "there is an old Jewish man. People come to his house Friday nights and on Yom Kippur. Until my mother die, she take me every Yom Kippur to the man's house. We drink tea and eat sweet mango cakes. The cakes are to remind us of God's sweetness, the old man say."

Myra's parents had always fasted on Yom Kippur. When she turned thirteen, they expected that she would fast too. Afraid to tell them how light-headed the fasting made her, she had stashed licorice under her mattress to help her get through the long day.

Eva smiles in a way that suggests she is remembering the sweet mango cakes. "Every year, on Yom Kippur day, my mother take me from the old man's house to the Catholic church so we can say confession and receive communion." She studies Myra's face. "The Jewish people, they don't do that here, do they?"

13

After a few weeks of Friday pickups, Caro and Omar fall into their own routine. Immediately after school, they walk to an ice-cream store on Columbus Avenue where Omar orders a scoop of strawberry in a cone and Caro orders whatever nonfat concoction is being offered from the machine. Ice cream in hand, they head south to the Museum of Natural History, where they visit first the dinosaurs on the fourth floor and then the African mammals off the rotunda. Afterward, they catch the bus up Central Park West, getting off at Ninety-fifth Street as Caro had during all of her high school years.

The salad Eva has made will be on the counter, the table set, the chickens her mother has cleaned and seasoned earlier in the day already in the oven. Omar plays cards with Eva until she leaves for evening services. A little before six, Myra climbs the stairs from her office. She and Caro have a glass of wine before calling the others for dinner.

After some toing and froing, Myra and Rachida have agreed that meals are not to be delayed for her since she rarely arrives before eight, and even that hour is unpredictable. On the first Friday in October, however, Caro notices two extra settings on the table.

"Who's coming?" Caro asks her mother when she arrives upstairs.

"Rachida. She invited another resident from the hospital. A woman named Layla who's also from Morocco."

A few minutes later, there are footsteps on the brownstone stairs. The front door opens and Rachida, in blue hospital scrubs, enters with Layla, a slip of a woman in a short skirt and sling-back pumps.

Layla's hands flutter as she reaches out to touch first Myra's and then Caro's arm. Adam comes down the stairs, unaware or having forgotten, Caro surmises from his unkempt appearance, that a guest will be at the table. Layla greets him with her arms pressed tightly to her sides.

Caro follows Adam to the kitchen while the others settle into the parlor. He opens a bottle of red wine and she pours a glass of juice for Omar, who has come downstairs, too. "Tuck your shirt in," she whispers as she leaves to bring the juice to Omar. "You look like something the cat dragged in."

Layla is draped in one of the Barcelona chairs, talking about the four years she spent at medical school in Iowa. Omar has taken Caro's seat on the couch, his head resting on his grandmother's shoulder.

When Adam extends a glass of wine toward Layla, she holds up a hand like a stop sign. "No thank you."

"A teetotaler?"

Rachida shoots Adam a sharp look as she gets up and heads to the kitchen.

"I don't drink because I'm a Muslim," Layla says softly.

"Excuse us, dear," Myra says. "We're all so parochial here."

"What's that mean?" Omar asks.

"You know," Caro says, "how some children love playing with action figures and you don't? Imagine if they couldn't understand that you don't."

"That would be mean."

"Well, I don't think it's meant to be mean, but it can feel like that."

Rachida returns with a glass of sparkling water that she gives to Layla.

"So, the two of you work together?" Caro asks Layla.

Layla glances at Rachida, who answers for her. "Layla is a second-year primary-care fellow. My track, the respecialization track, overlaps with the second-years."

Over dinner, Layla tells them that she was raised in a small village near the edge of the Sahara, not far from the Algerian border. "My father was the eldest son of the man who was the chief of the region. His grandfather was a sultan. When I was a child, my grandfather kept camels that he'd rent at the tent camps used by tourists headed out to see the Erg Chebbi dunes. He gave that business to my two uncles, and now they have the cell phone franchise for the area—which is very big because there are so few landlines."

"That's where Bertolucci filmed *The Sheltering Sky*, isn't it?" Adam asks.

"That was in Ouarzazate," Layla says. "In the Draa Valley. Where we live is totally desert."

"Layla was telling us about her family," Myra says, looking pointedly at Adam. "What is the village like where you live?"

"We live in an ancient town called Rissani. It was the home of the first of the Alaouites, Hassan the Alaouite. There is an old palace there that belonged to the royal family. Now, though, the area is very poor. Most people live off the meager incomes they receive from the government with a little extra money when they can get it harvesting dates in some nearby oases. My family has had electricity since 1990, but many families only got it in the last few years. Now everyone spends the hot afternoons squeezed into the houses of the people in the village who have televisions."

"Watching," Rachida adds, "dubbed sitcoms from the States. Layla intends to go back to southern Algeria and open a clinic. The electricity is too spotty to be counted on for refrigeration, so it makes antibiotic and vaccination use hard to manage. She's writing a grant proposal for the World Health Organization to fund solar generators for medical refrigerators."

"Blindness is the main problem," Layla says. "One out of eight children suffers from eye infections that place them at risk of losing their vision."

"You put us to shame," Adam says, pouring himself a second glass of wine. "Our father's a cardiologist, but he won't even take private health insurance anymore."

"How does your family feel about your being here?" Caro asks.

"When you call his office," Adam continues, "they ask for credit card information before they even ask what the problem is."

Rachida stands to clear the plates.

"Let me help you," Layla says.

14

After dinner, Adam heads upstairs to give Omar his bath while Eva does the dishes. Layla thanks Myra for having her, apologizing for leaving so early. "I haven't had more than ten hours' sleep all week," she says.

"Of course, you must be exhausted."

"I'll walk you to the cross-town bus," Rachida says.

"I can walk her there," Caro says. "I'm headed that way." Having assumed Rachida would prefer to have time with Omar before he goes to bed than to walk Layla to the bus, she is surprised by Rachida's expression, which suggests otherwise.

"Come back anytime," Myra says. "We'd love to have you."

Outside, the autumn air is damp and chill. Layla's heels make a clicking beat on the sidewalk. They turn south on Columbus Avenue, Caro folding her arms across her chest, Layla's gaze fixed on the sidewalk in front of her.

When they reach Eighty-sixth Street, Caro points across the street where the bus will stop, then extends a hand to say good night. Layla grasps Caro's arm.

"I didn't want to say it in front of the child," she says.

"Say what?"

Layla examines Caro's face. "You asked how my family feels about my being here."

Caro nods.

"My father and my brothers stoned me after they heard I'd been accepted to medical school in New York." Layla pushes up her jacket sleeve to reveal a long scar on her arm. "They broke my arm and my nose and three ribs, then dumped me as far out into the desert as their truck could go."

Caro gasps.

"They left me on the sand to be eaten by the vultures. My boyfriend heard about it. It took him until the next morning to find me, because I'd been half-covered by sand. He wrapped me in gunny sacks to hold my bones together and took me to a hotel where some French tourists had me flown to a hospital."

The bus pulls into the stop and Layla dashes across the street. When she reaches the curb, she turns to wave. Caro exhales, her breath held since she saw Layla's long scar.

15

Myra began her analysis with Dr. Klara Dreis after her parents' deaths, when she felt backlogged with grief from the miscarriages and achingly alone. At the time, she had not understood how unusual the analysis was. There was no chipping away at resistances, no gradual construction of unconscious thoughts. Rather, once she lay on Dreis's couch, everything poured out: the chill in her bones that had lasted her entire childhood; the fear of making a mess—of her puke, shit, toys, clothes impinging upon her mother's vigorously sanitized rooms, for that's what they had felt like, not a home, certainly not Myra's home.

Then, behind that torrent to Dreis, came the words *They didn't love me*, words sputtered with humiliating tears that backed into her nose and chafed her cheeks, followed then by something worse—the apprehension that the words were true.

For months, her only comfort was Dreis's reassurance that it would eventually become a relief to have it said, that her parents had not loved her, and then to look at this idea from a distance, as something of curiosity, how it had happened that two people had borne a child whom they then had not loved.

"When?" Myra demanded, her tears still abundant. "When will this relief come?"

"When you stop believing as you did as a child that it was because of you, who you are."

Not at five, not at eleven, at twenty, at thirty, had she been able to conceive of this possibility: that the sorry state of affairs had nothing to do with her, a reality which had its own quality of pain—the utter impersonality of it, the utter obliviousness to her, so that it would have made no difference if she were a saint or a psychopath. That these people whose offspring she was simply had nothing in them that allowed love: not for themselves, not for each other, not for her. The actual ease of their circumstances had never touched their belief that they were on the precipice of disaster, that living was a brutal grind that required unflagging vigilance.

"Had you been more difficult, had you enacted your sorrow," Dreis said, "they would have hated you for the interference. That might have been easier for you, since at least you would have had their attention."

For Dreis, the insight was just the skin of the beast. Myra still needed to face the ugly fact that she was like them—her own insistence on order and cleanliness, her stubborn, cruel belief that the state of pristineness was possible, be it in her thoughts, where she expected of herself to have only clean and generous responses, or her home, where she never allowed the paint to remain chipped, or with her body, where her torso by eight weeks after both of her children's births had been free of bulges.

"If your insistence on perfection was simply your identification with your mother," Dreis declared, "you would have given it up by now. No, it is more insidious. It is the expression of your grandiose defenses against the rage and despair you felt, as though you can conquer the natural order of disintegration and decay. You believe that you alone can keep a flower in bloom, that in your home, on your body, the petals will not wilt and the leaves not turn brown."

With this, Myra wept. What issued from her body was something more than tears, something closer to her own soul. She saw her insistence on having a third child as part of her demand for perfection: a tyrannical expression not only of her mother still alive and scrubbing inside her, but the invulnerability she had cultivated. With this, she was able to say out loud, "Well, I didn't love my mother and father either"—and then to weep at the great loss of this, not to have loved her own parents.

16

After Myra returned to New York from Tucson, the trip during which Larry had managed to delude himself for a scant few minutes that she might go to bed with him, he received a letter from her, her precise handwriting filling a single sheet of pale gray stationery.

Dear Larry,

I hope your ankle is okay.

I think you should know that I was tempted to sleep with you. Unlike you, I have been with no one else since you left. (I know you like to say that I kicked you out, but surely you can see that it was you who left me . . .) I am grateful that whatever small quantity of wisdom I have gained over the years was able to take the reins, because it would be a terrible mistake for us to become entangled again above and beyond what we will always have, which is to be the parents together of our children.

Once you severed the covenant between us (I am sorry to sound so Catholic here), it altered forever the path of my life. I had assumed that we would go hand in hand to old age, that our growth would come through learning about ourselves, through learning to love each other more deeply. I was very sad to give that up. I would have liked to take that path with you. Now, though, we will each take different routes. On my end, I do not believe that romantic love will be a central part of my life from this point on. Not that I don't think that I will have another lover—I imagine I will once the children are older, perhaps after they've left the house. Rather, I feel that I now have the children and my patients, and I suppose myself to nourish first. When I fell in love with you, I gave you all my heart. I will never be able to do that again, not because you broke my heart, but rather because I have moved on to a place where I can no longer give away that much of myself.

So, my dear Larry, you will remain always my ex-husband (my only ex-husband, I am quite certain) and the father of my children. If you take up with the women you take up with because you truly desire love, I hope that you will find it and be at peace, and that we will continue to work kindly together to parent our children. I think we've been doing a pretty decent job at putting aside our quarrels with each other in the service of their well-being. Sometimes, I even think that we're doing a better job as divorced parents than we might have had we remained together.

Yours in friendship,
Myra

For three nights after receiving Myra's letter, Larry made excuses to Linda for not seeing her, spending his evenings drinking brandy and watching television with his dogs on the couch beside him. On the fourth night, Linda came over unannounced with two filets mignons and a chocolate sour-cream bundt cake. She was three inches taller than he, six in her spike-heel sandals. He could discern the outline of her nipples beneath her white T-shirt. Pushing the dogs aside, he fucked her on the living-room couch and then, unable to control himself, cried in front of her.

In the morning, with Linda still asleep in his bed, he wrote Myra:

Dear Myra,
     Now it's my turn to be honest with you. I
wanted to touch you two weeks ago not because
I lusted after you but because I still love you.
That must sound like a strange thing to say after
what I did to you. There is no defense to my
argument other than to say, which, of course, you
must know, being in your line of work, that a
person is the final arbiter of the truth or falseness
of his own feelings and this is how I feel. I believe
that we could have a strong marriage. I have half
my life left. I would like to sit with you when our
children graduate from high school and college,
to visit our baby grandchildren together. I would
like to be grandparents together, doing all the
corny things that grandparents do with their
grandchildren.
     Maybe you're being a little selfish to hold on to your
grievances with me?
                                        Yours always,
                                        Larry

A week later, he received another letter from Myra:

Dear Larry,

Thank you for your letter. I am very warmed that
you still love me. In a certain way, I love you too. I do
need, however, to point out that your fantasies about us
are only an extension of our being parents together,
which we can, to some extent, continue to do. You can
sit with me when the kids graduate from high school
and then from college. We can both attend our grand-
babies' birthday parties.

You must, however, recognize that these images
do not constitute a marriage, or at least not the
marriage I would want (and will probably now never
have). Very few people actually have a marriage that I
think is worth having. My parents shared little more
than a roof together. Your parents are locked in
constant battle, which protects them from the
harsher reality that your father long ago outgrew your
mother. My cousins, Ursula and Alicia, carry on
with their husbands as in tawdry romantic comedies.
Only my friend from graduate school, Charlotte, who
you never met, has a marriage that looks good to
me. She and her husband are truly friends. They
discuss everything. They go to one another first when
they are in pain. They nourish one another's most
delicate hopes, the wishes most of us don't dare to
even say to another person. They treat each other with
a most gentle kindness, aware that they hold each
other's inner life in their hands. And they manage to
do all of this without sentimentality or banality,
their lives together leavened always with humor.
Perhaps we might have learned to treat one another
similarly, but during the years we lived together,

we never achieved anything even approaching this.

I think it best that we not correspond further.

Again, yours in friendship,
Myra

17

Before she has the key in the door, Caro knows that she is going to eat. There is no hunger, her stomach still filled with her mother's food. Rather, after hearing Layla's story, seeing the long scar on her arm, there is a craving for the oblivion of salt, sugar, chewing, all the while knowing, even before she has touched the refrigerator door, that what will enter her mouth will not be a comfort but rather a gorging—a debasement of what her mother would call the human spirit, that tiny flame it remains every person's mission to keep alive.

She starts with a leftover deli container of tuna and continues through a bag of pretzels and the remains of a box of cocoa she eats dry with a spoon. Hopelessness descends over her, accompanied by revulsion, not only at her behavior, but at the immorality of creating misery, of wasting her own life with this cycle of destruction. She subtracts dates in her head: fifteen years since her return from Morocco when she stumbled upon food as a drug—the disgust about her gluttony preferable to the disgust she felt that fall about herself.

Paris, Agios Nikolaos, Casablanca.

Slut.

Returning to Harvard, she ate so much food, she feared damaging her intestines. She prayed to be able to make herself vomit, but could not force her stomach to eject its contents. That semester, she'd read the Richmond Lattimore translation of *The Odyssey of Homer*, been pierced by the image of Penelope weaving a shroud by day for her father-in-law, Laertes, and then unraveling it by night. And so it seemed with herself when, by the end of the year, twenty pounds heavier, she settled on the seesaw of binging by night and starving by day.

Caro stares at her bloated face in the bathroom mirror. For Penelope, the unraveling at night served a noble purpose: the stalling of the suitors who would have had her abandon her husband, Odysseus.

Would there be suitors if she stopped?

She stretches out on her bed. She has her mother, whereas her mother had no one. How, then, is it that her mother can do so many things that she cannot? Her mother knows how to make herself lovely, something she does in the same way, for the same reasons, she arranges a vase of flowers—that it is ennobling to create beauty. With effort, Caro can make herself look passable, someone people won't notice one way or the other. Her mother knows how to take care of a child. Caro, child expert, lecturer at national conventions on the emotional and pedagogic needs of the three-year-old, has never tucked a child into bed, given a bath, taken a temperature.

Her mother knows how to make a meal: roast a chicken, whisk a salad dressing, roll out a pie crust. Her mother knows how to create a home, a garden, an office. Her mother knows how to heal a person.

Her mother has never slept with four men in a five-month span, one of whom tried to kill himself afterward, and then not been touched by anyone in the fifteen years since.

18

Adam watches his wife clip her toenails. Still in the hospital scrubs she wore through the dinner with Layla, she is seated in the middle of what, despite the four months they have occupied this room, he still thinks of as his mother's bedroom. Omar is asleep a floor below them. His mother has finished her piano practice. He can hear Eva climbing the stairs, the sound of her door shutting.

Rachida carries her weight in her back and arms. With her head bent over her small foot, she looks even more top-heavy than usual.

"Damn. I think I'm getting an ingrown."

Adam ignores his wife's comment. Rachida is a workhorse—she returned to work when Omar was three weeks old—but she maintains a habitual litany about minor ailments, a litany that seems like a nervous tic, an unconscious imitation of her mother's more insistent complaints. He's met Rachida's mother only once, on the trip she made with Rachida's father to New York for his and Rachida's wedding, but even then, she complained morning to night: her aching feet, her upset stomach, the terrible injustice that Rachida—hating shopping, soap operas, and anything to do with homemaking—has refused to act like a daughter and then, to add insult to injury, moved across an ocean.

"What do you think Eva does in her room at night?" Adam asks.

"She's studying Hebrew. She's taking a class at some synagogue."

"She told you?"

Rachida looks up from her feet. "What do you mean?"

"She hardly talks to me. Does she talk to you?"

"When I'm around. Your mother told me about the classes. I can't think of anything more stupid than learning Hebrew, a language spoken in one country with six million people. Why doesn't she learn Chinese?"

"Because they don't speak Chinese in Israel. And that's where she wants to eventually move."

Rachida makes a snorting sound. "So she can live in a settlement on the West Bank with an Uzi rifle under her bed? You should see the pictures of the places my mother's brothers and cousins live. The Israelis talk a good game about being the homeland for all Jews, but what they really mean is for all Ashkenazi Jews."

Adam regrets having come upstairs after putting Omar to bed. He'd had a vague idea of talking with Rachida about his remake of *The Searchers*—how he has changed Ethan to Moishe, a peripatetic rubber trader whose brother settled in Iquitos and fathered two daughters with an Indian woman, Ethan's issues about miscegenation recast as Moishe's rejection of his brother's daughters as Jews, but now, with Rachida's scowl, he already knows her response. She'd find the logical hole in the idea, the reason that Ethan cannot become Moishe, that Texas cannot be Iquitos.

Rachida stands. "I'm going to take a shower."

Through the half-open bathroom door, Adam watches his wife pull off the blue scrubs. It has been nearly a year since he and Rachida have had sex. What would happen if he put his hand on the white cotton underwear she is still wearing as she turns on the shower? Most likely, he thinks, she would laugh.

The first time he saw Rachida naked, he'd been surprised to discover a scattering of black hairs around her nipples and a faint dark fuzz that ran from her belly button down to her pubic line. He softly touched the fuzz. He'd never touched a woman in an intimate way, never imagined there would be an opportunity.

"My mother used to come after me with depilatory creams. She once threatened to have me restrained in an electrolysis chair if I didn't do something about the hair on my stomach."

"I like it," Adam said, and in a way he had. It alleviated his worries about his own scrawny arms, his lack of sexual experience, which he quickly learned didn't bother Rachida at all. To the contrary, she preferred his inexperience, since it made it easier for her to direct his fingers and tongue to precisely the places she wanted. For the first year, she had wanted sex every night, and she had come every time. As the months passed, he'd grown bolder—a liberation in knowing there was no other man he was competing with for her—and she had let him lead on occasion, moving her body the way he wanted.

At the end of their first year together, he'd started looking at magazines. The first few times, he had told himself that it was simply an overflow of his sexual feelings—that after Rachida would leave for the hospital, he was sometimes still aroused. He filled a brown envelope with photographs cut from the magazines: some of them *Playboy* girls whose photos he had never looked at in adolescence, pink nipples and firm buttocks pointed sky-high; then, as he ventured into edgier magazines, vaginas spread open, men with elephantine penises, handcuffs, anuses. Men kissing men. Men sucking men.

Terrified of tainting the screen, of blighting that refuge, he never looked at videos, at images on the computer. When Rachida had stopped wanting sex during her pregnancy with Omar, he'd been relieved, his orgasms, by then, more intense with the brown envelope than with her.

Rachida closes the bathroom door. Adam can hear the shower curtain being drawn shut. He goes downstairs to the piano room his mother has let him use as his study. "Do you remember?" she asked the afternoon they arrived when she showed him the table she had moved under the window for his desk and the closet she had cleared for his things. "I'd planned for this to be your room, down the hall from Caro. You insisted, though, on taking the room upstairs, across from mine. I tried to convince you that this room was nicer, larger, but you would have none of it."

The first thing he checked after his mother left was that the door had a lock. There were rice shades that covered the windows. Now he bolts the door, closes the shades, opens the closet, and retrieves the brown envelope from the back of the farthest file box.

19

"I love Eva," Omar says. It is a Saturday night and Rachida is home, sitting what Omar calls criss-cross-applesauce on the bath mat while he plays in the tub with his rubber sea animals and plastic submarine. For a moment, what looks to Rachida like a wave of worry passes over Omar's face. Is he afraid that he should not have told her that he loves Eva? That she will be mad? But he'd been so open about his love for Zahra, his Moroccan babysitter in Detroit. And Rachida had so clearly endorsed it, taking him each year to buy something special for Zahra's birthday, holding him in her lap when he cried after they had to say goodbye because they were moving here. Hadn't she told him that love is a bottomless lake? That loving one person does not take away from loving another?

Eva, though, is different. She is nothing like Zahra. She runs up and down the stairs with Omar. At night, after Rachida or Adam has tucked Omar in and gone up to their room, Eva, Omar has confided in Rachida, sometimes sneaks downstairs and climbs into bed with him because she is scared. Rachida had not been pleased to hear this, but the truth is, Omar seems happier than she has ever seen him. With Eva, to come back to that word Omar's preschool teacher used, Omar seems actually childish.

"It's very dangerous where Eva comes from," Omar says. "Her father once killed a poisonous spider in their kitchen. Her sister got leeches on her legs when they were playing by the river."

Rachida soaps Omar's back. When, as a baby, he was slow to pull himself up and late to walk, she assumed he had inherited Adam's lack of coordination and strength. It had taken her a while to realize that Omar is simply still—without the compulsive climbing-touching-spinning-top frenzy of so many young boys.

"Eva said she's going to take me to see the jungle. When she comes back from Israel to visit Iquitos, she'll stop and get me and bring me with her. The poor people come there on rafts they make into their houses. They bring banana leaves to make into roofs and their bathrooms are floating outhouses! And she's going to take me to the jungle lodge where she used to work. They have dolphins in the river and red howler monkeys like the one she gave me."

"That's nice." She is drifting into half-listening, something she finds herself doing too often in response to Omar's strings of enthusiasms—dinosaurs, jellyfish, asteroids, the moon, enthusiasms that center on science, her passion too, but are too melded with fantastical narrations to hold her attention.

She's had to delegate long hours of Omar's care to Adam and various babysitters, but this has never dented her feeling that Omar's well-being is entirely her responsibility. She alone has organized each step in his life: the cessation of the bottle and then the pacifier, the beginning of foods, toilet training, the adjustment to school. With a look, she can tell if he is well or sick, tired or rested. It has come as a disappointment, though, to discover her lack of patience, not only for Omar's enthusiasms, but for play itself. The discomfort she has felt when observing Omar belly-flopped beside Adam or Zahra or, these past few months, Eva, the two of them moving around Komodo dragons or killer whales or triceratops, Omar's hand resting on his companion's wrist or arm or shoulder. The fear that she resides outside the circle of his deepest feelings, the administrator of his life rather than a character in it.

20

Mid-October, Myra decides it is time to start Omar's piano lessons. With her own children, she had been too insecure to do many simple things for them. Looking back, she feels remorse that she'd taken them to a salon to have their hair cut, assumed that bakery cakes would be superior to those she could make herself, hired a tutor for Adam when he panicked at learning long division rather than working with him herself. With rare exceptions, the other parents around her had been equally intimidated, as though parenting was some new, complicated development that required expert handling. Now, with Omar, the foolishness of this assumption is apparent to her, accompanied by a sadness that she missed the pleasures of teaching her own children to read, to swim, to do, for God's sake, long division.

Afraid that Rachida might object to homespun piano lessons, Myra cautiously asks her permission.

Rachida pauses. Is she concerned that Myra's inexpert instruction might scar Omar's musical development, a realm that perhaps seems mysterious to her given that she cannot carry a tune, can hardly recall a melody? Having experienced the Moroccan music, the Gnaouan and Chaabi music that filled the squares Ramadan nights and the cafés on warm evenings, as primitive and bellicose, Rachida had as a child refused to learn either the indigenous instruments—ouds, kanuns, tan-tans, karkabats—or the European ones.

She grins. It is so rare to see Rachida's face relaxed, it actually looks strange, her mouth larger than Myra had realized, with bottom teeth that are quite cockeyed.

"You're a good woman, Myra. I'm lucky to have you."

Myra's eyebrows shoot up in surprise.

"I should have said that to you years ago. You're always thinking about what you can do for us."

"Thank you, dear. I'm lucky to have you too. Without you, Caro and I would still be shepherding Adam. But it's not an effort—lending a hand where I can. You're my loved ones. There's nothing more satisfying than helping your loved ones."

"You say that as though it's a given. But my mother is nothing like that."

When Myra met Rachida's family, on their trip here for Rachida and Adam's wedding, she'd been struck by the stealthiness of Rachida's mother's complaints, slipped in rather than directly lobbed—*That dish was a bit salty, wasn't it? The odor, it kept me up all night, maybe it was coming from the hotel room rug?*—her audience too uncertain if a complaint has actually been delivered to serve back a rebuttal.

"I'm not intending anything too ambitious for Omar. Some scales, some easy pieces from the Thompson series."

Myra gives Omar the choice between Wednesday afternoons or Sunday mornings for their lessons. With the concrete logic of childhood, Omar chooses Wednesday, which for him feels earlier in the week and will therefore mean more frequently.

Leaving to pick up Omar at school on the afternoon of their first lesson, Myra asks Eva if she could have a snack prepared for Omar when he gets back.

Eva is ironing a pair of Adam's jeans. She irons expertly, never getting trapped on sleeves or collars, singing along with the songs from a pop radio station. Myra has made a list for her of what to iron. Otherwise, Eva would iron everything: underwear, sheets, dish towels, Myra's nightgowns.

Eva holds the iron in front of her and smiles. "Snack. I never hear that word until I come to this country. Miss Caro, when she meet me at the airport, she ask me if I want a snack."

"What's the word in Spanish?"

"We have *porción* or *bocadillo*, but they are not really the same. Maybe we do not have this word?"

Eva places the iron on the leg of Adam's jeans. The meaning of her word lapse seems obvious: no one had offered her an after-school welcome.

When Eva looks up, it is with an expression that Myra

has learned means she wants to ask something but feels hesitant.

"Yes?"

"It would bother you if I listen when you give Omar the piano lesson?"

"No, of course not," Myra says, though by the time she has walked the seven minutes to Omar's school and then waited in the crowd of mothers and nannies for the children to be dismissed, she realizes, too late, it seems now, that she does not like the idea at all.

The lesson is uneventful. Omar, as expected, is an attentive student. He quickly learns the names of the piano keys, the C scale, and "Peter Peter Pumpkin Eater." By the end of the half hour, while Myra has not forgotten Eva's presence on the chair behind them, she is no longer monitoring Eva's response, so that it comes as an unwelcome surprise when Myra gets up from the bench and sees Eva's face, her eyes half-closed, her chin tipped heavenward in what looks like rapture.

21

A week later, Myra tells Eva that she is going to start having her lunch in her office. When she lived alone in the brownstone, she often made phone calls or looked over her patient notes while she ate her lunch at the farm table. Now, with others again in the house, her concern for her patients' confidentiality no longer permits this. Moreover, between Eva's puppy-dog looks and Adam's habit of plunking himself across from her to launch a lengthy anecdote about the Amazonian rubber trade, she misses the quiet hour she'd had to read and think and jot an occasional note for her own work in progress.

"I bring it down to you," Eva says.

"Thank you, but I can get it."

"I can do it," Eva insists.

And so it has come about that after her noon walk around the reservoir, Myra calls out a hello to Eva and heads down the front stairs to shower in the tiny maid's bath. With her hair still wet, she returns to her office where she finds her lunch tray on her ottoman. Like clockwork, at 2:20, ten minutes before Myra's first afternoon patient, Eva knocks on the rear office door, the door that leads to the back stairs to the kitchen. Myra looks up from the phone or whatever work she is doing and smiles as Eva retrieves the tray.

On the Friday that ends the first week of this new routine, Myra is reading in the armchair where she sits while she sees her patients when Eva knocks.

Eva pauses, looking around. "This is where your patients sit?" She points to the armchair across from Myra.

"Yes."

Eva touches the tissue box on the table next to the patient chair.

"They cry?"

"Sometimes."

"I can try the chair?"

"If you'd like."

Eva lowers herself into the chair. She yawns like a sleepy cat. How many times has Myra watched her patients respond to her office in this feline way, as though the upholstery itself stimulates an evolutionary regression?

"This is nice," Eva says. "I like it here."

Myra picks up the napkin on her tray. She folds it into a triangle. Aware from years of listening to patients talk about tempestuous relationships with nannies and housekeepers, relationships often more fraught than marriages, she has been careful not to ask Eva too much about herself, refraining from pursuing the clues.

"What do people talk about?"

"I can't say specifically. Everything my patients tell me is confidential. But, in general, people talk about what is bothering them."

"But what bothers them?"

"Events from their past. Their relationships. Aspects of themselves."

"When something bothers me, I ask God to take it away."

"Well then, you're lucky. Not everyone has your faith in God."

A fierce look Myra has not seen before settles across Eva's face. "I just said that. God never helps me. God hates me, I think."

"What do you mean?"

Immediately Myra regrets her question, the reflexive curiosity that she has come to understand is experienced as love—a recognition of something not yet spoken. If she believed in the kind of God Eva is talking about, she would ask to have the clock skip back five seconds and the four-word invitation disappear.

"If God love me, he does not let my father do what he do to me." Eva looks Myra straight in the eye.

Myra feels her breath catch in her throat.

The buzzer rings. Myra glances at the clock on the table next to Eva.

Eva stands. She is a good girl. "I am sorry. I take your lunch now." She picks up the tray with the remains of a turkey sandwich and carries it to the door. When she gets there, she turns halfway to look at Myra. "Do not worry, I won't bother you anymore."

22

By the time Myra comes upstairs from seeing patients, Eva has left for synagogue. Saturday, Myra is out all day at a friend's daughter's wedding, and on Sunday, Eva's day off, Eva leaves early in the morning and doesn't return until late.

On Monday, when Myra comes in from her midday walk, she calls out hello, but Eva doesn't respond. A tray is on the ottoman when she returns to her office after her shower. When Eva has not come to retrieve it by 2:25, Myra carries it up the back stairs herself.

Eva is folding laundry on the farm table. The room feels strangely quiet, and it takes Myra a moment to realize it is because Eva is not singing.

"Hello, Eva."

Eva keeps her eyes locked on the clothes in front of her.

"Is something the matter?"

Eva shakes her head.

"You usually come for my tray."

Eva shrugs her shoulders.

Myra stands watching the girl, trying to intuit what is going on inside her head, the atmosphere charged like the positive-ion-laden air before a deluge. Myra says the only thing she can feel any certainty about. "You seem not to want to talk with me."

With those words, Eva looks up. "We can do that? Not talk? You leave me a note about what you want me to do."

The truth is that Eva has verbalized precisely what Myra—at this moment, suddenly terribly tired, wishing more than anything that she were alone, without Eva in her kitchen, without her patient about to arrive—would love were it not so absurd, so ominous. She would curl up on the couch and fall into an immediate sleep.

"It's impossible not to ever talk."

"You write on a piece of paper what I supposed to do. I read it."

Myra inhales deeply, reeling her thoughts back from the world of desire to the reality of her kitchen, of this midafternoon hour. "Perhaps you were upset that I didn't have the time on Friday to hear what you were starting to tell me?"

"I never talk to anyone. I never tell anyone. When I was little, I stop talking for three years."

"What do you mean?"

It takes Myra a moment to recognize that she has repeated her question from Friday.

Eva shakes out one of Omar's T-shirts. She presses it flat with her hands.

"For three years, I say nothing to no one. My mother take me to a doctor, then to a priest, then to this lady in the Belén market who makes medicines from herbs, but I never talk."

"You must have a lot to say bottled up inside."

"Bottled up?"

"Things from the past that it would make you feel better to share with someone."

Eva looks at her strangely, as Myra realizes how incomprehensible her words must be. When new patients come to see her, they already know this. It is the premise for their coming— either their own or that of the person who has encouraged or, in some unfortunate cases, coerced them to come.

"No. I do not think it make me feel better. How does it make me feel better? Now I think about loving God. I study Hebrew. I work to go to Israel."

23

The next day, Eva knocks at precisely 2:20. Without looking at Myra, she sits down in the patient chair.

"I will tell you everything now."

Myra gets up from her seat and closes the door.

Eva pushes back her hair from over her ear, revealing an albumen-colored scar where her hair meets her neck. "This is where I try to shoot myself. I use my father's gun."

Myra stares at the scar. She can feel her heart pounding.

Out of her mouth comes the brief humming interjection "Mmmm" she sometimes thinks is the most important thing she does with her patients. "How old were you?"

"I was ten years old. The bullet didn't go in. It just scrape the side of my head. I never try again. My mother die a few months later and I don't want to go to Hell. I want to go to Heaven to see her."

The buzzer rings. Eva stands. "Your patient is here."

That night, at the piano, Myra cannot focus on the notes in front of her. She repeatedly misses the beat for the turns on a Beethoven rondo, cannot keep in mind the flats when she reaches the minor section. Her thoughts are on Eva. Is the girl too unstable to take care of Omar? Could she possibly be a danger?

Who, though, behind the veil of social appropriateness, does not have a hidden story? A teenage run-in with the law, a depression, a bankruptcy. It is naïve to think that there is anyone who does not have ghosts in the attic. If a Good Housekeeping seal of mental health were required to take care of a child, would Adam or Rachida or, for that matter, Larry or herself, have made the grade?

Myra switches off the piano light and tidies her music books. She sits in the wing chair that now faces the table where Adam works. Papers are scattered every which way, books piled in precarious towers. The closet door is flung open, revealing lopsided stacks of file boxes. She wishes she could simply tell Adam and Rachida what Eva has told her and leave her questions with them. Had Eva shown Myra her scar and told its story seated at the farm table, Myra would have felt able, but what is said behind the closed door of her office, unless there is a clear danger at hand, belongs to the speaker and is not hers to share. Besides, she knows what Adam and Rachida would say about Eva. That she is wonderful with Omar—playful and loving and responsible.

When asked how to decide if a child needs treatment, Anna Freud had responded, If his problems are interfering with his life. If a child is proceeding with the tasks before him—his schoolwork, his friendships, his growing independence—leave him be. Wouldn't the same apply to an adult? If Eva is doing her job well, should she be penalized for having had troubles as a child?

Too much talk, Myra imagines Dreis saying. *Why so much explaining?*

24

For the next two weeks, Eva comes to Myra's office every day at precisely 2:20. Sometimes she sits down, sometimes she does not. When she sits, she waits for Myra to give an indication that she is ready to listen—a tilt of her head, a lift of an eyebrow. Sometimes she stops before Myra's buzzer rings. If not, the moment the buzzer rings, she stands and heads upstairs to the kitchen with Myra's tray.

The story unfolds piecemeal, like a photo collage where the images don't quite match up, fractured so the mind needs to connect the lines to make up a whole. A courtyard behind the house where Eva's family lived before her mother died. In the courtyard, there was a chicken coop. Eva's father forbade anyone other than himself to kill the chickens.

"He drink from this brown bottle and then twist off their heads and throw the heads on the cement for the cats to eat." Eva shudders. "It was disgusting. In the morning, I see bloody chicken heads outside the door."

The next day: "When I do not eat the chickens, he come into my sister and my room and wave his hands covered with the blood over me. He smear the blood all over my blanket."

Then on the Friday: "He smear it in my hair."

It is 2:25. Eva has a faraway look in her eyes. "I scream so loud, my mother come running in with a butcher's knife. She chase my father outside into the courtyard. He trip and chip his tooth. When he get up, he spit a piece of his tooth onto the cement."

Myra prays for her patient to be late.

"My father take the rifle he keep in the chicken coop. My sister hide under the bed, but I watch from the door. He point the rifle at me, then at my mother. He shoot my mother in the thigh."

Eva holds her fingers a centimeter apart. "He miss the bone by this much. When my mother get home from the hospital, he tell her, If you ever raise a knife at me again, *putano*, I will kill you. I will twist your neck like one of those chickens."

The buzzer rings. Eva's eyes follow Myra's hand as she pushes the button to unlock the outside door. Eva stands. She takes Myra's tray. "When I scream the next time, my sister run and my mother know not to come."

After Eva leaves, Myra remains frozen in her chair. She feels the walls of her own house closing on her.

All weekend, her mind goes in circles. On the one hand, she feels bound by the confidentiality between therapist and patient. On the other hand, there are the strictures against dual relationships: not treating an employee, a friend, a relative. But Eva never stays in her office more than eight, nine minutes. How could these snippets of time be considered a treatment?

25

When Adam asks Eva if he can interview her as part of the research for his screenplay, she looks at him strangely.

"Would you mind?"

"No, I no mind."

After dinner, they sit side by side at the farm table while Adam attempts to construct Eva's family tree, beginning with Eva's great-great-grandfather, whose name and date of death Eva knows from the gravestone her grandmother showed her: Isaac Selgado, b. Rabat 1861, d. Iquitos 1895.

"Rabat, that's in Morocco," Adam says.

"Where is Morocco?"

"Northern Africa—where Rachida is from."

"I never know that. My mother never tell me that."

Slowly, Adam gathers what Eva knows. Isaac Selgado had a son, who seems to have been born around 1890 and was the father of Eva's maternal grandmother, Ana. It was Ana who showed Eva the Jewish cemetery, who took Eva and her mother to the Friday-night gatherings where Eva heard Hebrew read, watched candles being lit. Eva's mother, the great-granddaughter of Selgado, was born in 1945. She attended the convent school and slept beneath a crucifix. "We are Jews," she whispered to Eva, "but you must never tell anyone, not even your father."

Adam fills in the chart as best he can. Upstairs, his mother is playing the piano. Eva draws a finger along the lines. She glances overhead.

After his mother finishes her piano practice, Adam takes the chart up to the music room and settles into the wing chair to study it further. He can hear Rachida, who has managed to make it home in time to give Omar his bath, say a last good-night.

Eva knocks on the doorjamb. She steps toward him, thrusting out her closed hand.

"Here. I bring this to show you." She unfurls her fingers. In her palm is the piece of silver, the size and shape of a baby's hand, she showed Omar that night on the terrace after Adam had crashed into his father. There is a hole at the wrist where a chain could be threaded through. "My mother tell me this was my great-great-grandfather's. The writing on back, she say, is Hebrew."

Adam takes the amulet. He holds it under the reading lamp. Each of the five digits is engraved with a filigree design. On the back of the hand are Hebrew letters.

"I can't read Hebrew, but Rachida does. Can I keep it to show her?"

Eva nods. She bites her lip as the amulet disappears into Adam's pocket.

26

When Adam comes into the bedroom, Rachida, still in her hospital scrubs, is lying propped on pillows atop the bed.

"I'm so beat, I barely made it through one story with Omar. My eyes were closing as I read. I must have seen thirty patients today, half of them with no medical history on file and a presenting problem of I don't feel right, Doctor."

Adam sits on the edge of the bed. He lifts Rachida's foot, still in the heavy sock she wears with her hospital clogs, onto his lap. On the rare occasions when the hostility is not too thick between them, Rachida permits her feet to be massaged. He makes circles with his thumbs around her ankle.

She moans. "Whatever you're doing, keep doing it."

Adam removes his wife's socks and deeply massages one foot.

"Eva gave me something she says belonged to her great-great-grandfather who came from Rabat. When she showed it to Omar, she said it's called a hamsa." Adam reaches into his pocket and takes out the silver hand. He gives it to Rachida and then goes back to work on her foot.

Rachida examines it. "My father makes these. The Muslim women have their version that they call the Hand of Fatima. Both Jewish women and Muslim women wear them to ward off evil."

"Can you read the Hebrew on the back?"

Rachida turns over the hamsa. In Essaouira, women wear hamsas inscribed to Lilith, the demon who menaces the pregnant and newborn, so as to protect them from her nefarious deeds.

She reaches for her glasses on the bedside stand. "I think it says, I have set the Lord always before me."

Rachida studies the amulet while Adam moves on to her other foot. In the afternoon, he'd taken the subway to the Village to visit an Adults Only bookstore. The store had been empty except for a Gypsy woman at the counter eating a smelly sandwich and staring at a portable television. She looked at him with no more interest than if he'd come to search for shampoo. Perhaps because of her indifference (on past visits, there had been a skinny man with bad skin who watched his every move), he went for the first time to the Men and Men section.

Back at the house, he locked the music room door and looked at the magazine he'd bought. Most of the pictures were of men sucking other men's monstrous penises, images that held no interest for him. One picture, though, had mesmerized him: a tall, very erect, muscular man lifting another slighter, younger man high in the air, his mouth twisted into a lewd gesture that exposed his red tongue. Viewed in profile, the slighter figure, his penis hidden against the larger man's abdomen, might have been a woman. Not until Adam brought himself to a climactic gasp imagining himself held aloft, his genitals pressed against the hard belly of the tall figure, did he recognize the image as the one from *The Searchers* where Ethan lifts his niece Debbie high over his head.

During the months after his father had left, the apartment thick with the sadness Adam felt inside, he would lie in bed at night imagining that at any moment, soon, very soon, his father would bound through the door. He'd lift Adam high, out of his bed, and tell him he was back, it was all over, he was home. Instead, there had been Sheri with her cartoonish boobs and her cats who would jump on him as he and Caro slept on her pull-out couch. Then, later, after his father had moved to Arizona and transformed himself into a cowboy cardiologist, there was his father's relentless disappointment in him. *Jesus Christ*, he'd yell, *kids around here start riding while they're still in diapers, taking care of the animals not much later than that. Get on the goddamn horse.*

Adam presses his thumbs into his wife's arch. She lets out a guttural sound. He presses harder. In the dim light, with her broad torso and short hair, she could be mistaken for a man. He moves his fingers up to her calves.

Rachida lays the amulet next to her. Hidden beneath her scrubs, Layla wears a hamsa too. Rachida discovered this the first night she and Layla were on overnight call together. They exchanged back massages, something the residents often did for one another. Because it had been only the two of them that night in the residents' dorm, Layla had taken off her top. Hanging between her child-sized breasts, hardly filling her teacup-sized bra, was the hamsa. Rachida could feel each of Layla's ribs descending down to her waist, her back no wider than a twelve-year-old child's. When it was Rachida's turn to be massaged, Layla had teased that now Rachida had to take off her top too. She laughed at the size of the straps on Rachida's granny-style bra.

Now Rachida imagines unsnapping Layla's teacup bra, touching the tawny nipples. Pushing her tongue into Layla's cardamom mouth.

In the photo, it is unclear if the figure held aloft is aroused. Adam wants that to be the case. He wants the larger man's mouth against his ear, murmuring to him, pressing against him, Ethan, who wanted his brother's wife, Debbie's mother, now taking the grown girl instead. Adam moves up Rachida's body, massaging her thighs. She turns off the light and he pushes her onto her side and curls around her, his hands kneading her ample breasts until she directs them to the places where she imagines Layla's sweet fingers.

27

"It start before my mother die," Eva tells Myra. She runs her hand down the upholstered arm of the patient chair.

"What started?"

"My father, he pull me out of the bed after he kill the chickens. He drag me by the hair with his hands all bloody into the chicken coop. He pull down his pants and push my mouth over him. He push himself into me until his stuff squirt all over me."

Eva is softly crying. She takes a tissue from the box next to the chair and tears it into pieces. "I scream when he come into my room, but my sister put the pillow over her head and my mother is scared that he shoot her again."

The tissue falls in shreds onto the floor. Myra feels a sharp pain in the pit of her stomach. She knew this was coming.

"He is a dirty, dirty man. He keep magazines with dirty pictures under a floorboard in the bathroom. My sister tell me that if we spit on them, it destroys the evil. We spit so many times, the pages stick together."

When the buzzer rings, Eva immediately gets to her feet. Seeing the pieces of tissue on the floor, she bends over to pick them up.

Myra waits to call Dreis until her last patient has left. Two years after Myra had reached what both she and Dreis had considered the end of her analysis, she sheepishly went back to discuss her distress at a new permutation of Adam's phobias that had arisen at the time of his college applications. It had taken only a few sessions for Myra to see what was being set off in her by Adam. A few years later, Dreis, having finally decided to retire, called Myra to tell her.

"What if," Myra timidly asked, "there is something I need to talk with you about?"

"You'll telephone me. I'm not disappearing. I just won't be keeping regular hours or teaching any longer."

Since then, Myra has seen Dreis only once, perhaps three years ago, after she'd developed an inexplicable anxiety about one of her patients. She'd gone to Dreis's Park Avenue apartment. A housekeeper greeted Myra at the door, led her into the library, where her former analyst was seated with a blanket over her legs. It was a shock to see how old Dreis had become. But her mind remained as sharp as ever, and in one conversation, Myra felt back on track—not just with her patient, but with herself too.

"Would you like to come tomorrow? I know you wouldn't call me until it felt pressing."

"Would noon be okay?"

"Of course, dear."

28

After her last morning patient, Myra goes directly upstairs. Eva is at the sink washing lettuce. With the water running, she doesn't hear Myra open the stairway door.

She is singing to herself, and for a moment, Myra pauses to listen: "When the dog bites / When the bee stings . . ."

She has a beautiful voice. Sweet and pure.

"When I'm feeling sad . . ."

Myra clears her throat. Eva twists around. She looks shyly at Myra. "You are not going to the park today?"

"No. I have a doctor's appointment. I'll be back before my next patient."

"I make you a tuna sandwich for when you get back?"

"Don't bother. I'll have something while I'm out."

Eva turns back to the lettuce. Her shoulders pulse slightly. "I think you eat outside because you do not want me to talk to you today."

29

"She was right," Myra tells Dreis when she has reached the end of her description of Eva. "I don't want her to tell me any more, not today, not any day."

Dreis sips her tea and nibbles on one of the shortbread cookies the housekeeper has brought into the library.

"Of course you don't. We can't have our maids or our sisters or our neighbors as patients. It is too exhausting for us. There is no time off. If we can't attend to our own fantasies for some hours of the day, we burn out. Besides, it is dangerous."

"How so?"

"The transference is out of control. The girl wants you to really be her mother. There is no play in the work, no *as if.*"

"I haven't thought of it as a treatment. I've thought of it as a lonely, troubled girl unburdening herself to an older person."

"Myra, you know better. She sits in your patient chair. She tells you the things that people only tell their therapists."

"She sits eight, nine minutes at a time."

"My dear. All a patient needs sometimes is three minutes. Think of everything that is done in the last minutes of a session. For some patients, the entire treatment occurs in those few minutes. But here, you don't have a patient. You have a girl who sees you all day long. She wants to be at your feet, to suckle your breast without end. She wants you to be the mother she lost too young."

Myra sighs. She sinks back into Dreis's armchair.

"There is something you didn't tell me," Dreis adds.

"What is that?"

"How her mother died."

"She hasn't told me."

"And you haven't asked?"

Myra stares out the window. She can hear the Park Avenue traffic below. In her mind's eye, she can see Eva's father with blood dripping from his hands and his fly unzipped.

"So what do I do now?" Myra asks as she turns back to Dreis. "Now that I've allowed things to go this far."

"You explain to her what we've talked about and then give her the phone number of a clinic. You take her the first time if need be."

30

In the afternoon, when Adam comes downstairs, Eva is putting on her jacket, getting ready to pick up Omar at school. From the way she keeps glancing up at him as she does the buttons, he feels as if there is something he has forgotten to do or say or . . .

"Mr. Adam, did you show Mrs. Rachida what I give you?"

That's it. To give the amulet back to Eva. He was so thrown off balance by having sex with Rachida, he forgot to take the amulet back from Rachida. But where the hell is it? He remembers Rachida examining it, but what happened to it after that?

"I did. She said she's seen lots of them before. I'll get it for you while you're out."

Eva bends down to tie her shoes. She leaves without saying goodbye.

Adam climbs the two flights of stairs to his and Rachida's room. Rachida must have put the amulet on the bedside stand when she took off her glasses, he decides. He searches the drawers. He searches under the bed. He searches on top of the dresser.

He stretches out on the bed, reconstructing that night. Did he take the amulet with him after Rachida fell asleep and he crept into the music room to look again at the magazine? He had wanted to see the picture of the man lifted high, the one that reminded him of Debbie in *The Searchers*. Had the amulet dropped inside the file box?

Adam goes downstairs to look in the music room. He locks the door, pulls down the shade, and drags the file box from the closet, sweeping his hand between the folders. He removes the envelope from the box and empties the pictures onto the floor. A weird feeling overtakes him, as though the men in the pictures are hiding the amulet from him.

He calls Rachida's cell.

"Do you know where Eva's amulet is?"

"The hamsa?"

"The thing you said was a hand."

"I can't talk now. I'm with a patient and we're crazy backed up."

From the other side of the door, Adam can hear Omar knocking. "Daddy, I'm home. Can I come in? I want to practice the piano."

The photos are strewn across the floor. "One minute. I'm just finishing up something. Go have a snack and I'll come get you when I'm done."

"I already had a snack. Eva gave it to me."

"Well, go watch TV or something. I just need a few minutes."

"The TV is in here."

"Omar, I said I need a few minutes."

Adam can hear his son sighing and then heading to his room. He gathers up the pictures and puts them back in the brown envelope. He puts the envelope back in the file box and the file box back inside the closet, then opens the shades and the door.

31

"What should I tell her?" he asks Rachida after she too has looked everywhere for the amulet and cannot find it.

"You'll have to tell her the truth."

"She'll be devastated."

"I could ask my father to make her another hamsa, but I don't think it would be the same."

"Maybe she'd take it better if we had one to give her when we tell her hers is lost."

"Maybe." Rachida flops onto the bed. "There is an outbreak of croup. A lot of the children also have asthma, so we have to give them nebulizers. The nurses were so behind showing parents how to hook up the tubing that I had to do the blood tests and shots myself."

"Do you remember the inscription?"

"The inscription?"

"On the amulet, do you recall the inscription?"

Rachida presses her fingers over her eyelids. For a moment, Adam thinks he remembers the hamsa lying on the bedcovers next to Rachida's face. Had it been left there? Wouldn't Eva have found it in the morning when she made the bed?

"I have set the Lord always before me."

32

Eva sits motionless in the patient chair, her feet planted on the floor so her knees stick straight up.

"You look like you have something on your mind."

Eva stares suspiciously at Myra. "How do you know?"

"The expression on your face suggests you're thinking about something."

"I think about the silver hand my mother give me. She give it to me after my father shoot her in the leg. I never know if she give it to me because it stop working for her or because she think I need it more than she need it."

Dreis's question comes back to Myra. "You didn't say how your mother died."

"She die in a fire."

"A fire?"

"A fire in our house. My father set the house on fire."

Eva touches the chain that hangs around her neck. "My sister and I were in the courtyard. The house was one floor, so the fire catch the roof fast. The flames shoot up into the air."

"Your father set the house on fire on purpose?"

"He want to kill all of us. My mother, my sister, and me. But he kill only my mother. She burn to death."

Eva crinkles her nose. It is the same crinkle of disgust Myra has seen Eva make when she talks about the smell of cooking meat. She touches the spot under her shirt where something hangs from the chain.

"The only good thing is, he burn the dirty pictures. I never see them again after that."

33

Myra calls the clinic at St. Luke's Hospital. She speaks with the intake social worker, who promises a Spanish-speaking psychiatry resident, a man named Dr. Gonzalez, will see Eva.

Myra finds Eva in the kitchen. She's at the sink scrubbing potatoes.

"There's something I want to talk with you about."

Eva keeps her eyes on the stream of water.

"We need to find someone who will have more time for you than I do. Someone you can talk to about some of the things you've been telling me."

Eva nods as though she has known this would happen.

"I've made an appointment for you for Thursday at noon with a doctor, a man named Dr. Gonzalez, at a clinic nearby. They will only charge what they think you can afford. If it's still too much, I'll help you with it."

"You want a girl to cook meat for Omar. You think a growing boy needs meat and it bother you to have to do it yourself."

"This has nothing to do with your work. You are doing a fine job."

"I can cook meat. I will do it from now on."

A feeling of despair descends over Myra: it is too late with Eva, they are already in too deep. Don't be ridiculous, she chastises herself. You just have to handle this with clinical tact. "This has nothing to do with your cooking. This has to do with what you've been telling me about yourself, with your needing more time to talk and someone who can listen to you without interruption."

"You can listen to me. I will come down earlier."

"It's not good for your therapist to be the person you work for."

"After my mother die, my aunt take me to a doctor. He come out to the waiting room and listen to my heart. He pinch my cheek, then give my aunt some pills to give me."

"This doctor will talk with you before he decides what would help. The appointment is for noon. I'll go with you the first time."

Eva turns up the water; it splashes against the sides of the sink. Myra imagines Eva as a young girl, putting the pills under her tongue and then, when her aunt turns her head, spitting them into her palm.

34

On Thursday, Myra comes upstairs after her last morning patient. Eva is not in the kitchen. On the third floor, Adam has
the door to the music room closed. The beds are made in
Omar's room, in Adam and Rachida's room on the fourth floor,
and in Eva's room, but Eva is nowhere to be seen. At five minutes to twelve, Myra cancels the appointment.

"I forget," Eva says when Myra sees her before dinner.

"Are you sure you forgot?"

"Yes. I am more careful next time."

But the next week, the same thing happens. Again, when
Myra comes upstairs to get Eva, she is gone. She searches the
house, calling Eva's name before canceling the appointment.
This time, instead of waiting fruitlessly for Eva to reappear,
she changes her clothes for her reservoir walk.

When Myra returns to her office, a lunch tray is on her
desk. Eva is in the patient chair.

Myra sits behind her desk. Eva looks at her shyly, then giggles. "I am sorry. I forget again."

"Clearly, you did not forget."

"I cannot talk to a strange man."

"Would you feel better if the psychiatrist were a woman?"

Eva shrugs her shoulders. Myra wonders where Eva hid
today. In the synagogue on West End Avenue? In the back of
a closet, sucking her thumb, listening as Myra called her
name?

35

"Her mother burned to death?"

They are in Dreis's living room, where the housekeeper has
made a fire. Outside, the air is the murky white that harkens

a freeze. The room is exceedingly warm, but Dreis keeps her legs covered with a blanket. It occurs to Myra that it has been a long time since she has seen her former analyst standing. Even in full health, Dreis was tiny, hardly five feet. Myra wonders how tall she stands now or if she can, in fact, stand at all.

Myra nods.

"People die of smoke inhalation, of injuries from falling beams. Does she mean her mother was pulverized?"

Myra feels suddenly very foolish. Inept. Eva has said that her father set the fire and that she watched the house burn to the ground. Did she manage to get herself out or did her father change his mind and rescue her and her sister?

"I know that the picture doesn't quite fit together."

Now Dreis nods.

"She needs to tell her story. I know she shouldn't be telling it to me, but I don't think she's going to tell it to anyone else. If I refuse to let her talk to me, she'll never tell anyone."

In her mind's eye, Myra can see the newspaper photograph from the summer when Adam and Rachida and Omar traveled out West: a moose, antlers aloft, standing in the middle of the Salmon River, banks aflame.

36

Were it up to Adam, Eva would never be allowed into the music room, but his mother has gently insisted that Eva, whom he has instructed not to touch the papers on his desk or the boxes in the closet, be permitted once a week to vacuum the rug and dust the piano. Usually, Eva vacuums on Thursday afternoons while he is picking up Omar, Rachida's plans for doing pickup never having materialized, but this Thursday, the first Thursday in December, when he arrives home with Omar, he can hear the vacuum still running.

Adam forces himself to climb the stairs. Two weeks have passed, during which he's avoided telling Eva that he can't find her amulet.

Eva is bent over the vacuum, carefully guiding it between the piano legs.

"Eva, could I talk with you?"

Eva stares at him.

"Could you turn off the vacuum?"

The vacuum stops. Adam points at the wing chair. He drags the desk chair over for himself.

"I have bad news." He swallows, rests his clammy palms on his thighs. "I seem to have misplaced your amulet. I feel terrible about it. I've searched everywhere."

Eva sits motionless, her lips slightly parted.

"I'm sure it will turn up because I never took it out of the house. I showed it to Rachida. Then, when I went to get it to give it back to you, I couldn't find it. Rachida and I tore apart our room. We looked under the mattress. We even rolled up the rug."

Eva does not reply. She appears to be watching Adam's lips, as though they are strange doggish fish.

"Rachida's father—he's a jeweler—is making you another one. I know it's not the same, and I'm not saying we won't find yours. But in the meantime, at least you'll have something."

Adam's armpits are pouring sweat. He would not have felt worse if he were telling a kid he'd run over her dog.

"Can I go back to vacuuming?"

37

"My mother always say never tell anyone anything," Eva tells Myra the following day.

"Many children are told that."

"If I tell you things, you will think I am lying."

It is she, Myra, who feels like the liar. She told Dreis she would insist that Eva go to a clinic, that their talks cease. And she has tried. She made a third clinic appointment, which Eva also missed, but it was followed by a week during which Eva retrieved Myra's tray without sitting in the patient chair, so that Myra had thought, Well, she understands even if she won't go see another therapist. The following Monday, though, Eva was back in the patient chair. Before Myra could say, You can't sit here with me in the office, Eva resumed. Rags. Her father had stuffed rags soaked with kerosene in the corners. It was night, her mother asleep in the back bedroom. At the last minute, with the house already filling with fumes, he dragged Eva and her sister outside. He put them in the chicken coop and told them not to move. Then he crept into the kitchen and threw a lit match.

"All I have left from my mother is the amulet she give me." Eva touches something hanging under her shirt.

"Now you will quit me," she continues.

"Quit you?"

"Make me leave."

"Why would I make you leave?"

"The people who want it."

"Who want what?"

"When my sister tell her teacher that our mother die, my father hit her in the mouth with a rock."

Myra's buzzer rings.

After Eva leaves, Myra stands to stretch her back. She bends forward, her head and arms dangling down. A wave of dizzi-

ness, then nausea, comes over her, and for a moment she wonders if the sandwich Eva made for her was spoiled.

She walks toward the waiting room, not thinking, as she
usually does, about the patient she will greet, the mood she
might encounter, the link to what happened in his last session,
her mind still on Eva so that the sight of her patient's face comes
as a jolt, like a boat bumping against a dock, an undertow of
fear in its wake.

THREE

1

Since she was a child, Caro has dreaded Christmas. The dread begins the week after Thanksgiving, when the city falls down the rabbit hole into what is euphemistically called the holiday season but everyone knows is really the Christmas season. Vendors selling trees arrive from Canada with earmuffs and lumber jackets, the bound trees imprisoned along the sidewalks of upper Broadway. Drugstore windows are filled with squashed boxes of lights and neon tinsel on the verge of combustion. In the cramped supermarkets, carols blare through the loudspeaker systems.

When she was young, the dread had centered on the feeling that there are two groups: those who eagerly await Santa Claus and the mountains of presents, and then, in some alternate darker universe, the Jewish children who, like her, had been hoodwinked into accepting Hanukkah as their meager alternative. (Then it had not occurred to her that there are also Muslim, Hindu, and Buddhist children greeting Christmas morning without excitement.) Yes, her mother made latkes, and they had a holiday meal with her father's parents, who gave Adam and her chocolate gelt and fifty-dollar checks. Yes, there were dreidl games with Grandpa Max, who each year produced an outlandish dreidl—one that emitted gospel-style songs, one that lit up like a slot machine—but it all paled against the visions of her classmates running to their living rooms Christmas mornings to see the gifts piled under their trimmed and lit trees, their handsome bathrobe-clad parents sipping eggnog while the children rip wrapping paper from marvelous toy after marvelous toy.

Christmas had hit an all-time low the year her mother kicked their father out and Adam refused to go to Max and Ida's Riverdale house for Hanukkah without her. Gently, her mother attempted to explain that now that she and their father were getting divorced, she would no longer be attending his father's family gatherings. "Go," she urged. "Grandpa will be so sad if you don't." But Adam had been unbudgeable, so that Caro had to go alone.

Arriving home that night, Caro burst into tears. "I hate Christmas," she sobbed.

Her mother bundled her into her arms. "I think this is about the divorce, don't you, darling?"

"No, it's not about the stupid divorce. It's about Christmas. I hate being Jewish. I want Christmas."

In the morning, instead of their usual sensible breakfast of Irish oatmeal and fruit, there were waffles dusted with powdered sugar and mugs of hot chocolate capped with whipped cream. Adam pressed his moistened finger onto the plate until he'd captured every sugar morsel.

"Children," her mother announced, "I've been thinking things over. We live in the city where Christmas is the most beautifully celebrated, save perhaps in Rome, of anywhere in the world. Christmas is a New York tradition. We are New Yorkers. There is no reason we can't enjoy the part of Christmas that is about New York, not Jesus."

After that, her mother had taken them every year to see the tree at Rockefeller Center, the windows at Saks and Lord & Taylor, the Neapolitan crèche in the Medieval Hall at the Metropolitan Museum of Art, and, for Caro, the highlight of the season, the Balanchine version of *The Nutcracker* performed by the New York City Ballet. Each year, they would invite another Jewish family for Christmas dinner, and her mother would serve mulled cider and oysters Rockefeller and roast a leg of lamb bought from a butcher shop on Madison Avenue. For dessert, there would be a bûche de Noël and chocolate-covered strawberries.

Caro had loved the tree that magically grows to the ceiling as Marie's nutcracker transforms into her prince, the scent of nutmeg and rosemary that would fill the parlor floor Christmas afternoon. But the dread never fully disappeared, the feeling that she was counting the days until the holiday season was over.

2

The first weekend in December, Caro arrives at her mother's house for Sunday dinner to discover Eva and Omar decorating a tree in the parlor. Bing Crosby is singing carols while Eva, humming along, hangs red and green balls and Omar makes loops out of construction paper. In the kitchen, her mother is stuffing Meyer lemons into the cavities of two organic chickens.

"What's going on?"

"Eva brought home a tree. She carried it herself from Broadway. God knows how she did it. Omar was so excited when he saw it that I decided to leave the decision up to his parents. Rachida surprised me by being entirely gung ho. Adam tried debating with her about the capitulation to capitalism and the hegemonic culture until Rachida told him to do something I won't repeat. She took Eva and Omar to CVS to buy lights and ornaments."

"How do you feel about it?"

Her mother puts the chickens in the oven. She washes her hands and begins wiping down the counters with white vinegar, the way her own mother, a germ's worst enemy, Larry had called her, had taught her to avoid the parasites poultry breed. "At first, I felt uncomfortable. But when I saw how much fun it is for Omar and Eva, I thought what's the harm. The tree has nothing to do with anything religious."

"So are you going to have Santa Claus bring presents?"

"Omar already told me that Santa Claus is made up. Reindeer are the size of horses, he said. Nothing that size could fly. No. Of course not. We don't have to fall prey to the domino theory: that if you give way in one area, you're doomed to give way for everything."

Caro feels oddly chastised. Had she been a parent, she could imagine herself under the sway of this slippery-slope logic, as though a lollipop for a three-year-old would lead to Twinkies and cotton candy for dinner. "I'm surprised Eva wanted a tree."

"Before her mother died, she always had one. She thought it was a present for us. It never occurred to her that as Jews we might not want one."

3

When his parents were alive, Larry had come to New York every year for the week between Christmas and New Year's, a week when his office closed and the only heart procedures were on those persons unfortunate enough to have a coronary event over the holidays, when they'd be left in the care of the lowest-rung attendants.

This year, with Adam and Omar in New York, Larry feels a yen to again come East during this week. As long as he is home on Christmas Day—exclaiming over presents he doesn't want, accepting grunted thank you's from Betty's boys for the gifts he will learn he has given them—and for the New Year's Eve dinner dance at their club, Betty will not object to his being gone in between.

He decides to test the idea with Caro.

"Sounds great, Dad. Omar and I are both off from school, so we'll have lots of free time. Rachida probably has to work, but I'm sure she's not the reason you're coming. And Adam, well, he doesn't pay attention to the calendar."

"How about your mother? I assume I'd have to come to the house to get Omar. Do you think she'd mind?"

Caro hesitates. Her mother has always been the poster-child divorced parent; it never occurred to Caro that seeing her father might still be hard for her. "Why don't you ask her yourself?"

"She might not welcome a phone call from me. It's been a long time since we talked—since Grandpa Max's funeral, I think."

At the funeral home, Larry still recalls, Myra had kissed him on the cheek. Her eyes were damp as she told him how sorry she was about Max's death. Three years later, though, when his mother died, she'd not come to the service, sending, instead, a contribution to the B'nai B'rith fund they designated in memoriam. Part of his despondency at his mother's funeral, he'd known, was because Myra was not there.

"Maybe I could shoot her an e-mail."

"That's a good idea."

4

On the second Monday of December, Myra opens her e-mail to see larrymendelsohn@desertdocs.com:

Dear Myra,

I hope it doesn't shock you to hear from
me this way, but I thought you might prefer
the screen to the phone. I'm thinking of
coming East (by myself) for the week
between Christmas and New Year's to see
the kids and Omar. I'd like to take Omar
to do some things, which would probably
mean picking him up or dropping him off at
your house. Okay with you?

```
I would think I'd won the lottery if you'd
have dinner with me, but I won't even ask
since I know you won't. How about a line
or two to hear how you are?

There seems no way to sign this damn thing
without offending you, so I'll just say
Ciao.

Larry
```

Myra stares at the words. She puts her sandwich back on the plate. It pleases her that Larry has written his e-mail like a letter, not all in lowercase without punctuation, the way the kids do, or with the self-consciously casual diction so many affect, an excuse, she's always thought, for sloppy writing, which translates in her mind to sloppy thinking.

It surprises her that she does not feel adverse to the idea of seeing Larry, of having his bearish form lumber up her front steps. For a moment, she imagines him seated on her sofa, drinking a glass of red wine while Omar plays on the floor. They'd had only nine years together as parents. Omar will be seven in February, the age Adam was when they separated.

She glances at her watch. It is a little past two. Soon Eva will come for her tray. In the week since Eva told Myra about her father lacing the house with kerosene-soaked rags, she has not sat again in the patient chair.

Myra takes a bite of her sandwich and then gulps down half a glass of water.

```
Dear Larry,

I read in The Times that there are now websites divorced
parents can use to coordinate schedules and finances
without having direct contact. I'm not sure if we're lucky or
unlucky to have missed these developments.
```

Of course you may pick up Omar at my house. I'll decline the
dinner invitation for both of our well-being, but hope you'll
stay for a glass of wine in my parlor.

All best,
Myra

PS Don't be shocked when you see a Christmas tree. Eva
brought one home and none of us had the heart to
disappoint Omar by refusing to let her put it up.

5

"A Christmas tree?" Larry says to Adam when he calls to discuss his trip. "Why would Eva want a Christmas tree?"

Larry lies wrapped in a towel on a chaise longue on the terrace by his heated pool. Betty is inside baking her umpteenth
batch of Christmas cookies, this particular one a cardiologist's
nightmare since they are made with bacon fat, a recipe her first
mother-in-law told her is traditional in Sweden. All morning,
Betty fried bacon, plate after plate, which she and the boys ate
with eggs and then, for lunch, in sandwiches. When he came
inside for his own lunch of cottage cheese and salad, there was
a measuring cup filled with amber fat.

"Eva says her mother always had a Christmas tree."

"I thought Eva considers herself a Jew."

"Not considers, Dad. Is a Jew."

"How can she claim she's Jewish? She wouldn't know if you
ate matzoh at Passover or Hanukkah."

"It's not a question of claim. It's how she feels. She feels Jewish."

"Fine, I feel Chinese. That doesn't make me Chinese. She
was never in a synagogue before she came to New York. She told
me she went to Catholic grade school. It's absurd."

"To you. She feels in her bones that she's different, and she connects that difference to her great-great-grandfather. She believes that her life will be righted once she can live as a Jew."

"I don't live as a Jew. I haven't been in a synagogue since I moved out of my parents' home. But I am a Jew. It was the soup in which I was raised. We ate Jewish foods at home. My grandparents spoke Yiddish. My father was an atheist, well, until the whole Frank Lloyd Wright–God–nature nonsense set in, but that, too, for him was part of Jewish culture—the red-diaper-baby Jewish intelligentsia strain. For Eva, it's nothing but fantasy."

"Who gave you the mantle to decide what identities people can take? She's as much a Jew as you are. She's not Christian, she's not Yagua, she's not Moroccan. She's a Jew. Perhaps more so, because she feels that being a Jew makes her different from the people she grew up around—that it defines her. You're a passive Jew. You don't have to do anything to be a Jew. She struggles day by day to create herself as a Jew."

Adam senses that his father is thinking about what he is saying, that his father is torn between his intellectual honesty and his adherence to a crusty cynicism, which will inevitably win out in the exchange.

"You're getting a little liberal-artsy for me. A little theoretical-shmetical. Let's keep it simple. Does she eat bagels and lox on Sundays? Does she like celery soda? Does she cringe when she sees those bloodied dolls nailed to their plastic crosses? That's how you tell if she's a Jew."

6

Before beginning her writing project on the teleology of love, Myra had collected ideas: tsimtsum, wabi-sabi, the uncarved block. More accurately, she had collected distillations of ideas, since it is not in her nature to study an idea per se: its history, the semantic debates, the fiefdom struggles over its control. That would seem sterile to her, shallow in the way of careers based on the study of well-being via statistical analyses of self-report checklists by researchers who have never sat down with a human being to discuss the subject.

Now she thinks about wabi-sabi as she has come to understand it: the acceptance of not only the inevitability of decay but of the beauty within the process of decay. That from the moment we are born, a wall is painted, a cake baked, decay sets in, and that this decay, if accepted, if part of the object's organic conception, can be more beautiful, more satisfying than an artificial idea of perfection. An electronic gadget breaks and is done for, more expensive to repair than to replace. A stone wall smooths, rounds, nourishes green moss in its crevices. A woman's face can change from a plump peach to a sculpted oval of planes and bones and wisdom lines.

It has taken Myra a long time to accept this notion of celebrating decay, in her home, in the objects around her, in her garden, in her body. Now, though, when she looks in the mirror, she does not feel at war with the gray, with the wrinkles. True, she has been lucky—her body has remained lithe and limber—but she has let go of the idea that life is an arc with a build up toward an apex and then a slow winding down. She is no more accelerating or decelerating now at fifty nine than she was at nineteen. So it comes as a surprise that she feels nervous about seeing Larry—always trying with his young wives and horses and cars to vanquish time. About seeing herself through his eyes.

7

The phone rings on the bedside stand. It is three o'clock in the morning, the week before Christmas. Adam has the receiver in his hand before he realizes that Rachida, who came home after he went to bed, is asleep beside him.

"Rachida, Rachida, is that you?"

He recognizes the voice of Rachida's sister, Esther. "It's Adam. She's right here."

Rachida bolts up, grabbing the phone so violently that it smashes against his chin. As Adam turns on the light, he sees the tears already streaming down her cheeks, her face crumpling. From the tears, Adam knows it must be her father, Uri.

After she hangs up, he tries to put his arms around her, but she will not have it. She lies on her side, her back to him, and heaves into the pillow. Adam goes into the bathroom to look for a box of tissues. Not finding one, he tears off a wad of toilet paper. Rachida bats it from his hand.

Gingerly, Adam lowers himself back onto the bed, careful not to touch her. He's seen Rachida cry only once before, at Omar's birth, when she had cried from joy and exhaustion.

At seven, Adam wakes alone, ashamed that he fell back asleep. He goes downstairs where Rachida, dressed and dry-eyed, is seated at the farm table, drinking coffee with his mother.

"We've decided," Rachida says, "not to tell Omar until the afternoon. Can you give him breakfast and take him to school? I need to get on the phone with the airlines to make reservations."

"Okay."

"There's usually an eleven o'clock night flight direct to Casablanca. I'm going to try to get us on the one for tonight. If not, we'll have to fly to Paris and change there. Tomorrow's Omar's last day of school before the break, so he'll only miss one day. I'll call the school once we figure out when we're leaving."

Adam's mouth goes dry and his heart pounds. Dark spots float before his eyes. He clutches the lip of the table. Does

Rachida think he is going to get on an airplane with her? He sees his mother watching him. She nods slightly, as though to say, Just go along, don't challenge Rachida now.

8

When Adam returns from taking Omar to school, his mother is alone in the kitchen. "I've moved my first two patients," she tells him.

"Where's Rachida?"

"She's upstairs making phone calls."

"I can't fly."

"Yes, you can. You have to. You can't not go to your father-in-law's funeral."

"I'll be more trouble than help. You remember the time I tried to fly to Dad's? I had a panic attack on the runway and they had to let me off the plane."

"That was fifteen years ago."

"Well, that was enough for me. I'm not going to try again."

"I talked to Caro. Tomorrow's the last day of school for her too. She wants to go to Uri's funeral, and she said she'll miss a day of school so she can fly with you. I'll ask Jim Meyers, he's the psychopharmacologist I use for my patients, to write a prescription for something to help you relax."

Adam closes his eyes. He takes a deep breath. He tries to imagine buckling a seat belt, allowing a stranger, a man, he assumes, to take the controls and lift them into the air. "Rachida didn't even tell me what happened. How did he die?"

"A massive coronary. Apparently Uri told Rachida's mother that he'd been having chest pains and was going to make an appointment for January to go to the doctor. Rachida cannot believe that her mother or sister didn't insist he go immediately. And she feels guilty that she didn't know."

"I can't do it."

"Yes you can."

9

Adam sits on the sofa in the parlor reading *The Times* cover to cover, an attempt to distract himself from thinking about the night flight to Casablanca—two pairs of seats, with a return flight the day before New Year's Eve—Rachida has succeeded in booking them on. She is upstairs packing for Omar and herself. His mother has sent Eva to pick up the prescription for Xanax that Meyers called in for him. She is downstairs now seeing her late-morning patients.

He plows through a long piece in the Science section on the genetics of birds' innate migratory patterns. The thought of dissecting the birds to examine the differences in their pituitary glands makes him nauseous. By the time he reaches the second column of a piece on hormone replacement therapy, the meaning of each word dissolves with the arrival of its successor.

A little before eleven, Caro calls.

"How's everyone?"

"Off doing their thing."

"Do you even have a passport? You've never left the country, have you?"

"Good question, Sherlock. But the answer is yes. Rachida insisted I get a passport when she got Omar his. She thinks I won't fly as a way of annoying her."

"Maybe she has a point."

"I could dream up less unpleasant means of bugging her than breaking into a cold sweat and feeling like I'm going to shit my pants."

"You went on that rafting trip. That had to have been scary."

"Put me on a boat, on a train, I'm fine. It's things that go up in the air, where you can't get out, that terrify me."

"We have this theory at school that the kids do better approaching new experiences if we talk them through what it will be like first. Do you want me to do that for you with flying?"

"So I can go through it twice?"

"What exactly frightens you?"

"Taking off. I imagine this huge centrifugal force over-powering me as we lift off. Losing altitude mid-flight and fall-ing in accelerated free-fall straight down. Landing—crashing into the runway."

Caro sighs. "Let's take this a step at a time. There's no huge centrifugal force. At takeoff, you'll feel a slight pressure push-ing you back into the seat as the plane assumes about a ten-degree upward angle from the runway."

Adam shivers. "I better not talk about it. Just give me a bucketful of the Xanax and let me sleep through it."

"Did you pack?"

"Not yet. I will."

Caro imagines her brother's rumpled wardrobe, his stained T-shirts, his dirty sneakers. "Lay out everything on the bed that you're going to take. Then let Rachida check it."

"Ha, ha. Madame Rachida—arbiter of sartorial appropri-ateness."

After Adam gets off the phone, he heads upstairs. Caro is right. He should let Rachida give her seal of approval to his clothes. He doesn't want to be three thousand miles away with her berating him as to why he didn't bring his brown loafers. When he gets to the third-floor landing, he tells himself he will start by gathering up the papers and books he wants to take.

The outline for "Moishe in the Amazon" and some notes he took from the Internet about Iquitos are scattered across the desk. He tidies the papers, which he puts back inside a manila folder labeled *Research Iquitos*. Perhaps he will be able to do some research while he's in Morocco: Moishe, after all, comes from Marrakesh. He'll bring a notebook. With this thought comes a little relief to his anxiety—there will be a purpose to the trip aside from comforting Rachida, which seems already doomed, followed then by a new wave of terror since the thought implies that he will, indeed, board the plane.

What he wants to bring is the photograph from the magazine of the two men, the little one held aloft by the large one. He locks the door, lowers the shades, and opens the closet. The brown envelope holding the photographs is in the back of the bottom file box. He takes out the picture, averting his eyes so he doesn't actually look at it. He folds it and places it inside the blue notebook he used when he interviewed Eva about Iquitos.

He puts the envelope back in the file box, at the rear as before. But what if the plane crashes and someone has to go through his papers looking for insurance information or wills? Wouldn't it be safer to put the photos in a file where no one would look?

He can hear someone moving around in the kitchen—either Eva back from the pharmacy or his mother done with her morning patients.

He empties the envelope and puts the photos inside the manila folder labeled *Research Iquitos*. He puts the folder inside the file box marked *Moishe in the Amazon*. After the plane explodes on the runway, no one will care about Moishe.

10

In the end, Myra packs for Adam. Coming upstairs during her lunch break, she finds him staring at the contents of his top dresser drawer, the suitcase Rachida dragged up from the basement empty except for a notebook and a pile of books.

"How are you doing?"

"Caro said to lay everything out and have Rachida check it."

"Rachida has her hands full. Why don't we do it together?"

And so it is that Myra comes to see the shabby condition of her son's wardrobe. After five minutes' looking through his closet and drawers, she quickly writes a list for Eva to take to Macy's: six pairs of brown and black socks, two packages each of briefs and undershirts. Because they are largely unused, Adam's dress clothes are in better condition. She puts his suit in the bathroom to steam and gathers up the best sampling of khaki pants and shirts for Eva to press when she returns.

It has been a long time since she has involved herself with a man's clothing. With her lovers, she was careful not to make herself available in this way. Larry, though, had refused to pack for himself, claiming he couldn't fold as well as she could. "If I could fold the way you do," he'd say, "I'd have become a surgeon."

"Or an origami artist?"

"Just pack for me, baby."

Secretly, she had enjoyed handling his things, the vicarious pleasure of his immaculate wardrobe, his way, she thought, of holding on to the era before his father saw God in nature and renounced boxers purchased in dozen-count boxes from Brooks Brothers and Italian shoes each stuffed with a wooden shoe tree. Her own things are neat and lovely in a simple way, but fundamentally they were a peacock family with the male strutting the finery.

Betty, Caro says, is a slob. Myra smiles thinking about Larry living with muddy boots in the entry hall, the kitchen sink filled with the soggy remains of the morning's cereal, everything covered with hair from the three dogs and two cats.

It is probably good for him. To what had her own pristine ideals—the balanced meals, the orderly dresser drawers, the well-behaved children—led? A husband who had sex with his receptionist.

11

Caro calls her father to tell him about Uri's death and their departure in a few hours for Morocco.

"Let Rachida know I'm really sorry. What a shock. Did he have any cardiac history?"

"Not that Rachida knows of. Though he'd been complaining for a few weeks about chest pains."

"Adam's really going?"

"Rachida didn't give him a choice. Mom got him some Xanax. I want to attend Uri's funeral, but I'm mostly going to baby-sit him."

"Be careful not to overdo it with the Xanax. You know what a cheap date Adam is."

As always, Caro feels a twinge of surprise on hearing her father's concern—a residue of her childish belief when he first left that in so doing he'd stopped thinking about them. "You're going to cancel your trip now that none of us will be here?"

There is a long enough pause before her father's answer that Caro wonders if perhaps she is wrong. "Sure, no point now."

12

Myra holds Omar's hand as the car service driver loads the suitcases Eva and Rachida have carried to the curb. Adam is chalky with fear. Without saying goodbye, he climbs into the front seat where he'll have more air.

Caro counts their luggage. "Three suitcases, one duffel, and four carry-ons."

With Caro, Adam will be okay. Rachida and Caro each hug Myra. Myra hands a bag to Omar: some travel games she'd run to a toy store to buy. "Don't open it until you're on the plane," she whispers to Omar.

"Will we be back for Christmas?"

"No, darling. We'll have Christmas and open all of your Hanukkah presents on New Year's Eve—the day after you get back."

"Remember to put water in the tree, Eva," Omar says.

"I will."

"You can sleep in my bed while I'm gone."

Eva smiles awkwardly. As the van pulls away, she and Myra
stand in the dark waving goodbye. If Eva had somewhere to go,
Myra would tell her to take the week off. It would be a vacation
to have the house to herself. But there is nowhere for Eva to go.

Inside, Eva finishes the dinner dishes while Myra goes
downstairs to her office. She checks her phone messages, sorts
the mail on her desk. Then she turns on her computer.

In the middle of her inbox is larrymendelsohn@desertdocs
.com. She takes a deep breath and clicks open.

Dear Myra,

Well, I'm sorry for Rachida about her
father. Sounds like someone upstairs gave
him some warning calls and he ignored them,
which must be eating up Rachida. Uri and I
had a drink together at the kids' wedding
and I thought he was a decent guy—though
that wife of his reminded me of my mother,
which is not meant as a compliment. He
was tickled that my grandfather was a
jeweler too.

So I won't be coming East. I have to admit
that I'm sorry that I won't get a chance
to see you. I feel damn sheepish to tell
you I was really looking forward to it.
Don't give me any of your psychoanalytic
interpretations about wallowing in my
guilt and wanting what I can't have. I
just miss you is all.

```
In any case, I suppose I should say Merry
Christmas or Happy Hanukkah—whichever is
now your cup of tea. On my end, I could do
without the former. Kiss Omar for me when
he gets back.

Yours,
Larry
```

Myra reads the e-mail three times. She pushes the delete button so she won't read it again, then goes to get a tissue to wipe her eyes.

13

They have two pairs of seats: Adam and Caro near the front of the plane, Rachida and Omar twelve rows behind them. Thinking Adam might feel less claustrophobic on the aisle, Caro takes the center seat. Adam seems drowsy already from the pill he took at the airport. He closes his eyes and falls immediately asleep. When the flight attendand arrives with the dinner cart, Caro selects an entrée for Adam, balancing the two meals on her tray and then, when Adam never budges, miserably eating them both.

After the dinner detritus has been collected, the lights are dimmed. Caro lowers her brother's seat back and tucks a blanket around him. She climbs over his knees and walks back to check on Rachida and Omar.

Omar is sleeping with his head in his mother's lap. A maze book sticks out of his seat pocket. Rachida is seated upright, drinking a Scotch.

The seat across the aisle from Rachida is empty. Caro sits down.

"How's he doing?" Rachida asks.

"He's out."

"We could have just given him two glasses of wine."

"Probably. But this is good." With Rachida turned now toward her, Caro can see that her eyes are red and puffy. "How are you?"

"Fucked."

"Why fucked?"

"I can't stop thinking about how pissed I am at him for dying before I tried to make things okay between us. We were both so goddamned stubborn. I knew he wouldn't live forever, but I thought I still had some time."

Now, with Uri gone, Caro is struck anew by the strangeness of it having been her argument with him over the bracelet for her mother that had led to her, and then, through her, Adam, meeting Rachida. "What did you want to tell him?"

"Oh, stupid stuff. Like I understood why he never wanted to leave Morocco. All of my mother's family and most of his left for Israel and Canada, but he felt this loyalty to the Moroccan monarchy because they've historically protected the Jews. I would spit facts at him: Look at the torture Hassan II committed. Look at the current king. He'll irrigate a desert to make a golf course and let children in the south die from meningitis."

Rachida's voice breaks. She strokes Omar's hair. "He thought he'd never feel at home anywhere else, that if he gave up his business, he'd never be able to support my mother in the style to which she was accustomed. I'd argue with him about how dumb it was to keep living in the mellah just because his great-grandfather and grandfather and father had all lived there, on the rue Zerktouni, all of them jewelers in the ruelle Siaghine souk. He'd tell me other men wished for sons, but he was glad he had daughters because then his grandchildren would assuredly be Jews. I used to yell at him that he talked about me like I was a propagating cow."

"He was a generous man. I know that's a funny thing to say about someone I got to know because I thought he'd cheated me, but once we got past that, he insisted I come to your home for dinner and stay in Marrakesh at that lavish hotel where his friend worked."

"La Mamounia. Khalid is still the reservations manager there. When Omar and I visit in the summer, he always arranges rooms for us. In my father's mind, getting an extra thirty dollars from a tourist was not cheating. Cheating would have been selling inferior goods, which he'd never do. Selling anything but the best quality silver was out of the question for him."

Caro nods. The hotel in Marrakesh had been the most beautiful she'd ever seen: the lush gardens, the marble lobby, the intricately carved columns, the sound everywhere of gurgling water. She never knew if it was Uri or his friend who had refused to let her pay for the room.

Rachida leans down to kiss Omar's smooth forehead. He buries his face into the pillow on her lap. "My father was so happy when I asked him to make the amulet for Eva."

"The what?"

"Eva's amulet. Adam didn't tell you about it?"

Caro shakes her head.

"She had this charm kind of thing in the shape of a hand—in Morocco, the Jews call it a hamsa, something her mother had given her that had been passed down from her great-, great-, I don't know how many greats, grandfather who was from Rabat. Adam took it from her so he could have me translate the Hebrew words engraved on the back. Somehow he lost it."

"Eva must have taken that hard."

"Adam said she showed no reaction. But he felt terrible. My father sold dozens of them a year. He was going to look for an antique one and engrave the words from the original on it."

Rachida's eyes brim with tears. "He wanted to believe that my repeating the Hebrew words meant that I'd changed and accepted being a Jew." She dabs her eyes with a cocktail napkin. "He was so happy to do it."

14

A driver hired by Rachida's sister, Esther, meets them at the Casablanca airport to take them the six hours south to Essaouira. Adam sits in the front seat of the minivan with his window open, which leaves them all blasted by the hot desert air. The highway hugs the Atlantic coast, passing salt flats and oil refineries. Beneath the roar of the wind is silence. On occasion, they pass through a village where Adam stares at the women in chadors walking slowly along the road. Omar, accustomed to the sights from prior visits, never looks up from his book.

It is five o'clock by the time they arrive at the outskirts of Essaouira. Rachida and Omar will be staying in Rachida's mother's house in the mellah. Esther had offered her own home for Adam and Caro, but Rachida declined, though whether out of consideration for her sister or for them, Caro could not say. Instead, she and Adam are booked into a large Western-style hotel on the windswept beach road outside of town, a windsurfer's hangout, Caro recalls from her first trip here.

The driver delivers Caro's and Adam's luggage into the hands of a bellhop in a white embroidered tunic, pajama pants, and a tall, tassled hat—the uniform the only clue that the hotel is not in Miami or Rio or Capetown. Rachida's and Omar's suitcases will have to be wheeled on a cart through the narrow alleyways that lead to Rachida's mother's house.

Rachida tells Caro and Adam that the driver will return for them in an hour to take them to Esther's house, where Uri's cousins have already arrived from Manchester and Toronto.

"Is it far?" Caro asks.

"Five minutes by car."

"We'll walk, then."

The driver marks the route and address on Caro's map. She squeezes Omar's hand. "See you soon, pal."

At dusk, Caro sets out with Adam on the beach road toward

the entrance to the port. When they arrived, the wind was whipping the sand in sheets, but with the approach of night, it has turned to a balmy breeze.

"I read that Orson Welles filmed several scenes from *Othello* on these ramparts," Adam says.

"It rings a bell. I must have heard that last time I was here."

Adam looks at her with a moment of confusion, as though he has forgotten that she's been here before. "How old were you?"

"Twenty. It was the summer before my junior year."

"I could barely get downtown by myself at that age."

"And look what a big strong boy you are now. Flew on an airplane across an ocean."

"Don't remind me." Adam exhales loudly. "I want to see the ramparts where Iago is put in a metal cage. Do we have time?"

Caro studies the map. With her finger, she traces a detour that will bring them past the fish grills and then north along the Skala de la Ville. "If you don't walk like a slug, we could do it."

She takes her brother's arm. They pick up their pace, neither of them talking until the walls come into view.

"There!" Adam points. "That's where Iago is hung over the sea."

To Caro's relief, Adam does not embark on a treatise on *Othello*, sinking instead into a silent reverie as they pass under the ramparts and then by the woodworking shops selling carved chess sets and marquetry boxes fashioned from the local thuja wood. Not until they fall behind a band of blind musicians in burgundy robes blowing wooden flutes and banging on hide drums does it occur to Caro that this is the first time her brother has been anywhere more foreign than Tucson.

15

It is dark when they reach Esther's house: a low modern structure built around a courtyard. Esther greets them at the door with tearful hugs. She has grown plump in the decade and a half since Caro met her, but her face remains pretty and girlish.

Caro and Adam follow Esther into a living room rimmed with banquettes covered in printed fabrics, maroons and yellows and azure blue, with loose cushions resting against the walls. Rachida is seated next to her mother, holding her hand the way she might a soiled tissue. Raquel is half-reclining with her feet on a leather pouf. She closes her eyes while two women fuss over her, adjusting a wet cloth on her forehead, loosening the straps to her shoes. On the other side of the room, a group is gathered around a brass tray perched on a stand, passing photos among themselves.

"Raquel felt faint," Esther's husband whispers to Adam. "Where's Omar?"

"In the courtyard, with the other children."

Adam leans over his mother-in-law to kiss her cheek. He has not seen her since his wedding, seven years before. She opens her eyes, her hand fluttering in front of her chest as though to indicate the limit of the energy she has to expend on him. Rachida stands. "I'm going to introduce Adam and Caro to everyone."

The men seated around the brass tray grip their thighs and hoist themselves to stand. Two of them look to be past eighty, one around fifty. The women, of an indeterminate elderly age, smile and offer hands and cheeks to be kissed. They are, Rachida explains, two of her father's cousins, one of the cousin's sons, and their respective wives, though Adam cannot tell who goes with whom.

After the group has settled back down, adjusting themselves on the banquettes to make room for Adam, Caro, and Rachida, they resume looking at the photographs. "These are from a Mimouna we had at a park in the early sixties, before the war, before the family dispersed," the youngest man says, handing a photo to Adam.

"The war?" Adam asks.

"The Six-Day War, in Israel," says one of the cousins. "After that, it became clear that we could not stay. Mobs ransacked the mellah. Many homes were destroyed."

"Well, it was clear to everyone but Uri," says the cousin's son.

Adam examines the photo. A white tablecloth laden with food and flowers is spread on a rocky ledge. People sit on the ground, smiling at the camera, holding up glasses filled with red wine. He passes the photo to Caro.

"What is a Mimouna?" asks Caro.

"It is a festival we hold after Passover," one of the women answers. "My sister still participates in one in Negev, but we don't have them any longer in England." She hands Rachida a photograph. "That is your father, the one on the left."

Adam peers over Rachida's shoulder. In the photograph, two men in long djellabas, their heads wrapped with white cloth, are on camels against a backdrop of dunes.

"Where was this taken?" Rachida asks.

"By the village in the Anti-Atlas where your grandfather was born."

"Berber through and through," Rachida says.

Esther looks up from across the room, where she has taken over holding her mother's hand. She places a finger on her lips. The cousin who has not yet spoken turns to Adam and Caro while the other cousin gathers the photos. "We are *toshavim*," he whispers. "Jewish Berbers. Our family have been here for nearly fifteen hundred years. Raquel's family are *megorashim*, the exiles from Spain. Because our father and Uri's father grew up in a remote village, speaking only Berber, she thinks we are inferior to her family which six hundred years ago lived in Seville."

A young woman emerges from the kitchen to clear the tea glasses from the brass tray. Her hair is covered with a head scarf, only her slender hands and sandaled feet visible outside her kaftan. Her toenails are painted bright red. A moment later, she returns with two chairs, and then an enormous platter of a steaming lamb and date and almond tagine she sets on the tray. "Take the chairs," the cousins urge Caro and Rachida, while the others squeeze together on the banquettes so everyone can reach the food.

There are no plates, no utensils. A basket of flat bread is passed, pieces broken off to scoop up the food. Adam has seen Moroccans he knows in Detroit share food in this manner, all eating from the same platter, but he has always begged off, his stomach turning at the thought.

When Adam does not take a piece of bread, one of the cousins' sons places a piece in front of him. "Come. Eat some tagine with us," he says.

"A little later. I'm going to find my son first."

Relieved to be away from the food, Adam goes into the courtyard. The walls are tiled in a blue-and-white geometrical design that looks almost Escheresque. In the center is a fountain, defunct or perhaps turned off in deference to the occasion. Four boys and two small girls are racing back and forth with a soccer ball. Omar gives the ball a long sturdy kick and then calls out something in Arabic.

Adam knows, of course, that Zahra, Omar's Moroccan nanny, spoke only Arabic to Omar and that during the summer trips to visit Rachida's parents, there is no English, but it still surprises him to hear these inexplicable words coming from his son's mouth.

He sits on a stone bench at the back of the courtyard. Rachida has told him that, including her family, there are only four Jewish families remaining in the mellah, the other homes abandoned or broken up for itinerant workers from the sardine canning plant. Other than something hanging on a line in a courtyard a few houses away, there is no evidence of anyone else living here at all.

A high-pitched wail pierces the air, and then the raised voices of the women inside. The children, absorbed in their game, ignore the hubbub. Adam rests his elbows on his knees: Ethan on the porch of his brother's house, listening to the laughter of the children, the murmurings of the women, the camaraderie of the men—imagining the forbidden breasts of his brother's wife.

16

Caro wakes at three with a burning sensation across her pelvis. She can hear her intestines gurgling. A cold sweat blankets her forehead as she races to the bathroom.

Not wanting to insult Uri's cousins, she had eaten the figs served after the tagine, knowing, all along, that the unpeeled, uncooked fruit was risky.

For the rest of the night, she lies atop the bed, unable to tolerate the feeling of the sheets on her clammy skin. Between trips to the toilet, she drifts in and out of sleep, wakened periodically by the violent cramping in her gut and then at some still dark hour by the first of the day's calls to prayer.

At seven, she knocks on Adam's door. A look of terror washes over his face as she tells him she won't be able to attend the funeral.

"You can ask the bellman to arrange a taxi for you. The synagogue is very close."

"What if he takes me somewhere else?"

"You're too ugly for anyone to sell you into white slavery." Her bowels are gurgling again. "Go. If I could take you I would. But I can't."

Back in her room, she lies on the floor, curling her knees to her chest to try to arrest the cramping. She has shit so many times, there is nothing left inside her. The last time she was here, she'd also been sick—though not from unpeeled fruit. Then it was August, deathly hot. She'd been the only Westerner on the third-class bus from Casablanca. Halfway down the coast, the bus stopped by the side of the road, the call to prayer coming from some unseen place. While men laid their prayer rugs in the sand, she stumbled off the bus and vomited a few feet from the road.

She had spent three days in her hotel, in a tiny room with a Juliet balcony overlooking the Place Prince Moulay Hassan, unable to keep anything down other than a few sips of bottled water. A young maid with a lovely oval face had brought a tray with a pot of tea and a small green cactus she cut with a pocket knife. From the maid's gesturing, Caro had understood that the cactus was for her ailing stomach. She drank the pungent tea, but left the cactus untouched.

17

Adam grips the armrest of the taxi as it bumps along the Boulevard Mohammed V. When they reach the Place Prince Moulay Hassan, the driver slows to accommodate the street traffic.

"Are you okay, monsieur?" the driver asks in a clipped English. He studies Adam through the rearview mirror.

"Yes, thank you."

"You are going to a funeral?"

"My father-in-law."

"Father-in-law? What is that?"

"My wife's father."

The driver nods. "He was Jew?"

A metallic taste fills Adam's mouth. Should he answer? But it seems absurd not to since the address he has given is for the synagogue.

"Yes."

"And you too? You Jew?"

The words seem hostile, but the man's face in the mirror looks gentle, even friendly. "My family. I'm not really anything."

"At one time, there were many Jews in this town. More than one-third the people here Jews. Jews, Arabs they all got along. Now there are maybe twenty Jews in the entire town."

They are passing through the medina, past the clock tower, the mosque, onto the Avenue de L'Istiqlal.

"Over there, a few meters by foot, is the jewelers' souk. When I was a boy, two dozen Jew jewelers had stalls here. They worked in gold and silver. My mother bought all her jewelry from a Jew man there. Now"—the driver shakes his head—"now only a few old men there. No gold anymore, just silver."

"One less now since my father-in-law died."

"A jeweler?"

Adam nods.

"*Lhamdu llah.*"

18

In the afternoon, Caro risks a brief trip down to the pool. It is chilly outside, more from the wind than the air, the pool empty save for two Japanese children giggling as they splash each other while their mother, dressed in gabardine pants and alligator pumps, snaps photos.

Caro stretches out on one of the chaise longues, covered by two of the long pool towels, the weak winter sun warming her face. She wonders if the hotel on the Place Prince Moulay Hassan, where she stayed fifteen years ago, still exists. There was no air-conditioning, no pool, no hotel bar, but with the kind maid who brought her the tea and cactus and bottles of water, it had been a haven. Emerged from her room on the third day, she discovered the rooftop terrace, where breakfast was served on tile tables, the view of the ramparts and the Ile de Mogador below.

Then she was obsessed with the question of her sexual experience, which for so long had been too little, and then in the space of a few months was too much. The pianist's husband had left her determined to bring her sexual education in hand, to rid herself of the embarrassment of naïveté. Camped out on her friend Anne-Marie's floor, she had taken her first lover, Francis, whom she'd met in the Jardin du Luxembourg, where she'd been reading on one of the iron chairs adjacent to the basin where children launched model sailboats. He had offered her a cigarette, and when she said, *Non, merci, je ne fume pas*, he'd shot back, *Et pourquoi pas un café?*, and when she said, *Je n'ai pas soif*, he stood up and did a handstand on his short muscular arms, landing so close to the water, the nearby children gasped, thinking he might topple in.

On their first date, Francis, a factory worker during the day and university student at night, had made her laugh with absurdist quotes from Saint-Exupéry while he picked bread crumbs from his closely cropped beard. On their second date, he came to get her in his tiny Renault and took her to his sister's apartment, where it turned out no one was home. His beard left a prickly rash across her chest. He made an omelet for them while she scrubbed blood from the couch cushion.

Francis was followed by a Romanian music student, Mikel, whom she met through Anne-Marie. Mikel lived with two other Romanian music students, the three of them having devised a schedule so each had the two-room apartment to himself one night a week. Mikel's night was Thursday. Every Thursday he would meet her at eight and race her back to the fourth-floor apartment, where he behaved like a madman who'd had no food or drink for a week. On Fridays and Saturdays, he would chastely escort her to student recitals at the homes of various friends who would cook pastries stuffed with meat and breads filled with dates and nuts.

In June, she and Anne-Marie bought cheap airline tickets to Crete, where Anne-Marie had a cousin who worked at a bar in Agios Nikolaos. Meeting Caro, Anne-Marie's cousin smirked.

"Andreas, my boss, will give me a raise for inviting you here. He has a thing for American college girls. You are all Marilyn Monroe as far as he is concerned."

The bar was a beach club during the day, with umbrellas and chairs laid out on the coarse sand and a motorboat that took out water skiers. At night, it was more a nightclub than a bar. Anne-Marie spread her beach towel on the sand. Belly down, she untied the back string of her bikini top. She had long angular shoulder blades, a tiny waist, and a big bottom. Caro read under an umbrella in the only bathing suit she owned, a navy tank she'd worn for her high school swim class, now stretched out and falling off her.

The motorboat sputtered onto the sand. The driver had gray hair pulled back into a ponytail and deeply tanned skin. "You girls want to ski?"

Caro had never been on water skis and was too terrified to try, but Anne-Marie loved anything fast where the wind would blow in her face. Caro sat in the boat with the suntanned man while Anne-Marie skied off the back. When Caro hugged her arms, he gave her his shirt to put over her suit. Wiry gray hair curled on his chest. "You and your friend come to my club tonight," he instructed. "You will see the real Greek dances."

At the club, couples danced on the tables and men threw plates against the stone hearth. Caro and Anne-Marie drank the raki that Andreas kept sending to their table. When Caro stumbled outside to be sick, Andreas followed her with a wet dishrag. He led her to the apartment he kept over the club. When she woke at dawn, he was nuzzled against her, kissing the nape of her neck. "I love you with every bone in my body," he whispered. He guided her hand into his briefs. Afterward, he lay on his back smoking and asked her name.

In Athens, she saved two baggy outfits but threw out the rest and the old tank suit. She bought two batik print skirts, one short, one long, and a striped bikini Anne-Marie picked out for her. In Barcelona, Anne-Marie insisted she have her hair straightened. A man with rubber gloves brushed Caro's hair so it fell in soft, chemical-scented waves over her shoulders. "And where is my ugly duckling?" Anne-Marie asked.

By the time they reached Casablanca, Anne-Marie had had it with third-class hotels. Using Papa's Carte Suisse, she took a room for them in a hotel with air-conditioning and a swimming pool. Tired of the beating sun, Caro remained in the room while Anne-Marie went to the pool. When Anne-Marie returned, she announced that they were going to a nightclub with two brothers she had met in the lobby. Very refined men, she declared. Their mother was a third cousin of the king.

The brothers, Abdu and Yosefa, arrived in golf shirts and khaki pants. They had manicured hands, each with a long left pinkie nail. Anne-Marie touched Abdu's nail. He whispered something in her ear. Her eyes opened wide.

They drove to a club along the corniche where Abdu danced with his hands cupping Anne-Marie's butt. At the table, Yosefa told Caro his story: that first Abdu, then, two years later, he had been sent to boarding school in Switzerland. Abdu, who loved to ski, had gone to university in Toulouse; Yosefa had attended in Aix. For the sake of propriety, they lived with their parents and would continue to do so until they were married, though they shared an apartment as well for . . . and here Yosefa left the sentence unfinished.

The next evening, the brothers took Anne-Marie and Caro to a restaurant overlooking the sea. Anne-Marie wore a halter dress that left her back bare. Abdu ordered a sparkling wine that Anne-Marie drank like soda. When Abdu suggested they return to his and Yosefa's apartment so they could listen to some music, Anne-Marie shimmied her shoulders, her small breasts jiggling beneath the shiny fabric of her dress.

"No. N-O," Caro whispered in Anne-Marie's ear. "I am not going."

"Do as you please. I'm going." Anne-Marie dug her nails into Caro's upper arm. "Bitch," she hissed.

Afraid to leave Anne-Marie alone, still thinking she could convince her to go back to the hotel, Caro followed Anne-Marie to the brothers' car. Yosefa stared at Caro with a silly grin. In the car, he touched her hair. "You are so beautiful. I am in love with you."

Caro removed his hand from her straightened hair. "That is impossible. You just met me yesterday."

"I know my heart. I want to marry you. I want to be with you forever."

Abdu turned off the corniche road and began driving away from the ocean.

Caro leaned over the front seat. "I'm not feeling well. I want to go back to our hotel."

"We will give you something to make you feel better," Abdu said. "A special Moroccan tonic." Anne-Marie snorted and then hiccuped.

They parked in front of a five-story building and climbed the four flights of stairs to the brothers' apartment: a large room with a refrigerator and sink in the corner, a table, and a mattress on the floor with a curtain strung in front.

Anne-Marie and Abdu disappeared behind the curtain. Caro sat with Yosefa at the table. He handed her a Coca-Cola in a glass bottle. That was the last thing she remembered.

When she woke, she was naked on the mattress with a blanket that smelled like an old dog over her. There was a red scratch on her abdomen. Yosefa was sleeping next to her, fully dressed.

Her panties were missing. She found the rest of her clothes and her bag. Yosefa stirred as she tiptoed to the door, but he did not waken. Using the sun to direct her westward, she made her way back to the corniche road, where she gave a waiter scrubbing an outdoor table fifteen dirhams to call her a taxi.

Anne-Marie was not in their room. She was not at the pool. At the front desk, the clerk said the other young lady had come in earlier, but had left again with a gentleman. He pursed his lips in disapproval.

Caro returned to their room. She lay on the bed staring at the ceiling until the phone rang.

"I must see you," said Yosefa.

"No."

"I will come now."

"I never want to see you again. You took advantage of me." Her eyes filled with tears.

"I made love to you. It was from my soul, a beautiful thing."

Caro hung up the phone. Her heart was beating too fast. She felt scared—of Yosefa, who she imagined already in his car, speeding to the hotel, but also of herself, that she'd crossed a line to become someone unrecognizable to herself.

The phone rang again. Hoping it was Anne-Marie, she picked up.

"If I do not see you, my heart will crack into little pieces."

"If you come here, I will call the police."

For a moment, she thought she heard Yosefa snicker, but she must have been wrong, because what he said next was more frightening. "I love you. Allah has chosen you to be my bride. We must marry immediately. By the end of the week. I will tell my mother and sisters and they will prepare everything."

Caro left the phone off the hook. She stuffed her things in her duffel and scribbled a note to Anne-Marie.

The bus terminal was a ten-minute walk away. The next departing bus was for Essaouira. She had heard the name, but wasn't sure where it was. She boarded the bus.

19

Uri's casket is in the front of the synagogue, adjacent to the cabinet where the Torah scrolls are stored. Before Adam has a chance to find Rachida and Omar, Esther's husband is at his elbow, asking if he will be one of the pallbearers.

"My back," Adam murmurs, ashamed to decline but unable to bring himself to touch the casket.

When Rachida arrives with her mother and Omar, she seems oblivious to Adam's presence. Not knowing whether he should sit in the front pew with Rachida and Omar, he sits a row back between Uri's two cousins. The old men hack so loudly, he can barely hear the rabbi, not that he would have understood the Hebrew.

Afterward, they walk to the Jewish cemetery on the outskirts of town, a dusty, downtrodden place with headstones decimated by the sun and the wind. Adam holds the arm of the frailer cousin, though whether he is supporting the old man or the old man him, he cannot say. Three horse-drawn carriages, either commissioned for the occasion or perhaps simply queued outside the walls, bring them back to Raquel's house, where Esther and her maid have prepared a buffet: lamb kebabs, tomato and cucumber salad, merguez, sweetened mint tea, sticky almond pastries. Omar and the other children sit on Raquel's bed watching reruns of *Friends*. Like the other boys, Omar is dressed in a blue embroidered tunic with Western pants and sneakers beneath.

Embarrassed at not having been a pallbearer, Adam sits alone on a chair in the corner, nursing a soda. Again, Raquel holds court, her feet again raised on a leather pouf. He has not seen Rachida since the cemetery.

A slight, thin-faced man approaches him. "I am Hamid. I was Uri's assistant." He holds out his hand. "I worked for your father-in-law for thirteen years. In the mornings, when he was in the workshop, I tended the customers. I have been looking for your wife, but I do not see her. Sadly, I must leave. My own wife is expecting our second child any day now, so I do not want to be away too much longer."

Adam knows that he should say something, that Caro or his mother would know the right thing to say, but he cannot think what that something is. Instead, the words *I've got to get the fuck out of here* cycle on an endless loop through his mind.

"Rachida had asked Uri to make something for her. He finished it the day before he died. I was to have mailed it to her for him." He removes an envelope from his kaftan pocket and holds it against his chest. "It is a silver hamsa. He looked for an antique one, but he could not find one that he would be able to engrave, so he made this himself. Could you kindly give it to your wife? Please tell her I am very sorry I could not give it to her personally, but I worry too much now about my wife to wait any longer."

Hamid gives the envelope to Adam. He wipes his eyes with the back of his hand. "It was the last thing he made."

Adam nods soberly. "Thank you. I will tell Rachida."

When Rachida arrives, she is accompanied by a boy carting bags of ice.

"Where were you?" Adam asks. He does not like the sharpness in his voice, but half an hour has passed since Hamid left, during which he has been unable to quiet the *I've got to get the fuck out of here* tape in his mind.

Rachida looks at Adam and then the ice with disgust.

"Your father's assistant gave me something to give you." Adam hands Rachida the envelope. "It's the hamsa for Eva."

Rachida opens the envelope. Inside is a silver hand with engraved writing on each of the five fingers. She turns it over and reads the Hebrew on the back: "I have set the Lord always before me."

The new hamsa looks entirely different from the original: shiny and crowded with letters, the fingers more elongated. Adam wonders if it will only upset Eva.

"He said it was the last piece your father worked on."

Rachida inhales so sharply Adam feels himself recoil, the way he might with a dog baring its teeth or, he thinks, seeing Rachida's face, his wife refusing to weep.

20

The day after the funeral, the weather turns unseasonably warm. Seagulls caw from the beach across the road. Rachida brings Omar to the hotel so he can swim. Caro rests on a lounge chair sipping a vile concoction Rachida has given her, a local remedy for intestinal ailments. Twenty feet away, Rachida dangles her feet in the water, watching Omar. Adam stretches out on the lounge chair next to Caro.

"I've got to get out of here," he says.

"What do you mean?"

"This town gives me the creeps. There's too much light. It's too—too blue."

"So . . . ?"

"Go home. You and I leave. Now. Yesterday."

"I can't fly now. I barely made it from the room to the pool. Besides, it would cost an arm and a leg to change our tickets."

"I'll pay."

"Right. And who'll pay your credit card bill? It's charming here. You just hate being away from home. You used to feel the same way when we went on vacation with Dad."

Adam squeezes his eyes shut. He does look miserable. For that matter, Caro thinks, so does Rachida.

"Maybe you're right. Maybe it's being with Rachida's family. They're so conniving, they actually make me appreciate Dad's bluntness. Esther pulled me aside to check out if we are going to continue sending her mother money, which I told her was news to me. That shut her up. And then there's some issue about the jewelry business. Whether Uri's assistant has a right to the store or whether it can be sold."

"You've never spent any time with them. All families are horrid at times like this."

Omar climbs out of the pool, shivering like a tiny dog. Rachida wraps a towel around his shoulders and briskly rubs him dry.

Caro scoots over to make room for Omar. He nuzzles against her. Rachida pulls up a chair.

"Can I play a game on your cell phone?" Omar asks his mother.

Rachida reaches in her bag and hands the phone to Omar. "Ten minutes. That's it."

"It works here?" Adam asks.

"We've been paying for international service for three years. How do you think Omar and I call you every night when we're here?"

Adam angles his face into the weak sun.

"Let me guess. You're trying to recruit Caro to escort you home early."

"No comment."

Caro puts another towel over Omar. He's too absorbed in the game on his mother's phone to pay attention to her jabs at his father.

Rachida sighs. She turns to Caro. "Not that he deserves it, but I do feel bad that he won't see anything more of Morocco than Essaouira. It's like coming to the States and going only to Cape Cod."

"He'll survive. He can watch movies about the rest of the country."

"Esther's husband is going this afternoon to Marrakesh for business. I was thinking maybe we should go with him. I'm so wiped, I can't even think right now about all the things I need to do. We could stay tonight and tomorrow night at La Mamounia—Khalid would give us rooms—and then drive back with Esther's husband Tuesday morning."

Rachida bites her lower lip. "My father loved La Mamounia. We went every spring for a week. Esther and I would order room service breakfast. It would come on a cart with pink cloth napkins and platters covered with enormous silver domes. We played tennis on the clay courts. In the evening, my father and Khalid would have chess competitions in the library bar."

She pokes Adam's stomach. "When Roosevelt visited Casablanca during the war, Churchill insisted he could not leave Morocco without seeing Marrakesh."

"Wow. That's the nicest thing you ever said to me. To put me in the same category as Roosevelt."

"They had to carry Roosevelt up the tower of the ambassador's residence."

Is this it, Caro wonders, the glue between her brother and Rachida? A relentless teasing that for the first time strikes her as a parroting of the way her father talks to Adam. "You'd have to carry me. I'm in no condition for a road trip. But go. Rachida's right, Adam. You really should see Marrakesh."

Rachida stands. She claps her hands next to Adam's ear. "Up. I'll call Khalid while you pack."

Rachida gives Caro a peck on the cheek. "We'll see you in two days. I'll leave Esther's number for you at the front desk in case you need anything. Come on, Omar. We need to let Auntie Caro rest."

21

Still on the lounge chair, Caro sleeps covered with towels—a long deep sleep cut by a river of dreams: a room she has escaped to from menacing dogs, a rooftop where Yosefa threatens to jump to the ground.

She wakes to a ringing sound coming from her feet. Inside the balled-up towel at the bottom of the chaise is the cell phone Omar had been playing with. It is probably Rachida calling to find her phone. Caro flips it open. Still groggy, she searches for the talk button, surprised when she hears a voice, the connection automatically made when she unfolded the top.

"You naughty girl. You made me wait all this time." It's a woman's voice: young, accented, throaty. "I'm in the closet, the one we go in. I'm so wet, it's going to drip out of my panties."

Caro looks around. The pool is empty. An old man is scooping dead mosquitoes from the water with a net.

"Talk to me. Now. Talk very, very nasty."

Caro's stomach is cramping, her mouth dry. The voice is familiar. She needs a toilet.

"I have my finger on it." The woman moans. "You cunt. Why aren't you here to do it for me?"

Layla. It is Layla. Caro pushes the red OFF button. There is a tearing sensation in her bowels. She races upstairs to her room.

22

They are an hour outside of Essaouira before Rachida realizes she doesn't have her phone.

She wants to ask Omar if he remembers what he did with it, but he and Adam are both sleeping. She feels a moment of panic. What if she left the phone at the pool and Layla calls and Caro picks up?

She borrows her brother-in-law's cell phone and tries calling her own phone, but no one answers. She calls the hotel and asks to be connected to Caro's room, where Caro is lying on the bed, trying to gather the strength to go back to the pool to retrieve her things.

"Hey, how are you feeling?"

"About the same."

"Did you see my cell phone?"

Caro massages her temples. She has a band headache, which she'd once read is a sign of being dehydrated. With the throbbing, she can't decide if she should mention Layla's call.

Rachida continues, apparently having taken Caro's silence to be a "no."

"Shit. I never took it back after Omar was playing that game. It probably got mixed up inside the towels."

"Probably."

23

Arriving at La Mamounia with its palatial Moorish arches and carved columns, the four doormen dressed like sultan's guards, Adam thinks first of the *Arabian Nights* and then of the novels of Wharton and James: a young man on the obligatory year of travel between his college days, in what his crowd referred to simply as New Haven or Cambridge, and the banking house he would join in New York. The classic tour with a transatlantic crossing to England, then Paris, Rome, and Nice for the winter with an apartment overlooking the Promenade des Anglais. A boat to Tangier and a roadster into Marrakesh. Beautiful but well-worn calfskin luggage, tended to by his manservant while he took a stroll through the orange-scented gardens.

Omar knows his way through the marble lobby to the billiards room, to the pool, to the gazebo circled by silvery olive trees. Standing on their balcony, he points out the Koutoubia Mosque in the distance.

"I want to go to the square," Omar tells Rachida. "Remember, last time there were snake charmers and fire-eaters there? And children boxing?"

"Which is dangerous—and debased."

Rachida looks at her watch. "He wants to go to the Djemaa el-Fna. It's an enormous outdoor market with lots of food and handicrafts and street performers. We could go for an hour and then eat somewhere nearby."

Adam is reading the history of the hotel he found in the leather folio on the desk of their room. For nearly two decades, he reads, Winston Churchill, accompanied frequently by his wife, Clementine, wintered at the hotel, setting up his easel on his balcony or in the thirty-two acres of flowering gardens. In 1935, Churchill had spent the Christmas holidays here alone. "My darling Clemmie, my beloved pussy cat," he wrote, lavishing her with his verbal portraits of what stretched before him:

"a truly remarkable panorama over the tops of orange trees and olives, and the houses and ramparts of the native Marrakesh, and like a great wall to the westward the snow clad range of the Atlas mountains."

"I'm too tired. Omar, you go with Mommy. I'm going to stay on the balcony and watch the sun set."

After Rachida and Omar leave, the sky turns purple, then orange and crimson. Adam tries imagining himself as Winston Churchill with Clemmie, here on the balcony. Clemmie, his little kitten. Clemmie, his tiny bird perched in her white dressing gown on the edge of the bed. But he cannot imagine whispering endearments to a woman, unfastening a corset, much less donning a top hat, leading a nation, commanding a war.

He tries to imagine himself as Moishe, Moishe of the Amazon. But La Mamounia was not built until after all the Moishes and Jaimes and Leons left for the jungle.

Inside, he draws the curtains and puts the DO NOT DISTURB sign on the door. He rummages in his duffel bag for the notebook he packed at the bottom with the photograph of the two men folded inside.

What he can imagine is himself as Debbie, lifted high above John Wayne's head, himself as the younger, smaller man held aloft by the older, bigger one.

24

Caro wakes in the morning with the sensation of the calm after a storm. Her intestines are no longer cramping. She does not need to race to the toilet. She wants grapefruit and toast with jam and butter. Then she hears Layla's voice in her head.

She buries her face in the pillow, thinking back to the evening when Rachida brought Layla to her mother's house. How could she have missed that the two were lovers?

She showers and dresses, her pants loose, very loose, after three days without food. Downstairs, breakfast is being served on the terrace next to the pool, where, after debating just leaving Rachida's phone, she'd taken it to give back to Rachida on her return.

Planters overflowing with crimson bougainvillea rim the terrace. Small birds fly between a persimmon tree and a lemon tree. Caro nibbles her toast, sips her tea. The toast is delicious. She chews slowly, enjoying each bite. After a few mouthfuls of the grapefruit, she puts down her spoon, her shrunken stomach full.

She will have to tell Rachida about Layla's call, only not now, days after her father's funeral. And won't Rachida look in her call log and know? And is Layla the first for Rachida? The first woman? The first infidelity? Strangely, it is easier to imagine Rachida with Layla than with Adam, though the image has been unwelcomingly assisted by Layla's filthy talk.

In the distance, Caro can hear the wind on the beach. On her first visit to Essaouira, her first meal after she left her room had also been breakfast, also served on the terrace. Then, too, she'd nibbled at toast and tea. She had heard the wind against the ramparts, the screeching of gulls as they dove for fish. Not until she returned to the States, to her dorm at Harvard, where the nausea continued, did she understand that what she'd suffered in Essaouira had nothing to do with anything she'd eaten. At the Cambridge Planned Parenthood, she had been mortified to tell the counselor that she wasn't a hundred percent sure who the father was. She'd gone alone to what was called the procedure, lying that someone was coming to escort her home. It was then that she'd begun to use food as a drug, the up and down of her jaws, the sweet or sour or salty taste on her tongue, an eraser for her mind.

By Thanksgiving, she had gained twenty-two pounds, a full suit of armor on her small frame. Her mother blessedly did not comment, but at Christmas, when her father was in New York, he poked her stomach, more hard than affectionately. "Pizza and beer, hey?" By Valentine's Day, she had settled into a pattern of nighttime binges and daytime starvation, which stopped the scale's ascent but left her locked in a cycle of disgust.

For months, there had been letters from Yosefa, forwarded by Anne-Marie, pleading that Caro let him visit. Then, in the spring, Anne-Marie called. Yosefa's brother Abdu had come to see her in Paris, begging, then threatening her for Caro's address.

"Do not give it to him."

"He says that Yosefa will not eat, that Yosefa will kill himself if he cannot see you."

"Do you hear me, Anne-Marie? Do not give him my address. If you do, I will move and never speak to you again."

Anne-Marie began to cry. Caro could picture her flat stomach, her skinny shoulders, the big buttocks where Abdu had cupped his hands. She wondered if Anne-Marie had let him fuck her again when he'd come to Paris. "Don't blame me if he jumps out of a window," Anne-Marie said.

The letters stopped. In the fall, she marked the anniversary of the abortion with weeks of preliminary dread and not leaving her bed on the day.

At first, she had thought of her celibacy as expiation. By the time she settled into her job at the school and her apartment on West End Avenue, it was a way of life, a necessity between the nights of gluttony and the mornings with her stomach bloated with congealed greed. In August, it would be fifteen years. Fifteen years with a tire around her middle, like a bumper on a bumper car. Longer than Penelope sat at her loom, weaving by day, unraveling by night. Stalling the suitors.

She picks up a knife to spread butter on more toast, then puts it down. Enough. She has had enough.

25

Christmas Day, Myra wakes with a sense of apprehension, an achy nervousness, a premonition, she worries, of physical ailment or disaster. The present she bought for Eva sits wrapped at the end of the farm table. She eats a bowl of cereal while she thumbs through the holiday's skeletal newspaper.

When Eva comes downstairs, Myra points at the wrapped box.

"For me?"

"Yes, for you."

Eva gingerly touches the wrapping paper. She fingers the ribbon. "I never had anything before that came like this."

"You just rip off the paper."

Eva tears at the paper carefully, then lifts the box lid. Inside is a yellow ski jacket with a matching black-and-yellow-striped scarf. Eva puts the jacket on over her nightgown and drapes the scarf over her neck. She twirls around. "It fit me perfect. I love it!"

At noon, Myra leaves for her walk. With the holiday, the day has lost its shape. If Eva were not at the house, she would go back to bed with a cup of tea and a novel. Instead, on her return she decides to play the piano.

The door to the music room is closed, which is strange, since only Adam ever closes it. She pushes it open. At first, she doesn't see Eva. Then she sees her kneeling by the closet, the black-and-yellow scarf still wrapped around her neck.

Eva turns, an odd expression on her face that reminds Myra of Eva's night terror her second week in the house.

"You scare me." She stands, waving the dust cloth in her hand. "The boxes are very dusty." She picks up the trash basket and leaves the room.

Myra opens the closet door. Piled inside are Adam's file boxes. She leans over to read the words written on the lid of the top box: *Moishe in the Amazon*. She lifts the lid. Inside, there are files, each with a white label bordered in blue.

She feels tempted to take out one of the files, to read the papers inside. So many of her patients have talked about searching their kids' pockets and backpacks, reading their journals. With her own children, though, she's never gone through their things. Nothing she might find, she's always thought, would justify the damage that snooping would occasion.

The files are in alphabetical order: Amazon, Boats, Dogs, Herzog, Marrakesh, Rabat, Research Iquitos. Myra closes the lid.

She plays the Bach Prelude in B-flat Major. She plays the Schubert Impromptu in G-flat Major. She plays three Chopin mazurkas. But still, she cannot rid herself of the thought that Eva was looking at something inside Adam's file boxes.

26

Adam wakes with a start, unable to place where he is, confused as to why his legs are so cramped, what all the noise is around him.

Caro is shaking his arm. "We've landed." She hands him a bottle of water. There is something different about her, something unfamiliar. When she stands to get their carry-on bags from the overhead luggage rack, he realizes that she has lost weight.

"What happened to you? You're thin."

"That's what happens when you can't eat for three days."

In the van back to the city, Omar and Rachida sit in the rear, with Caro and Adam in the middle seat. Adam opens the vent and drinks in the cold air. Tomorrow is New Year's Eve. He twists around so he can see Rachida.

"Do you want to give Eva the amulet tonight?"

"Fine."

Rachida is staring out the window. Omar has fallen back asleep with his head on her shoulder. Caro has her eyes closed. Difficult as the time away had been, Adam feels a dread of returning descending on him.

"Did you want to give it to her or do you want me to do it?"

"It doesn't matter to me."

They drop Caro at her apartment first. When they reach the house on Ninety-fifth Street, his mother comes outside to greet them. She hugs Rachida, then Omar and Adam.

"Where's Eva?" Omar asks.

"She's out. There's a lecture at her synagogue."

"Daddy brought her something. That hand thing you wear around your neck. Grandpa Uri made it for her."

Omar yawns.

"I made some tortellini and fruit salad," Myra says. "You can all have a quick bite and then get to sleep."

Jet-lagged, Adam wakes at four in the morning. He is alone in the bed. He goes downstairs, where Rachida is already dressed in her hospital scrubs, drinking coffee at the farm table.

"I'm going in early. Your mom has no patients in the afternoon because it's New Year's Eve. She wants to take Omar to Rockefeller Center to see the tree."

"What are we going to do for New Year's?" Seeing Rachida's strained expression, Adam regrets his question, which he fears Rachida has experienced as a slap in the face of her grief. What, after all, do they ever do on New Year's Eve?

"Your mother wants to make a holiday dinner for us and Caro. She bought a leg of lamb. She put Omar's Hanukkah presents under the Christmas tree."

"So what do you think? Should I give the hamsa to Eva today? Or wait for tonight when you are here?"

Adam can feel Rachida's annoyance—the effort it takes her not to snap at him to stop asking her the same question over and over.

"I don't care."

More than anything, Adam wants to put his arms around his wife, to say, Please, for the new year, let's start fresh, let's be kind and good to each other, but the gesture feels impossible, his arms inert, his tongue trapped in his mouth.

27

After Rachida leaves, Adam takes the newspaper and lies down on the couch. His eyes feel heavy. The paper drops onto his chest.

When he wakes, Eva is in the kitchen sorting laundry. Adam stretches, then swings his legs to the ground.

"Hi, Eva," he calls out.

Eva doesn't turn. She bends over to load clothes into the washer. Did she not hear him?

Adam stands. He'll shower first and then give Eva the amulet. Under the stream of hot water, he rehearses what he will say.

When he comes back downstairs, Eva is at the sink, washing the dishes he and Rachida left there last night. Adam holds out the envelope with the amulet inside.

Eva keeps her gaze on the running water.

"This is the hamsa Rachida's father made for you. I know it's not the same as the original, but he inscribed the same words."

Eva turns up the water.

"We went to Marrakesh. We stayed at La Mamounia. It

was Winston Churchill's favorite place." He feels ridiculous, this foolish attempt to fill the silence. Why would Eva care about Winston Churchill? Would she even know who he is? "Many of the rubber traders who came to Iquitos were from Marrakesh."

Eva leans down to get the cleanser from under the sink. She scours the white porcelain. She scours until the basin is covered in gritty circles.

Not knowing what else to do, Adam sets the envelope next to the drain board.

He climbs the stairs to the music room. He unpacks his papers and opens his notebook. The photo of the two men embracing falls onto the desk. He can hear Omar moving around down the hall. He locks the door and pulls the top file box out of the closet. He takes the brown envelope from the folder labeled *Research Iquitos*.

His stomach clenches. He has never kept the photos in a particular order, but he has always kept the most important ones, the ones he responds to most strongly, at the back of the envelope. Now the photo of a man licking another man is at the front.

Adam flips through the photos. Two of them are stuck together.

His mouth tastes like sawdust. He peels the photos apart, then adds the photograph from the notebook to the envelope. He puts the file box in the closet and goes back downstairs.

Omar and Eva are sitting with their arms touching at the farm table. They are both eating bowls of cereal and giggling over a copy of *Tintin* that Omar bought in the Casablanca airport.

"Look at Snowy," Omar says. "He's biting the bad guy on the butt."

Adam sits across from Eva. He can see a chain peeking out

from the neckline of her sweater, but if there is anything hanging from it, it is hidden beneath her clothes. He hopes she is
wearing the amulet Uri made.

Eva pushes back her chair. She stands and leaves the room.

28

Rachida comes home early. Eva is peeling potatoes. "Omar
went out with Dr. M.," Eva tells her.

"And Adam? Do you know where he is?"

Eva shrugs her shoulders.

On the second floor, the door to the music room is closed.
In her room, the suitcases are open, still unpacked—as though
there was any chance Adam would have unpacked.

She lies down on the bed and closes her eyes. Layla is angry
with her. She claims that Rachida hung up on her and did not
return her call.

"I left ten, twenty messages for you and you cannot be
bothered to call me back."

"I left my cell phone in Essaouira. I didn't get it back until
we returned from Marrakesh." They were in the cafeteria, at a
table in the center of the room.

"Liar. You let me do what I did in that closet and then you
hung up on me." Layla covered her face. "I never did that with
anyone."

"What are you talking about?"

"Don't play Missy Innocent with me. You got off on
what I said to you and now you're getting off on humiliating
me."

"I left my phone at the pool where Caro and Adam were
staying. Caro found it. By the time I got it back, the battery
was dead, and then I couldn't find my charger."

"Don't insult me. I'm not your deadbeat husband who you

can tell anything and he'll believe you." Layla's voice had risen in volume, and Rachida glanced around to see if anyone was watching them.

The table jerked as Layla stood. Rachida reached out to steady her coffee cup.

"Layla, I had other things on my mind. I was there to bury my father. I had Omar to take care of and my mother, and then Adam was useless and Caro got sick."

"Fuck off, you control-freak pervert. Go fuck your ugly little husband. Go tell him your stupid lies."

Now Rachida can hear Adam climbing the stairs. The bed reels as he sits down. He takes her hand and begins stroking it in a way she knows he intends to be comforting but only feels irritating.

"I gave Eva the amulet."

"And?"

"I don't know. She didn't open the envelope. She seems not to want to talk to me."

Adam pulls off her clogs and begins massaging her feet. She can see the fine black hair in Layla's armpits, soft like a baby bird's feathers, Layla's nipples, small and brown, like fine buttons sewn onto her flawless skin.

"Did she say anything to you about it?" Adam asks.

"What?"

"Eva. Did she say anything to you about the amulet?"

Rachida turns her head and looks at the wall. She is afraid that she might cry, and even though she knows it must be about her father, it feels as if it is about Layla. She knows there are good reasons why she married Adam. She just cannot re-call any of them now.

"Can we talk about this another time?" She turns onto her side and curls her knees into her body so her foot moves out of Adam's reach.

29

Another time to talk with Rachida about Eva, Adam thinks
the following week, seems never to arrive, the days passing
with Rachida either too tired or testy or gone. It is strange how
quickly he has become acclimated to Eva not speaking to him. In
an odd way, it is as if they are now more intimately involved—
a secret collaboration in which they both endeavor to not
draw attention to the silence between them. On Adam's part,
he takes care not to ask Eva anything in front of Omar. If he
needs to know something from Eva, he asks someone else to
ask her. On her part, whenever possible, she slips from the
room if Adam enters. Once, she actually caught his eye before
she left, and although she immediately averted her gaze, Adam
had been left with the sensation of their having, like certain
pairs of children, a shared wordless language.

Omar returns to school on Monday. On Wednesday, as
usual, Myra does pickup. She leans against the door frame,
already bundled into her long coat and scarf as she steps into
her winter boots.

"I'll come with you," Adam says. He grabs a jacket and his
sneakers.

Outside, it is cold but sunny, the air winter white, an hour
left before the dusk chill descends. They walk east on Ninety
fifth Street, Myra refraining from motherly reprimands about
Adam's jacket, more appropriate for April than January.
When Caro was six months old and they moved her from the
bassinet next to their bed into a crib in the adjacent room,
Myra had cried. "I feel like she's going to college," she told
Larry as she settled the sleeping baby. Three years later, leaving Caro at nursery school had felt like leaving her own leg
behind. By the time the same moment arrived with Adam,
she could already see the chain of breaches by which her
children would move from being part of her to their lives

becoming entirely their own. Now, as adults, their need for her respect, she has come to understand, means that even her advice, unless invited, has to be withheld.

She had been acutely aware of this on New Year's Eve, when she saw Caro for the first time after the trip to Morocco. It was a shock to see her slender. Only once before, after Caro's semester abroad, had she seen her daughter with visible hip and collarbones. Hugging Caro, Myra could feel the ribs in her daughter's back and the sinew of her arms, and the same wave of alarm she'd felt fifteen years ago.

"Darling, you look lovely, but are you okay?"

"I had a vicious case of tourista in Essaouira. I lost twelve pounds. Usually, people just gain it back, but something clicked in me afterward and I thought, Why not make hay out of this? I've been eating carefully since then."

Myra has known for a long time that there is something amiss with Caro and food. Caro is too pointedly abstemious. Too often, at their Sunday dinners, she will order a salad and tea, begging off that she had a late lunch, the classic pattern of a secret eater: skimping in public and stuffing in private, so that food becomes a hidden torment.

When Caro first moved back to New York, Myra had anguished about raising the subject with her. "I could encourage her to see someone, work on it," she told Dreis.

"Did she ask for your help?"

With Dreis's question, Myra felt the slap of shame—the precise feeling, she realized, she would cause in her daughter by uninvited inquiries. "No."

"You want to tell her that you, her mother, do not trust that she will find her way?"

"I feel like I am putting my head in the sand, abandoning her."

"I do not see anyone abandoning anyone. I see a young woman who needs her mother to treat her with the dignity she deserves as an adult."

Adam stops to zip his flimsy jacket. Shivering, he turns up the collar. "Something is going on with Eva. She refuses to talk with me. I can't figure out what I've done to offend her, but she seems very angry with me."

Myra unwraps her scarf and hands it to Adam, who takes it as though it were his own. She has been keeping at bay her concerns about Eva. For the first few days after the kids left for Morocco, it seemed that Eva was more stable. She was so happy Christmas morning, hugging the yellow parka before she put it back in the box, keeping on the scarf. By the afternoon, though, when Myra found Eva kneeling in front of the music room closet, dusting Adam's file boxes, she claimed, Eva's mood was entirely changed, her eyes locked in a squint that had left Myra worried that she was becoming unglued.

"At first, I thought it was because I'd lost her amulet. But she didn't seem so upset about that."

"What did you lose?"

"She showed me this amulet, it's called a hamsa, that had been passed down in her family for several generations. She wore it around her neck. I took it to show Rachida, so she could translate the Hebrew inscribed on it. And then, moron that I am, I lost it."

"You're not a moron. When was this?"

"A few months ago. Maybe November."

Myra feels a tilt of confusion, her thoughts misaligned: Didn't Eva say someone was trying to take something from her? But wasn't she playing with a chain around her neck when she told Myra about her father setting their house on fire?

This week, with Myra's patient schedule back to normal, Eva has resumed leaving Myra's lunch tray on her ottoman, but she has not come back to retrieve it, as though avoiding the temptation to sit in the patient chair. Although Myra has been relieved, she has been troubled by bizarre thoughts about Eva.

"I've been thinking that we should reorganize the schedule so Eva doesn't watch Omar."

"Why is that?"

"She's going through a lot. She's preoccupied. Let her stick with the housework. As it is, she only picks up Omar on Tuesdays. Maybe you should do Mondays and Tuesdays."

Adam refrains from saying, *And Thursdays. How many Thursdays do you think Rachida really makes?* He looks at his feet, not wanting his mother to see his face. The truth is, he frequently goes back to sleep after he drops off Omar. By the time he gets up and eats, it is often past noon. How will he get anything done if he has to turn around three days a week to fetch Omar?

They are nearing the school. A group of mothers dressed for their daily pickup with heeled boots and fur-trimmed parkas is gathered outside, the street clogged with the SUVs they drive, or in some cases are driven in by uniformed chauffeurs.

If he could get to bed at a reasonable hour instead of wasting time at night looking at filth, instead of being such a disgusting turd, he wouldn't have to sleep half the day and it wouldn't be a problem to pick up his kid. In his screenplay, Moishe, nineteen years old, gets up every day before dawn to begin his river journeys, twelve, thirteen hours on the dark murky water to reach the Indian settlements where balls of rubber and nothing to eat other than piranha fish and an occasional banana await him. And Adam can't take care of his child three afternoons a week?

30

On Friday, Caro walks from work to pick up Omar at his school. The day after New Year's, she'd gone to Lord & Taylor and bought herself two pairs of pants, a cashmere turtleneck, and two tailored shirts. At work this week, everyone made a big fuss about how terrific she looks. Emboldened by the com-

pliments, she went to a Tribeca hair salon where a stylist named
Rolando examined her features, holding a sheet of cardboard
first over her eyes and then under her chin. "Time, sweetie," he
instructed, "to lose the blow dryer and the Miss School Marm
pageboy." He cut Caro's hair in long layers, smeared a gooey
gel throughout, and then scrunched it up with his fingers so it
curled wildly around Caro's face in a way, he pronounced, that
made her look fetchingly reckless.

Without the nighttime eating, she sleeps deeply, then
bounds out of bed. Instead of waking to a disturbing memory
of the previous night's debacle, her gut distended and gassy,
she wakes hungry, looking forward to her morning cereal and
fruit, to her day. With the extra time gained with her carefree
hair, she has taken to walking to work, across Central Park
and then north along Third Avenue to her school. Instead of
averting her gaze and sucking in her gut, she walks with her
eyes on the trees, the bare limbs delicate as dancers, the small
patches of snow clutching the exposed roots, the birds who
winter in the park darting from branch to branch.

Caro stands outside Omar's school, watching the children
coming through the door, some of them racing toward their
mothers or babysitters with backpacks half-fastened and clothes
askew, others exiting slowly, their faces pale, their eyes narrow-
ing at the winter light.

Omar neither runs nor drags. His backpack is zippered, the
catches fastened.

Next month, he will turn seven. He touches her arm, and
she leans down to kiss his forehead.

"Pizza or ice cream, pal?" Caro asks.

"No thank you, Auntie Caro. I'm not hungry. It's Katie's
birthday, so we had cupcakes just before dismissal. Can we go
straight to the museum?"

At the museum, they go to the exhibit of miniature poison dart frogs. The button-sized creatures are so brilliantly

colored—royal blue, Kelly green, sunflower yellow—it is hard to believe they were not painted. Transfixed, Caro and Omar stand for a long time, hand in hand, watching the tiny frogs in their terrarium universe.

It is dark outside by the time they leave. Still hand in hand, they walk up Central Park West, passersby, Caro imagines, assuming they are mother and son. When they reach the house, it is already past six. Her mother is in the kitchen, a chef's apron over her clothes, the sleeves of her white shirt rolled up to her elbows as she checks the roasting chickens.

"Did Eva leave already?" Omar asks.

"Yes. But there's a surprise upstairs for you."

"What's that?"

"Your mommy came home early. She's in her room."

Omar goes upstairs to see Rachida. Myra sets the oven timer and hands Caro a glass of wine. They head into the parlor, Myra settling onto the couch and Caro onto one of the Corbusier chairs. "Did you two have a good time?"

"We went to see the poison dart frogs. They're so gorgeous. And then, of course, we had to see the dinosaurs on the fourth floor."

"Adam lived in that museum too. Do you remember? Until he moved, your father took him every weekend. It was one of the few things they enjoyed doing together."

"Where was I?"

"You were busy all the time with soccer games and hockey practice and sleepovers." Myra smiles. "I hope I'm not staring at you. I'm still getting used to this new you."

"Me too." Caro swivels on the chair in quarter circles. She can sense her mother waiting to see if she wants to say anything about her new, thin self, and then registering that she does not.

"Actually, there's something else I'd like to talk with you about." Myra pauses while Caro stills the chair. "It's Eva. She's been acting strangely. She's developed this aversion to Adam. She refuses to speak with him. I can't go into details, but she's shared with me some things that have made me think she has the potential to be quite unhinged."

"What do you mean?"

"I just don't think she's very stable. I talked with Adam, and we agreed that we're not going to have Eva pick up Omar anymore, that we're going to have her stick to the housekeeping."

Caro looks at her mother, at the worry in her eyes. She has seen her mother troubled before, mostly about Adam, on rare occasions following a late-night call from a patient, but she has never before questioned her mother's judgment—worried that she is in over her head. It leaves her uneasy, and then filled with guilt to be doubting her mother's reasoning.

"I think the emotional intensity of our family is too much for her. With only the housekeeping, she'll be a bit more buffered." Myra curls her legs under her. "I've tried three times to take her to see a therapist, but each time she has missed the appointment. She says she doesn't want to talk to a stranger."

The oven timer goes off and her mother stands. "Today, I made an appointment for her with Meyers. Sometimes a little medication can help a lot."

"And what if she doesn't go to that appointment?"

Omar and Rachida are coming down the stairs. Her mother puts a finger to her lips.

31

Caro waits until the first week of February before calling Rachida.

"I need to talk to you."

"What's the matter? Is something the matter with your mother? Your father?"

"They're fine. But I want to talk with you alone."

Saturday will be Omar's birthday party, which Myra has suggested they have at the house. Rachida has found a magician who will do gross seven-year-old-boy tricks in the garden: water and slime and crawling critters. Afterward, Adam will show Laurel and Hardy movie clips, and they will end with cake and ice cream. Caro has agreed to help out.

"How about after Omar's party?" Rachida suggests. "Omar will just want to play with his new toys."

The party goes without a hitch. No one gets hit or hurt, no one throws up or spills his juice or cries. Unlike some of the magicians Caro has seen at children's events over the years, creepy guys with short fuses who are annoyed when the kids act like kids, crowding close to look and calling out their ideas about the tricks behind the magic, this magician seems to actually like the children.

Watching the magician, Eva laughs along with the boys. Afterward, she helps Caro set the table for the cake and ice cream while Myra, Adam, and Rachida take the boys upstairs to watch the Laurel and Hardy clips. Eva studies the cake Myra has made for Omar, with a T. rex drawn in colored icing on top, jellybeans for eyes and shaved chocolate for scales.

"I have never seen such a wonderful cake," she tells Caro.

Caro thinks back to her own birthday parties, the usual events at bowling alleys and gymnastic studios with bakery sheet cakes. It wasn't until she returned to New York after college that her mother began baking Caro's birthday cakes, which she has done every year since, making up for the lost time, she's told Caro, when she lacked the confidence to do things herself.

"What were your birthdays like?" Caro asks.

Eva looks down at the dinosaur paper plates she is setting around the farm table. "Some of the girls at school have parties for their birthdays. But not my sister and me. My mother always make plantains on my birthday, because that is my favorite food, and she buy me new shoes, but I did not tell my father she buy them. I have to say they are from my grandmother."

The children troop down the stairs. Rachida and Adam herd them to the table while Myra lights the candles on the cake. Rachida lowers the lights and Adam starts the video camera. Rachida holds Omar's shoulders as his grandmother places the cake before him, his face aglow in the candlelight as everyone sings "Happy Birthday."

Standing next to her brother, Caro looks for Eva, but she is nowhere to be seen.

32

After the children have left and Caro and Eva, who reappeared when the cake was over, have helped Myra clean up, Caro gathers her things to leave.

"I'll walk you," Rachida says so matter-of-factly it alarms Caro to think how natural the habit of deception must be to her sister-in-law. "I could use some air."

Omar is seated at the farm table, building one of his new Legos with Eva. Caro leans over to kiss him. "See you Friday," she says.

They head south along Central Park West, past the doormen hailing taxis and ribbing one another, the bare trees in the park across the avenue ghostly in the falling dark. Caro waits in the quiet between her sister-in-law and herself—a silence that after so many years of knowing each other is usually comfortable but is now weighted with what must be said.

At Ninetieth Street, Caro tells herself, she will begin. When they reach Eighty-eighth Street, she renegotiates with herself: Eighty-sixth Street, at Eighty-sixth Street, she'll begin.

At Eighty-sixth Street she points to the benches along the
park wall. "Are you too cold to sit so we can talk?"

Rachida raises her eyebrows, surprised, Caro suspects, that
she would suggest the park side of the street after dark.

"It's only six o'clock. There are dozens of people out. Two
doormen standing here looking out."

They cross and sit. Sit for what feels like a long time, both
of them facing the street, their legs stretched in front of them,
while Caro's thoughts go in circles: Does she really need to tell
Rachida that she knows about Layla, is it truly necessary? But
what about Adam, how can she keep this from him? Couldn't
she wait and tell Rachida some other time?

"I know"—Rachida leans over her legs, gripping her knees—
"that you know about Layla. She told me. About the call. It took
me several days to convince her that it hadn't been me on the
line."

Caro hugs her arms, blinking in the dark.

"I'm sorry you heard that," Rachida says. "It must have
been shocking."

"Layla seems to specialize in shocking."

Rachida looks up.

"The stoning by her brothers. She told me about it the time
I walked her to the bus."

"What did she tell you?"

"How her brothers almost killed her when she said she
wanted to go to medical school."

Rachida hoists a foot onto the bench so she is sitting with
her knee level with her chin. It is the way a teenager might sit,
though there is nothing youthful in her expression.

"I'm in love with her."

Caro nods.

"She is very brilliant, the most brilliant woman I've ever
known. But very vulnerable."

"I can imagine. After what she's been through."

"That was a crock of shit. She has two older sisters, no brothers. One is a lawyer, the other's an architect. Her father is a professor of surgery. He planned for her to be a doctor since she was in diapers."

Caro feels a flush spread over her cheeks, as though she has been slapped. "So how did she get the scar on her arm?"

"She was in a motorbike accident a few years ago."

A bus pulls in front of them, exuding its belchy fumes. Two elderly women, one wearing a turban hat, the other wearing a hat with a pom-pom at the top, descend. They hold each other's arm as they cross the street.

Caro waits for the bus to leave. "Is she the first?"

"First what?"

"Woman you've been with? Infidelity with Adam?"

"Yes. Yes to both. And I'm the first woman for her too. At the beginning we were like two kids, unsure even of how to make love."

Caro fights the impulse to snap at Rachida that she's heard enough details already. "What are you going to do about Adam?"

"I don't know. He lives so much of the time in his own world, I don't really even feel that guilty about him. I feel guilty at the thought of our separating and putting Omar through all of that."

"Does Adam have someone else?"

"I wish. That would make things easier. But there's so much going on all the time in his head, I don't think he has the mental space."

Somehow the conversation has gone off track. Learning that Layla's story about the stoning was made up, a lie, feels, in some ways, more of a violation than hearing her pathetic panting over the phone.

"I don't want to judge you. How you lead your life is up to you. But you can't expect me to keep this kind of secret from my brother. Believe me, I wish I hadn't answered your phone. But if you don't tell Adam, I'll have to."

Rachida lowers her leg. A second bus is pulling up to the stop in front of their bench. "I know," she says, raising her voice over the bus's whooshing halt. "But I need a little time."

They cross the street, hugging quickly at the corner as they say goodbye.

Caro is unlocking her door before she realizes that Rachida, in fact, has told her nothing: does she intend to end it with Layla? To end it with Adam? And how much time is a little time?

For the first time since their return from Uri's funeral, Caro feels the urge to put something in her mouth, but now, her key still in hand, the awareness of how much worse food would make her feel overpowers the urge. Inside, she stretches out on her couch, the room still dark, wondering if her father had debated telling her mother about Cheryl or Shirley or whatever the woman's name had been. Or had both phone calls— from Cheryl or Shirley or whatever her name had been and from Layla—been fated from the start, the impossibility, as her mother would say, of an equilibrium ever lasting, the inevitability of entropy, tumult, and decay.

33

Myra plays the Bach Invention Number 8 in F Major. It is the most difficult of the two-part inventions she has learned thus far and her favorite because the challenge of following the patterns between left and right hands, the alternations between legato and staccato, the way the melody moves across hands, does not allow her thoughts to wander. With the Schumann *Kinderszenen* she played at the beginning of her practice, the left hand by now automatic, she found herself wondering why Eva had disappeared when the lights were lowered and she carried the cake with the lit candles over to place in front of Omar's sweet, excited face.

Before Christmas, Myra had assumed that what has happened with Eva is a kind of regression: having lost her mother so young, having been left unprotected with a brutal father, the girl is starved for mothering. Watching Myra with Omar and, to some extent, with Caro and Adam too set off this ravenous wish to be mothered herself.

Since Christmas, though, Myra has found herself feeling confused, feeling that behind her formulation, she understands nothing. She knows that she should go back to Dreis and try to sort it out, but she is in a state where she cannot even articulate what is bothering her. All she knows is that she has begun to worry that the girl's troubles run deeper than she thought. When she told Eva that Adam would be taking over the Tuesday pickup so he could spend more time with Omar, Eva had looked at her suspiciously, with the immediate, unguarded perception of another's intent that Myra has seen in her most disturbed patients, in vicious animals, and in the unhappiest of children.

Myra turns off the piano light and heads downstairs. Eva is at the farm table eating a piece of the leftover birthday cake.

"I put stain stick on the tablecloth where the children left marks."

"Thank you." Myra points at Eva's plate. "You missed the cake before."

Eva digs her fork into the butter cream icing and licks her lips. "It is so good. I cannot believe you make it!"

Myra pulls out a chair and sits across from Eva. She folds her hands on the table. "Eva, we need to talk."

"I do something wrong?" Eva glances at the kitchen drawer where she told Myra she couldn't find the matches Myra had sent her to get. When Myra went to look herself, the matches were, as always, at the front of the drawer.

"I want to take you to a doctor who will give you some medicine to help you feel less nervous all the time."

"I am not nervous."

"Less bothered by thoughts of the past."

"I do not want to talk with anyone else. I go to synagogue Friday nights, I go to my class on Tuesday and Thursday. I never bother anyone."

"I'm not saying you're bothering anyone. I want you to feel better."

"I bother you when I talk in your office. You cannot eat your lunch. It is very bad of me. But now I stop."

"I've made an appointment for you to see a doctor I often work with. The appointment is this Tuesday. He won't ask you to tell him a lot of details about your past. Just how you are feeling now."

Myra looks at Eva's empty plate. She wants to offer Eva another slice of cake. Maybe all the girl needs is another slice of cake, a glass of milk, and to be tucked into bed.

"I have to insist."

Eva touches the chain around her neck. She goes to the sink and washes her plate.

After Eva leaves, Myra putters around the kitchen, putting away the silver cake server and the box of birthday candles. She feels terrible. Eva did not make her say it, which she'd been prepared to do if needed—that if she does not go to see Meyers, she will have to leave. Instead, Eva looked at Myra as though she'd been asked to gouge out an eye.

Rachida unlocks the front door. Without saying a word, she goes upstairs.

On the corkboard is the schedule Myra made last June for Eva. Myra takes it down. Behind it is the editorial about the misguided Smokey Bear policy she clipped from the paper the summer Adam and Rachida and Omar took the rafting trip down the burning Salmon River: the snuffing out of the small,

natural fires without which the overgrown underbrush becomes perfect tinder for out-of-control burns. She had read the
article at the table on her deck, nibbling her sandwich, a map
of Idaho beside her. A lifetime ago, when she lived in this
house by herself, without Adam and Rachida and Omar and
Eva, not always tracking their enthusiasms and moods.

34

On Tuesday, Myra takes Eva to see Jim Meyers. She sits in the
consultation room with Eva while Meyers gently asks Eva
about troubling thoughts, sleep patterns, preoccupations, hearing voices that other people don't hear, seeing things that other
people can't see. Eva stares past the doctor's face, saying no to
each question. Afterward, he asks Eva to sit for a moment in
the waiting room while he talks with Myra.

"Obviously, she's very guarded. From what you've told me
and the way she acted, I think there's a lot going on that she's
not saying. I'd like to give her a low-dose antipsychotic and see
how she does. We'll give her one pill at night so she's not too
drowsy during the days. If she tolerates one pill, we can try
doubling the dose."

"I think we're going to have a compliance issue."

"So give it to her yourself. Just make sure you watch her
swallow."

Myra gives Eva the first pill with a glass of water.

"I don't need water. I can swallow pills without water." Eva
puts the pill in her mouth and makes a swallowing motion.
She smiles at Myra, keeping her mouth closed.

The following evening, Myra goes to get the pill vial from
the kitchen cupboard, but it is no longer there.

"I put the pills on the table next to my bed," Eva says when
Myra asks what happened to the vial. "It is easier for me to take

the pill after I get into bed." Eva smiles sweetly. "Don't worry, I won't forget."

35

Dressed in a blue kaftan and white flip-flops, Ursula is in the garden of the San Isidro house, inspecting the peonies the ugly, brooding gardener put in this year when her cell phone, on the table next to the coffee her husband left half-drunk before leaving for his Saturday-morning golf game, rings.

She stubs her toe as she rushes to get her phone, cursing under her breath and rubbing the China red nail while she listens to Myra's concerns about the girl whose name had slipped Ursula's mind until Myra says it now. Eva.

"Sweetheart, how terrible for you. And I am entirely to blame." The polish is chipped on a corner of the toenail. She doesn't have the color herself. Now she will have to drive all the way to Miraflores to get it repaired.

"Perhaps New York is too much for her," Myra says. "Certainly our family is. I can't think of anywhere she could go except back to you."

"Of course, if she is not a help to you, send her back." Ursula mouths *Goddamnit*. Well, Alicia will have to figure it out, will have to manage her maid, Marina, who will undoubtedly be unhappy to find Eva returned. Over the last few months, Alicia has given Ursula an earful about this Marina: emboldened by her plan to marry her boyfriend, Marina has turned from sassy to brazen. Twice, Alicia has caught her washing the foyer tiles with a bucket of filthy water, too lazy to fetch clean water. When Alicia chastised her, Marina let her know who was boss by telephoning in sick the next morning for herself and the two other girls with whom she shares a room in a boardinghouse. "All three of you?" Alicia asked, certain she could hear the others laughing in the background. "We are so sorry," Marina said. "We all ate spoiled *anticuchos* last night."

"Does she clean or is she one of those girls who just moves around the dirt?"

With her cousin's question, Myra realizes that Ursula has let herself absorb the outlines of what she's been telling her without actually listening. And doesn't Ursula recall that she herself recommended Eva as someone Alicia said was one of the most thorough cleaners she'd ever had? As she sometimes does with a distracted patient, Myra lowers the register of her voice and slows the pace. "The problem is not with her housekeeping. The problem is Eva herself. She's a disturbed young lady."

"You mean cuckoo?"

"Yes."

Her cousin, the psychologist, wants to send the cuckoo girl back to her? "You can't take her to get some help?"

"I have tried. Several times. She is not willing. I think the best course is to return her to a more familiar environment where she might do better."

Ursula looks at her watch. Her husband will be gone for another hour. Twice last month, she screwed the ugly gardener in the garden shed. Dirt under his fingernails, but an enormous prick. And he likes her tits. She is feeling fat this morning, which makes her less in the mood, but she might feel less like eating if she took him in there again.

"Sweetheart," Ursula says, "you can't keep her just until May? What is there for her here? None of the synagogues here will welcome her. Alicia is going to Tel Aviv in April. She can look for something for the girl there. It is only three months. What can happen in three months?"

36

On the first day of March, a snowstorm blankets the city. Rachida wakes to see snow piled like meringue on her windowsill. She has, of course, seen snow before, here in New York and lots in Detroit, but it still leaves her filled with wonder that everything can be covered with something so clean and white. Then she remembers Layla and everything feels gray and sooty again.

She goes down to the kitchen. Myra is on the phone, measuring coffee as she talks. After she hangs up, she turns to Rachida. "Schools everywhere are closed. Caro wants to take Omar sledding in the park. She thinks there are some old sleds in the basement."

The garden is entirely white. Snow is swirling in eddies. Nearly three weeks have passed since she and Caro had the talk about Layla. Although Caro had not set a deadline, Rachida can feel the clock ticking. Now, though, the deadline does not feel as much about telling Adam as about deciding what will come next, after the end of her fellowship in late June, when they return to Detroit in July.

The problem is not Layla. Being in love with Layla has never blinded her to the awareness that a life with Layla would be more maddening than a life with Adam. Without the built-in limit of the fellowship, she probably would not have allowed things to go as far as they have. And if Layla were honest with herself, Rachida feels certain, she would admit the same. Layla has no intention of spending her life with a woman—especially someone as plebeian as Rachida. She'll marry an Arab banker or a sheik. She'll live somewhere with servants and a driver and round-the-clock nannies to bathe the children and entertain them during the long, hot afternoons.

As has happened too frequently since her father's death, Rachida feels herself on the verge of tears. No, the problem is not Layla.

37

Caro arrives as the snowfall is ending. As a kid, she and her friends had sledded all the hills in Riverside Park and Central Park—their favorite, the steep one at 116th Street, the Hudson River on the horizon, bales of hay arranged to prevent sledders from crashing into the trees.

It has been years since she's been in the basement of her mother's house. Behind the stacked air conditioners and the bike she always intended to take, she and Omar find two wooden sleds, hers well-worn, Adam's hardly used.

"Would it be okay if I ask Eva to come along?" Caro whispers to her mother after she has carried the sleds onto the front stoop. "She's probably never been sledding."

Myra glances at Eva, leaning over the ironing board. Caro imagines her mother debating the pros and cons. Would inviting Eva to join them send a wrong message about Eva's position in the family? It would be cruel, though, to deprive the girl of the fun.

"Sure. Go right ahead."

Eva claps her hands when Caro asks her. "I saw that once in a movie. Children going down a hill on their sleds, with a dog running behind them." She unplugs the iron and follows Omar and Caro up the stairs to change into warm clothes.

On the third floor, Omar knocks on the closed door of the music room while Eva continues up to her room. "Daddy, Daddy, open up."

"Give me a minute," Adam calls out.

"Auntie Caro's going to take Eva and me sledding. Please, can't you come?"

Eva stops midway up the stairs. She twists around to look at the music room door.

"Okay, I'll be right out."

Caro helps Omar find his snow pants and a heavy sweater.

She adjusts the suspender straps, then heads downstairs to gather hats and gloves while Omar goes to tell Eva he is ready.

When Omar comes back down, Caro and Adam are in the front hall pulling on their boots. "Eva's not coming," Omar says. "She's feeling sick."

Adam catches Caro's eye. He clears his throat, then turns back to his boots.

Outside, there are children trooping toward the park, plastic saucers and red sleds and trash-can lids in tow. Caro looks up at the top-floor window of the room that is now Eva's. The curtain is cracked.

38

Slowly, Winston Churchill at La Mamounia has crept into the screenplay. A rich man after his Iquitos ventures, Moishe, now middle-aged, has become a regular at the hotel for lunch. On several occasions, he has seen Churchill walking in the gardens. Then, in the winter of 1937, they meet on the terrace. Moishe invites Churchill for a drink, over which he tells him about the years he spent in the Amazon, while Churchill talks about his fear for the Jews of Germany and Austria, who are already escaping to England. The main story is now, in essence, a flashback that occurs during this conversation.

Although Rachida does not roll her eyes when Adam tells her about Churchill, she might as well have. "I thought Frank Lloyd Wright was in the movie—that he and your Moishe guy were on the same boat."

"That was 1909. This is nearly thirty years later."

"So they're both in it?"

Adam can feel his teeth grinding. Whenever he talks about his screenplays, Rachida finds a hole in the narrative logic. Exasperated and embarrassed too, he has on occasion seized the bait, backing himself into ridiculous corners in which he is defending pompous and vague notions of fictive truth. The truth is, he had forgotten about the idea of having Frank Lloyd Wright in the story. Besides, it has never been Wright who interests him. It's the gruesome scene at Taliesin: the fire set by the deranged Barbadian servant who then ax-murdered Wright's lover, Mamah Cheney, and her children.

"I still have to work that out."

In the afternoon, when Adam leaves to get Omar, Eva is in the kitchen. She is emptying the dishwasher. He debates saying goodbye, but there is no point. Eva would not respond. "Lucky you," Rachida said when he raised again the subject of Eva's refusal to speak to him. "I wish half the people in the world who chatter at me would just shut up."

Outside, it is warmer than he expected. He leaves his coat unzipped. The streets are slushy with clumps of wet, black-flecked snow. Over the weekend, his mother told him that she had called Ursula to discuss having Eva return now to Peru and that Ursula had urged her to let Eva stay until May. His mother sighed. "In that case, I might as well let her stay until the beginning of July, our original plan, when you go back to Detroit. No matter how tactfully I put it, she would take it very badly to have to leave early."

He had been about to say Jesus Christ, I can't imagine another season of this, when he heard the front door opening, Eva coming in with grocery bags, and he felt that he should exit the room.

He stands outside the school, the only father in the group of waiting adults. What he really cannot imagine is July, returning to Detroit, living alone again with his wife and son.

39

After Omar finishes the peanut-butter-and-jelly sandwich and glass of milk Eva has left for him, Adam follows him upstairs to his room. They play chess. They build a model apatosaurus with a long snaky neck and tiny head and a protoceratops with elephantine legs and a stubby tail. They look through an old set of the World Book Encyclopedia. For a while, Adam's mind stays on their play, but then his thoughts drift to the pool at La Mamounia, to the view of the medina walls from their room. He imagines Moishe and Winston Churchill strolling through the lavish gardens at dusk, the red embers at the tip of Churchill's burning cigar. Moishe walking in leather slippers back to his home, past the Koutoubia, beyond the Djemaa el-Fna.

"What exactly is a fossil, Daddy?" Omar asks. They are thumbing through the F volume.

Adam doesn't really know. Is it the animal bone turned to stone or the imprint of the animal? Once, his father told him that in a mirror the images are reversed so we never see ourselves as we are seen. His mother told him that dreams do the same with desires. We dream we are giving a ruby ring to the brother we want to rob.

Omar abandons the F volume and turns onto his belly. He holds the apatosaurus in one hand and the protoceratops in the other, softly speaking to himself. Not long ago, Adam asked his mother about Omar's still talking to himself, the way he spins out loud the stories his toys stimulate in his head.

His mother looked surprised at the question, surprised, he realized, that he'd asked her opinion about Omar at all—something he has refrained from over the years out of fear of Rachida's anger.

"You were the same. You talked out loud to yourself for a very long time. But no, there's nothing to worry about. That's just his inner stream of thought."

"It sounds like the inside of my head when I'm working."

"Exactly. It's the child's creative work."

"Or maybe it goes the other way. Maybe my work is just child's play."

His mother smiled. "That was essentially Freud's position. He thought imaginative writing is the mark of an immature personality, an escape into florid fantasy—that there is only a thin line between the creative writer and the psychotic. I think he was just envious because he was probably a novelist at heart himself."

Omar pokes a finger into Adam's side. "Come on, Daddy Let's play."

Adam did not want to say so, but he understands entirely Freud's point. Who wouldn't prefer to live in his mind, moving around creatures who do what they are told and never snap back?

He lowers himself onto his stomach and tries to pay attention to Omar's story about the dinosaurs and the cave and the meteorite that is coming. For two weeks now, he has not looked at the photographs. Not since the morning of the big snowstorm when he'd been interrupted by Omar knocking on the door, by his plea that Adam join the sledding. It had gotten to him, his son's little voice on the other side of the locked door, the glaring white of the snow outside, and then, himself, with his pants unzipped and a dirty picture in front of him.

Lying in bed this morning, he had a reverie. He'd known it was not a dream because he was sufficiently awake to be aware that he was creating it in his head, but the images had the same hazy, effortless quality of a dream. He was the younger, slighter man—the one being lifted high. The older, heavier man was lying on a bed. He beckoned to him with one finger. "Come on over here," he said. His voice was gravelly. Adam lay down. He curled his body into the older man, resting his head on the broad chest. The older man hooked an arm around Adam's shoulders and then looked off, away from him. Adam began to kiss the man's chest, his neck. Slowly, with a look of amusement, the man turned to him and covered Adam's mouth with his own.

"I have some work calls to make. You play by yourself for a while. I'll come back as soon as I'm done."

Like a criminal, he creeps across the landing in his stocking feet, locking the music-room door, lowering the shades, dragging the file box out into the middle of the room.

He finds the file and takes out the envelope with the photos inside. He has never counted them. At least twenty. There are at least twenty. But why are they sticking together? It is as though the folder got wet. Adam examines the file box. He can see no evidence of water. He will have to get a flashlight, check the closet ceiling, the floor.

The photo he wants is near the rear of the clump. It is stuck to the photo in front of it. Carefully, he peels it apart. Splotches of white spread over the image, part of the photo imprinted on the back of the prior picture.

Adam stares at the photo. The men's faces and their shoulders are covered with white. Erased.

He feels like crying. He feels as though the older man has jerked away his mouth and stood up from the bed. He gathers up the photos and puts them back in the envelope. He puts the envelope back in the folder and the folder back in the file box.

He leaves the box in the middle of the room and returns to his son's room. During the time he has been gone, Omar has taken out a set of iron knights one of the children gave him for his birthday. Adam lies on the floor next to Omar, staring at the ceiling. Omar leans against his arm.

He tries to conjure again the kiss from the reverie, but all he can see are the white splotches on the ruined photograph. He sits up. He feels sick, disgusted with himself, to be thinking about the photographs with his son next to him. He pinches his cheeks hard enough to make himself wince, to wipe out the splotched photograph, but the moment he releases his fingers, a new thought arrives: he needs another magazine.

"The knights are coming to save the good vegan dinos from the meteorite." Omar hands him the model apatosaurus. "You be the dino."

Adam takes the apatosaurus.

"When the meteorite comes, the carnivorous dinos are going to get burned up."

There is the bodega five blocks away. The bodega doesn't have much, but the place in Times Square is too far.

He looks at his watch. Four twenty-five. His mother is still with her patients. Rachida will not be home until after nine. Eva is in the kitchen. He could be back in twenty minutes.

"I need to run to the store to get something. I'll be right back. If you need anything, Eva's here."

Omar will be fine.

He gets to his feet. Twenty minutes. There will be no need to mention to Rachida or his mother that he left Omar with Eva for twenty minutes. For twenty minutes, no need to go through the awkward exercise of telling Eva that he is leaving.

He places the apatosaurus next to his son, leans over to kiss his dark glossy hair, and shuts Omar's door.

40

Myra's office is chilly. She puts on the wool cardigan she keeps on her desk chair and buttons it over her cotton shirt. Then she goes to fetch her patient from the waiting room, a young woman with tight jeans and high-heeled boots who ruins every relationship with a cruelty that emerges as soon as any closeness evolves. The gorgeous viper, an ex-boyfriend called her.

Is she smelling smoke? She's definitely smelling something strange. "Excuse me," she says to her patient. "I smell smoke. Just wait here a moment." She returns to her office and opens the back door.

There is definitely smoke.

She hurries back to the waiting room. "I'm sorry, but I need to go upstairs. I'm going to have to ask you to leave. I'll call you tonight to reschedule."

She races up the back stairs. No one is in the kitchen. The smoke is pouring down the main stairs. She dials 911.

Then she hears Omar's cry. "Eva. Eva. I'm scared."

She drops the phone and bounds up the stairs. If Omar is here, then Adam is too.

"I'm coming, Omar," she yells. The fire seems to be in the music room. Is Adam inside? The laundry basket in the doorway bursts into flames. Where is Eva?

Omar is at the top of the stairs, gripping the rail. His face is streaming with tears, his cheeks black with soot. The door frame of the music room is on fire.

She reaches Omar, peels his fingers from the rail. She is hollering, "Adam, Adam, Adam . . ." The smoke is so thick, she can barely breathe. She pulls Omar down the stairs.

The railing catches fire. A piece of wood crashes toward them. Omar screams.

A clump of hair over his ear is on fire.

Myra smashes Omar's burning hair into her wool sweater. She rolls Omar's head against her body. He goes limp. She picks him up and stumbles with him the rest of the way down the stairs. She is still screaming, "Adam, Adam," but she is heaving, struggling for air, and her voice is hardly a whisper.

Neighbors are on the street. A man is on the stoop. He takes Omar. "His hair caught fire. Over his ear." She is barely audible. "Cold water. Run his head under cold water."

The man dashes with Omar across the street.

"My son . . ."

The sirens are drowning out her words. She can see fire trucks turning the corner, firemen running toward the house.

"Get her off those stairs," one of the firemen hollers. Someone drags her to the curb.

There is a terrible pain in her abdomen, where she pressed Omar's burning hair into her side. "My son," she gasps to the fireman now holding her arm. "The third floor . . . front room . . . our housekeeper . . ."

Ambulance workers are racing down the street and people are pointing them toward the building where Omar is inside. Dark spots are invading her eyes. Her knees buckle. Everything goes dark.

FOUR

1

Rachida, called by the neighbor because Adam was crying too uncontrollably to speak, waits outside the pediatric operating room. She paces, kicking the toes of her hospital clogs against the linoleum floor. She perches on the edge of a chair chewing a cuticle. She rests a cheek on the rough plaster wall.

When the surgeon emerges, he places a hand on her shoulder. "Your son is going to be okay. The good news is that because his face was pressed into his grandmother's abdomen, there doesn't seem to be serious inhalation injury. The burns, though, are serious. He has third-degree burns on 25 percent of his scalp and the top of his right ear. We shaved his head and debrided the dead skin on his scalp. Where the dermis was destroyed, we applied a porcine xenograft to prevent loss of fluids and infection until a skin graft can be done."

Caro, called by Rachida, waits outside the adult operating room. She sits with her eyes locked on the wall, a sensation of something black and heavy filling the cavity from her throat to her groin.

The attending doctor on the burn unit comes to talk with her. He pulls his chair so close, their feet are almost touching. Her mother has a second-degree burn the size of a handkerchief on her torso, the injury complicated by the cotton fibers from her shirt that adhered to her skin from rolling Omar's burning head across her middle. "More concerning is your mother's coughing and wheezing, evidence of smoke inhalation damage. We've intubated her so as to prevent her airway closing from edema."

Adam waits in the hospital lobby with his head in his hands and a plastic bag at his feet.

2

Rachida is not allowed to see Omar until after he has left the recovery room and been delivered to the pediatric burn unit. When an aide finally escorts her to Omar's room, she hurls herself toward the bed where her child, having surfaced from the anesthesia, is now sleeping, his head wrapped in white gauze, an oxygen mask over his mouth and nose, an IV in his left arm.

Rachida buries her face in Omar's belly and weeps.

Someone grabs her arm. "What the hell are you doing?"

Rachida looks up. A wiry man with gray hair drawn back into a stubby ponytail and a badge that says HOWARD TALIS, R.N. is scowling at her. As he pulls her away from Omar, she realizes that her hospital scrubs have confused him. "Dr. Amzalag. The mother," she whispers.

"You know better than to put your germy head so near to a burn site."

Talis draws a chair next to the bed. "You can sit here. He's going to be out for a while. Actually, I'm going to keep him sedated for the rest of the night since we're going to have to open that bandage in six hours to check for exudate, and that can hurt like hell."

Rachida sits in the chair. She wipes her eyes on the sleeve of her scrubs. Talis hands her a box of tissues and pours her a glass of ice water from a wet plastic pitcher. She drinks. The surgeon told her that had the burn extended another eighth of an inch, Omar would have lost the top of his ear.

"You're lucky. Scalps are good. They're thick. He's got a third-degree burn, but it didn't hit bone. The porcine graft lets us avoid the dressing changes. We can keep it there until he's strong enough for the autologous graft procedure."

"I'm a dermatologist. Or was. I'm a respecialization fellow in primary care now."

"Well, you probably know all this, then. He won't get hair from the skin graft, but when he gets older, you can do a tissue expander from the adjacent scalp hair. It usually works pretty well."

Rachida takes Omar's hand. She rubs her wet thumb over her child's dry skin. He breathes into the oxygen mask.

"Your mother saved him. She jammed that head right into her belly and put the fire out on her sweater."

"Mother-in-law." Rachida wants to climb into the bed with Omar and cradle him in her arms. She inhales the smells of her injured child, pushing out of mind what might have happened if it had, in fact, been her own mother.

3

At first, Talis worked the graveyard shift, eleven at night until seven in the morning, only when he had a foster baby living with him, but now he has come to prefer it. The doctors, save the skeletal crew of residents and the occasional on-call attendant, are gone. The visitors, save the parents dozing on chairs or cots next to their children, are gone. The night has a rhythm: the fussing of tired children accompanied by the anxious nursing calls of their parents as midnight approaches, calls that have more to do with their fears about their children's futures than any present needs, then the quiet as children and adults fall into exhausted sleep, the rounds every two hours, the inexorability of the sky lightening from black to steel to pale blue to, on days he has come to think contain hope, streaks of peach and boysenberry.

The first foster baby was three years ago after he'd gotten so angry he'd nearly come to blows with the hospital administrator. For three weeks, a little boy, burned with an iron by a crack-addict mother, had been on the unit, the nurses and the social worker praying that a foster parent could be found for him before he was discharged. When no foster parent had been willing to take on the continuing wound care, the child was sent to a group home to be watched by shifts of child-care workers. That day, with the child's sad face stuck in his head, Talis submitted an application to be a foster parent. Since then, he has taken home five children from the burn unit, all cases of neglect or abuse. Two stayed only a few days, until a longer placement could be found, but three, including a seventeen-month-old girl who'd been left to wander the apartment with a pot of boiling water on the stove while her father slept in front of the television, remained with him for more than a month.

During the times he has a foster child, Mrs. O'Connor, his landlady, stays overnight with the child while he is at work. He always tries to pay her and she always refuses. "Dearie, a human being doesn't get paid for doing God's work." When he arrives home after dawn, the child will be sleeping, rows of onesies and socks and feeted pajamas Mrs. O'Connor has washed by hand hanging on a wooden drying rack she has her husband bring up from her own apartment.

The healing children and Mrs. O'Connor and his nursing supervisor, who somehow always finds personal days and vacation time to give him when he has a foster child, have made him believe, in the face of the inhumanity he sees inscribed on the flesh of these children, that the world is still more good than evil.

4

At three o'clock, Talis checks Omar's pulse and blood pressure. The mother is snoring softly on a cot set up by the child's bed. The vitals are fine.

The shift supervisor told him that the father is in the lobby, too scared to come up. The grandmother is on the floor below. Her daughter is with her, the supervisor said.

On his break, Talis goes downstairs. He reads the grandmother's chart. Her breathing is labored. If it doesn't stabilize by morning, they will do a bronchoscopy. Talis peeks in the door. A handsome woman, younger looking than the fifty-nine years it says on her chart, is sleeping propped on pillows. She has a thin nose and a high forehead. Her lips are parched from the tube that goes into her lungs. Even in sleep, she appears to be in pain.

The daughter is curled up in the chair with her knees pulled into her chest. She is tinier than her mother, with a mop of curly brown hair. Her hand rests on her mouth. Talis covers her with a blanket from the closet. In her sleep, she pulls the blanket up over her shoulders.

Talis takes the elevator down to the lobby. It is empty except for a guy with a scraggly beard and dirty sneakers. A ratty jacket and a plastic bag with what looks like some magazines in it are on the floor next to him. A television, bolted to the wall, is playing with the sound turned off. The guy stares at the screen, his neck arching back from his hunched shoulders like a turtle poking its head out of its shell.

Talis sits next to him. From Omar's chart, he knows the father's name is Adam. Talis looks at the TV. It is an old movie, vaguely familiar. His mouth goes dry. "I know that movie," he says. "It's about smoke jumpers."

"*Red Skies of Montana*," the guy says without taking his eyes from the screen.

"It's about the fire at Mann Gulch where twelve smoke jumpers died."

"Richard Widmark, Jeffrey Hunter, Richard Boone."

Talis saw the movie with his mother when he was maybe nine or ten. He'd always known that his father, Kip Talis, had been a smoke jumper, but it wasn't until he saw the movie that he connected the image he'd had in his mind, his father sailing through blue skies with a red-and-yellow parachute overhead, with an inferno of smoke and flame and crashing trees.

Talis turns from the screen. He looks at Adam. The grandmother and kid were admitted a little before six. Has this guy been sitting here since then? Talis takes the remote from the magazine table and turns off the television. The guy blinks like a kid whose glasses have been stomped on by a bully.

"Let's get you something to eat." Talis picks up Adam's coat and the plastic bag. He leads Adam to the section of the cafeteria that stays open all night. Only a few of the tables are occupied: people drinking coffee or sodas to help them stay awake, eating sandwiches or chips. Adam follows Talis through the line, not reaching for anything.

"Hey, man," Talis asks, "what do you like to eat?"

Adam doesn't respond. Talis puts a yogurt container and a piece of pound cake and a turkey sandwich on the tray. He fills two cups with coffee and adds a bottle of juice. Adam trails after him, bumping into the rail.

Talis pays for the food and leads Adam to a table in the corner. He hangs Adam's jacket and the plastic bag over one of the seat chairs. He wants to tell the guy to go take a piss and wash his hands and face, but that seems like crossing a line. He opens the juice bottle and hands it to Adam with one of the sandwich halves.

Adam chews the sandwich without looking up. He gulps down the juice. Talis puts the other half in front of Adam. He unwraps the pound cake, breaks off a piece for himself, and passes the rest to Adam.

When Adam finishes the food, he looks up at Talis. "Who are you?"

"I'm your son's nurse. I'm on break. He and your wife are both sleeping."

Adam covers his face with his hands. From behind his hands come snorkeling sounds. Talis pulls a wad of napkins from the dispenser and pokes the backs of Adam's hands with them.

"He's going to be okay. It's a bad burn, but it's contained to his scalp. They put a porcine graft on it. Pig skin. In a couple of weeks, when he's stable, they'll replace it with a skin graft from his buttocks. It should heal fine."

Adam takes the napkins from Talis. Tears stream down his cheeks, falling unheeded on the table.

"Your mom's burn is less severe, but she inhaled a lot of smoke so they have to keep her on close watch."

Adam blows his nose. "It's my fault. I left him to go to the store. I thought it would be only twenty minutes but it took longer. It took thirty minutes."

Talis's jaw tightens. Every time he hears this story about kids having been left, it is always thirty minutes. The adult who was supposed to be watching the kid was gone only thirty minutes.

"You left him alone?"

"Eva, she's the housekeeper, she was there. And my mother was on the ground floor seeing her patients. I thought he would be okay."

"So you didn't leave him alone? The housekeeper and your mother were there?"

"I went to buy these." Adam lifts the plastic bag off the back of the chair. He hands it to Talis.

Talis looks at the bag and the tear-streaked man. Whatever is in the bag, he knows he doesn't want to see it. Adam is staring at him. It reminds Talis of the way he has seen certain patients with terrible disfigurements study his face, as though testing their own humanity. Would he be able to look at the horror they've become and still see them as human?

Talis pulls one of the magazines partway out of the bag. On the cover, an Oriental woman with her naked butt stuck up in the air is being led on a pearl leash by a black man in a leather thong. "Christ, man, are you crazy?" Talis stuffs the magazine back in the bag. Adam stares at the remains of the pound cake.

"You left your kid to go buy porn?"

Adam nods. Talis's hands have formed fists, his thoughts sirening: *Break the fucking pervert's nose, break the fucking pervert's nose.* As a kid, he'd been on a hair trigger. One word about his mother, Dot—the town widow, too comfortable, some thought, from the insurance money she got after her smoke jumper husband disappeared packing out from a fire west of Yellowstone, too popular with the married men—and his fists would rise.

Talis stands. He ties the plastic bag shut and picks up the tray filled now with their debris. He drops the plastic bag into the garbage can and dumps the trash on top.

5

At five, Myra wakes. Caro is sleeping in the chair beside her with a blanket pulled to her chin. Adam. Where is Adam? Then she remembers that he arrived while she was being lifted into the ambulance.

Her throat aches from the tube. Her chest feels tight. Her abdomen is burning. She pushes the buzzer.

A Filipino nurse comes. Myra pantomimes for pencil and paper. The nurse leaves, then returns with a small pad and a pen.

"My grandson," Myra writes. "How is he?"

"You want to see your grandson? No children are allowed on this floor."

Myra shakes her head. She takes the pen and adds. "He's here."

"Your grandson is here. He's a patient here?"

Myra nods. She writes *Omar Mendelsohn* on the paper.

A pleased look, as though she has figured out a charades clue, forms on the nurse's face. "I'll call."

Caro sits up as the nurse leaves. "How are you feeling?" she asks her mother.

Myra moves her hands in a wave motion. *Mezzo. Mezzo.* She points to the pen and paper the nurse put on the bedside stand.

Caro stands to get them. In her haste to get to the hospital, she'd grabbed without looking an old pair of jeans from before she'd lost weight. Now she has to hold them up. She hands her mother the pen and paper, then drags her chair next to the bed.

Her mother writes something, then sinks back on her pillows. She turns the pad so Caro can read it.

"Eva?"

6

When Rachida wakes, Omar is still sleeping. The oxygen mask has been removed. With the white gauze wrapped round his head, he looks like a small Sikh.

She does not want to think about what she knows is under that gauze: the skin burned to a pasty white or a leathery gray, the pig skin placed on top. The skin graft that will follow. Then the series of operations, perhaps years from now, to replace the hairless grafted skin with a skin flap created by an inflatable balloon from the adjacent scalp that will hopefully allow for hair growth.

It could have been worse. It could have been much worse. As a dermatology resident, she saw children whose hands had been charred to stumps, whose lips no longer existed. She saw legs so badly burned, amputations were required. Watching her drugged, sleeping son, she thanks the God in whom she has never believed. She vows that if Omar is okay, she will give up Layla and her button nipples. She will eat her tongue before saying a sharp word to Adam again. She will take care of her mother, let her come live with them if she wants, or visit for however long she wants. Take her shopping at every outlet she can find. Then she closes her eyes and silently cries because she cannot believe in a God who will bargain with her.

7

Caro tightens her pants with the safety pin one of the nurses has given her and goes to see Omar, asleep, with Rachida holding his hand, and then on to find Adam, seated in the lobby staring at the morning talk shows. After promising her brother—*Cross my heart, hope to die*, she says in their oath from childhood—that no one is too scary, Caro leads him first to their mother, groggy from having been sedated again, and then to Omar, still sleeping, where she leaves Adam while Rachida goes to see Myra and she goes to look for Eva.

She takes a cab to her mother's house. Strips of yellow plastic printed with DO NOT ENTER are strung across the walkway to her mother's office and the steps that lead to the parlor level door.

Caro studies the house. The windows on the second and third floors are boarded up. The glass has been swept from the sidewalk, but the steps are littered with shards. The stench of wet burned wood and smoke permeates the air.

A man comes out of the brownstone across the street. He asks about Omar and her mother, tells her that he carried Omar into his apartment and held his head under cold running water until the ambulance arrived. No one had realized that her mother was also injured.

"She was so brave, your mother. A fireman had to restrain

her from going back in to look for your brother. That's when she passed out. She came to for a few minutes while they were lifting her into the ambulance, and we dragged your brother over to her so she'd see that he was okay."

"Did anyone see the housekeeper, Eva? A young woman from Peru?"

The man shakes his head. "The firefighters went in to check for other people, but no one else was inside. We were all here on the street for over an hour. I never saw her."

"Could I borrow a piece of paper and a stapler? I'd like to leave her a note." When the neighbor returns, she writes: *Eva, I hope you are okay. Please call me on my cell.* She adds her cell phone number, then staples the folded paper with Eva's name on the outside to the yellow police tape.

She walks to the synagogue where her mother has told her Eva attends services. The sanctuary is empty except for a man sweeping between the pews. No one has been here today, he says, other than the rabbi and the Misters Finkelstein and Mandelbaum, who come together every morning.

At home, she brushes her teeth and washes her face. Her mother gave her the name of her insurance broker and the number for her colleague Jim Meyers, who she wants to call her patients. Caro sits down at her desk with a pad of paper. She writes the two names at the top of the page and underlines them both. Then she calls her father.

8

As far as Talis can tell, the family is pretty shaky. When he returns from sign-off rounds to check on Omar a last time before he goes home, Carol, the day nurse, tells him that the mother, the Arab woman doctor, went to visit the grandmother. The aunt asked for a safety pin to hold up her pants and then left the father, weeping in a corner of the room, alone with the sleeping boy. Omar woke up a few minutes ago, but so far the father hasn't been able to say a word to him.

"Get your skinny ass to bed," Carol tells Talis. "You should've been out of here an hour ago."

"I'm just going to bring in some games for the kid."

"Do you like checkers?" he asks Omar.

"Do you have chess?"

Talis rummages through the shelves of the children's day room for a chess set. The box is missing two black pawns. He takes two black checkers and carries the set into Omar's room, where he pushes back the IV rack and sets up the board on a stand that rolls over the bed.

Omar picks up one of the checkers.

"Just pretend these are pawns."

Even on painkillers, the kid plays a wicked game of chess. The father watches from the corner. After Omar has beat Talis, Talis motions to Adam to come sit by the bed. "Play with your son," he says.

9

Except for those times when he has a foster baby with him, Talis has the post-graveyard-shift routine down to a science. Immediately upon getting home, he pulls the blackout shades and makes a cup of elderberry tea sweetened with milk and honey. He drinks it while he takes a hot bath, then puts on a sleeping mask to cover his eyes. He is usually asleep within a few minutes.

This morning, though, he feels restless. He puts on the teakettle, trying to stick to his routine, but already he can tell that he isn't going to fall asleep anytime soon.

It's that damned movie, *Red Skies of Montana*. It has set him to thinking about his father, Kip.

In his twenties, Talis had tried to locate his father. He went to Tennessee, where Kip had grown up, to find out if anyone had heard from him. But his father's father, the town preacher, Howard Talis, after whom Talis had been named, had died the year before and his grandmother was lost to Alzheimer's, leaving Talis with only the stories his mother had told him. How his grandfather had inculcated in his father the belief that war, all wars, even the war against Hitler, was evil. How Kip, drafted in '43, registered as a conscientious objector and was assigned to the Civilian Public Service. With so few able-bodied men to fight fires, some of the CPS guys, Kip heard, were being used in McCall, Idaho, at the newly formed smoke jumpers' base. He immediately volunteered.

"Your father was just nineteen," Talis's mother, Dot, told him. "I think he needed to prove that he wasn't a conscientious objector because he was a coward. And it suited him. He was a loner. He loved trees. He loved the animals that live in the forests. The elk, the bears, the raccoons, the deer. And the birds. The ravens, the hoot owls, the sparrows."

Talis's father had made his 238th jump into a fire near Yellowstone two days before Talis's first birthday. After an hour on the ground, Kip Talis told his crew leader he wasn't feeling well and was going to pack out. He was never seen again.

Talis's mother refused to believe that Kip was dead. "Your father knew the forest too well to die in a fire. He just wasn't suited to being a family man. Too many people around all the time." Until Talis was ten, she waited every day for the mail, hoping Kip would send a clue. She imagined a postcard from Alaska, the smoke jumpers' base at Fort Wainwright, the idea so vivid that in the fourth year Kip was gone, she called the Wainwright base and asked for someone with a cowlick in front and a scar on his right cheek.

On the tenth anniversary of his father's disappearance, Talis's mother gave away his father's clothes. She cut the thick

red hair she'd worn in a long braid down her back since she
was a girl. The new hairdo brought out her green eyes and
gave her a come-hither look. She threw out her oxford shirts
and sensible shoes and started dressing in tight skirts. The kids
in town took to calling her Red Hot Dot.

At twelve, Talis dropped his first name, the embarrassing
Howard that made him think of his Tennessee preacher
grandfather. Anyone looked at him cross-eyed, he bloodied
their nose. He did bungee jumping from cliffs over the Snake
River. He married his high school sweetheart, only to learn on
their honeymoon, from which he came back alone, that she'd
been fucking his best friend for the past year. He did a dozen
parachute jumps landing on a farmer's six-hundred-acre corn
field. He moved to San Francisco, where he worked construction and discovered that if there was any genius in him, it was
in his hands. He learned to fit pipes, tape walls, pull wires, lay
tiles. He learned to do Venetian plaster and dirty washes and
gold filigreeing on egg-and-dart moldings.

On his thirtieth birthday, Talis woke up with a girl whose
name he couldn't remember on a mattress on the floor of the
otherwise empty studio apartment he called home by default.
For the first time in his life, he felt old—with too little time left
to be wasting it beautifying the already sufficiently beautiful
homes of people with too many beautiful things. He enrolled
in nursing school.

During his second year of nursing school, Talis did a rota-
tion in a pediatric burn unit. Classmates who had tolerated
gunshot wounds and stillbirths threw up in the bathroom
sinks when they saw children with feet burned off, gray dead
flesh. Children who screamed when their dressings were
changed. Talis, though, felt immediately that he understood
burns. The dermis needs to be prepared for its new layers in
the same way as old walls do for paint. No rushing, no cutting
corners.

Although Talis would never say it out loud, he believes his work is his father's legacy. His father cared about the trees and the animals, large and small, on whom fire inflicts its damage. He cares for the children whose delicate skin depraved adults, on purpose or by neglect, have let fire destroy.

10

Larry hangs up the phone after talking with his daughter and instructs his secretary to cancel his afternoon patients and to book him on the next flight to New York. He calls Betty and asks her to pack him a suitcase, enough for a week, and to meet him at the airport. From the car, he pages his partner and signs off his hospital patients and then calls the Stanhope Hotel in New York, where he always stays, to reserve a room.

As a cardiologist, he has learned that you don't ask stricken people what you can do to help. A drowning man might say, Go ahead and finish your lunch. Or, I'll be fine. Or, Don't bother. You take off your shoes and jump in.

Arriving in New York, he takes a cab directly to the hospital. Between the billions of lights and the shadows from the buildings and overpasses as the cab exits the FDR Drive and turns into the hospital entrance, he feels as though he is piercing the hide of a dangerous animal.

He goes first to see his grandson. Omar is sitting up in bed. Rachida and Adam are in chairs flanking his bedside. They are all staring at the television set mounted on the wall. Omar does not appear to be in pain, but his lips are cracked and his eyes glassy.

Larry brushes his grandson's cheek with his lips. Omar's skin feels too dry.

"He looks dehydrated to me," he says to Rachida. "Are they giving him IV hydration?"

A look of panic crosses Rachida's face.

"Did you check the chart?" Larry asks. Rachida's eyes fill with tears.

Larry walks out to the nurses' station. He presents his Tucson hospital ID and asks to read his grandson's chart. The IV hydration was halted three hours earlier. He asks to speak to the resident on call and then, using all the tact he can muster, outlines the clinical signs of dehydration.

When he comes back, Omar is sleeping with his mother holding his hand. The sound on the television has been turned off, but Adam is still staring at the screen. Caro has told him that, for tonight, Rachida is going to stay in the room with Omar and that Adam will stay with her.

"Did you have some dinner?" Larry asks Rachida. It occurs to him that he hasn't kissed his son or, for that matter, his daughter-in-law either. Now it seems too late, too awkward to maneuver himself close enough to reach their cheeks.

"Caro went to get sandwiches. She should be back soon."

"I'm going to visit Myra."

"Okay."

"Your mother," Larry says to Adam, who nods without looking at him.

Larry waits for the elevator. He hasn't seen his ex-wife since his father's funeral nearly six years ago. He holds his breath as he enters her room.

Myra appears very thin and frail under the bedsheets. She is intubated. She waves her fingers in a way that makes it clear that Caro told her he was coming.

He kisses her forehead. She feels slightly hot. He looks at the IV rack by her bed to check what she is being given, resisting the impulse to lift her gown to see how extensive her burns are. He sits in the chair next to the bed, overcome with sadness, followed by remorse as he recalls the years of her miscarriages when she lay in bed, racked more with emotional than with physical pain, when his response to her pain was to stay away.

Myra pats his hand. At Adam and Rachida's wedding, they had stood side by side under the huppah in Myra's garden, exchanging no words other than the expected politenesses. At his father's funeral, she gave him a ceremonial peck on the cheek.

"So, I have to wait for you to be injured to have some time alone with you?"

Myra points to the pad next to the bed. He gives it to her. "Take care of Omar," she writes. Her hand shakes.

"I will. I checked his chart first thing. He needed his hydration reinstated."

"Thank you," Myra writes.

"He's my grandchild too." Larry pauses. He wants to hold Myra's hand but fears that she does not want that. "How are you feeling?"

"Worried where Eva is," she writes, turning the pad so he can see it. She fixes her eyes on Larry, then picks up the pen again. "Keep having thought . . ." She puts down the pad.

Larry reads the words twice before they sink in. Then he leans over and whispers in his ex-wife's ear, "You think she set the fire."

Myra looks at him solemnly—the look he remembers from the first time he made love to her.

"Police?" she writes.

Larry tears off the paper and places it in his inside jacket pocket. "Caro and I will handle it. You need to rest now."

Myra lifts his fingers to her cheek. She closes her eyes.

11

Larry goes with Caro and Adam to Caro's apartment. Caro turns on the shower and marches her brother into the bathroom. She hands him a fresh towel through the door.

With Adam in the shower, Larry sits next to his daughter, his sensible daughter, as Myra used to call her, always left to pick up the pieces, and talks to her softly.

"Your mother seems to suspect that Eva might have set the fire."

Caro nods. All afternoon she has struggled with the same thought.

"Why?"

Caro sighs. "I don't know. I know she thought Eva was kind of unstable. She'd stopped letting her watch Omar."

"There's a big leap between kind of unstable and setting a house on fire." Her father pauses. "Your mother was wondering if we should notify the police."

"This is terrible to ask. Would that invalidate the insurance claim?"

"No. I called my broker in Tucson and ran it by him as a hypothetical. The claim would only be threatened if the fire was purposefully set by the policy owner. But it could hold it up."

Caro can hear the water turning off in the bathroom, her brother stumbling around. "Look," her father says. "Everyone is understandably very upset. It's not as though there's any concrete evidence here. I think we should wait a few days and see if Eva shows up. Maybe she just got overwhelmed and went to stay with a friend. If she doesn't show up by the end of the week, we'll go down to the precinct and file a report."

Caro rests her head on her father's shoulder. "I never heard Eva mention any friends."

"Where do you think she is?"

"I checked Mom's house, the synagogue where she goes. I don't know where else to try. She's never been anywhere, as far as I know, other than the time she came with us to your house in Willow."

Her father looks at her. As a child, she'd felt as if she could hear his thoughts—the glances they exchanged, silent consul-

tations about Adam and how to circumnavigate his emotional
landmines.

He puts his arm around her. "We'll go in the morning."

12

Caro has not used her mother's car since the trip to Willow,
seven months ago. She opens the glove compartment to check
that the registration papers are still there. Beneath them is the
snapshot of Eva that Ursula sent, the picture in which Eva
looks like a deer caught in headlights.

She waits on the corner of Ninety-sixth and Broadway for
her father to arrive.

Her father lumbers out of the cab, maneuvering a bag with
takeout coffees and bagels with too much cream cheese.

"Do you want me to drive?" he asks through the open car
window.

"Okay."

Not until they are out of the city, on the New York State
Thruway heading north, does her father mention that he went
to the hospital early this morning so he could talk with the attending doing the morning rounds. "I was worried about your
mother running a fever last night. With the smoke inhalation,
she's at risk for pneumonia."

There are patches of snow between the highway and the
stands of trees. She doesn't tell her father that she'd also gone
back to the hospital. It was one in the morning when she crept
into Omar's room. Both Rachida and Omar were asleep. She
sat in a chair watching the two of them until a male nurse doing
rounds discovered her. She was sure he would throw her out,
but he acted as though it was entirely natural to be visiting in
the middle of the night.

"The aunt?" he whispered. He had pale gray eyes and pale

arched brows that suggested the towhead he'd been before his long hair, pulled back in a ponytail, turned the color of steel.

"Yes," Caro whispered back. "How's he doing?"

"He's got a lot of painkillers in him. But he's going to be fine, medically speaking. He's so young, he won't suffer self-consciousness from the scarring and alopecia for a while. When he's closer to full-sized, they'll be able to cover it with skin cultured from his scalp."

Talis, that was the name on the man's badge, checked the gauges on Omar's IV and, without waking him, took his blood pressure and pulse. He left the room, then came back with a glass of apple juice that he handed to Caro. She drank it, aware only then of how thirsty she was.

"How's your brother?" he asked.

"Asleep in my second bedroom. He didn't even stir when I tried to tell him I was coming here."

"You're a little late for visiting hours."

"I'm just going to check on my mother, and then I'll leave."

"Don't think that's going to fly there. The nursing staff on that floor are more of the cross your *t*'s, dot your *i*'s school than we are here."

With the thought of her mother all alone, Caro had to hold herself back from crying.

"Tell you what. I'll go check on her and bring you a report."

"That would be so great." Caro tried to smile, but her mouth barely moved. "Could you give her a note from me?"

"Sure." Talis stood loosely in the doorway, a man who was comfortable in his body, while she wrote a note to her mother: *Dear Mom—Dad and I are going to drive up to Willow in the morning. I'll come see you when we get back.* LOVE, *Caro.*

When Talis returned a quarter of an hour later, he beckoned for her to join him in the corridor. Caro had appreciated that he gave her the update on her mother without sugarcoating. Her mother was in pain. The resident had been called to increase her analgesics. Her mother nodded after she read Caro's note.

Caro rests her head now against the passenger door. She thinks about Talis, the way he leaned against the doorjamb. The way he watched her as she wrote the note to her mother.

13

It is nearly noon by the time they pull into the driveway at Willow. Larry had not expected to see the house again. A couple from the city with two young children have signed a contract to buy it. The closing, which his brother, Henry, will attend, is scheduled for next month. They amicably divided most of their parents' personal belongings two years ago, after their mother's death, when they sold her Riverdale house, so that this second household of things seems superfluous. Henry has taken the files their father kept on the construction of the house: the correspondence with Frank Lloyd Wright and the Taliesin studio, the bound architectural drawings. Larry took his father's gardening gloves and a collection of his grandfather's jeweler's tools: a magnifying glass that fits over an eye, miniature pliers and screwdrivers and mallets, pincers for closing links of gold chain. The realtor sold the kitchen table and chairs, the Ping-Pong table and the bunk beds to the buyers, and arranged for everything else to be picked up by the Kingston Salvation Army.

Opening the car door, he inhales the cold air—mulchy smelling after a winter of decomposing leaves. The heavy brocade drapes, so out of character with the house, which his mother insisted on hanging to cover the drafty casement windows, are drawn. He walks behind the house to the flagstone patio where they have always kept the spare key under a chipped clay pot. It is possible, Larry tells himself, that the realtor drew the drapes.

The clay pot is turned over, the key gone. Larry feels his pulse quickening. Calm down, he orders himself. Perhaps Henry directed the realtor to remove the key.

Larry can hear Caro coming around the house to meet him. He points to the overturned clay pot, then tries the kitchen door.

It is open. Larry holds the door for his daughter. Inside, the house is cold and dark, with a sharp, bitter smell, as though a small animal has died behind one of the cabinets.

Caro sidles next to him. In August, she recalls, Adam never carried a key. Eva would have seen him using the one under the pot. Gripping her father's forearm, she walks with him through the living room and then back to the master bedroom wing. The room where her grandparents had slept is empty except for a few pieces of stray packing tape left on the floor. Her father opens the closets, the shower stall door.

They cross the living room to the second bedroom wing. The guest room is empty. The door to what her grandmother called the children's room is closed.

Caro looks at her father. She steps back, leaving it for him to do the deed. Slowly, he opens the door.

Eva is asleep on the bare mattress of the bottom bunk. She is wearing a wool cap pulled low on her forehead and the yellow jacket Caro's mother gave her. The black-and-yellow scarf is balled up in her hand. She clutches it against her neck and chin. She is sucking her thumb.

The thumb in mouth, so familiar from her preschoolers, sets Caro's mind in motion, the balls and cylinders falling into place with the clarity she depends upon when faced with a crisis with a child at her school. She leads her father into the kitchen.

"We should let her wake on her own. Can you go get some food? She probably hasn't eaten anything since she's been here."

Caro tries to remember what Eva likes to eat. Candy. That was what she'd wanted when Caro asked her that first day at the airport if she would like a snack. And no meat. "There's that New Age sandwich place in the center of town. Get her one of their vegetarian sandwiches: cheese and avocado, something like that. And candy."

After her father leaves, Caro drinks some water from the tap. Is Eva being here evidence that she set the fire? Isn't it equally plausible that Eva was out at the time of the fire? That she returned to see the house roped off and everyone gone? Scared, she came here, the only other place she knew?

Either way, Eva's job is over. There is no house now to keep.

14

Caro sits on the floor watching Eva sleep. Eva has rolled onto her side, facing Caro, her thumb no longer in her mouth. The scarf has slipped out of her hands onto the floor. There is something hanging around her neck, an antique-looking charm shaped like a hand. Is this what Adam lost or what Uri made to replace it?

Eva cracks her eyes, then closes them again.

"Eva. Wake up."

Eva curls into herself. She clutches the charm. Then she opens her eyes. She sits up, covering her face as though expecting blows.

"It is not true," she whimpers.

"What is not true?"

"She was not in the house. She was at the neighbors' house playing a tile game. It is a lie. The wicked lady, the one who said my mother went back to our house, she is a witch."

Caro gets to her feet. Looking down, she can see the albumen color of Eva's scalp.

"Only my father was in the house. Looking at his dirty pictures. Drinking his nasty stuff."

Caro takes Eva's hand. "Come," she says, pulling Eva to her feet. "You're still half-asleep." She leads Eva to the bathroom, where someone has left a roll of paper towels on the counter. "Use the toilet. Wash your face."

15

Caro waits in the kitchen for Eva to come out from the bathroom. She can hear the water running. It sounds like the tub. Perhaps Eva is giving herself a sponge bath with the paper towels.

What was Eva talking about? Her mother and someone she thought was a wicked lady.

Caro wishes she could talk with her own mother about what to do. Should she ask Eva if she set the fire? Should she tell Eva what happened to her mother and Omar? Do they need to turn Eva over to the police? Or should they take her to a hospital?

She hears the car coming up the driveway.

She goes back to the bathroom. The water is still running. "Eva," she calls through the door, "we have some food for you when you're ready."

The water continues to run. Caro's heart starts to pound. She knocks on the door. "Eva. Answer me, please."

She hears the car engine turning off, the car door opening and closing, and then the crunching sound her father's shoes make on the gravel path.

Caro knocks again on the bathroom door. There are no sounds other than the running water. She turns the handle. The bathroom is empty, the water running into the empty tub.

The door to the children's room is closed. Caro can hear her father unpacking the bags in the kitchen. She knocks on this door. "Eva?"

She knocks again, then opens the door. The casement window is open wide, the screen propped against the wall.

On the floor is Eva's scarf, on the bed the key to the house.

16

Caro knows her father does not believe they will find her. She knows Eva is like one of those nocturnal animals who sense where the shadows fall and how to find caves and hidden burrows, an instinct for where a bat will swoop or an owl pounce. But Caro needs to try. Needs to give Eva a chance to explain herself. For two hours, her father circles the roads near the house with an increasingly larger radius while Caro peers out the car window.

Before they return to the city, Caro writes Eva a note with her phone numbers. *Call me as soon as you get this*, she writes. She underlines her phone number. *Look in the mailbox at the end of the driveway. I left your scarf and a sandwich and candy for you inside where the animals can't get at them.* She tapes the note to the front door.

Her father lifts the screen back into the casement window and closes the window. She puts the key back under the clay pot.

"I'll call Henry," he says, "and ask him to remove the key and the things from the mailbox when he's here next week for the closing."

Her father registers her unhappiness that he does not think Eva will come back. Caro refuses to tell him that she thinks the same, that she has already decided that if she doesn't hear from Eva by the morning, she will call the Willow police and go to her mother's precinct to file a report.

At the end of the driveway, her father stops the car so she can put the scarf and the food inside the mailbox. She pushes the door to the mailbox tightly shut and climbs back into the car.

Her father takes her hands and holds them between his own. "She's a survivor," he says. "She did what she could to make herself safe."

17

On the week anniversary of the fire, the day Myra is discharged from the hospital, she realizes that they have already begun to acclimate: the crisis, ceased as a crisis, having shifted to their new circumstances with its own order and logic.

Rachida, who has been staying in the residents' dormitory, will remain there until the end of June, when her fellowship will be over, after which she and Adam and Omar will return to Detroit. Adam will stay at Caro's. When Omar is discharged, he will move into Caro's as well. Larry, who has rescued and had cleaned what of their clothes could be salvaged, will go back to Tucson at the end of the week.

On her end, she has made decisions with a certitude that has rendered them simple despite their magnitude. Most significantly, she has decided not to return to living in the house. The insurance adjuster, a surprisingly gentle and patient man, visited her on her second day in the hospital. Her policy will cover six months of temporary housing. He has given her the names of two contractors who specialize in fire renovations. Her office suite is luckily undamaged. Once she is ready to resume seeing patients, she will be able to do so there. After the house is presentable again, she will sell it and buy an apartment where she can also keep an office.

Caro has found her a furnished apartment to which she goes straight from the hospital: the home of a soap-opera star who has been written out of her part so that she is subletting her Trump Tower thirty-sixth-floor one-bedroom to go live uptown herself. "A seesaw," Myra says to Caro. "One person's misfortune, another's opportunity."

The apartment is extravagantly comfortable, with towel warmers and a heated floor in the bathroom and a remote control that operates the sunshades, but impersonal and bland, so that Myra feels as though she has been airlifted into an advertisement in a glossy design magazine. On her first day out of the hospital, she lies on the couch looking down at the city so far below it is sanitized of garbage and rat droppings and sound, save for a whooshing that, were she not able to see the horse-drawn carriages lined along Central Park South and the cars, tiny as toys, rounding Columbus Circle, she would have mistaken for wind.

In the evening, Adam comes to visit. His fingernails are untrimmed and he needs a haircut.

Myra waits for him to settle into the white leather slipper chair before telling him that she will be selling the house.

"Are you sure?" Adam blurts, as though she might have jotted down a piece of information incorrectly.

"I am, darling. The fire was just the kick in the pants. I love the house. It's where I raised you and Caro. But the two of you have been gone for a long time now. It's time for me to live a different way." She doesn't say what she has thought countless times since the fire: that if she hadn't delayed for so long selling the house, an avoidance, really, of acknowledging that the era of raising her children is long past, she would not have taken in Adam and Rachida and Omar. Would have left Adam to figure out how to manage here in the city without her. Would not have hired Eva.

18

The day after Caro settles her mother into the temporary apartment, she returns to work. It is a relief to find everything the same: Simon, still wearing her old Harvard sweatshirt, still lingering by the bakery stoop, the Christmas lights strewn over the door even though it is late March, the yeasty smell of the soft Spanish rolls ready for the slabs of orange cheese.

"Hey, gorgeous," Simon says, "long time no see. You been in Tahiti with your boyfriend?"

"I wish. My mother had a fire in her house."

"Bummer. Real bummer."

"It is. How've you been?"

"You can keep a secret, right?"

Caro raises an eyebrow.

"This kid in the neighborhood spliced some wires and got me cable in my squat." Simon grins. "I got HBO now!"

Caro smiles. It is the first time she has smiled since the fire. For a moment, everything feels okay. "Come on," she says. "Let's get us something to eat."

19

It is late afternoon, Myra's first excursion out of the soap-opera star's apartment since she left the hospital four days ago—a doctor's appointment and a visit with Omar. Her porcine dressings have been removed and the burn doctors have declared what they describe as good epithelialization on the wound site, but she still feels a deep fatigue, a heaviness in her limbs, a constant awareness of her sapped energy.

She and Larry are seated on opposite sides of Omar's hospital bed, watching him sleep. Adam has gone back to Caro's. Rachida will be arriving soon. Mumbling so that at first she's not even sure what he's saying, Larry asks if she will have dinner with him tonight, his last night in New York.

"Okay."

"Really?" Larry grins like a fifteen-year-old. "The concierge at the Stanhope is usually able to get early reservations at Daniel."

"It would be wasted on me. Especially now. And I don't feel like dressing up with bandages still covering half my stomach. Let's just go someplace simple."

Myra suggests a small French restaurant on upper Broadway, a place where she's been with Caro. Seven o'clock, so she can rest first but still not be out too late. When she arrives, Larry is already seated at a table in the window alcove in the front. He stands to kiss her cheek. His skin is smooth, just shaven. In his cashmere sports coat and Cartier watch, he looks overdressed and too prosperous for the place.

She recommends a few dishes that she's had before—the fluke, the ocean trout, the vegetable terrine—and leaves Larry to select the wine. They chat for a few moments about how well Omar is doing. Then Larry leans forward in his chair. "Henry called me this afternoon from Willow. The walk-through before the closing was today. He went to check the house first, and it seems that Eva did come back. The note Caro wrote was gone and the mailbox was empty."

Myra nods. When Caro told her that Eva had left the scarf Myra had given her at Christmas, Myra had thought she would come back.

"I haven't told Caro yet. Do you think I should?"

"Why not?"

"She felt terrible about making the police report. I think she imagined Eva in one of those nightmare scenes from the movies when dogs and men with nightsticks surround some poor, vulnerable person. Then, afterward, she said she had the impression that the report would go in a filing cabinet and nothing would be done. She didn't like that either."

"She was filling in for me. Eva was my responsibility."

"So you wouldn't tell her?"

"I would tell her. She has a right to know. And we don't need the burden of another secret."

Larry looks at her quizzically.

"Eva had a lot of secrets."

The waiter arrives with the bottle of wine. Myra stares out the window while Larry goes through the silly tasting ritual. She waits until they are alone again to continue. "I think there are only two people whom I've failed with a capital *F*. Eva was one of them."

"She was crazy long before she came to New York. If anyone is to blame, it's your cousin. She should have warned you."

"Ursula really didn't know her. She just wanted Eva out of Alicia's and her hair. Eva's troubles go way back. But we, I, made her come entirely unglued."

It surprises Myra that she does not feel with Larry a sanction against talking about Eva. Perhaps it is because he is a physician, so it seems in some way almost collegial, within the confines allowed by professional ethics. Or has what Eva's done—or, to be fair, what Myra suspects Eva did—released Myra from any covenants?

"I only understand a part of it. She wanted me to be the protective mother she lost too early or probably never had. I think seeing so many of us—Rachida, Caro, me—taking care of Omar made that longing overwhelming for her. But there was something more, something that had to do with Adam. After the kids got back from Uri's funeral, she stopped talking to him. She set the fire in the music room, the room Adam was using as his office."

The waiter arrives with their first courses: the terrine for Larry, a green salad for herself. She feels so tired, she hopes she will be able to make a respectable attempt at eating.

"But why a fire?"

"Her mother was killed in a fire. Her father set the house where they lived on fire and her mother was burned to death."

"How do you know that?"

"She told me."

"And she never told the police?"

"I suppose not."

Larry puts down his fork. He has finished the terrine before Myra has even begun her salad.

Without thinking, Myra switches their plates, then flushes as she recognizes the gesture from the years they were married, when Larry's hunger always outstripped hers. "I'm still getting my appetite back," she murmurs.

It is true about her appetite, but she switched the plates, she sees now, as distraction—because she feels unnerved by the skeptical way Larry is looking at her. It reminds her of Dreis, of the doubt she, too, seemed to have about Eva's story.

"Adam must have gone to town with that," Larry says between forkfuls of Myra's salad. "You know his obsession with Frank Lloyd Wright and the fire the servant set to his home."

"To the servant's own home?"

"No. To Taliesin, Wright's home. Adam never told you that story?"

"I suppose he did. I must have forgotten."

The waiter clears their plates, brings their entrées. Larry ceremoniously tops off her wineglass and refills his own empty one.

"So," Larry says, raising his glass, "let's not waste all our time on Eva. Or Adam's obsessions. We're finally having our dinner. Only twenty-five years later than I wanted."

Myra clicks her ex-husband's glass. "We've been separated for twenty-six years."

"It took me six months to know what I wanted to say to you."

"Well, please don't say it now." She touches Larry's arm to soften her words.

"My intentions were pure in inviting you to dinner. Not that I wouldn't drop everything if you said you'd take me back."

"That's ridiculous. You just like that fiction. You'd be irritated by me within a week. Besides, you seem to be genuinely happy with Betty. Happier, in fact, than I've seen you before."

Larry props an elbow on the table, rests his chin in the cup of his hand. He is aging well, Myra thinks, as lean as he was at forty, his hair gray now but thick as ever. "I am happy with Betty. The kids think she's crude, and she is a little rough around the edges. But she has a big heart."

"They know that. Adam told me how nice she was with Omar when they visited you in Willow."

"But what about you? Don't you miss having a man?"

Myra takes a long drink of water, which makes her feel better. In the habit of therapists who've spent too many sessions hearing patients' observations of them in movie theaters or at the grocery store, she surveys the room to be certain none of her patients is watching her. "At times," she says. "When there's a blizzard and everyone's housebound and I imagine I'm the only one not playing Parcheesi and drinking hot cocoa. Sometimes in August, when I don't want to travel by myself. But, at heart, no. I feel like I've moved beyond romantic love."

"You wrote me that after I came to the place you were staying in Tucson. When I made an ass of myself by trying to get you to go to bed with me."

"You didn't make an ass of yourself. You were very sweet and sincere."

"You didn't seem to think so at the time. You said some pretty strong words to a guy who could barely walk. I ended up on crutches for two weeks after that night, with a nasty sprain."

Myra takes a forkful of her trout. "Poor Larry. I was using every ounce of self-control not to let things happen between us. It would never have worked. We would have just ended up confusing the children and hurting each other again. People always think they can go back. I can't tell you how many of my patients spend hours on the Internet looking for their high school crushes."

"I've read that a lot of those relationships turn into something. People marrying their long-lost sweetheart."

"No one writes about what happens three years later."

The restaurant is filled now, a low din in the room, the candles lit on all the tables. "I like this place," Larry says.

"A place to eat rather than a destination to be discussed like most of the restaurants where I seem to go when I'm here. It's genuine—like you." He pauses, embarrassed, it seems, that she will think he's saccharine, then plunges ahead. "I still remember what my father said about you—that you had soul. I was so hurt when he said that, because I thought what he meant was that I did not."

Myra pushes her plate slightly to the side. She folds her hands on the table. "One person can't be another's soul. And you're wrong, Larry. You have soul. You have your own soul, different than mine, but every bit as good."

Myra leans over and kisses her ex-husband, father of her children, grandfather of her grandchild, lightly on the lips.

20

During the second week Myra is in the soap-opera star's apartment, the city has a two-day cold spell. Ice crystals form on the windows. Looking out from the thirty-sixth floor, it's as though she has traveled to another latitude. Preoccupied with ice, she reads about Ultima Thule, the mythic last stop of civilizations, about the king penguins who march hundreds of miles each year back and forth from their glacial breeding grounds. She imagines ships gliding through water bound by glaciers, the fractured ice-splintered light. She recalls her beloved childhood stories. The Snow Queen who abducted children to her crystal palace. Guinevere wrapped in furs as she was carried off to Arthur's castle.

The renovation of her house begins, the fire department having caused as much damage as the fire: windows smashed to release the pressure from the hot air, floors flooded with the water from the hoses so that blowers and dehumidifiers have to be installed to dry out the soaked woodwork and plaster.

She cannot tolerate warm sheets, hot beverages, woolen sweaters. She turns off the heat, drinks her coffee iced, flings off her covers. She cannot stop thinking about the little girl she saw the first day she visited Omar whose leg was kept submerged in a bath of cold water. Otherwise, she would scream in pain.

Prone on the soap-opera star's sofa, she pieces together a story line, each action illustrated as in a picture book. *A child setting fire to a house laced with gasoline-soaked rags. The drunken father racing out. The child crouching behind the chicken coop. The mother she'd thought was next door playing a tile game, trapped inside.*

An e-mail arrives from larrymendelsohn@desertdocs.com. She cracks the window. A cold wind blows across the table where she has set up her computer.

It's eighty degrees here today. The bougainvillea on the trellis by the pool are in bloom. Betty's boys are both swimming.

When you kissed me in the restaurant, I had the most vivid memory of the first time I ever kissed you—a girl I'd met seated behind a table of books who read highbrow novels and spent her meager salary on nosebleed seats at Carnegie Hall. It's so strange to say this, but I saw for the first time that you were my love but that you will not be my only love. For the first time since I threw our lives together away with that stupid Sheri, I felt truly released.

You didn't say who the second person was you failed. Not that I agree with your assessment of the first.

Myra hits Reply.

You. I failed you.

21

On the day that a piece of skin $1/100$th of an inch thick is removed from Omar's left buttocks and sewn onto his scalp, Adam tells Caro that he and Rachida are separating.

"She told me about Layla," Adam says. "She said you knew and had told her she had to tell me."

It is six o'clock. They are eating in the hospital cafeteria. If all goes well, Omar will be discharged at the end of the week.

"She says she's in love with Layla. That she would never have made it through this without her."

Caro tastes a piece of the baked fish, dried out from too many hours under the warming lights. If she were alone, she would spit it into a napkin.

"Layla's going to move to Detroit with Rachida in July. They're both going to look for jobs as primary care doctors there."

It is hard to imagine Layla in Detroit. "I'm sorry."

Adam takes off his glasses and rubs his eyes. "Yeah. I am sad. But I'm kind of relieved too. The main thing is Omar. I told Rachida I want him to live with me."

"You think she'll go for that?"

"I don't think she's going to fight me on it. At least not for the first six months while she's getting settled into a new job. Only, I want to stay here with him. She doesn't know that part. I'm going to put the screenwriting on the back burner and try to get a teaching job. I'm almost looking forward to it: being part of the mainstream, so that days like Memorial Day and Presidents' Day mean something to me. I'm going to see if there are any openings at Omar's school, since I could get half tuition for Omar that way."

There are so many holes in Adam's plan, Caro doesn't know where to start. And even if Rachida were to agree to let Adam keep Omar in New York, how would he afford an apartment large enough for the two of them?

By bedtime, against her will, a solution comes to her. Once she has the idea, she wishes she could send it back to the recess of her mind from which it has escaped. But it is so logical, so right, as she tells her mother the following Sunday, it grows legs on its own.

They are sitting in the soap-opera star's living room, a room at odds with the green tea and bran muffins they are sharing.

"Right?" her mother asks. "Do you mean morally right or the best-fit solution?"

"Both. Doesn't it seem that the two usually coincide?"

Myra tucks her legs under her. In the past week, the pain from the burn has finally abated and, with this, the compulsion for cold. She doesn't want to know what it is that Caro has dreamed up. Already she can feel that it entails a sacrifice. Another sacrifice for Adam.

"Adam and I will buy your house."

Myra laughs. She cannot help herself. Then she feels tears come to her eyes. "Darling, you don't have to do that."

"I know. But behind the feeling that I should do this, for everyone, there's a feeling that I want to. Having Adam with me this past month has cured me of the need to keep everything perfect. And the house is so large. I'll take the top floor, and Adam and Omar can have the third floor. We can rent out your office. I've talked to Dad. He says he owes Adam a down payment, since he helped me with my apartment. Between what I'd make if I sold my apartment and what Dad would give Adam, we'd be fine."

Myra can see it already, Caro in what had once been Myra's room, Adam using the music room for his bedroom and office, Omar in the room where he'd stayed before the fire.

She would leave the furniture—what survived—as her gift. On the fourth floor, the bed frames and dressers were saved, but the mattresses had to go. On the third floor, everything had been destroyed by flames or smoke or water. The piano had suffered all three. It was the only item over which she cried. Afterward, she gave herself a stern lecture. Her family was spared. Omar is recovering nicely. Objects, not even pianos, do not deserve tears.

On the parlor floor, all the upholstered items—the stuffing infused with smoke—were added to the garbage heap. That left the farm table, the Indo-Pakistani and Tibetan rugs, the Empire sideboard she and Larry bought when they were first married. The secretary Larry's father gave them when he closed his office. The stools the children sat on doing their homework at the soapstone counters. These items she will leave behind.

22

Rachida departs for Detroit before dawn on the first day of July. Omar says goodbye to her the night before. As her parting present, she gives him a cell phone. "You can call me now, whenever you want. I programmed my number in." She shows him how to use the pre-set dialing. She will be back in two weeks for a visit. In August, when his camp is over, Adam will take him on the train to Detroit.

Omar does not cry. He wanted to, he tells Adam as they walk to camp the next morning, but he felt that he should not. They are staying in New York, Adam has told Omar, because he has taken a job as a teacher. He hopes, he has explained, to eventually get a job at Omar's school, but there are no openings. For now, he will be teaching seventh-grade English at an all-boys school.

With his baseball cap on, Omar looks like any other kid. Before he left the hospital, the social worker had met with Rachida and Adam to counsel them on how to help Omar with the questions he would inevitably be asked about the bald part of his head or the headgear he might wear to cover it. "We need to help Omar understand that most of the time children who stare at him or ask questions are not doing it to be mean. They're doing it because they're curious, just as he would be if he didn't know so much about burns and scars." On Omar's first day back at school, he took off the baseball cap to show the kids in his class where the graft had been stitched. "I can't show you where it came from," he told them, "because I don't think the teachers would like me showing you my butt!"

Adam takes Omar's hand as they cross the street. "Auntie Caro will be picking you up for the next few weeks. Her school's out for the summer, and I'm trying to finish my screenplay before my new job starts."

"Can Eva pick me up sometimes?"

Adam feels a moment of panic. Has no one explained to Omar that Eva will not be coming back? Before the fire, he would have mumbled something and left it for Rachida to talk with Omar. Now he forces himself to look at his son. "You wish Eva were still here?"

Omar nods. "But I know she's not."

They reach the sidewalk and Adam releases Omar's hand. "Do you know where she is?" Omar asks.

"No, I don't."

Inside the camp classroom, Adam rubs the special sunblock they keep stored in a cubby into Omar's scalp. He reminds Omar to keep his baseball cap on when he goes outside and to rinse off his head in the shower after he goes swimming. He kisses him on the cheek and watches his son turn to join the table of children making potato block prints.

23

Caro spends the afternoon in her apartment in cutoff jeans, packing books. When the time comes to get Omar at camp, she looks outside at the hot haze, thinks screw it, and walks out the door as she is. Over the past few months, she has put back a few of the pounds she lost in Morocco, but the seesaw of secretive nighttime eating followed by daytime starvation has blessedly not returned. No weaving and unraveling. Rather, she feels as though she has settled into the body she was meant to have: no tire of shame hiding her shape, but still flesh covering her bones.

She walks north on Columbus Avenue, past Dominican grandmothers in long dark dresses and vendors selling coconut and lemon ices. Inside the school, she waves to the camp's security guard and makes her way upstairs to Omar's group's room. She gathers up Omar's wet bathing trunks and towel and stuffs them inside his camp bag. "It occurred to me," she says as they leave, "that you don't have a bike. Did you have one in Detroit?"

"A baby one with training wheels. I never learned how to ride without them."

"Well, seems like now's as good a time as any. There's a bike store on Ninety-sixth Street."

It is surprisingly simple. Budget or better construction, red or blue for bike and helmet.

"Better construction," Caro says.

"Blue," Omar says.

Caro wheels the new bike down the hill and into Riverside Park. Omar is wearing the new blue helmet. She taught Adam how to ride a bike after their father had been too impatient. She finds a wide, deserted path and runs alongside Omar, holding the handlebars. "Pedal faster," she yells.

Omar pauses and the bike slows.

"The faster you pedal, the steadier you'll be."

Caro watches her nephew absorbing the paradox with the pleasure of a seven-year-old wrapping his mind around an idea. He licks his lips, lowers his chin, and pedals fast. She runs beside him, and then, at the instant when she feels the balance shift from her hands into his body and the bike itself, she lets go and he sails forward.

24

They celebrate with cheeseburgers and fries and icy sodas at the outdoor café in the park where Caro ate years before with her mother when their conversation had veered in a direction her mother always claims inspired her teleology of love. Since Caro was last here, the enormous sandlot has been outfitted with circus rings. A few accomplished swingers are now making graceful arcs from ring to ring, the movement all in their hips, while the rest of the adults laugh self-consciously at their own clumsy attempts and children climb on top of an overturned trash can to reach the rings.

"Look," Omar says, holding up his half-eaten burger. "That's Nurse Talis."

Caro looks up to see Talis dip his hands into a plastic bag filled with ground chalk. His arm muscles bulge as he loops, pelvis first, from ring to ring.

"Nurse Talis, Nurse Talis," Omar cries. Omar stands to wave.

Talis squints in their direction. He waves back. He does a final course over the rings, agile as a monkey, then climbs the steps toward Omar and Caro, wiping his hands on the back of his jeans.

Caro pulls out a chair and extends her hand. She wonders if Talis will remember her from Omar's second night in the hospital, when she came at one in the morning. "I'm Caro, Omar's aunt. We met once."

"I don't think you want to touch these hands." He looks at her in a way that seems to take in the moistness across her collarbone, the grease smudge on her shinbone. "You gave me a note to take to your mother."

"Have a seat." She is embarrassed at the sound of her voice. Too high and thin.

Talis sits. He leans back in the chair, stretching his legs out to the side. "So how are you, bud?" he asks Omar.

"I just learned how to ride a bike."

"No kidding. That's a big deal. I'm going to have a beer to celebrate that."

"Can you teach me how to do the rings?"

"Sure. If it's okay with your auntie."

Caro nods.

Omar jumps to his feet. He forgot to put on his baseball cap after taking off the helmet. "I'll go practice until you're ready."

Caro looks at his half-eaten food. "Are you done?"

"I'm full," he calls as he heads for the steps.

"Do you think he needs to cover his head?" she asks Talis.

Talis glances up at the sky. "He'll be okay. The sun's low now." He waves over the waitress and orders his beer. "How's he doing?"

"Very well, I think. I was worrying about him today because his mother went back to Detroit this morning. His parents are separating."

"Sorry to hear that. It happens a lot after a fire."

It is hard to tell how old Talis is, but she guesses ten years older than she is. She dampens a paper napkin and rubs the grease smudge off her shin. Then she sneaks a look at his left hand.

25

Larry has insisted on managing the sale of the house, the price of which he has had determined by an appraiser. "What you have will eventually go to the kids," he e-mailed Myra. "But it's not good for you to be cash poor now." She knew immediately that he was right, that she should maintain her assets so she will not be dependent on Adam and Caro when the time comes for her to stop her practice. And although he doesn't say it, she is certain that he also means that it is not good for Adam to be subsidized.

In May, she found a two-bedroom apartment on Central Park West with a layout that with slight modification will allow her to have an office at home. It has high ceilings and egg-and-dart moldings and a newly renovated kitchen entirely unlike the earthy one of her brownstone but pleasing to her, with stainless-steel counters and ash cabinets opened by chrome pulls. There are picture windows in the living room from which she can see the great green rectangle of Central Park with the blue oval of the reservoir. There is an alcove that will fit a grand piano. In the room that will be her bedroom, French doors lead to a small Juliet balcony with cream balusters where she imagines having her morning coffee.

It is a perfect apartment for a woman living alone, and that, she realizes, is precisely what she desires now. She buys a hundred-year-old Series O Steinway with the original ivory keys, the only antique she intends to have in the new apartment. She hires the super to do the alterations needed to convert the second bedroom into an office from which the rest of her apartment will not be visible. She hires a good painter to turn the already skim-coated living-room walls a silvery gray and those of the office a café au lait, leaving the rest to be done in a color, white dove, whose very name brings her pleasure.

She takes her summer break earlier than usual, moving into the new apartment at the end of July. The city feels empty save for her children, Adam about to take Omar to Detroit for a visit with Rachida, Caro involved in supervising the renovations on the house. Without the constraints of her patient schedule, she takes her walks in the morning, circling the reservoir, some days on the jogging path, other days, as she does this morning in early August, on the more ample bridle path. From the eastern side of the reservoir, she can pick out her new building in the skyline that towers over the trees. It is a magical, almost mythic view: the water, the trees, the sculptural buildings, stately as dowagers.

It is just ten o'clock, but the sun is already hot, the waistband of her shorts chafing against the new skin that has formed where she was burned. Now, five months after the fire, she can see what happened with Eva more evenhandedly: as with her marriage, the ending involved a mutual rupture, a mutual betrayal. Although she would never have chosen either, both shook her loose, catapulted her forward.

Moving her things out of the house, she found the Smokey Bear editorial, the edges curled and rimmed with soot, still stuck with a pushpin to her bulletin board. Across the top, in her own hand, *The Tragedy of Good Intentions.* She removed the pushpin, crumpled the newsprint into a ball.

She stops to rest on the stone battements between the reservoir and the tennis courts. What Eva did was what fire does in the forest. She cleared the tangled underbrush: protection against greater catastrophe, preparation for a new season's growth.

26

Adam takes Omar to visit Rachida—a fourteen-hour overnight train trip to Toledo and then an hour bus ride on to Detroit. They will stay three weeks, Layla decamping to a friend's apartment while they are there. Adam will watch Omar during the first week while Rachida still has to work, then stay alone in what was once his home so he can pack up his remaining things while Rachida and Omar spend two weeks at a resort on Lake Michigan.

Rachida meets them at the bus station. Her face is pasty

and bloated, with a painful-looking blemish on her chin. She kisses Omar without smiling.

The house is even dingier than Adam recalls. He sits in the dank living room drinking orange juice and flipping among the four channels available without cable while Rachida settles Omar for a nap in his old room. When she comes back downstairs, he turns off the television.

"Was Layla mad about having to stay somewhere else?"

Rachida sits next to him on the couch. She puts her feet up on the coffee table. "She moved out."

"For three weeks?"

"For good."

Turning to look at Rachida's face—the bloat and blemish, Adam now understands, marks of misery—he feels sad for her. It is not her fault that she doesn't love him. It is hard to imagine how anyone could.

"She decided she doesn't want to be with a woman. She's dating a guy now, a neurosurgeon."

Adam pats Rachida's leg, cautiously, the way he might touch an unknown dog. "Do you want a sip of my orange juice?" he asks.

"Okay."

He hands the glass to Rachida. She drinks most of it and gives the glass back to him. "He has blond hair," she says. "He wears those shirts with alligators on them."

"I hate those."

"He plays golf. Layla claims now that she loves golf. She's full of shit. She went on a golf trip once with her father."

"He sounds like a jerk. The neurosurgeon, I mean."

"Hassan II irrigated deserts to build golf courses while there were people in the south of Morocco without enough water to have schools."

Adam puts an arm around Rachida. She rests her head on his shoulder. She feels like an old friend. This is what they should have always been: friends comforting each other over their heartbreaks.

27

Wanting to move into the house free of clutter and junk, Caro plans to use the days with Adam and Omar gone on a blitz-krieg purge of her apartment: weeding through her files, bag-ging up old clothing to bring to the Salvation Army store, throwing out chipped dishes and frayed towels. Instead, she feels a strange combination of anxiety and lethargy. She spends the first day alone in her apartment in bed until noon, and then reading the newspaper and a novel until dusk. On the second day, she goes through her books, managing to identify only a dozen to give away. She gives up by three o'clock, puts a magazine and a bottle of water into a tote bag, and walks over to the park.

Since seeing Talis at the circus rings, she has not been able to get him out of her mind: this man who can swing from ring to ring and take care of children with burns. The thoughts are more unpleasant than pleasant, unpleasant because they have made her aware of how many years have gone by, not only since she let herself be touched by a man, but since she has even wanted to be touched.

She walks by the sandlot. She sits at the café. She orders a diet soda. She orders a salad. She orders a beer. He does not come.

At night, she cannot get comfortable. Her back hurts, the air conditioner is too loud. The sheets feel rough, then clammy. She gets out of bed and makes tea. She watches the five o'clock morning news, the sky lightening with the approach of day. With the end of Talis's shift.

She sits at her desk. On a pad of lined paper, she writes out a script, word for word, inviting Talis for breakfast to talk about a program for teaching fire safety to the kids at her school.

She bites her lip as she dials the hospital number, which she still remembers from the month Omar was there. She asks for Talis, then waits for what seems like a very long time. Had she not given her name, she would hang up.

It gets only worse once he is on the line. "This is Caro. Omar's aunt."

He doesn't respond right away. She imagines him trying to recall who she is. Or remembering her and trying not to smirk.

"I didn't tell you this, but we'd met, well, I'd seen you before that night I let you stay after visiting hours."

Her heart is pounding so hard, she can feel it against her ribs.

"It was the first night your mother and Omar were in the hospital. You were sleeping in the chair in your mother's room. I covered you with a blanket."

She looks at the piece of paper, with her script written on it, the words a blur through a scrim of tears.

"You were so damned cute, I had to use my willpower to be professional about it."

"Don't use your willpower," she whispers into the receiver.

28

He has the next night off. In all the years she has lived in the apartment, she has never had a man for dinner other than Adam or her father. Now, with the still empty boxes piled in her living room, she makes a summer salad of frisée greens and chopped shrimp and corn she takes off the husk herself. She makes gazpacho and bakes dinner rolls from a paper tube. She washes her hair, taking care to scrunch it the way Rolando had instructed to bring out the curls, puts on a summer shift that flatters her curves.

He is taller than she remembers. He wears knee-length khaki shorts and a pressed cotton shirt with the sleeves rolled up. His forearms are long and thin, his wrists graceful. He brings yellow dahlias.

"I looked for you in the park on Tuesday," she tells him.

"I haven't been there in a while. I had one of the babies with me last week."

She doesn't understand.

"Some of the kids on the unit can't go back home. I do short-term foster parenting until longer placements can be found for them."

"How old was the baby?"

"Nineteen months. A pip, into everything, talking up a storm. At the last minute, his grandmother from Louisiana agreed to take him, but she had to wait for the weekend to travel up here."

She wants to ask more questions, but she senses that between the baby and the grandmother lies a moat of misery and for the first time in a very long time she yearns for something else for herself.

They eat. He eats quite a bit. She swallows a few forkfuls. Then he pulls her up from the table, into her bedroom, where she feels herself falling, falling, like one of the trust exercises she'd been led through at camp as a teenager, backward onto the snowy white quilt never touched by hands other than her own.

He tastes of wine and tomatoes. His back is taut. His mouth travels from her eyes to her neck to her collarbone.

She pushes him away, props herself up on an elbow. She tries to steady the whirling inside her. "I need you to tell me some things about you. Something before the babies."

"Now?"

"Yes. Now."

He lies on his side, facing her, his limbs sinewy like an animal that hunts.

"How did you learn to do the circus rings?"

"Climbing trees. I grew up in McCall, Idaho. There are a lot of trees there."

"McCall, Idaho?"

"There was a smoke jumpers' base there. My father was a smoke jumper until he disappeared."

He pauses but does not make her ask how, why, when. "I was one. My mom thinks he staged it to look like his death so we could get the insurance money, but I think he might really have been killed."

"A smoke jumper?"

"Guys who fight fires by jumping from planes into the middle of a blazing forest. Sounds crazy, doesn't it?"

"And dangerous."

"He'd been a conscientious objector during the war. A lot of the COs trained to be the first smoke jumpers. Most of them left the Forest Service after the war, but my father stayed on. The CIA was just forming, and some of the smoke jumpers were recruited. They passed over my father, my mom said, because he'd been a conscientious objector."

"Why were they interested in smoke jumpers?"

"They don't panic in circumstances that usually make people panic. They take risks but still follow orders."

Talis pushes the hair off Caro's forehead. "With fires, my father told my mother, you know whose side you're on. Later, when half the fires were ones the Forest Service set themselves to prevent other fires, some of them lacking the good manners to stick to the perimeters drawn in the home office, having to be fought themselves, he stopped thinking fires have definable sides."

He smooths her forehead with the palm of his hand, so that for a moment Caro sees her mother's face, feels her mother's hand. "Is that why he left?" Caro asks, stumbling over her words, unsure if she should refer to Talis's father as someone who chose to disappear or as someone who was killed. "I mean, is that why your mother thought he might have left, because he no longer knew what he was fighting?"

"Sometimes. Other times, she thought it had to do with us. That he couldn't stand all the people that came along with family life. Too many relatives, too many neighbors."

He runs a finger along the outline of her mouth, then kisses her again. "Enough with the Q and A."

29

They are each amazed at the other's lack of hesitation, un-questioning of their own.

"I knew the first time I saw you, when I covered you with a blanket."

"I was sleeping."

"I could see everything about you. How sweet and loyal and tough you are. How hard you work at everything."

"But you didn't do anything."

"I didn't think you were ready."

"I knew when I watched you on the rings that day."

"That I am more monkey than man?"

"That you are all heart and muscle with no bullshit."

Because he works nights, during the week, there are only mornings, every morning until the end of the month, when Omar and Adam will return and Caro will need to go back to her job to get ready for the school year. They grab each one, Caro waking early and walking in the morning cool to his Riverside Drive apartment so she arrives before him. Letting herself in and then preparing breakfast—breakfast without coffee, since she goes back to bed with him afterward.

On the last morning before Omar and Adam's return, he

asks if she wants to have kids. She stares out his bedroom door, at the table still littered with juice cups and waffle remains. It is a question that fills her with shame, a subject she has not discussed with even her mother. "I don't think so. I've never made a definitive decision, but I think I'm just letting time run out."

"But you're so close with Omar."

"It's totally different being an aunt. Being an aunt is like swimming in a lake. There's a shoreline all around. Being a parent has no shoreline. I'm too selfish. I don't want to give up my routines, my time to read the newspaper, walk to work, talk on the phone, sprawl on the couch."

"It will change," he says. "I'm sure of it."

30

When Adam and Omar return, a week before Omar will go back to school, neither of them seems surprised that Talis is now part of her life.

"Second grade," Talis tells Omar, "that's prime baseball time." He takes Omar downtown to buy a mitt. He shows Omar how to soften the mitt in the clothes dryer, instructs him to sleep with it under his mattress.

For the rest of the week, every afternoon after Talis has slept, he brings Omar to one of the baseball diamonds in Riverside Park. He teaches him how to catch, first without the mitt—"You gotta know how that ball feels in your hand"— then with the mitt. He teaches Omar how to bat. How to bat like they did in McCall, Idaho, so each hit makes a fat cracking sound. He teaches Omar how to slide so his feet touch the base first.

On Friday, Caro meets them in the park. Talis has gathered a group of kids so with the grown-ups they can have teams of six each. Omar has his baseball cap on backward. He is playing first base, jumping and whooping.

Caro sits on a bench watching, marveling as her nephew hits ball after ball into the outfield. "Must be Rachida's genes," she says to Adam that night as he kneels by the tub carefully washing the sand and dirt from Omar's scalp.

Talis asks Caro to show him the work being done on the house. The woodwork has not been sanded to his standards. He talks to the crew leader, insists on a finer-gauge paper. He shows Caro photographs from design magazines about how the molding can be painted a shade darker or lighter than the walls. He takes her to a paint store, has them custom mix a blue for her room that will have no sweetness in it—pure sky and water—so it washes out in sunlight and is phosphorescent at night. He has her rethink the lighting, encouraging her to add wiring for bedside sconces, channel the parlor ceilings for art lights, install under-the-cabinet halogen bulbs.

He chips out the concrete slab in front of the decorative fireplace in the parlor and lays copper tiles in a railroad pattern for the hearth. He does a dirty wash on the plaster surround so it looks like limestone. He paints a dinosaur on one wall of Omar's room. He draws plans for floor-to-ceiling bookshelves around a long counter to make an office area in the room that will be Adam's and finds a cabinetmaker to construct them. He clears the shattered glass from the garden, installs a trellis for Spanish flag and trumpet vine, and plants mums and flowering cabbages for the autumn and daffodil and iris bulbs for the spring.

Packing the last of her books, Caro finds her tattered copy of *The Odyssey*. A bookmark is still at the Penelope passage: "In the daytime, I would weave at my great loom, but in the night, I would have torches set by, and undo it." She takes out the bookmark and puts the book in a box.

31

The weekend before they are to move into the house, Talis brings over a ceramic dish and the ingredients and utensils to make a peach cobbler. In McCall, he'd grown up with kids from the Nez Percé tribe. From them, he'd learned that a new home should be blessed with something homemade. Peaches, he tells Caro, are symbols of contentment. She sits on the kitchen counter, watching while he puts the cobbler together.

Caro invites her mother to see the house and eat the cobbler. Myra walks through what had once been her home, slowly, from top to bottom. "It's more beautiful than ever," she says. "Polished like a jewel."

Talis serves the cobbler on yellow paper plates. Myra bites into the flaky biscuit floating over the honeyed fruit and pro-claims it the most delicious thing she has ever tasted.

Talis goes outside to inspect the garden. Myra reminds her-self, as she has over and over since Caro told her about Talis, not to entrap Caro by comments that she knows however lightly intended will feel like leg irons—not to jinx this late, first love with ominous hope.

Caro finishes her last bite of cobbler. "I worry that he's too good to be true," she says.

Myra tries to figure out how to say what she wants to say without condescension, then, turning an about-face on her weeks of prudence, says, "He's perfect for you."

"I could hear Dad biting his tongue when I told him I was involved with a nurse. I'm sure he thought I meant a woman."

"He probably imagined a girl with nice buns and a little white cap."

"I had to tell Dad he was in the Pliocene, that there are male nurses even on sitcoms these days. I told him it comes down to love or money—there are guys with worldly success gained at the cost of not being able to love deeply and guys who can love deeply gained at the cost of worldly success—and asked which he wants for his daughter. That shut him up."

Myra studies her daughter, who knows, of course, that her father had been the former kind of man. It had been Myra's own failings that had not let her fall in love with the latter.

Myra can hear Talis moving about below, in what was once her haven. She waits for Caro to tell her that Talis will move in too, and when Caro does, Myra leans over the ceramic dish filled with sweet peaches and kisses her daughter on the forehead. She holds her breath so no tears will tumble on the blessing cobbler.

32

By December, they have settled into the house: Caro and Talis on the fourth floor, Adam and Omar on the third, a young psychiatrist in the street-level office, a music student in the au pair suite. Because Talis does not hang up his clothes and leaves his books and mail in heaps on the floor, Caro has made the front bedroom on the fourth floor, the room that had been Eva's, Talis's own. During the week, when he works nights and sleeps days, he stays in his room. On his days off, they sleep together in Caro's room.

They fall into an easy pattern. Except for Wednesdays, when Myra picks up Omar, Talis wakes in time to get Omar at school. Talis and Omar walk the eight blocks to the school where Adam teaches, after which Talis leaves Omar with Adam while he does errands or takes a run or works in the garden. By the time Caro arrives home at six, he has dinner ready. They all eat together. Then Caro does the dishes while Talis takes a nap and a shower before going to work.

On this afternoon, Omar has a classmate over. The children are upstairs in Omar's room playing with a train set. Talis is cutting cauliflower into florets and eggplant into chunks when Adam sits down at the farm table. He fidgets in the chair and picks at the crevices in the tabletop.

Talis positions himself so he is looking at Adam. "Something on your mind?"

Adam glances at the stairs, then changes chairs so he is sitting closer to Talis.

"I figured out why she set the fire."

"Who?"

"Eva. Our housekeeper who disappeared." Adam clears his throat. Talis can feel his impatience rising: impatience with Adam's mumbling, unfocused quality, like a thirteen-year-old kid who needs a kick in the pants to pull himself together. No wonder he has chosen this age to teach; he must be right at home with the kids. Other times, recalling the night he met Adam and the plastic bag with the dirty magazines, Talis feels overcome with disgust, so that he has to remind himself that it makes no sense to be angry at a person for being himself. When he told this to Caro—not about the magazines, that he decided to keep to himself, but about his irritation with Adam—she put her arms around him. "Poor Talis, instead of a girlfriend, you got a menagerie. You're still getting used to Adam. He's so much improved. He has a job. He gets up every morning and puts on a tie. Last year, he spent all day locked in the music room, sleeping, for all I know."

"Do you remember those magazines I showed you?" Adam asks.

"Kind of hard to forget them."

"There were pictures . . ." Adam looks at his hands arched like spiders on top of the table. "Pictures I'd cut out from other magazines in a file box in the music room closet. I think Eva found them, and that's why she set the fire."

One of the few words Talis remembers from the year of French he took in high school is the word for eggplant:

aubergine. In San Francisco, he painted the bedroom of a potter with gray hair coiled around her head a color called aubergine. All he'd wanted for this evening was to chop aubergine,
grind coarse salt, drizzle extra-virgin olive oil on the gorgeous
purple skin. Fortify himself for a night of dermis, puffy and
red or white and blistered or ashen gray. Now, though, Adam
is staring at him, waiting, it seems, for Talis to say something.
Something different from the snarl Talis is rolling around inside his mouth: *Hey, I'm a nurse, not a priest. Or a rabbi, or who-
ever the fuck you want to absolve you.*

"Do you think I should tell my mother and Caro?"

Talis puts down the eggplant. He dries his hands on a dish
towel. To his relief, the disgust for Adam has never been concern that Adam would do anything wrong with Omar or with
his students. Rather, the porn seems to Talis a sign of weak-
ness, a substitute for a real human being, as pitiable as a grown
man who can't throw a punch reading superhero comics. A
guy scared of horses writing Westerns.

"Do you?" Adam repeats.

"What good would it do?"

"They'd understand how fucked-up I am." Adam clenches
his hands, the spiders disappearing into his fists. "I haven't
looked at any of that stuff since the fire, but I'd be a liar if I
said I don't still think about the pictures."

Talis's mother had taught him how to live with a secret. He
can't recall her ever having actually instructed him not to tell
anyone that she didn't believe his father was dead, but he'd always known that this was more forbidden than anything else
he might do. For a long while, he resented the burden of something that could not be said, but as he grew older, he'd been
able to see the situation through his mother's eyes: the secret, a
small price for not living hand to mouth as they would have on
her supermarket cashier's salary alone, for not worrying about
buying her kid shoes or having the electric turned off, for not

asking for handouts from her sisters, who looked down on her, or her parents, who kept accounts of every penny given.

"So you want to tell them so they can then forgive you?"

And the kids were right. His mother had been Red Hot Dot, screwing married men on their late-night trips for milk and diapers in the manager's office, where she was the one who closed out the registers each night.

Adam digs his nails into his arm. He looks like someone who could gouge out his own eyes.

Parachuting from a plane was easy next to what Talis wills himself to do now: to pull it out of himself, the goodness to respond, to grant the healing of one soul revealing itself to another. "Let it go, man. Let it go."

33

At first, there are only hang ups. Three on Caro's cell phone in January, two in February. When Caro calls back, there is no answer. Trying the numbers again, a few hours later, she discovers pay phones at a gas station, a laundromat, a convenience store. No girl from Peru anywhere near.

From the area codes, it seems that Eva is moving west: Pennsylvania, Ohio, then a leap to Colorado. Six calls. Six hang ups.

In April, there is a call without a click. Caro can hear breathing. *Eva? Eva, is that you?* Caro asks over and over again. On the second of these calls, Caro just talks into the receiver. The monologue comes surprisingly easily. Omar is doing well, she says. His skin graft has taken, and he doesn't seem too self-conscious about the bald patch he will have until he is old enough for the tissue expansion. Her mother, Dr. M., has healed well, too. The house has been repaired.

The calls stop. Caro wonders if Eva is satisfied, having

heard that everyone has survived, or if she is afraid of her whereabouts being traced.

34

When Caro gets home, Adam is in the kitchen making dinner.

"Where's Talis?" she asks.

"He left about an hour ago. He was called in for an emergency. A fire in Queens, I think. One of the burn-unit nurses has a stomach flu. Something like that. He said he'd call you later."

Caro turns on the television, which they keep now in the parlor. She flips to the local news, watches reports of the mayor's press conference, beach closings due to sewage. Then, the report of the fire. It was in the basement apartment of a semiattached house. An Iranian family lived in the apartment. Only the baby survived. Someone broke a window and threw burning paper inside. A neighbor, a man whose son died in Iraq, is the prime suspect. Another neighbor, an old man wheezing beneath a checked shirt with buttons strained against his girth, is interviewed. "Twice, I seen him go after those people. Once, he threw garbage at them, rotten eggs. Screamed something about go back to your caves. Another time he chased them into their house with a crowbar. I tried to tell him these people are from Iran, not Iraq, they don't live in caves in Iran, but all he'd say was all of them's out to destroy us."

The reporter wears a sleeveless turtleneck and gold hoop earrings. Her arms are lightly tanned. "And no one ever called the police?"

"Me? Call the cops? On my own neighbor? I don't think so, ma'am."

She speaks directly into the camera. "A case of racial prejudice. An Iranian family mistaken for Iraqis."

Caro turns off the television. After dinner, she calls the hospital. Talis is with the baby in the pediatric intensive care. "Don't bother him," Caro says. "Just tell him I called."

She wakes early, having forgotten to pull the blackout shades, the northern light filtering through the glistening leaves of the neighbors' maple tree, the warmth of the coming day hinted at in the sheen of the still air. Talis is lying on her bed in his nursing uniform. His hands are behind his head and his eyes are open.

She turns toward him.

"Bad?"

"Bad." Talis blows air out of his mouth. "Three kids. No one knows how old exactly. Maybe five, three, and an infant. The father, best we can figure, grabbed the baby, put her under his shirt, and got her out. Dumped her on the sidewalk, then went back to try and get the mother and the two other kids. The kids and the mother were dead by the time the ambulance arrived. The father died in the ambulance."

Caro touches the V of skin over the blue of Talis's uniform. She lays her hand over the fine hairs, mostly blond but a few grays too, her fingers curling around his exposed neck.

"The baby has a third-degree burn on one foot and an arm. Which is serious at her age, especially on the foot and the inside of the arm. The skin is like paper. We don't know how old she is, but little. Maybe eight weeks."

Talis unfolds his arms. His hands move into fists. "Assholes," he cries, pounding the mattress.

35

No relatives appear to claim the baby, either because there are none here or they are too frightened to identify themselves. Her foot and arm are kept in traction so she doesn't knock off the dressings or disturb the compression bandages. It is hard to know if her screams are because of pain at the burn site or a protest about the traction. On her chart, she is identified as Baby3, the three because she was the youngest of the three children in the house. Talis names her Chicky on account of the dark curl on the top of her head.

At the end of her first week in the hospital, Chicky develops an infection in her foot. For four days, Talis fears she will lose the foot. Her fever cannot be brought under control. He refuses his two days off, not trusting anyone else to stay with her overnight. During the hours when he isn't on the unit with her, he is on the computer reading about other cases of severe infant burns. When her fever finally breaks, she is sedated so that the dead and infected tissue can be surgically removed. A week later, the surgeon sees between Chicky's toes the hoped-for beginning signs of epithelialization.

Once Chicky is removed from traction, the nurses hold her constantly, singing to her, cooing, kissing her miraculously unscathed forehead. Over the Fourth of July weekend, Talis agrees to switch to the short-staffed day shift. Caro does not object. She hates traveling on holidays, likes the city on summer weekends, when there are no lines for anything and the streets are empty. She meets her mother for brunch, then walks across the park with a sandwich for Talis.

Caro knows most of the pediatric burn unit day staff from Omar's stay. She waves to the nursing supervisor, who is writing charts in the center station, says hello to one of the attending doctors. In the dayroom, Irene, a Scottish woman with five children and nine grandchildren, is rocking a baby.

Caro leans over to look. The baby is tiny, with a little tuft of black hair. She has a bandage on one arm and her foot. "Is this Chicky?"

"That's our ducky."

"How is she?"

"Drowsy, as always. She opens her eyes for a few seconds, and then it's back to sleep. Once we get her out of these dressings, we're going to have to lower her morphine, because she's got to start exercising those arms and legs of hers."

"Can I hold her?"

"That would be nice, dearie. I could use my afternoon tea. There's hand sanitizer on the table."

Caro holds the baby while Irene hoists herself up. Carefully, afraid of jostling Chicky's bandages, Caro sits down in the rocker. The baby nuzzles against her shoulder. She tucks her knees under her so her shins are resting on Caro's breastbone and her tush is sticking out, the curl of a baby in the womb.

Gently, still worrying about disturbing the dressings, Caro rocks back and forth. She sings "Mary Had a Little Lamb." She sings "London Bridge." She sings "Rockabye Baby."

The light filters through the half-closed venetian blinds of the children's dayroom, sketching golden trellises on the linoleum floor. On the low shelves, Caro can see Monopoly, Connect 4, Clue, Uno. She played all these games with Omar during the weeks he was here. Across the room are bookshelves with *Olivia, Where the Wild Things Are, Pippi Longstocking*, a collection of the Harry Potter books.

She cuddles Chicky, no longer worrying that the rocking will hurt her. She sings "Hush, Little Baby," all ten verses, the way her mother sang it.

When Caro gets to "If that cart and bull turn over, Mama's gonna buy you a dog named Rover," Chicky twists her head to locate the voice.

For the rest of her life, Caro will never forget the moment when Chicky's eyes—two brown pools, not of pain, but of curiosity—first find her own. Chicky's tiny perfect lips part and a smile breaks over her face, revealing her pink toothless gums and the crimson tip of her tiny tongue.

Caro is so stunned, her own mouth drops open. She bursts into tears, flooded with the feeling that this injured bird is hers.

36

For Talis to bring Chicky home as a foster baby would be simple. The complications would arise if they were to make an appeal for permanent placement. Translated into legal language, Caro feels the impulse of the afternoon fracturing into doubts.

"I don't want to take her home if she won't be able to stay with us," she tells Talis.

"There are no guarantees. No one's showed up now for six weeks, but anything could happen. A relative from anywhere might appear. But we'd have priority over any nonrelative."

Talis narrows his eyes. Has he taken a baby home so many times, Caro wonders, that he can't understand that it would be better not to take Chicky home than to have to give her back—that Caro can already imagine fleeing the country with Chicky and abandoning everyone else in her life, including him, rather than losing her?

At work, the numbers on the school's budget spreadsheet lie inert, incomprehensible on the page. Her thoughts are caught in a spiral. If they were able to adopt Chicky, what would they tell her when she is old enough to understand? Should they try now to find her relatives in Iran? What would happen if relatives appear five years from now?

It is a relief when her father calls and asks the same questions. "You have to consult with a lawyer." He clears his throat, unaccustomed, she knows, to giving her, his practical child, advice. "And how about getting married? Wouldn't an adoption be easier if you were married?"

"What if," she asks her mother the following day, "what

I've always thought about myself, that I don't have it in me to raise a child, is true?"

Caro can see her mother studying her anguished face. She wants her mother to tell her what to do: wear the brown or the navy shoes, choose the grilled cheese or the tuna, invite Allie or Helen for a sleepover.

"No one has it in them ahead of time. We grow into the task, grow with our child. You're strong, darling. Stronger than you think."

Adam takes off his glasses when she asks what he thinks. It is late, Omar asleep, Talis at work. They are in the parlor, both in pajamas. He rubs his eyes. "You'd be a fantastic mother," he says.

Her eyes are pathetically watering. She hadn't realized how desperate she is to be reassured. "You think so? I love Omar, but I know it's a hell of a lot different."

"You half-raised me. I know so. And it would be great for Omar to have a little cousin. I already asked him how he'd feel. He said he'd share his room and teach her how to build Legos."

Caro hugs her brother. Chicky and Omar look like cousins, she thinks. Both with brown skin, skin seared by fire, skin that for the rest of their lives will elicit questions about where they are from and what happened to them.

37

Rachida calls after midnight. "A few days ago I remembered that Layla has a friend who works at the Iranian embassy. I called her and asked her to see if her friend could make some inquiries."

Caro flips on the bedside light. Her thoughts are racing too fast for her to focus on how difficult it must have been for Rachida—who, Adam has told her, has an endless loop in her head of Layla fucking the blond neurosurgeon, a sapphire ring gleaming on his pinky finger—to call Layla.

"Layla's friend found out that the baby's father came to Queens eight years ago. He drove a cab. He brought his wife and the two older children over sixteen months ago. That's when they moved into the basement apartment of the house. The baby was the only one born here."

"Are there any relatives that anyone at the embassy knows about?"

"Not here."

"But there are in Iran?" Caro asks.

"I'm sure there are." Rachida pauses. "Layla says you can't send the baby back. They'd never accept a scarred girl in a rural village. It would be cruel."

Layla is not to be trusted. She told Caro her brothers had stoned her and left her for dead in the sand. She told Rachida her panties were wet when she thought about her, and now she is sleeping with the blond neurosurgeon.

About this, though, Caro knows Layla is right. Chicky has to stay.

38

When Talis gets home from the hospital, he sits on the edge of the bed where Caro has been lying, unable to sleep since Rachida's call. "A specialist from Boston came to look at Chicky's foot. The dermis is basically intact. She's beginning to grow new skin on the ball of her foot."

Caro opens the covers and beckons Talis to come into the bed. Still in his nurse's uniform, he climbs in next to her. He buries his nose in the hollow of her neck.

Caro strokes his hair. "Don't you want your own baby?" she whispers.

"You mean with my genes?"

Caro nods, the top of her chin grazing Talis's hair.

Talis turns onto his side. He smiles sadly at Caro. "Genes don't make people belong to each other. I haven't seen my father since I was one. If he's still alive, if I ever meet him, I'll probably recognize certain things about myself in him, maybe my hairline or the way my third toe is longer than the second. But he never raised me. Never taught me anything. Never made me his."

The adoption attorney they had consulted told them that as soon as Chicky is ready to leave the hospital, they can bring her home as foster parents while their application for adoption is being processed. "Nothing is guaranteed," he said, "but I don't foresee any problems." Just hearing the word "problems" had made Caro so anxious, she had to excuse herself for the ladies' room.

Talis takes her hand. "Sometimes you just have to jump."

39

Now, when Myra picks up Omar on Wednesdays, he asks to come straight home to see his cousin. He races to wash his hands and then flings himself on the floor to play with Chicky, who can sit up supported by pillows. Afterward, he eats the snack that Caro, on maternity leave, gives him, and goes upstairs to do his homework or play on his own for a while. Caro then commences her weekly report to her mother on the things Chicky is doing: babbling, pointing, smiling at certain books.

"I know I must sound ridiculous, as though I have the only baby in the world."

"When you were little, Grandpa Max used to visit us on his lunch hour every Friday. I was exactly the same way: de-

scribing your and Adam's incredible feats. Who else can
you go on and on with about your children other than their
grandparents?"

"You mean, with whom else can you abandon restraint and
good taste?"

"You're doing so well. It's such hard work, taking care of a
baby. And it's doubly hard for older mothers. Not that you're
old to be a mother, especially these days. But with the twenty-
two-year-old mothers, they haven't yet developed a self they
have to put aside for the baby's sake. There's less for them to
give up."

"Chicky couldn't give a damn that I've written grants total-
ing nine million dollars or that I'm used to running a staff of
eighteen. All she cares about is that I feed her when she wants
to be fed and entertain her when she want to be entertained
and hold her when she wants to be held."

Over the years, Myra has treated half a dozen mothers unable to keep at bay the resentment of having to put her own
desires on the back burner for the good of her baby. The more
strongly the mother resists the immersion in her baby, the more
the baby senses the rejection, the baby's pain manifest in a
disorganized flailing that the guilty mother experiences as
condemnation of her, a vicious cycle of neither enjoying the
other because they are profoundly out of sync. The mothers arrive in her office, so stressed they seem ready to explode, filled
with inane advice from parenting magazines about taking
more time for themselves. Time for exercise and manicures
and romantic meals with husbands. They are shocked and often furious when Myra prescribes the opposite: more time with
the baby.

Caro snaps Chicky into her bouncy seat. Chicky bats at the
toy bar, squealing when the clown flips over the top. "Talis
showed me something he's been reading. There's an idea that's
part of Kabbalist thought called *tsimtsum*. It has to do with the

way that God had to contract himself, absent himself, in order to create the world. It made me think about Chicky—the way that I have to constrict myself, my own wishes, so as to leave her room to unfold."

Chicky pushes against the belt of the bouncy seat. She scrunches her face and punches the air with her chubby fists. Caro unbuckles her and Myra holds out her arms to take the baby. It seems pointless to tell Caro that she, too, had once been fascinated with the same idea. Myra bounces Chicky on her knees while the child, her face now so relaxed it is hard to believe the protest was only seconds before, examines the hair on a purple giraffe.

"I have to learn to do the same thing with Talis," Caro says. "He's such a slob. I can have everything put away before I go to bed, and by the time he's been home fifteen minutes, he's left a sticky spot of orange juice on the counter and toothpaste smeared in the sink and his clothes on the floor. Before Chicky, I coped by keeping his stuff in the front bedroom, but now it's Chicky's room. I have to keep reminding myself that he's the one who's normal, that a pristine environment is what's unnatural."

Caro leans over and kisses the top of her baby's head. "What in nature is pristine? The leaves fall from the trees, animals shed their skins, dead birds rot in ditches. Nothing."

"I'm afraid you got that from me. The notion that the pristine is something to aspire to. It's like any idea: it turns on itself. There's that precarious line over which something worthwhile becomes a horror."

Myra turns Chicky around so Chicky can see Caro's face. She hooks one arm across the baby's tummy and strokes her soft dark hair with the other. Like with Eva, she can see the scalp underneath—only with Chicky, this is because she is half-hatched.

What Chicky wants is to drink in the world. What Eva wanted was to pour herself out.

"Da!" Chicky shrieks, pointing at the giraffe she has flung to the floor. Bracing the baby against her arm, Myra retrieves the toy.

With Eva, Myra had let herself be deceived about the necessity of the boundaries she maintains with her patients, the way that the limit on their access to her serves as a firewall. Eva lit the match, but it had been she, Myra, who had laid the tinder with her foolhardy good intentions. The *yes* to Adam's request to live with her, not even a request, rather an implied request—or had it even been that? had the idea, in fact, first been hers?—that should have been a *no*. The girl from the Amazon who should never have come to New York. The story she should never have let Eva tell.

40

Thanksgiving morning is cold but bright. When Talis comes in, he gives Chicky her bottle and she goes blissfully back to sleep.

At nine-thirty, Caro bolts awake. Talis is asleep beside her with an arm stretched like a tree limb across the white sheets. She bounds out of bed. She told her mother, who'd promised to help with the dinner, that they would start cooking at nine. Yesterday, Talis made the pies and the cranberry sauce, but there is still the turkey to stuff and the vegetables to prepare.

She finds her mother in the kitchen mixing corn bread to put in the stuffing.

"Oh my God, I'm so sorry. How'd you get in?"

"Omar. He was up reading and eating cereal. I'm glad that you got to sleep in. Omar and Adam and Rachida just left to watch the parade from my apartment. Omar invited one of his friends to go with them. They plan on meeting your father at his hotel afterward."

Rachida had come in late last night. Seeing Rachida for the first time since the summer, her hair grown out so it falls in a glossy bob, Caro did a double take. It had been Rachida, though, seeing Adam without his beard, his delicate features uncovered, who did the real double take.

"Look at you," Rachida said, touching Adam's smooth chin. "When did this happen?"

"Ten days or so ago. I got tired of the boys and the other teachers at the school pigeonholing me because of the beard. And," he paused to wink at Caro, "Chicky pulling on it all the time."

Her father, who'd taken the red-eye, should have arrived by now—Betty, off to her brother's for Thanksgiving, not having objected to his coming East for the long weekend so he could meet Chicky. Before Chicky came home from the hospital, he'd sent Caro a check for nursery furniture, enough, she joked, to furnish the entire house. This past week, he consulted with her by e-mail half a dozen times about what kind of toy Chicky would like, until she finally wrote him: *Calm down. We're talking about a six-month-old. Just bring yourself and a wooden spoon and an old pot.*

The coffee is made, which Caro knows her mother must have done. She takes the cup her mother hands her, and for a confused moment, it is as though the year she and Talis and Adam and Omar and now Chicky have lived here dissolves and it is her mother's kitchen again.

She inhales the coffee. "Do you miss the house?"

"Not really. Not that I didn't love living here. I had wonderful years here, but it's not as though I want to be back in those years now. I feel very lucky to have been able to move on."

Myra puts the pan of corn bread in the oven. She takes the sausages she brought out of the refrigerator and begins dicing them into cubes. "And I love my new apartment, the sun rising over the reservoir, the lights reflecting on the water at night."

"Sounds like you're burning the candle at both ends."

"I've been working hard on finishing my project—the last stage, I think, of my teleology of love." Myra raises her voice on the word "teleology," as though mocking herself.

"And?"

"Oh, it's too early in the morning . . ."

"I'm interested. Truly." Caro sips her coffee, enjoying the moments before Chicky will wake up, before she will turn to washing the turkey and cutting the vegetables. The kitchen is filling with the sweet and savory smells of the corn bread baking and the sausage pieces now cooking in the cast-iron pan. Her mother smiles, her way of saying, Caro has learned, that although she takes her work seriously, she doesn't expect anyone else to do the same.

"It's life its very self," Myra says. "I hope that doesn't sound too corny. And, of course, I'm only using myself as a case study. After the breast, or the longing for the missing breast, and words and mastery of the body and romance and children and then— again, for me—my patients and my garden and my piano and my feeble attempts at something spiritual, something transcendent, it has come round to being able to love life its very self."

Caro nods. The words are her mother's, the ideas ones she could not have found syllables for herself, but the sentences feel so inevitable, they seem almost to be coming from her own head, like a reverse déjà vu—a glimpse of a state of mind she will reach one day herself.

"The greatest art, the apex of love, I've come to think, is to be able to love life its very self." Her mother cracks two eggs into the bowl where she will mix the stuffing. A froth forms as she whisks together the yolks and whites. "I see it in my mind as one word: *Lifeitsveryself.*"

Only now does Caro recall that corn-bread-and-sausage stuffing is her father's favorite. Her throat catches as she is filled with gratitude, gratitude at her mother's generosity. Gratitude that she'd not had to build herself entirely from scratch as her mother had. To have grown up in Rome, not on parched sand.

41

After dinner, Caro and Myra do the dishes while Rachida plays chess with Omar. Larry, done with his mock groaning that he ate enough to slay three cardiac patients, lies on the floor flying Chicky on his knees while Adam shows Talis portions of *Fitzcarraldo*, which he has discovered Talis has never seen.

Myra takes the sink, washing the oversized platters that were once hers and that she left for Caro and Adam. Caro dries the platters with the tea towels her mother gave them as a housewarming present.

"You did a lovely job, darling," Myra says. "With the dinner."

"It's very strange to be stepping into your shoes." Caro looks at her mother's face.

"It's your turn. And I would never have been able to manage here, with the garden and the stairs, once I got really old. With my new apartment, I can see myself able to live there until the end of my days. I'll be one of those women with a caregiver, a nanny for old ladies, wheeling them to the park for air."

"I'll wheel you."

"Hopefully we've got a while before we're there."

To Caro, her mother seems lighter since the fire, since leaving the house, as though the luminous air of her new home, the sky over the park, the sun on the reservoir, has penetrated her skin. Her mother has become happily unencumbered while she has become happily encumbered.

Myra gives Caro the last platter to dry. She scrubs the sink and dries her hands on the apron wrapped around her. For the first time, Caro notices the age spots on the backs of her mother's hands, patches of skin where the pigment is failing—the inevitability of the day when she will touch her mother's hands and they will be cold.

She sets the platter on the counter and wraps her arms around her mother's slender torso. She rests her cheek on her mother's breastbone. Over the last year, she has seen crow's-feet emanating from her own eyes, a heaviness under her chin, the telltale signs of her own body's slippage, her own decay.

Through their breathing, beyond it, Caro can hear her mother murmuring something like *there, there*, or perhaps it is that phrase, *lifeitsveryself*, murmured over and over like an incantation. She sees herself burying her mother—Adam and Rachida and Omar and Talis and Chicky with her at the graveside, each of them throwing a handful of dirt against the mahogany coffin. Then twenty-five more years until it will be herself lowered into the earth. And who will be standing there to kiss her forehead, to bid her farewell? It is hard to imagine Adam or Talis outlasting her. Omar, yes, sad, of course, but not filled with grief. It will be Chicky who will be grief-stricken. Chicky, tall and graceful, her hair dark and sleek, her long lashes rimmed with tears, her slender arms, one of them still marked by fire.

The spring after a forest fire, Talis has told her, is always gorgeous. Lush from the nutrients unlocked by the burn, the razed land fills with a riot of wildflowers. Larkspurs, poppies, and hyacinths thriving on the nitrate remains. Sweet peas, lupines, and paintbrushes. Berries and grasses. Vines of wild cucumbers, bulbs of pink onions. A tempest of crimson, lavender, and gold. A feast for hummingbirds, woodpeckers, and deer.

In a few seasons, the underbrush grows thick again, a new tinderbox. Lightning strikes, flames dance through the fallen branches and nimble saplings, and then, again, yellow forget-me-nots, pink snapdragons, blue Canterbury bells.

ACKNOWLEDGMENTS

I am indebted to a number of sources for background informa-
tion critical to this novel. For my understanding of the Jewish
community in Iquitos, Peru, and the links with Moroccan
Jewish communities, I drew heavily on Ariel Segal's *Jews of
the Amazon: Self-Exile in Paradise* and Susan Gilson Miller's
"Kippur on the Amazon: Jewish Emigration from Northern
Morocco in the Late Nineteenth Century" in *Sephardi and
Middle Eastern Jewries: History and Culture in the Modern Era*,
edited by Harvey E. Goldberg. Daniel J. Schroeter and Joseph
Chetrit's "The Transformation of the Jewish Community of
Essaouira (Mogador) in the Nineteenth and Twentieth Centu-
ries," also from Harvey E. Goldberg's anthology, and Daniel J.
Schroeter's "Jewish Communities of Morocco: History and
Identity" in *Morocco: Jews and Art in a Muslim Land*, edited by
Vivian B. Mann, were invaluable sources on the history of
the Jews of Essaouira. In the Mann anthology, Moshe Idel's
"The Kabbalah in Morocco: A Survey" and the photographs
in the incorporated catalog helped me to understand the mean-
ings and varieties of hamsas. Although we did not meet until
the near completion of this novel, I am grateful as well to Jorge
Abramovitz, president of the Sociedad de Beneficencia Is-
raelita (Kehila de Iquitos), who generously allowed me to interview him and provided introductions to other members of the
Iquitos Jewish community.

My interest in the politics and ecology of fire was ignited
by both my experience rafting under the expert guidance of

Gary Lane on the Salmon River in Idaho during the wildfires of 2000 and reading Richard Manning's *New York Times* op-ed piece "The Politics of Fire" (August 24, 2000). My understanding of this topic and of the history of smoke jumpers in America was enriched by Stephen J. Pyne's *Fire in America: A Cultural History of Wildland and Rural Fire*, *Ashes to Wildflowers: A Promise of Renewal Springs from Destruction* by Wayne P. Armstrong, and the websites of both the National Smokejumper Association and the McCall Smokejumpers.

Code of Honor: The Making of Three Great American Westerns by Michael F. Blake, *The Western Genre: From Lordsburg to Big Whiskey* by John Saunders, and *The Searchers* by Edward Buscombe were all important sources with respect to Westerns, and *Herzog on Herzog*, edited by Paul Cronin, provided invaluable material about the making of *Fitzcarraldo*. For helping to unlock the work of Frank Lloyd Wright, credit is due to *Essential Frank Lloyd Wright* by Caroline Knight and to *Loving Frank* by Nancy Horan.

I am indebted as well to the report of the International Society of Hair Restoration Surgery on their pro bono Operation Restore, and to their member Dr. Antonio Mangubat for a phone interview regarding his work with tissue expansion in cases of scalp burns in pediatric patients. Other sources include Dr. Robert L. Sheridan's article "Skin Substitutes in Burn Care" in the *Karger Gazette* no. 67 (August 2004) and Dr. Monique Aurora Tello's article "Eyes Wide Open" in *Yale Medicine* 36, no. 4 (Summer 2002), an account of her treatment of a three-year-old burn victim in Guatemala City.

Thank you to Dan Cahill, Henry Dunow, Anne Edelstein, Claire Flavigny, Selin Gulcelik, Dan Piepenbring, Jane Pollock, Jill Smolowe, Meg Spinelli, and Lucy Stille for their generous feedback at various stages of this manuscript; to Rebecca Ascher, Jessie Byrnes, Mark Epstein, Jenny McPhee, Linda Morton, Shira Nayman, Susan Scheftel, Arlene Shechet, Ana

Sousa, Nancy Star, and Barbara Weisberg for their help and sustenance; to the wonderful caregivers of my children—Mag Brown, Bernadine Roberts, and Glory Khan—who through the decades have given me the peace of mind necessary to focus on my work; to the amazing Montclair Writers Group for their sisterly support, wisdom, and humor; and to the Gornick family—Fred, Janet, Marian, and Vivian—whose narrative gifts raise the bar on what constitutes a story. Without my loyal agent, Geri Thoma, who has impeccable taste and believes in novels for grown-ups, and my fiercely independent and breathtakingly intelligent editor, Sarah Crichton, who knows when to reach out and when to say enough, this book would never have found its way into print. Finally, a bottomless thank-you to my husband, Ken, for gifting me the time to work on this novel, and to my sons, Zack and Damon, voracious readers and artists both, who teach me something new every day.

A NOTE ABOUT THE AUTHOR

Lisa Gornick is the author of the novel *A Private Sorcery*. Her stories and essays have appeared widely, including in *The Agni Review*, *Prairie Schooner*, *The Sun*, and various psychoanalytic journals, and have received many awards. She has a B.S. from Princeton and a Ph.D. in clinical psychology from Yale, and is a graduate of the writing program at New York University and the psychoanalytic training program at Columbia. She lives with her family in New York and is completing a collection of linked stories.